Passion Transcended

Southern Dom Book 2

Lorelei Tiffin

Baby Boomer Romance

Contents

Meet The Rollinses   1

1. Chapter 1   3

2. Chapter 2   10

3. Chapter 3   18

4. Chapter 4   26

5. Chapter 5   35

6. Chapter 6   47

7. Chapter 7   60

8. Chapter 8   68

9. Chapter 9   75

10. Chapter 10   82

11. Chapter 11   89

12. Chapter 12   99

13. Chapter 13   107

14. Chapter 14   116

15. Chapter 15   126

16. Chapter 16   137

17. Chapter 17   148

18. Chapter 18   155

19. Chapter 19   164

20. Chapter 20   174

21. Chapter 21   186

22. Chapter 22   198

23. Chapter 23   211

24. Epilogue   223

Bonus Material   228

Acknowledgements   255

About the Author   257

Meet The Rollinses

Tommy Rollins

Business genius and D/s Master all rolled into one studly package. Living proof that 60 is the new 40. For years, he had settled for vanilla in the Carolina interior, holding onto the Southern Gentleman persona that hid his darker side, always searching for that one woman who could fulfill his wildest dreams. And when he had found that rare, singular woman who completed him, who spoke to the deepest, darkest part of his nature and drew out the Dominance he longed to share, he had collared her and married her and never looked back. Because, even after 18 months, that intoxicating woman was still "the one"…

Clare Aullwood Rollins

A woman looking for a simple life, somewhere to find some peace in her retirement years, hoping the Carolina interior would be the answer to her prayers. She was a survivor of all the horrible things Life could throw at one woman, but still hoped to find love in the dusk of her life. And then Fate placed her in the path of the one man who could be everything she needed, everything she wanted, if she could just reach out and grab it. And she had grabbed that chance at love with gusto, and held on for dear life. Because even after 18 months, he was still a curse and a reward all wrapped up in masculine mystique, the only man who had ever been able coax out the woman she longed to be. Not such a bad choice after all, he had turned out to be "the one"...

Follow Tommy and Clare's continuing journey through life's ups and downs, and the evolution of their relationship, as they explore the more formal BDSM lifestyle that he craves. See if he can guide her through the lifestyle changes he wants to make, and still keep their marriage intact. And see if Tommy can survive a fundamental change of his own, just as his BDSM dream is coming true. When all is said and done, will he still be "the one"? Will she still be "the one"? The answers to these questions, and more, are right inside.

Chapter 1

"Something's different, Big Man. Something's very different. Ohhhhh!" And a shiver overtook her whole body, stopping them both for just a moment.

"What do you mean, Baby Girl? What's different? Do I need to stop?"

"Well, I mean – either you're a little bigger this morning, or I'm a little smaller than usual. It just feels a little fuller than normal, if you know what I mean, and not in a bad way. And please, don't stop. You need to just keep on doing what you're doing!!"

Clare shivered again, breaking out in telltale good bumps, signaling that the man at the center of her world was pushing all her love buttons with renewed vigor. Tommy had always been a masterful lover, since the day they had met, but there was something noticeably different that morning, deeper, more arousing than they had achieved in all the months they'd been together, and their short conversation stopped him long enough to let her catch her breath.

"I changed up the angle, Baby Girl, I read about it in one of your porn novellas, and I'm thinking it's working pretty well!! It's sure working for me! Every time you clench those tiny little muscles, it makes my toes curl!" Clare had been about to tell Tommy to stay the hell away from her erotic romance books, but he had just changed her mind on that subject. Instead, she moaned again.

Tommy, feeling he had her permission to continue, started up again, thrusting from behind like a man possessed, pushing them both up the hill toward their version of heaven on earth. Intuitive lover that he always was, he realized she was lagging behind ever so slightly. Wanting them both to come together, he reached around and pinched her tiny bundle of womanly nerves, and she screamed, clenching again, and pulling them both over the waterfall into a mind-numbing shared orgasm.

When her eyes uncrossed, Clare whispered "Oh, fuck, Big Man, the things you do to me! That's probably illegal in all fifty states." Her breathing was still extremely labored, but who could concentrate on a little thing like breathing when every ounce of her being was focused on that one little part of her that only he knew so well.

Clare had been kneeling on the edge of the bed with Tommy standing behind her, and when he leaned over to rest his weight on her for just a moment, their combined weight threw them both off the bed onto the floor. And they laughed like idiots. Not bad for a pair of sex crazed 60-somethings.

"Merry Christmas, Master."

"Merry Christmas, my beautiful Baby Girl. That was spectacular, even if I didn't allow you the opportunity to ask for permission to come. I may still spank that sexy ass of yours, but it won't be for punishment, it will just be for my enjoyment – and yours."

"Yes, Master, I look forward to it." And she leaned over to place a kiss on his naked chest, over his heart, just like she had always done.

Master. Yes, there it was. What their relationship was morphing into. Could she do it – for him? That still remained to be seen.

As they lay on the floor wrapped in each other's arms, dizzy from the strain of their amorous Christmas morning activity, Clare thought back over the past 20 months, thinking again how blessed she was to have Tommy in her life. And what a long, rocky road it had been to reach that Christmas morning in their Carolina paradise.

When they met, Tommy was a part time ER nurse and a full time business genius – and a sex god with a rocket hot body, looking more like 40 than 60. Clare was emotionally damaged and needy, trying desperately to reclaim what was left of her life in her retirement years. They were introduced by mutual friends on a beautiful little golf course on a lovely, warm Carolina Spring day and had been together ever since. They'd already been through a lot together, even though they'd known each other for less than two years, married for less than 12 months. Clare still marveled at her luck, finding such an incredible man to share her retirement with, the one man in all the world who completed her, even though he was a huge control freak. She would never have admitted to anyone, especially him, that maybe she needed that immense level of control over her life. But he did make her feel incredibly loved, even when he was driving her absolutely crazy. The 'Master' thing was new, but the love they had for each other had been there from the beginning, and they hoped it would be a strong foundation as their relationship changed.

Tommy and Clare knew they wouldn't have the long years together that some couples had, so they lived each day together with gusto, making the most of the time they did have. Time – such a precious commodity – at their age, they never knew when time was going to run out. In such a hurry to start their life together, Clare had let Tommy talk her into moving into his house with him the day after they met – the afternoon after the hottest sex she had ever had. So yes, she moved in with him because he was hot and she was needy and in lust, but she married him a year later because they were madly in love.

In their less than two years together, they had experienced meteoric highs and bottomless pit lows, but the middle ground was so fulfilling that neither of them could imagine being anywhere other than side by side. In the past year, Tommy's long lost psychotic, murderous brother, Shane, had descended on them, tortured them for hours in their home, and had almost gotten them both killed. Shane had ended up committing suicide by Cop – when he was gone, their whole small Carolina town breathed a collective sigh of relief. But it took another few weeks of tension between Tommy and Clare to finally put Shane behind them and move forward. In the end, Clare had to force the issue to get Tommy to face his own demons and let them go.

With Shane unable to hurt anyone anymore, and Tommy and Clare back on solid footing together, they settled into a routine that filled them both with peace and contentment. When Tommy proposed marriage on a flight to Hawaii, Clare said yes. The surprise wedding on Maui, surrounded by their closest friends and family members, was perfect. Even though Clare didn't get the enjoyment of planning her wedding, she couldn't imagine that she would have done any better than Tommy had done on her behalf. By the time they got home from Hawaii, they didn't think anything could possibly cause them any more difficulty than they'd already had. And then a rapist from her past resurfaced with plans to torture and then kill both Tommy and Clare.

Surviving Shane's attack had made Clare realize that she was not the weak little thing her rapist thought he remembered. In order to save herself and protect Tommy, she and the rapist finally faced off, in the middle of the living room in the house she shared with her husband, and she ended up killing him with his own gun. Again, Tommy and Clare were able to put a violent event behind them and move on. But the house itself suddenly seemed less hospitable than it had before. There were too many violent memories lurking in the corners. Tommy had suggested moving, but Clare had come to love his house as her own, and she wasn't about to let a few maniacs drive her away. Rather than move, they settled on some rather sweeping changes to the house that they thought would dispel the ghosts and make them comfortable in their home again. But just as the planning for their home remodel was wrapping up, Tommy stunned Clare with a request that would also remodel their relationship, and she questioned whether she would be able to make the changes he wanted to make. That remained to be seen.

Clare and Tommy had gone to Vegas to celebrate her birthday in October of that year and had a wonderful time, but because she was a horrible eavesdropper, she knew there was a serious conversation to be had once they got home. They had been back from Vegas only a few days when Tommy suggested they have dinner out one evening. They were just about to jump into remodeling hell and still had a lot of prep work to do, but they both needed a night out.

He took her to her favorite restaurant and they drank more than a little wine – at least Clare did. When they got home, they headed to their BDSM playroom in the lower level of the house for a little fun. Even in her slightly intoxicated state, Clare knew where the evening was headed – they were about to have "the talk". Tommy had barely gotten her stripped and into the restraints on her favorite piece of bondage equipment when she just couldn't keep her mouth shut any longer. Quietly, tentatively, Clare said "I know what you want to do – what you need me to do." And he looked at her and nodded.

Before they went to Vegas, she had overheard Tommy's end of a phone conversation with his friend Jackson. She was well aware that Jackson was very involved in the D/s lifestyle, and he had tried several times to get Tommy back into it. And she knew Tommy had walked away from that lifestyle many years before because his sub had gotten injured attempting something he wanted to try, and he felt guilty. When Tommy and Clare first started playing with bondage all those months before, they had a brief conversation about it, and she had expected they would have more conversations, but they never did – he had never brought it up again and neither had she. Clare assumed from the silence for all those months that Tommy just wasn't interested in getting that deep into the lifestyle again – that maybe marriage was enough for him. But it looked like either she had been wrong or he had changed his mind.

There was no more conversation between Clare and Tommy that night until she had been orgasm'd and then fucked almost to death and could barely move a muscle. Once he thought she had been subdued enough to listen and not talk, Tommy took her out of her restraints and carried her to the sofa in the family room outside the playroom, wrapped her in a warm, comfy blanket and started "the talk".

He pulled her into his lap and absentmindedly caressed her cheek, combing his fingers through her hair, thinking about all the things he wanted to tell her, never taking his eyes off hers. Then he began to speak.

"Clare, I'm not sure what you think you know, but here's the deal. Jackson has been getting a lot of requests to start up his dungeon again – from men and women he trusts. It would be the only dungeon for 100 miles around us and he's gotten a LOT of requests. He's also been getting a lot of requests from his friends to get some training – they want to learn how to be the best Dom they can be for the subs they have or for the subs they hope to find. Some of these dominant men and women have lots of experience, but nothing recent, and some have no experience at all – only the feeling that D/s might be the right lifestyle for them, but they need to learn more. He's also been getting requests, mostly from submissive men and women he knows, looking to get into, or back into, the lifestyle, but needing some training themselves. He's trying to weed out abusive Dom's like your ex, so that no other woman or man has to go through what you did with that cocksucker Edward.

"Jackson wants me to do the training – on how a Dom should behave, what expectations there should be for a sub they might take, how to safely use the equipment they might find in the dungeon. I might need a little practice on a few things, but I can do this training, I've done it before.

"The Doms in training will have to submit to anything they might want to do to a sub so they know how it will feel. Beyond that, some things I can demonstrate on a dummy, but other things would mean more, be more educational, on a live model. That would have to be you, unless you're willing to let me put my hands on some other woman, which I doubt. I can do some demonstrations with you clothed, but the ideal situation would be with you nearly or completely naked.

"I know your hard limits about doing things in front of people, of being naked in front of anyone other than me. People would see the scars on your ass, baby, and want to know how you got them. They would wonder if you got them from me. I don't know how willing you are to tell your story about your past experience, but there would be people who would want to know. You know there are still a lot of people who see our lifestyle as physical and emotional abuse, and it would be very helpful for potential club members to hear your story and your perspective. They'll learn more from that than anything I can demonstrate on a dummy. I'm just not sure I want to put you in that position.

"Baby Girl, these people being trained would want realistic feedback on how they're doing and they can't get always get that from a dummy. They can train with their own subs if they have them, but I think a lot of our potential members would be single – both Dom/me's and subs. I would never let anyone else fuck you, and the thought of another man putting his hands on you makes steam come out of my ears, but if you were willing, other men and women might gain good experience playing with your tits, maybe clamping your nipples, or you might get spanked by someone else from time to time. And there might come a time when you would be asked to help train subs who are looking for a good Dom. You would be much better suited to that training than I ever would.

"But even if we could get past all of that, there's discipline to be considered, Clare.

"You can't be pulling attitude every time something happens that you don't expect or don't like. And you can't just say every little thing that comes to mind – you have a smart mouth sometimes and that will get you into trouble. Other subs can't learn from you if you can't handle it yourself. All this isn't exactly the experience you might find in a larger, established location, but we have to work with what we have and what we know.

"Clare, I know this crosses into so many areas you've considered hard limits in the past, and I'm not sure I want to put you on a path that could lead to heartache, or any discord between us."

And he finally shut up, and gave Clare a chance to talk.

"Tommy, let me say what I need to say and then we can talk through everything together, okay? You know that because I'm a nosy eavesdropper, I've had some time to think about this. I know why you stepped away from the lifestyle but I also know that you've never really let it go. I'm a little surprised it took this long for someone to try to get you back into it. Tommy, you've helped me to grow so much as a woman since I've known you. When I first moved in here, I was so needy, so afraid, I had so many hard limits, I'm not sure how I let you touch me that first night.

"Maybe it's the natural Dom in you, but I trusted you to take care of me, to teach me, to push my limits – and even to keep me in line. I love the strong woman I am now, I'm proud of who you've helped me to become. Baby, I owe you so much, I can never repay you for everything you've done for me."

When Tommy started to respond to her statements, she stopped him because she wasn't done yet.

"No, don't say anything yet, I'm not done. Tommy, I don't know if I can do all those things you just talked about or not, I don't know what hard limits I have left. But I do know that this is something I need to try. I need to give this my best effort, not just for you, but for me too. It's something I WANT to try. As bad as things were with Edward, there was something about D/s that really spoke to me then, and still does now. There will be a transition from Husband to Master that will take a little time, but you know I've always been sexually submissive, we'll just have to see if I can take the next step, and be more submissive outside the bedroom as well. I don't know what Jackson's timetable is, how soon this would all start, how much time I have to prepare, but I think we probably need to start very soon. There's a certain dynamic to D/s that will challenge you as much as it does me. You're very possessive of me, even when we're with close friends. You may have as much difficulty with this transition as I do, maybe even a little more.

"You said a long time ago that our D/s relationship would be whatever we want it to be – whatever we make it. We can talk this to death forever, baby, but that isn't going to help either of us. If this is something you want to try, then we need to just jump in and see what happens. I'd like you to call Jackson and tell him yes, we're going to try."

And she pulled him to her to gaze into his eyes, to see into his heart, and let him see into hers. And they kissed like the world as they knew it was about to end.

They both slept fitfully that night, but the next morning, after they had both talked to Jackson, they were ready to see where this change in their relationship would end up, hoping like hell that they'd still be together at the end of the road.

Chapter 2

Tommy's idea of 'training' caused difficulty between him and Clare almost immediately, and those early weeks were some of the worst. He wanted her to call him Master, sometimes even when they were out around town. She had difficulty putting her BDSM side on display when they were not in a private setting, it was one of her bigger struggles with their new relationship.

His control freak nature blossomed as his inner Dom came out more and more. He seemed to know intuitively what would piss Clare off, and he would do those things just to see what her reaction would be. Like the night he wouldn't let her into bed until she had crawled across the bedroom floor and licked his feet – because he knew that she thought licking his feet was as demeaning as any activity he could insist on. He tried to make her sleep on the floor that night because she had hesitated too long before starting her crawl across the floor – it was almost the last night they slept in the same room.

"Tommy, I'm not sure I can make this change for you. I know you love and cherish me, but when you order me to do things like this, it makes me think you don't respect me. I have difficulty respecting myself when I think you don't respect me as a human being. I'm not your toy, I'm not your possession, I'm your wife, and I would think after everything you know I've been through in my life, you would appreciate how important respect is to me. You've asked me to do a lot of things lately that I didn't like, but I went along with it, trying to make this work. But making me crawl on the floor and lick your feet after everything you know happened with my former Dom could be my last straw. I'll put up with the ball gags and the slave poses and the extra discipline, but not this. Not this."

"Clare, baby, I know this is a hard transition for you. And no one could ever respect you more than I do, just for the fact that you're trying to make this change for me. But this is considered standard behavior between a Dom and sub in many places. I'm trying to find what your hard limits still are and get to some kind of middle ground for the two of us, not put so much stress between us that we break as a couple. I won't let that happen. So how about we put aside the crawling and the licking for the time being, maybe we can come back to it later, when you're more used to the Master/sub relationship. Come here, Clare, get into bed and let me hold you."

"I'm sorry, Master, I feel like I'm failing you because this isn't second nature to me and I'm struggling with so much."

"No, baby, I love you, you could never fail me, don't ever feel like that. Just come to bed and we'll put this behind us for tonight."

She took his hand and he helped her into bed. They got into their comfortable spooning position and he held her as she cried herself to sleep, placing soft kisses on her cheek to settle her. Before he faded off to sleep himself, Tommy wondered if he was making the biggest mistake of his life, risking his marriage and the woman of his dreams for the possibility of a relationship he could probably live without.

In the early days of her submissive training, Tommy had started calling Clare slut and whore, trying to convince her that when he called her those names, they were terms of endearment – but knowing that it took her right back to the night when the rapist had called her those names to humiliate her. Another ugly conversation ensued and he did stop calling her whore very quickly after, seeing by her continued reaction that it was the one word that brought back her worst memories. He was her loving husband after all, and even though he was trying to push her past her terrifying memories, he came to see that that particular 'endearment' might be another hard limit they had to work around.

And, of course, to add to the stress between them, right in the middle of their training, the home remodel project started in earnest.

In those early weeks, the stress of the remodel, combined with the strain of their new relationship, really took its toll on Clare and on her trust in Tommy. Many times she wasn't able to stop herself from screaming at him at the top of her lungs, calling him every vile name she could think of, begging him to take them back to the relationship they had before, knowing that they were probably past the point of no return on that. She went to bed too many nights in tears, her ass on fire from the latest punishment, but she never went to the spare bedroom to sleep, even when her bed seemed on the verge of being on the floor. She was afraid that once she made that break with Tommy, the best of what they were as a couple would be gone. All in all, the month of November sucked, but eventually the fights became fewer, Clare's ability to obey Tommy's simple commands was more consistent, and her trust that he would always protect and cherish her grew strong again.

They had jumped into home remodeling construction too naïvely, thinking that by Christmas, their home would be comfortable again, and reflective of both their tastes. Remodeling being what it is, their four week construction project quickly turned into eight to ten weeks. Thanksgiving came and went with no end in sight to the construction nightmare.

But the highlight of Thanksgiving was Clare's official collaring ceremony, in the living room of their home, attended by their closest friends. They were circled around Tommy, with a small opening on one side, through which Clare walked, wearing a long, sheer gauze cape, which she clutched tightly around her. She was all but naked for the first time in front of them, so nervous, she almost vomited on a very dear friend who was just trying to help Clare get ready. Once inside the circle, she released her death grip on the cape, and as it fell to her sides, everyone in the circle could see the pink flush of her embarrassment across her whole body. But the minute Clare saw Tommy's face, how seriously he was taking their commitment ceremony, nothing else mattered.

Once she was inside the circle, Tommy motioned for her to stand before him. His voice choked with emotion as he said one word – "Kneel."

And she did, careful to keep her eyes cast down and not look at his face again, as a sign of her own commitment and respect. He took a deep breath and said in a low voice "Clare, do you accept my collar as a sign of your devotion to me? Do you accept me as your Master? Do you trust that I will guide you and protect you and love you for the rest of our life together? Look at me now and answer me."

And Clare gazed up at his face, into his eyes, and responded with equal emotion, "Husband, I do accept you as my Master, deserving of my submission, my devotion, my trust, my love. I would be honored to accept your collar as a sign of my submission to you for the world to see. Whatever makes you happy will make me happy for the rest of my life."

And a single tear ran down her cheek as Tommy placed his hand on her head, signaling that he had accepted the gift of her devotion and her submission. And he replied quietly, "Good girl."

Tommy reached into his pocket and pulled out the beautiful gold and platinum chain, placed it around Clare's neck, and locked it in place with a small gold heart shaped padlock.

"Never take this collar off without my permission, love."

"Never, Master."

When the lock clicked into place, there was quiet applause from their friends. Clare didn't move from her knees but continued to look into Tommy's eyes.

When the applause died down, she asked "Permission to speak, Master?"

"Permission granted, slave."

"Master, I would be honored to be of service to you now."

And she licked her lips and stared at his zipper, which seemed to be straining at the force of his cock trying to get free.

He smiled at her and said "Permission granted, slave. Make your Master a happy, satisfied man. And while you pleasure me, I want you to pleasure yourself as well. Rub your clit and fuck your pussy with your fingers while you take me to your throat. Feel free to come if you can."

"Thank you, Master, you're very generous."

Clare shivered and broke out in a body full of goose bumps, then reached up with trembling fingers to slide the zipper of his pants down. She reached in and freed that beautiful hard cock that she knew and loved so much, and she pleasured her Master/husband until he was sated and relaxed. And she pleasured herself at the same time, coming with a surprising orgasm by her own hand, humming across her Master's cock just before he came. As she licked him clean, he pulled up her hand and licked her juice off, moaning a little at the taste he loved so much. She kissed his cock one last time, and then placed it gently back inside his slacks, zipping his pants closed again. Tommy helped Clare to her feet, caressed the chain and lock, then kissed her soundly, to more applause from their friends. And then the party began, filled with champagne, her favorite food, laughter and the love of their closest friends. It was an experience that she would hold in her heart for the rest of her life.

As much as she had dreaded the thought of the ceremony and everything about it in advance, it turned out to be one of the most liberating experiences of Clare's life. And the most meaningful she would ever remember. When Tommy had her kneel in front of him within the circle of their friends, and he put the gold and platinum collar around her neck, locking it in place, she felt connected to him in a way she never had before. When he allowed her to devour his cock in acceptance of her submission, and allowed her to experience an orgasm at the same time, his eyes were full of love. The fact that they had done all of that in front of their friends made her feel strong in a way she never had before. Because of him. That night was the pause and the celebration they both needed to get through the rest of Clare's training, as well as the damned construction project. And it was the start of the rest of their lives together.

The original plan was to remodel the kitchen along with the rest of the house, but the contractor convinced Tommy and Clare that the kitchen was too big a project, and should wait until it was the only room left to be done. So for most of December, the only rooms in their house not covered by plastic and drywall dust were their second floor bedroom/bathroom, the spare bedroom across the hall, and the first floor kitchen, most of the time. Even their BDSM playroom in the lower level of the house was undergoing a makeover, which was why her collaring ceremony had taken place in the living room instead of the playroom – it wasn't ready for anyone to see yet. The construction crew on that room was limited to Tommy's closest friends, the work was usually done at night, and the progress was going slower than the rest of the house.

Not everyone who knew Tommy knew about his long time interest in BDSM, and his penchant for a little couples bondage play with his loving wife, and Tommy planned to keep it that way. Clare wasn't allowed to see what changes were going on in their playroom, and the wait was killing her. She had fallen in love with her husband in that playroom, faced her past and conquered her fears there. She was hesitant to see anything about the room change – but Tommy assured her that she would love it when it was done.

And then, room by room, they started to see the light at the end of the construction tunnel. By Christmas Eve, there was still finish work to do in every room, but the really disruptive construction was almost done. And Tommy was pleased with how Clare's submissive training continued to progress.

They had agreed to skip Christmas presents just because there was nothing either of them really needed or wanted, other than time together. But he just couldn't stop himself. She had been looking online at new cars for quite awhile, something to replace her way too old Ford Escape, and she kept coming back to the latest Escape model. She would stare at it, picture herself sitting in it, driving it, speeding past all those jackass men in their pickup trucks on the highway, and then she'd close the browser and decide that her car would last another year. Christmas Eve morning, Tommy took her car instead of his own Mustang, calling over his shoulder to her that he'd be back in a little while, as he headed out the door. Clare didn't think too much about it, and she was busy in the kitchen anyway, doing weekly meal planning, making a grocery list, all the un-fun things that went on in a kitchen before getting to the fun baking and cooking part.

Tommy was back a few hours later, all 6 feet 3 inches of him stalking into the kitchen looking like hot monkey sex on two legs. Seeing Tommy always made Clare stop and take a deep breath – she just didn't know how a man in his 60's could still look so fucking hot, could make her so wet with just a look, but she was grateful for him every day. Ice blue eyes greeted her with a devilish sparkle and his close clipped reddish brown ex-Marine hair, finally showing a little grey at the temples, was always that unexpected turn-on. Not to mention the powerful chest, broad shoulders and those biceps that made Tommy look like he could pick up a car with no effort at all.

Clare turned her back on him to clear her head and get something out of a cupboard and he came up behind her, pressing her into the counter. She turned her head to look at him over her left shoulder. When he put his chin on her shoulder and looked back at her, he had a twinkle in his eye that suggested he'd done something she wasn't going to like, and he was trying to distract her – wrapping his arms around her from behind, fondling her breasts, kissing her neck, nibbling on her shoulder, pushing his hard cock into the crease between her ass cheeks. All the things he knew were guaranteed to make her lose track of everything, including what year it was. She was sure that whatever he had done had to be big – BIG!!

When Tommy thought Clare was adequately subdued by his sexy shenanigans, he pulled a strange car key out of his pocket and put it on the counter in front of her, along with the title to her old car, and for good measure, a pen. And the fight began.

"What did you do?!? Where are my car keys??"

"Now, Baby Girl, just calm down."

"Don't tell me to calm down! Where's my car?!?"

"It's at the dealership, where it's going to stay. Your lovely new car is in the driveway. It's the one you've been staring at online for three months. It's even the color you want. Let's go look at it and take a drive."

How could he stay so calm when all she wanted to do was scream and throw something?? "I want my car back, jackass – NOW!"

Tommy unleashed that deep, rumbling, no nonsense voice, the one he seemed to think always made Clare toe the line, and said "That's twenty – do you want to go for forty? On Christmas Eve?"

Not wanting her ass punished severely on Christmas Eve, as fun as it might have been, she changed her tone and said, as sweetly as she could, "Please, Master, I'm sorry, I just want my car back."

Tommy changed his tone a little too, trying not to be quite so stern.

"No, we're not going to do that, Clare. That old car of yours is a menace. It's not safe for you to drive, it leaks oil all over the driveway, and I'm really tired of trying to piece it back together again every time it breaks down. You've been looking at new cars for months but you're too cheap to just buy one. So I did it for you."

"Then you can just undo it. Take it back and bring mine home!"

"No."

"Yes!"

"No."

"Damn it, Tommy! Arghh!!" She screamed in frustration and he knew he had her. He turned her around in his arms to face him, planting a kiss on her forehead.

A gentler voice spoke now – "You act like I'm some pussy Dom that will let you get away with attitude but you know I'm not. That's ten more, for your spoiled brat attitude, at the time and place of my choosing."

Knowing she was not going to win the argument, she pouted, thinking how sore her ass might be on Christmas Day. But the thought of it, as usual, got her hot.

Luckily, Tommy wasn't without a little sensitivity – "Clare, I know that car has been a symbol of your hard won independence, but it has to go. It's done. The appropriate thing to do now is smile, say thank you, and maybe put a sweet little kiss right here on my cheek."

And he pointed to his face with that smirky smile she'd come to know and love – and hate. There were lots of things Clare could think to do with his cheek, but kissing it wasn't one that immediately came to mind! She tried to stare him down, but she'd never won that contest before and she knew she never would.

So she stopped – took a deep breath – smiled – and said "Thank you, Master, I'm sure I'll be very happy with the new car."

And she pulled herself up his 6' 3" sex rocket body to give him that kiss he was looking for. And he smiled back at her – that smile that he reserved for every time he won an argument – the one Clare had seen all too often since they had met.

"That's better. It's not going to get you out of your well deserved punishment though. Now sign the title to your old car – with the correct name, please – and we'll take a drive in the new car. We can drop off the title at the dealership on our way home."

"Yes, Master. Whatever you say, Master. I live only to serve you, Master."

He swatted her ass as a warning, then gently ran his fingers around the gold and platinum chain link collar around her neck, caressing the tiny lock with his fingers.

"Clare, have I told you lately how much I love you, and how much you please me?" Then he smiled and kissed her forehead again. Her loving husband and Master helped her into her favorite leather jacket, grabbed her purse off the kitchen counter and handed it to her. And they were off to take Clare's new Christmas present car for a drive.

Chapter 3

Tommy's Christmas Eve gift to Clare was not the only gift given that day – she had one for him as well. About six months after she had moved in with Tommy, there was a disastrous pre-Thanksgiving reunion with her family. The aftermath of that disaster was Clare having to reveal to Tommy yet another embarrassing secret about her past – her sister's misguided attempt to have Clare committed to a mental institution because she thought she was unstable and couldn't conduct her own affairs anymore. All because of what she considered Clare's routinely bad choices in men. Obviously, the district court did not agree with her sister's opinion and Clare was not committed. But as a health care professional, and because he was a huge nosey bastard control freak, Tommy had insisted on seeing the paperwork from her final psychiatric evaluation and the court transcripts of her final competency hearing.

As Clare was digging through a large box in the spare bedroom to find the documentation he was dying to read, Tommy put his hands on a book that she wasn't ready for him to see. It was a journal that she had kept for the ten years before she met Tommy, filled with frustration, despair, detailed accounts of her time with a rapist and an abusive

Dom, comments from and about opinionated "friends" and family, ups and downs of life in general, right up until a few months before Clare and Tommy met.

She didn't want him to read the journal yet and she asked him not to. He knew at a high level all of the things Clare had experienced before she met him, but not the graphic details that she wasn't prepared at the time for him to read yet. She hid the journal but she was pretty sure he always knew where it was. She was also very sure that since he had promised never to read it until she gave it to him, he had never opened it in all those months. In the interest of Clare keeping no more secrets from her Master, she decided it was now time for him to have the journal and the option to read it – or not – she was leaving it up to him. Earlier in the day, while Tommy was out buying her new car, she retrieved the journal from its hiding place, flipped through the pages quickly, and then wrapped it and put a card on it with just a few words to let him know that she was ready to put her past behind her, and face their future with a clean slate. Clare slipped the wrapped journal in Tommy's Christmas stocking along with a few other small gifts, hung it back on the fireplace mantle in the living room, and went back to what she had been doing in the kitchen.

After the argument about her new car, they took that drive, dropped off the title to her old car at the dealership, had lunch at a fabulous little bistro in the neighborhood and headed home. She went to the kitchen to work on their Christmas Eve dinner, and Tommy went to his office to do some work. A few hours later, she knocked on his office door to let him know that dinner was about 30 minutes away.

He looked up at Clare, smiled and said "Come here, little slut. Strip and put yourself across my lap. I think we have time to get your punishment out of the way before dinner."

She opened her mouth to protest, then closed it again without saying anything. She only hesitated a second before scampering to his desk. Clare stood the required 18 inches from him as he sat in his office chair, and she started to remove her clothes. She took her time unbuttoning her blouse, and when all the buttons were undone, she slid it teasingly off her shoulders, down her arms and off, folded it carefully and laid it across Tommy's desk. He moaned a little as he looked at her. Then she unbuttoned and unzipped her jeans, pushed them down off her hips, down to the floor and stepped out of them. They also got folded carefully and placed on the desk with the blouse.

Since Tommy didn't like for Clare to wear panties except for special occasions, that left her standing 18 inches away from him wearing only her pale pink lace La Perla bra and a little smile, her newly aroused state obvious to both of them. And he groaned, his stare fixed on her freshly waxed naked pubis, right at eye level.

She started to reach behind her to unhook her bra, and he said "Stop. Step closer."

Anticipation trapped her breath in her lungs and her core clenched as she closed the distance between them. Almost before she had stopped moving, Tommy's hands were on her hips, pulling her close. He buried his nose in her bare crotch and took a deep breath, and then growled. The sound of his breath and his growl made her lower half clench tight again, and Clare could feel the dampness between her legs growing. He licked around her smooth, waxed mound, uncovered her swelling clit with his tongue and bit down sharply, making her squeal and rise up on her toes. And the dampness between her legs became a small stream. And Tommy's groans got louder and raspier.

He finally pulled his hands away from her hips and reached up to caress her breasts over the lace of her bra. Clare's body broke out in goose bumps and her nipples hardened at Tommy's touch. He gave them both a good pinch between his thumbs and forefingers through the lace, making her squeal again.

And he said "I love that little sound you make, baby, it makes my cock hard."

"Your cock is always hard, Master."

"Whenever I'm around you, little slut. You do that to me." And he played for a few more minutes, while she gasped and moaned.

Then he looked up at her and said "Step back, little slut, finish stripping so we can get to the good stuff."

"You mean where you light my ass on fire, Master? That good stuff?"

"Yes, that good stuff, slave. And don't be surprised if I don't stop at twenty because of your impertinence."

She giggled a little when she said "Whatever you desire, Master, you know I live to please you."

"And you always do please me, love. Now get out of that bra and assume the position on my lap." And then HE laughed.

Clare removed her sexy bra and draped her naked self across her Master's lap so that he could make them both groan and breathe heavy. Feeling his hard cock against her belly as she lay across his lap made getting settled a little difficult, but she finally stilled as he put his hands gently on her ass cheeks, caressing her as only he had ever done. He slipped a finger between her ass cheeks and moved down to inspect her pussy, finding it already showing the evidence of her arousal. What he found there made him groan, and what he did next made Clare groan.

Clare's twenty punishment spankings turned into twenty-five, delivered slowly and methodically by her expert Master spanker – a hard slap, then a soft caress, then two hard slaps, another soft caress, running his fingers through her increasingly wet pussy and checking after every few spanks to see if she was enjoying her punishment. Moans escaped her throat after every few swats, and tears flowed from her eyes as she absorbed the blaze of fire on her ass. She melted as the fire became sensual heat, and the small stream between her legs turned into a river of her desire.

When her punishment was done, Clare remained spread across Tommy's lap while he caressed her burning ass, bringing both of them slowly back to the real world. He let his hands wander between her legs, feeling the small flood there, laughing a little and feeling like a king because he had done that to her. He played lightly with her clit, enough to maintain her arousal, but not forceful enough to take her over the edge.

She whispered "Master, please…"

And he said "No, slave, this was for punishment, not for pleasure."

"Yes, Master, I understand. I was just hoping, since it's Christmas Eve, that it might be both punishment and pleasure?" And she sighed audibly, raising her ass just a little to bring his fingers closer to her prize.

"Topping from the bottom again, my love? Will you never learn to leave well enough alone?"

He delivered three more hard slaps to her already red butt cheeks, causing her to gasp and moan again. Then helped her to stand up and step away from him, whispering in her ear, "Your acceptance of my discipline always makes me proud, love."

"You deserve nothing less, my Master."

He stood before her, pulled her close, and kissed her – tenderly at first and then building to a lip biting, demanding kiss that left them both breathless and overheated. And then the oven timer rang out from the kitchen, interrupting their passionate interlude, and Clare knew she had some work to do. Tommy released her with a little laugh.

She grabbed her clothes from his desk and yelled over her shoulder "Dinner in the dining room in 15 minutes, Master." And she ran to the kitchen to put dinner on the table.

·❤·❤·❤·❤·❤·

This being their first special dinner since becoming Master and submissive, as well as husband and wife, Clare wanted to make it a very special occasion. She set the dining table with one place setting, and brought all the food to the table. When Tommy came into the dining room, she was at her place, wearing nothing but an apron, kneeling on the floor on a pillow next to his chair, ready to serve him whatever he needed. This dinner was about her commitment and her service to him, and she could eat later. She wasn't all that hungry at the moment, she was too nervous about what his reaction would be, and her ass was still pretty sore from her spanking.

Tommy was absolutely silent as his eyes scanned the room and took it all in, especially Clare, mostly naked, kneeling on her pillow on the soft area rug that covered the hardwood floor under the table.

She heard him take a deep breath and say "Everything looks lovely, little slave. You worked very hard today."

Clare let out a long sigh and said "Thank you, Master. It's my pleasure. May I serve you dinner?"

Still very emotional, he managed to croak out "I'd like that very much."

She rose from her kneeling position and pulled out his chair for him. When he was seated, she served him a little of each dish she'd prepared and poured him a glass of wine that would go well with dinner. After she set the plate and the wine glass in front of him, she returned to her position on the floor, her eyes burning a hole in the rug under Tommy's chair, hoping he'd be happy with his meal and with her submissive behavior. It was important for her to show him that she was actually learning all the things he'd been trying to teach her about their evolving relationship.

"Everything is delicious, Clare, would you join me?"

"Thank you, Master, I would be happy to join you."

As Clare rose from the floor, she thought she would go to the kitchen and get another plate and glass, but Tommy had other ideas. Before she could walk to the kitchen, he took her hand and patted his lap, wanting her to sit with him.

"Here, little slut, sit on my lap and I'll feed you."

"Whatever makes you happy, my Master."

As she settled on his lap, Tommy said "I've always wanted to do this, Clare, but there was never anyone I wanted to do it with until I met you. Every time I turn around, you fulfill another of my fantasies. You enrich my life and fill my soul. I can never make you understand how much I love you. Maybe I'm a pussy Dom after all."

She kissed him gently on the cheek and said "We complete each other, my love. I walked a long, hard road to reach this day with you. It's been worth every sad, lonely moment that came before, just to share this with you now. I look forward to nothing but the best with you in the years to come. And my ass would say that you are not a pussy Dom at all, Master."

And he laughed and kissed her lips sweetly, and her body exploded in those goose bumps that always said so much about her feelings for him.

They sat and talked quietly as he ate, and he fed her along the way. And when they were done eating, they continued to talk into the evening, until the weight of her sitting on his lap made the poor man's leg start to go numb.

While Clare cleared the table and cleaned up the kitchen, Tommy went to the living room and lit a fire in the gas fireplace, checking out the stockings hanging on the mantle, like he'd been doing for the past ten days. He noticed something extra in his stocking and was dying to know what it was. When she came into the living room, Clare had changed from her apron into a very short red lace nightgown and a Santa hat, hoping Tommy would see the humor and desire in her wardrobe change and wouldn't require her to be naked for the whole evening. When he saw her, he smiled approvingly and patted the sofa next to him for her to sit.

Clare pulled the stockings off the mantle and brought them with her to the sofa, handing his to him as she sat down and snuggled next to him. They opened all the little gifts and kissed after each one was opened, but he saved the larger unknown package for last.

"Clare, what is this?"

"Please open it and find out, Master."

He opened the card first and read what she'd written – "*T, this is my past, you're my future. Do with this book whatever you wish. Read it or don't, it's your choice. I don't want this past anymore, I have you and a bright future to look forward to. Your loving slut, C*"

"Clare, is this what I think it is?"

"I guess once you open it, you'll know for sure. Please go ahead and open it, you're making me a little nervous by not."

Tommy very gingerly opened the package and saw the journal inside. He seemed hesitant to touch it, and he looked at Clare, almost as if asking permission. She just nodded a little and he picked it up, thumbing through the pages quickly, looking at the date on the first page and the date on the last page.

"Clare, this is almost 10 years of your life."

"Yes."

"And it stops right before we met."

"Yes. I had decided that it was time to look forward and not back, and I had a feeling that 2013 was going to be a good year, I didn't need to keep that journal anymore. Tommy, the book is yours to do with as you please. If you choose to read it, fine. If you choose not to, that's okay too. I just don't want there to be any secrets left between us."

"You haven't been keeping a journal about our time together."

"No, I'm sorry, I haven't been. Early on, it seemed like journaling was too much like living in the past, and I didn't want to do that anymore. Then once we settled into a routine, there wasn't time, and not really any way I could write something private with you snooping around all the time."

"I don't snoop."

"Really? You don't think you're just a little snoop-ish?"

"I do not snoop. Besides, it's my house, and everything in it belongs to me."

"I guess I can't argue the fact that I belong to you – body and soul. How about if someday I write a book about our life together – a grand tell-all about the adventures of Big Man and Baby Girl – Master and slave girl. That would be a best seller, don't you think? Maybe even a blockbuster movie?"

"I know it would be a best seller, I'm just not sure I want our personal life put out there for the world to read. I'll think on it and let you know later if you have permission to write that book."

"Fine, my love, you just let me know when you're ready. Now would you like some more wine? A snack? Perhaps some chocolate and a cigar? We never finished what we started in your office, maybe I could get on my knees and serve you again? Would that please you, my Master?"

Clare put her hand to Tommy's cheek, caressing his soft bottom lip with her thumb, gazing into his distractingly ice blue eyes. He leaned into her palm and sighed.

"Everything you do pleases me, slave. I think another glass of wine would be very nice, and maybe a little snack for later. But let's take everything up to the bedroom and finish what we started earlier. I certainly wouldn't want you to have to go to sleep tonight unfulfilled."

"You're such a kind, generous Master. I think I love you." And she leaned up to kiss him gently on those soft, full lips.

"And I love you too, little slave."

They kissed again, building another fire between them. While Clare went to the kitchen to get more wine and some of Tommy's favorite snacks, he shut off the fireplace and headed upstairs. She joined him in their bedroom where they toasted Christmas Eve, and let the fire of their passion rage until only the glowing embers of their lovemaking remained. And then they were sound asleep, spooning together, bare skin to bare skin, in their usual position.

Chapter 4

The Christmas morning sex was spectacular, and a little more primal than they'd had during the past few months, because Tommy had called a moratorium on their Master/slave relationship for the holiday, putting them on the same level for a change. Clare took advantage of the opportunity to top from the bottom a little. The hot monkey sex that threw them off the bed onto the floor was only round one, and by the time the passion was finally on simmer, they'd had sex as many ways as a man and woman can have. And she was a little sore. They spent some time soaking together in the Jacuzzi tub in the bathroom to ease some of the discomfort and then had some dessert sex in the shower just to finish things off. Clare's husband was a manly man, as he had been since the day they had met.

They spent Christmas away from the house and the construction mess that still remained, helping to serve Christmas dinner at a homeless shelter about 30 miles away, and then visiting with friends around town. Clare had tins of homemade cookies, brownies and fudge to deliver to their special friends and it took up most of the afternoon and evening. By the time they got home, she was ready to snuggle in with whoever was in her bed that night – she was never sure if it would be her husband or her Master – she was just ready for some sleep with a strong, protecting arm around her, holding her close.

But Tommy had one last thing he wanted to do before they turned in for the night. Clare had just undressed and was about to get into bed when Tommy came into the bedroom, took her hand, and led her back downstairs. She didn't even have time to grab a robe as they exited the bedroom. He pulled her by the hand down the stairs, made a right turn through the kitchen, and down another set of stairs to the family room, and the door that led to their playroom. The room she thought was still under construction. Still off limits to her.

As they stood before the door, she could tell Tommy was a combination of apprehensive, excited, and shortly thereafter, horny as hell.

"Clare, I know I told you that I didn't want you to see the playroom until it was done, but I can't wait any longer. There's still finish work to be done, but all of the big stuff is complete and I want you to see it. I need to know that you love it as much as I do."

"Husband, if you love it, I know I will also." And he unlocked the door and held it open for her to enter.

The room was dark when they walked in, and Tommy closed the door before he turned on the lights. When the room was illuminated, Clare gasped – it was so different – and so beautiful. The space was relatively the same size as the old playroom but a few walls had been shifted.

Everything had been rearranged or replaced, making the room look so much larger and more open. Recessed lights had been added near the ceiling all the way around the room, and the color was a dark rich gold, making the whole room seem to glow. The walls were covered in dark gold brocade paper, and the floor was covered in dark brown marble, with flecks of gold that sparkled under the glow of the lights.

All of the furniture was wood, stained a rich oak color, and the pieces that were covered were spread with deep red or gold leather or dark red velvet. The colors of the wood and the leather were made all the richer by the muted gold of the recessed lights.

It was all so beautiful, Clare wasn't sure where to look first, but eventually she made her way around the room, taking in the new furniture, touching everything, imagining all of the erotic things Tommy had envisioned when he found each piece.

To her left, close to the door, was a wide wooden chair with a tall, somewhat reclined, velvet covered back, a shallow leather covered seat, and substantial scrolled wooden arms and legs that extended well beyond the edge of the seat. Putting a hand gently on one of the padded, upholstered arms, her mind went to all of the possibilities the chair would afford.

If Clare sat on the chair, her ass would be almost hanging off the edge, and she noticed that the height of the seat would be just perfect for Tommy to stand between her legs and fuck her blind. When she looked closer, she could see that there were D rings anchored into the wood in many places, just begging for Tommy to strap her in.

Once he had her firmly restrained, he could stand and fuck her silly or get on his knees and eat her pussy all day long, and she wouldn't be able to make a move. If she knelt on the seat of the chair, facing the velvet back, Tommy could restrain her arms and legs in different positions for other forms of pleasurable punishment. Her breath caught in her chest and she started to get very aroused and very wet, just thinking about everything he could do to her. The chair was torture and bliss all wrapped up in one, and she couldn't wait to try it out. But there was much more still to see and touch.

On the wall facing the door was an honest to god St. Andrew's Cross, mounted to the floor and the wall. The wood had been sanded and finished smooth as silk and there were already padded cuffs attached, anticipating its use. Again, there were D rings anchored into the wood so that Tommy could tie her to the cross in different positions, perfect for a good flogging. They hadn't done that yet, but she knew he'd been practicing so that he could train other Dom's how to use different kinds of floggers, and it was only a matter of time before he started practicing on a live model. Clare hoped Tommy wouldn't keep her waiting too long, she couldn't wait to try it out. And her "wet" became a small stream in anticipation.

Across the room, opposite the multi-purpose chair, was her favorite spanking bench, the perfect item for a good spanking or a sound butt fucking. It was the only piece of furniture that remained from the original playroom, and she was glad that Tommy had kept it. The spanking bench was the last piece of bondage furniture Clare had allowed Tommy to use with her in the original playroom, and it had quickly become her favorite. Just looking at it, even in its recovered state, conjured highly erotic memories with her Master.

As part of the room remodel, Tommy had the bench recovered in dark red leather, to coordinate with the rest of the room, but other than that, it was the same spanking bench Clare had learned to love. Funny that it was the one piece of original furniture that she had resisted at first. Tommy had to get her stoned one night to introduce her to the bench because she had refused anal sex. It was too much a reminder of what she had experienced being tortured by her rapist. But again, her husband had helped her through that nightmare of her past. Once she trusted that Tommy wouldn't hurt her, and she realized what an intense orgasm she could achieve with anal, she learned to really enjoy it.

The final piece of furniture in the room was angled into the corner on the door wall. It was a beautiful double wide oak fainting couch covered in soft, dark gold leather. It had a gentle rise at the head, the perfect elevation for lounging, and there were no sides to get in the way. This piece of furniture also had D rings available to attach restraints at the head, down the sides and at the foot end. And Clare started thinking maybe she could actually get Tommy restrained on this piece of furniture for a leisurely blow job or with her on top riding his cock to glory.

There was beautiful erotic artwork scattered throughout the room, on the walls and on small tables tucked in the corners, but it wasn't until she looked up from the fainting couch that Clare noticed a large, beautifully framed photo on the wall above it. It was a photo of Tommy and Clare the night of their collaring ceremony, at the moment when he placed the collar around her neck and clicked the lock closed. The two of them were in focus, with everyone around them faint and blurry. The photo captured the devotion on Clare's face and the love in Tommy's eyes as he looked at her and caressed the collar. And it made her cry to look at the simple beauty of it.

By the time they finished their tour of the room, Tommy was almost breathless. He'd been waiting for Clare to say something about the changes to the room, and she realized that she had barely said a word since they'd walked in. She also realized there were tears streaming down her cheeks. Clare turned and threw her arms around his neck and continued to cry. He hugged her tight for a minute and then pulled her away from him.

"Clare, why are you crying? Do you hate the room?"

"Oh no, my Master, it's spectacular. I know it's not quite finished, but it's already perfect, just the way it is."

"Oh, my little slut, I'm so glad you love it. The colors make you positively glow. Every piece of furniture and art reminded me of you. This room was inspired by you."

"I do love it. I'm already wet thinking about how we're going to use this room. Christmas isn't over yet, Husband. There's wine waiting in the bedroom and you have a very aroused wife dying for your attention before she sleeps."

And she snuggled up close to him and wiggled on his cock, feeling it growing with every passing second.

"Baby Girl, you really are such a brat sometimes. You're really lucky I love you so much. Let's go upstairs and I'll let you make me come inside your juicy cunt."

"No slave ever had a more generous Master, my love." And they kissed again, then headed upstairs for a glass of wine and some screaming orgasms.

The fire of her Master's passion flashed red hot, singeing them both as he pulled her up the stairs. Half way up, he sat Clare down on a step and spread her legs wide. When he stared at her exposed pussy, the pupils of his eyes grew so large and were so dark she wasn't sure how he could see. But he could see just fine.

He seared her with that look, igniting a bonfire inside her, as he whispered "I can't wait, baby. I need a little taste and maybe a little something else to tide me over. It's a long way up to the bedroom."

Yes, it was maybe 15 whole steps to the bedroom, but Clare wasn't prepared to wait either. Her erotic thoughts as they had toured the remodeled playroom already had her dripping wet, and having him leer at her with that "I have to have you now, slut" look on his face just amped up her arousal. She rested her back and head on the steps above and Tommy leaned in toward her mound with those magic lips and that tongue he'd been tormenting and teasing her with for almost two years. It still hadn't gotten old. He leaned so close she could feel his fevered breath on her pussy lips, and her clit jumped out from its hiding place to greet him.

With a tight voice and labored breath, she begged "Please eat my pussy, Master. Eat me like only you can. Please suck my clit and fuck me with your tongue. You know I live for it. Please, Master, I'm desperate for your touch." And she spread her legs as wide as she could in invitation, making her Master growl in anticipation at the sound of her dirty talk and the scent of her arousal.

That first lick from her rear hole to her clit made Clare gasp so hard she thought she might have inhaled Tommy, but he just laughed and licked again. He attacked her clit with his thumb and fucked into her pussy with his tongue, starting the goose bumps and the panting breath that only he had ever given her. Over and over, he swirled around her sensitive little bud, his tongue flicking in and out of her slit. Her soft moans and garbled words seemed to be music to his ears, and she could hear him groan a little as well. When she was right on the edge, just about to jump off the cliff, he stopped and looked up at her.

"Please, Master, please make me come, please!!!" He laughed and started swirling around her clit again, but not enough to send her screaming.

She moaned long and loud and he said "I'm not sure you deserve to have an orgasm, slut, you made me wait so long to tell me whether you liked the playroom changes. That was very unkind and I'm thinking you need to be punished just a little."

"No, Master, please. You can punish me later. I need a Christmas orgasm and I need it really bad!"

And he laughed again and whispered "Oh, my love, I crave the sound of your begging. And you did it so sweetly, I will grant your request."

And he leaned back down, shoved two very talented fingers inside her pussy, stroking that G spot he knew so well, and bit down on her clit with just enough pressure to send her to the moon. Clare screamed through the waves of her orgasm and stopped breathing for just a few moments. When she came back to the world, her Master was clutching her hips tightly, pinning her to the step, and he was pumping that mighty cock into her with perfect aim, hitting that G spot again and again, sending her falling into another orgasm that rolled through her entire body. Her pussy muscles clenched that cock so tightly, Tommy gasped and shot off his own orgasm, and they rode their combined release together, clutching each other as the waves rippled through them.

The full weight of Tommy's body fell on her and they held onto each other as if their lives depended on the connection. They didn't move for a few minutes, slowing their breathing, gently caressing each other, nibbling each other's lips, relishing the quiet moment. And marveling that they hadn't slid down a few steps from the intensity of their combined release.

"Oh, my Master, you are the best fuck I've ever had. You don't just fuck my body, you make love to my mind and my soul. I thank the heavens every day for the love I have in you."

"We certainly did wait a long time to find each other, little slave, but it was worth the wait, don't you think?"

"I'd go through it all over again if I knew I would end up right here with you. Take me to bed, love, let me show you just how much I love you. I want to fuck your cock with my mouth. I want to tickle that little spot just under the head with my tongue. I want to take you all the way to my throat and swallow everything you can give me."

That growl rolled out of Tommy's chest again and Clare knew that he would grant her request. With his big cock still inside her, she squeezed him ever so gently with her tiny but strong pussy muscles, over and over again, making him grow as he carried her to the bedroom. He lifted her off and allowed her to remove what was left of his clothing, depositing everything on the floor. As each piece of clothing came off, she licked a little across his skin – the hollow of his throat, his chest, his peaked nipples, his navel, down the smooth center of his six-pack-covered core to the root of his cock as his pants came off. She gave him one kiss on the head of his cock and then he stretched out on his back on the bed, making a place for her on her knees between his legs. The sight of him, looking like a grand Christmas feast, made Clare lick her lips in anticipation.

He lifted the two glasses of wine off the bedside table, and handed one to her. They clinked glasses and toasted Christmas and their love for each other, and downed the wine in one gulp. He took the glass from her hand, put both glasses back on the bedside table, then gave her his darkest Dom look.

"I believe promises were made, slave."

"Yes, they were, Master."

"Then be about your business, little slut. You know what I expect. Devour your Master. Suck my cock, play with my balls, make me come down your throat until this painful erection is tamed."

"It would be my pleasure, Master. I live for these opportunities. I want nothing more tonight than to satisfy your every desire and then sleep peacefully beside you – if that pleases you." And he growled again and smiled.

She started slowly, with her hands, gently caressing his cock with one hand and his balls with the other, marveling as she watched him grow second by second. He slid down on the pillows a little lower, spreading his legs a little wider, giving her more access. Clare grasped his cock tighter, stroked him a few times, up and down, up and down, hearing his breathing change as she did. That little bit of pre-come on the tip drew her like a magnet and she bent to swipe it with her tongue.

As always, the taste of him took Clare to a place inside her head where her desire was savage and her libido was overpowering. She licked his cock from root to tip, cupping and rolling his balls as she did. When her Master's breathing picked up, she took his cock inside her mouth and began to suck, just the head at first, but then moving lower and lower. She tongued his dick on her way down, sucking her way back up so that only the head remained in her mouth.

With each pass, she went lower, until her lips touched his soft, curly pubic hair. She paused for just a second and swallowed on him, then sucked her way back up to the tip. She leaned down lower to suck his balls into her mouth, one by one, and roll them with her tongue, then went back to suck the head of his cock, giving him that little bite she knew he loved.

"Oh, little slut, you have such a talented mouth, I consider myself the luckiest Master in the world." And she smiled a little, humming her joy down the length of his cock.

He began to pant and Clare could feel the shudders in his body that told her he was close. She took his cock to her throat with one pass and swallowed – he groaned low in his chest and started shooting come down her throat. She swallowed over and over, not wanting to lose anything, licking her way back up until she finally let him slip from her mouth. One final, gentle kiss on the tip of his cock showed her Master how much she loved him and how glad she was to be his. He leaned forward and took her in his arms, giving her a kiss that showed her how much she was loved in return.

Tommy turned off the lights and they both stretched out on the bed under the covers. He pulled Clare to his side so that they could sleep skin to skin, spooning like they had since their first night together. As she fell asleep, the grandfather clock in the living room chimed Midnight, signaling the end of another magical Christmas with the only man she had ever really loved.

When Tommy knew that she was asleep, he reached behind him to the little basket on the bedside table that held the TV remote, and pulled out a small remote that he was hoping Clare had never noticed was there. Pointing to the ceiling fan in the center of the bedroom, he hit the little remote once and turned off the hidden video camera that had just recorded yet another of their sexual interludes – the Christmas blow job she'd just given him. He smiled to himself, knowing that being videotaped or photographed during sex had always been an almost "hard" limit for her. He laughed quietly when he imagined the reaction she would have when she saw the video and knew other people were seeing it also. He hid the little remote under his pillow and fell asleep, snuggled next to the love of his life, satisfied that he had captured some more excellent training video for the classes they were about to start teaching.

Chapter 5

The weeks that followed Christmas were filled with work, friends and Clare's continued submissive training. She and Tommy took a break to celebrate New Year's Eve with a party at a close friend's house, but she was still mostly naked that night, as were all of the other established submissives in their group of friends. She was getting more and more comfortable being naked in front of their friends, but because Tommy still had some issues with his Dom friends who might inadvertently touch her, she again wore the flowing gauze cape she'd worn for her collaring ceremony. And she didn't mind at all. More than once that evening, Clare had to tend to her Master – kneeling at his feet and rubbing against his leg, putting her arms around him and placing a kiss over his heart. He always seemed to settle once she placed her hands on him and showed him she had no interest in any other man, no other Master but him. It got to be a long night, and they were both relieved to be headed home shortly after midnight – before her Master had the need to punch some friend in the nose.

They practiced many things during the month of January, but she also found Tommy frequently taking a break, sitting in the family room reading the journal she had given him for Christmas. He chuckled at comments in the early parts of the journal –

Saturday, May 29, 2004

Picking up men is harder than I remembered. Spent the day on the golf course and the evening in the bar and ended up with nothing more than a sunburn and a hangover. Maybe I just haven't invested enough time. Sure would like some help – I'm not doing a very good job giving myself an orgasm and it's not helping my mood at all.

(Tommy's thoughts – "Oh my god, is she kidding? This is hysterical!!")

And she caught him laughing openly a few times –

Saturday, August 21, 2004

Well I got what I needed but I can't go back to that golf course again. Thought I was alone on the back nine, got caught with my hand in my panties by a guy wanting to play through. He had a condom in his wallet and a big cock to put it on, and he knew how to use what nature gave him. Got some abrasions on my back and on my ass from the tree bark, but he made me come and got his rocks off in the process. He even said thank you as he played through.

(Tommy's thoughts – "Tree bark burns!! She does like sex outdoors. I wonder what she thought of my cock the first time she saw it. Oh, yes, she called it 'magnificent'! And I do know what to do with what nature gave me!")

But when he got to the passages about her abusive former Dom, it was all she could do to calm him.

Sunday, October 14, 2007

Guess I'm lucky to still be alive. Survived my stupidity one more time. Spent 6 months in hell with Edward and when the torture was over, I left with my car, a key to a storage locker, a bunch of scars on my ass, and a check for $75,000.00 – hush money, I guess, so I don't go to the police. Not that I would – I walked into that nightmare with my eyes wide open. And signed a contract. Fucking A-Fib is back – the stress of the last 6 months, I guess. Back in the monthly Cardiologist blood test cycle again. I could just kill that bastard Edward.

(Tommy's thoughts – "Me too, baby.")

Sunday, November 25, 2007

It's 5:00 am and I'm in the mood to clear some shit out of my head. So here it is – the Edward Chronicles. Foreplay always started with spankings, which I didn't mind, but escalated to getting paddled hard with whatever implement was close by. The few times I tried to get away from the beating or defend myself, I got beat worse...

(Tommy's thoughts – "God, no wonder she didn't fight me that first time I spanked her! She must have been terrified. And I was such an ass that night!")

May 1ˢᵗ I woke up with his collar on me, had to start calling him Master Edward. We had talked about a collar a few weeks before – I said I wasn't ready for that level of commitment – he wasn't happy and finally made the decision for me. It had a lock on it so there was no way I could get it back off. So much for that sacred BDSM symbol.

(Tommy's thoughts – "Does she really want to wear my collar, or was she just afraid to say no?")

He had a party for Summer Solstice in June – lots of people invited – I was chained in the dungeon naked, on display – Edward gave tours – brought guests down so they could look at me, call me names, touch me, beat me, fuck me, deep throat me – sometimes two or three of his friends going at me at the same time – whatever they wanted – Master was the consummate host.

(Tommy's thoughts – "Jackson has been watching out for this prick to apply at the new dungeon. I will kill the bastard if he ever comes near Clare again!")

Early August, he beat me with a cane so bad I passed out – woke up – passed out again – don't even remember why – there may not have been a reason – it was days before I could walk again – longer for the cuts from the cane to heal. God awful scars on my ass.

(Tommy's thoughts – "The scars are awful, even now, but I look at them as a sign that she's strong and she survived. This pig is going down!")

I watched and waited, and when everyone's back was turned, I snuck out. Almost made it to the road before he caught me. That night he dragged me down to the dungeon naked, handcuffed me to the wall again with a bucket between my legs so I wouldn't pee on the floor, and he left me there in the dark for the weekend.

Three weeks later, the contract had expired, the doctor said I was well enough to leave, and that was that. I left with my car, the key to the storage locker with all my stuff in it, and a big check. Didn't see Edward that last day and never looked back – hope I never see him again.

(Tommy's thoughts – "I don't know how she survived all of this. I can't even read about it without crying, without getting so angry I want to find him and kill him with my bare hands. I think I have to put this journal away for awhile – maybe come back to it in five or ten years! I need to find Clare and hold her.")

Tommy's anger toward Edward for some of the things he'd done to her had seemed to be a living thing, and Clare wasn't sure if he was more angry at Master Bastard for doing it, or at her for allowing it and never reporting him to the Police. Tommy had become obsessive about Edward, and she worried that something ugly would happen.

But just as she was contemplating having a talk with Tommy's best friend and fellow Dom Justin, Clare noticed that Tommy had put the journal away and they didn't speak of it again. Which was a good thing, because by the end of January, they were ready to start doing some Dom/sub training with Tommy's friend, Master Jackson, and his friends at Jackson's soon to be opened dungeon.

She was excited to do this for Tommy, and for Jackson – and for herself – but she was so nervous that she would screw up and embarrass her Master and his friend.

Their first training night was a Friday, a rare day off for both Tommy and Clare, and the closer they got to the dungeon, the more nervous she got. Tommy pulled into a parking lot next to a few other cars that were already there. She recognized Jackson's car but no others. The parking lot was next to a nondescript two-story building in a commercial part of town. There was no sign on the building and as Tommy escorted her to the front door, carrying two garment bags with their dungeon clothes, she noticed that the two windows on the first floor were blacked out, and the solid metal door was protected by an electronic card reader. Tommy used his key card to open the door and ushered her into the building.

Tommy handed Clare her garment bag and pointed her in the direction of the women's locker room, saying he'd meet her at the top of the stairs when she was ready. She'd already put on what little makeup she was going to wear, so it didn't take her long to change into her little outfit – little being the operative word. Tommy had shopped for Clare's outfit earlier in the day and it was already in her garment bag so she hadn't actually seen it until she was in the locker room. It was so skimpy, she stared at it for a few minutes, just shaking her head, wondering why he didn't just put it in a baggy instead of a garment bag, thinking "Master, you must be joking! I might as well be completely naked!" But the buildup to naked was always Tommy's favorite part of an evening, so she just laughed a little and changed.

Clare was just coming out of the locker room when Tommy, standing outside the door, had just opened his mouth to yell in at her. When he saw her in the outfit he'd selected, he stopped short and stared. And she smiled. And dropped to her knees on the floor and assumed the greeting position Tommy loved best.

He circled her as she knelt on the floor, one fingertip gently brushing the exposed skin of her shoulders. His breathing became somewhat labored by his growing lust.

Her red satin bustier barely covered her nipples and stopped a few inches above her waist – it pushed her breasts up, practically into her throat. It was so tight, breathing was a challenge.

The red plaid latex 'skirt' was more of a 'belt' – it started at the top of her ass crack and ended six inches later. It barely covered her pussy when she stood. Kneeling on the floor with her knees spread, directly across from the front door, it covered nothing.

The front door opened and closed quickly, Clare blushed, and Tommy laughed. Their friend Jackson whistled as he caught sight of the view and grunted "Uh, Master Thomas, you might want to move that luscious pussy away from the front door!! We're trying to keep this place a secret at least until it opens!"

Tommy punched him in the arm as Jackson made his way up the stairs, and then he offered Clare his hand and helped her to her feet – which were bare, because he hadn't put any shoes in her garment bag. Probably just as well. She was way too nervous that night to try walking around in 4-inch stilettos.

Finally on her feet, she had an opportunity to check out her Master, dressed in his tight leather pants and a leather vest that accentuated his biceps, his pecs, and his washboard abs. And that delicious package that was so obvious behind the laces of his fly.

"May I say, Master, that you look so hot tonight? You don't wear your leathers nearly often enough."

"I'm so glad you approve. I may have to get a few more sets to keep here and at home. And maybe a separate set for when I actually get to ride my Harley."

"Oh, Master, I love the look of you on that bike. Just thinking about the sight of you straddling that vibrating beast makes me wet. You're such a manly man."

She stepped close and wiggled on his leather covered cock, and they both moaned. Then he swatted her on her ass in warning for her comment and her behavior, before they headed to the second floor.

They had just reached the top of the stairs when more people started coming in, four men and three women heading into the locker rooms and then joining the rest of the group already in a conference room at the top of the stairs.

When everyone was settled in the conference room, including Clare on her knees on a large floor pillow at her Master's feet, her head resting comfortably on his thigh, Jackson started the meeting.

"I want to thank you all for being here tonight. You're helping me to achieve a goal I set for myself eight years ago when I was forced to close my first dungeon. A few of you were with me in that first dungeon, and you've stuck with me through the process of getting this going again. A few others are established in the lifestyle, but new to this area, and we appreciate the roles you've played and will continue to play over time as we get this location going again.

"I'd like to start with introductions, in case some of you don't know each other. First, we have our chief architect, Master Rodney Day and his lovely submissive and wife, Bella. Master Rodney has been involved since the beginning. He helped me scout this location, helped me with the design and created the detailed floor plan drawings, which incorporated everything on my wish list, and then some. Thank you so much, Master Rodney, for your extraordinary talent and your complementary vision for our new dungeon." And Master Rodney nodded to the group, but didn't speak.

Jackson continued with the introductions – "Master Rodney then found Master Marshall Hawthorne to take over as general contractor for the actual renovation, which I believe you'll all agree is spectacular. Well done, my friend. Master Marshall is here this evening with his sweet submissive, Portia Greenbriar. Portia is somewhat new to the lifestyle, but she seems very eager to learn more. And as an interior designer, she's had some great ideas along the way, especially in the area of finishing touches that will make our female members more comfortable." Master Marshall nodded and Portia gave a little wave and a smile from her place, seated on Marshall's lap.

And the introductions continued. "We're also honored to have our Training Master here tonight. Master Thomas Rollins is here with his beautiful submissive and wife, Clare. Clare and Master Thomas have been married for several years now and have been a bondage couple for almost all the time they've been together, but they've only been in a Master/submissive dynamic for a few months. Master Thomas has many years of experience in the lifestyle, and he's been an excellent Training Master in the past. I'm sure you'll all learn much from Master Thomas. Clare will be assisting Master Thomas with many of his training sessions, and he's told me several times that she has obedience issues from time to time, so I imagine we'll all learn quite a bit about discipline in the days and weeks to come." Tommy nodded to the group, and Clare turned her face into his thigh in embarrassment, raising her hand a little above the table with a slight wave and a quiet giggle.

"Our general manager is Mistress Desdemona Wyatt. I've known Mistress Desdemona since I was ten and she was nine. Way before we got into D/s. She's been running her own very successful business for many years, and she assures me that she will have no problem managing daily operations in our little dungeon. She's also quite handy with a single tail whip so I have complete confidence that she will keep our dungeon running smoothly as we continue to grow our membership. Mistress Desdemona relocated to this area specifically to help us with this endeavor and I can't thank her enough for making the move. Mistress Desdemona brought her new submissive, Clay Fiehrer, with her when she moved. I hope you'll both be very happy here." Desdemona smiled at the group and nodded knowingly, while Clay gave a quick wave from his place beside her on his own floor pillow.

"Our final founding member is Master Will Portman, who will be filling the role of Sergeant At Arms, responsible for the safety of the dungeon members anywhere on the premises, including the parking lot, which will be undergoing some recommended changes over the next two weeks. Master Will was a Navy Seal for 20 years and has experience with all types of firearms, as well as facility security, which has very recently been updated, thanks to his suggestions. Master Will also relocated here just a few weeks ago, but until he moved, he was a member of a premier regional SWAT team that served a number of large southern metro areas. In addition to his security responsibilities, Master Will has agreed to assist with member recruiting and vetting. I just hope that Master Will doesn't get bored and leave us for more exciting locations." Master Will nodded to the group from his place at the far end of the table, and it was then that Clare noticed he was there alone. She wondered if his sub was not available to attend or if he was between subs, and flying solo.

"Master Will, if you need any backup with security or any rowdy behavior, I'm sure Mistress Desdemona would be happy to assist." And Desdemona just smiled and nodded.

"Master Will is between submissives at this time, just as I am, but once things settle into a groove and we are able to grow the membership a little, that could change for both of us.

"I know that everyone here knows me, at least a little, but I should probably give you a little bit of background about myself. I am Master Jackson Kelley. I've been in the lifestyle since my early 20's, and I've always been a member of some dungeon, wherever I could find one close to my home. Twelve years ago I opened my own dungeon about 100 miles from here, in a barn on the farm I owned. It was a little rustic compared to what you'll all see tonight, but it was very special to me and to the other members. Unfortunately, our recruiting processes weren't quite what they should have been, and we opened our doors to a couple who were hired by an enemy of mine, specifically to get enough dirt on me to ruin me. Needless to say, they were successful. I lost everything, including the farm, forcing me to close the dungeon. In the process, my enemy was killed and I was charged with his murder. Thanks to Master Thomas and a few of his shadier friends, the real killer was brought to justice and I was cleared of all charges. And my reputation was rebuilt – or more accurately, re-formed.

"For every friend and supporter I had before what I refer to as 'the incident', I gained two or three more, thanks to the sweeping popularity of erotic romance in recent years. It appears that everyone has at least a passing interest in the D/s lifestyle so I anticipate that we will have no problem growing our membership, while at the same time maintaining a rigorous background check process to weed out any potentially dangerous would-be members. Master Will, I am very grateful for your participation as the Membership Master.

"And now, the information you've all been waiting so patiently for – the name I've selected for our new dungeon. As you recall, you were all invited to submit potential names that you thought would be appropriate and in keeping with the theme and the initial drawings. And we received some excellent suggestions. But the one I thought was the most fitting was submitted by Master Thomas.

"Our new dungeon will be called Asylum. As you know, the word asylum has two meanings. In earlier times, and in other countries even today, the word asylum stirred up horrible visions of mental institutions where 'crazy' people lived in terrible conditions and went wild on a regular basis. I have no doubt that our little dungeon will at times feel like that kind of asylum. We want our members to revel in their sexual kink, live it with abandon, while we watch and protect from the wings, ready to bring them back from the dangerous brink if needed.

"But the word asylum also has another meaning – a meaning that conjures a different vibe. Asylum also refers to a haven, a place of safety and comfort. As popular as erotic romance has made our lifestyle, many people in the vanilla world still consider us sick, dirty, perverted, in need of mental counseling – that other kind of asylum. This is still the conservative South, so keeping our lifestyles to ourselves is a must. But we're ready to provide welcome and shelter, as it were, to those who are interested in seeking a little more kink in their lives. We want to provide that kind of asylum to those we deem appropriate to join us.

"So, without further ado, welcome to Asylum. Let's all go downstairs and see the main floor, check out the privacy rooms, and have some wine and snacks. Mistress Desdemona tells me our Bar Manager and Chef will be joining us next week. They are a Mistress/slave couple who are well respected and highly recommended. I met them last week and I look forward to adding them to our little group. It's all coming together, friends, thanks to all of you, and I couldn't be more pleased. Now, let's head downstairs so I can give you a tour of your new dungeon."

Clare appreciated Jackson's introductions and his little speech, but she was ready to get up off her knees for a while. When her relationship with Tommy changed, so did her relationship with Jackson. Because of his Master status, she would never be able to tell him he was a little longwinded, without suffering a seriously red ass for her disrespect, but she could think it to herself all she wanted! Tommy helped her up off the floor but kept her from leaving the room with the rest of the members.

"Clare, wait, I want to talk to you for a few minutes alone."

"Are you alright, Master? Did I do something wrong?"

"I'm fine, Clare, and you didn't do anything wrong, your behavior has been impeccable tonight. But I need to clear something up before we go any further. I have to ask you – did you agree to wear my collar because you wanted to? Or were you afraid to say no? I need you to be really honest with me on this, Clare. Are you comfortable with our Master/slave relationship?"

"Tommy, why would you ask me that? Have I given you any indication that I was unhappy or uncomfortable with how our relationship has progressed?"

"Clare, you know I've been reading your diary. It was all fun and games at first and then I got to the part where you described your time with the bastard. Edward wasn't happy with you when you said no to his collar, and he beat you on a regular basis until he finally took matters into his own hands and collared you without your permission. And then he continued to beat you frequently. I know you were afraid of my love of bondage at first and it took you awhile to settle into that. I know you were seriously afraid of me when I spanked you the first time. Were you afraid of me when I first talked about collaring you? Is this new relationship we have what you really want? Or did you say yes out of fear? Clare, I don't ever want you to do something you don't want to do just because you think it's what I want. Is that what this is all about?"

She took his face gently in her hands and said "Oh, Tommy, my love, how long have you been worried about this? Why didn't you just ask me about it right away? Yes, you know that I'm resistant to change, and this has been a big change for us. But I'd been waiting a long time for you to suggest taking our relationship to a new level, even after we got married, so I've been thinking about it for quite a while. It was so obvious that you longed for a Master/slave relationship, especially after you introduced me to Master Tucker and his slave/wife Ava last summer. I was actually about to bring it up myself when I overheard your phone conversation with Jackson last fall."

"You mean the conversation you were not invited to, but listened in on anyway, Mrs. Nosey?"

"Yes, that conversation. And I may be nosey, but you love me anyway. And I love you, so very much. Tommy, I admit that I was nervous when you collared me, because there was a part of me that worried I would let you down or disappoint you in some way, maybe embarrass you in front of your friends. I still worry about that. But please hear me, and believe me, when I tell you that I was thrilled to accept your collar, and I will never regret doing it. I promised I would never take it off. I intend to be buried with it, hopefully a long, long time from now, so that we can still be together in Heaven."

And she leaned in and pushed his leather vest aside, placing a kiss on his chest, over his heart.

Taking her hands in his and pressing them to his heart, the love of her life said "Oh, Clare, I don't know what I ever did to deserve you, but I'm the luckiest bastard who ever roamed this earth. You're the treasure I searched for 60 years to find. No matter what happens with this dungeon, you will never disappoint me or embarrass me. I promised something as well the night I collared you. I promised to love you and protect you and cherish you for as long as we both live. Promises that are maybe more important to me than our wedding vows. I take all of those promises very seriously. All you have to do is trust me, Clare, as hard as that might be sometimes, and nothing else you ever do will be less than perfect. Okay?"

"Okay, my Master. Now can I get you a glass of wine and a snack to celebrate the new dungeon?"

"Yes, slave, I think that would be lovely."

Tommy and Clare caught up with the rest of the group in the bar area on the first floor and Jackson made a beeline for them, with a very concerned look on his face.

"Master Thomas? Clare? Is everything okay? Is there a problem I can help with?"

"No, Master Jackson, everything is just perfect. My slave and I were just having a little conversation and a little alone time. You know how I worry sometimes. I needed to clear up a little confusion on my part, and my slave was able to put my mind at ease. As she always does."

"I'm glad to hear that, Master Thomas. You know, I hope to find a submissive like the one you have some day. I think she's the perfect soul mate for you and you are one lucky bastard. Clare, if you have any like-minded friends who might be interested in learning more about the lifestyle, I would be more than eager to assist."

"I'll keep that in mind, Master Jackson." And she just couldn't leave well enough alone. "And that was a lovely speech, by the way, Master Jackson, it gave me lots of time to exercise my knee joints.Thank you very much for your kindness, sir."

"Master Thomas, I think maybe you might want to demonstrate the art of spanking for our fellow Masters sometime soon. Perhaps show them how to handle a brat."

"I already have discipline planned as the first lesson – since I have such a willing and deserving training assistant."

Knowing she was in trouble for her wayward comment, Clare bowed her head and said quietly, "I'm sorry, Master. I never meant to offend or disrespect Master Jackson, I just wanted to compliment him on his speech. May I please apologize to Master Jackson?"

"I would expect nothing less, brat."

Keeping her gaze firmly on the floor, she whispered "I apologize, Master Jackson, my words have displeased you, and that was never my intent."

"Apology accepted, little one. I believe I'm going to enjoy tonight's training immensely."

And Clare was sure that she would not.

Chapter 6

The members of the group all chatted in the elevated bar area, getting to know each other a little better, enjoying some wine and some heavy hors d'oeuvres while they waited for their tour of the dungeon.

After about 15 minutes, Jackson got everyone's attention and led them all toward the main dungeon area and all of the equipment there. He showed off his pride and joy first – a mahogany St. Andrew's Cross mounted to the wall on a platform in the corner of the bar area. It was positioned so that a wide audience, including everyone in the bar, could enjoy whatever show happened to be going on there.

Angled into the corner as it was, the platform was large enough to provide plenty of swing room for a Dom/me to administer an erotic blend of pain and pleasure to their lucky submissive. There was a selection of restraint cuffs, canes and floggers mounted to the walls on either side of the cross, waiting to be used to make some sub's dreams come true. It was obvious that new submissive Portia was apprehensive about the cross, but interested enough that she whispered something to her Dom Marshall, making him smile and nod his head. And she giggled softly.

Jackson led the group down the center of the very large room, and the first thing that caught their attention was all the different kinds of lighting. Beautiful gold and crystal chandeliers were spaced on the high ceiling down the center of the room, bathing the room in a soft golden glow. There were additional smaller crystal lights attached to the dark slate gray walls at different places around the room.

Each different play station was lit by overhead can lights aimed perfectly to bring maximum attention to whatever action was going on. Many of the overhead lights could be changed to whatever color would set the mood the Dom/me was looking for. Just the lighting alone was so breathtaking that Clare had trouble concentrating on Jackson's answer to a question from someone in the group.

As they continued their tour, Jackson pointed out spanking benches, stocks, and other pieces of equipment just waiting for someone to be restrained and brought to a glorious state of arousal and orgasm. In two different locations, one on each side of the room, there were winches attached to chains hanging down from the ceiling, ready for a submissive to be attached and dangled at whatever height best suited the Dominant's pleasure.

At the far end of the room was another stage that stretched almost the entire width of the room. On the stage, at the back wall, there was another larger St. Andrew's Cross, surrounded by additional restraint cuffs of varying sizes, plus a number of whips of different sizes and styles, ready for a seasoned Whip Master to show off his or her skills. Currently only Desdemona and Will were Whip Masters, but Tommy had started working with them both recently to hone his skills with a single tail. Tommy and Clare were both very excited at the prospect of snaking that whip across Clare's ass and thighs and shoulders, marking her lightly as she crested a wave of erotic pleasure.

On each side of the room there were two large mahogany chests filled with toys – butt plugs of various sizes, gags of different sizes and styles, nipple and clit clamps, so many vibrators of different styles and sizes – a toy overload that made Clare's head spin.

And there were an equal number of sensual torture and restraint devices and toys – cock rings and chastity cages, strokers, humblers, penis pumps – perfectly suited to bring a male submissive to screaming release as well.

Finally, Jackson pointed out the floor down the center of the room where tape marks on the shiny, slate colored cement indicated where black and dark red leather couches and love seats would soon be positioned.

Finally, Jackson pointed to a hallway beside the bar, leading to an elevator and another set of stairs that led to private rooms on the second floor. Each of the private rooms sported a different theme, covering a wide range of kink, and he invited the group to check them out at their leisure.

All in all, the dungeon provided the perfect combination of institutional sterility and intimate warmth to welcome members and guests alike. Clare couldn't wait to become familiar with every piece of furniture and every erotic toy in the room.

Jackson concluded the tour and asked for questions from the floor about anything they had seen during the tour. There were no questions raised, and a few people had turned to go back to the bar, when Jackson spoke to the group at large, and Tommy specifically.

"Hold on just a moment, friends. Master Thomas, I believe you have a little training session planned for this evening."

"You are correct, Master Jackson. My slave finds herself in the 'enviable' position of being the first to star in a training video. Then she will have the distinct honor of receiving the first discipline inside our new dungeon. I'm sure she considers herself highly favored right now, and more than a little apprehensive, thinking about what discipline I'm going to rain down on her."

Clare turned to Tommy and all but buried her face in his chest, whispering "Master, permission to speak in private, please?"

"Permission denied, little slut. You've said just about all you're going to say this evening. On your knees – assume the position. Now let's all watch a little video, shall we?"

Jackson smiled an evil smile at Clare as she lowered herself to her knees on the hard concrete floor at Tommy's side, and he pushed the button on a remote that lowered a movie screen from the ceiling on the stage. He then pushed another remote and a little video started to play – and Clare's worst fears were realized.

As soon as she heard her husband's voice on the video – *"Then be about your business, little slut. You know what I expect. Devour your Master. Suck my cock, play with my balls, make me come down your throat until this painful erection is tamed."* – she knew exactly what everyone was about to see – their Christmas Night blow job.

Everyone was going to see her service her Master – except Clare, of course, because in her current position, her head was bent low and her eyes were boring holes into the cement floor. Her whole body was covered in excited goose bumps, and embarrassment tinged her skin a lovely shade of pink.

But as she heard quickening breaths around her and quiet moans beside her as the group watched her impromptu little porn video, she allowed herself to enjoy the sounds of her Master brought to orgasm by her lips and tongue and hands. And it was as erotic as anything she'd ever heard.

When the little video was done, and the screen had been returned to the ceiling, there was a short round of applause, and Tommy reached down to help Clare back to her feet. When she was on her feet again, Tommy held her close and kissed her passionately. He whispered in her ear, "You're so good at that, my little slut. And you looked great on the video. We'll have to do that again sometime soon."

"Master, I…"

And Jackson interrupted her, driving her to frustration again with his next comment.

"That was quite a little video, Master Thomas. Your slave is quite skilled in the art of blow jobs. Perhaps she could do a little training with the other subs at some point, just to improve their skills."

"I believe that could be arranged, Master Jackson. She is quite skilled, as you say. Just watching the video got me quite hard, but I believe the next blow job my slave gives me will be in private, and unrecorded." And Clare blushed Tommy's favorite shade of pink again, breaking out in another round of goose bumps.

"I'm sure that will meet with your slave's approval, not that you need her approval for anything. Now I believe the last event for this evening is a spanking demonstration. Master Thomas?"

"Yes, that's correct, Master Jackson."

Taking Clare by the hand, Tommy said "Slave, come with me." And they walked to one of the mahogany cabinets so that her Master could retrieve a ball gag and a wicked little wooden paddle, much like one they had at home. One that would probably hurt like hell at first, and then turn into raging arousal.

Tommy walked Clare to one of the spanking benches, twirling the paddle by its rawhide cord, and just looked at her, daring her to make any snarky comment at all. So she smiled sweetly and asked "How would Master like me to position myself on the bench?"

He smiled wide and said "Very good, little slut. You make me proud. Now tell the group why you're receiving the inaugural punishment tonight."

And she turned to the small crowd with her head bent low and said "I said something that could be considered disrespectful of Master Jackson."

"COULD BE considered disrespectful, slave?"

"I'm sorry. What I said was disrespectful and I apologize again for my comment."

In the back of the group, Will leaned over and whispered to Jackson, "Someday you'll have to tell me what it was she said!"

Not waiting, Jackson offered, "She implied that my speech was a little long winded."

"It totally was, dude! Necessary, but a little long. You really do enjoy the sound of your own voice sometimes, I almost yawned near the end!" And they both chuckled quietly.

"I know. But Master Thomas's slave doesn't need to know that I agree. This should be quite fun to watch. T has always been really good at this."

Then Tommy took the attention of the crowd back and said to Clare, "Come close, slave, let's get this gag on you. You have a tendency to scream loudly when you're being spanked and we don't want to subject the group to that tonight."

So Clare obediently stepped very close to her Master and opened her mouth wide, allowing him to stuff the gag into her mouth and then hook it behind her head. When he was satisfied that the fit would allow her to breathe – and drool – he took a moment to review with the group the proper use of a ball gag. He discussed the different kinds of gags, when and how to use each different kind, and used Clare as his model to demonstrate the proper fit and snugness.

Tommy's last word of caution for everyone when using a gag of any kind was to have an alternate method to call a safe word when needed. He discussed the popular method of using a bell, and also demonstrated several different hand gestures that had worked for Clare and him in the past. When all of the Masters and the Mistress nodded their understanding, Tommy turned his attention back to Clare.

"On the bench, slave. Lay over the center bar, hands and knees on the side rails. Up you go."

Unable to speak, she just nodded and crawled up onto the bench, positioning herself the way her Master had instructed. Luckily, by then her bustier had slipped below her breasts so she was able to rest more comfortably on the bench, one breast on each side of the padded center rail. Not so lucky for her, the 'skirt' had long since ridden up to her waist and everything below it was in full view for the crowd.

Submissives in this dungeon, including founding members, would learn immediately that any modesty they might bring from the vanilla world had no place in their kinky haven. It was less of a hard limit for her now than it had been in the past, but she still had some work to do to put that all behind her, considering that she again turned a rosy shade of pink when she realized her behind was on display.

Restraint cuffs appeared out of nowhere – thanks to Master Rodney – and by the time Tommy had finished cuffing Clare's wrists and ankles to the outside corners of the bench, she was spread wide and not going anywhere. She was hoping for a short, fast count and not too much pain, but she would take whatever she got for her punishment and maybe learn to keep her fucking mouth shut in the future.

Standing by her head, addressing her, but facing toward the crowd, Tommy said "How are you doing, slave?" And she gave two thumbs up from her restrained hands, making Tommy laugh.

"Very well then, slave, let's get this punishment started. You've earned a count of 20 for your rude behavior tonight."

As he walked slowly to the other end of the bench, he stroked his hand gently down Clare's back and across each rosy ass cheek, admiring the pink color of her embarrassment, muttering almost to himself, "So beautiful, you're so beautiful. I could stare at you all day when you're restrained like this."

That mental picture made the lower half of her body clench tight at the thought, and she felt a little trickle of arousal start to drip down her thigh. He leaned down and kissed the small of her back, and then he gave her two medium intensity whacks with the paddle, bringing immediate tears to her eyes. He leaned back to look at her and asked, "Are you still breathing, slave?"

She gave another two thumbs up. Which prompted another reminder from Tommy to the crowd about never turning their attention from their subs any time they were restrained in any manner – good Dominants took the responsibility for their submissives very seriously, safety was always top of mind.

And then without warning, he laid another three smacks on her ass with the paddle, a little more intense than the first two, causing Clare to scream through her ball gag. He soothed her ass cheeks with the palm of his hand for a few seconds, gauging the changing color of her skin, listening for changes to her breathing and checking her hands for any signs of distress.

He applied five lighter intensity smacks with the paddle to the backs of her thighs, and then instructed the group, "My slave isn't a pain slut and the backs of her thighs are fairly sensitive. I don't want to not give her attention there, but I try to be a little more gentle when I'm using anything other than the palm of my hand there. It's all about getting to know your sub's pain and pleasure limits. We all know it's okay to push the envelope, but obviously we want to be sensitive to body language at all times."

Suddenly there was another voice, one from the crowd, Master Will asking a question Clare had hoped wouldn't come up. "I have to ask, Master Thomas. About the scars on your slave's ass. They look pretty bad. Did they come from you?"

"I'm glad you brought that up, Master Will, but let's table that conversation until the punishment is done, and then I'll let Clare share as much as she cares to on that subject."

Will nodded and Tommy stroked her thighs gently to remove some of the remaining sting, then focused the paddle on her ass again. Another five quick hard smacks had her tears flowing and her mouth drooling, creating a puddle on the concrete floor and making her scream again.

"My slave loves a nice erotic spanking from time to time, but this is a punishment spanking, meant to teach her a specific lesson.But sometimes she enjoys a punishment as well, and I like to check a few things when I'm getting close to the end."

He leaned back to her ear and asked "How are you doing, my lovely?" And she flipped up two index fingers to let her Master know that she needed just a minute to collect herself before the last five whacks. So Tommy took the time to explain their hand signals.

"My submissive and I have a set of hand signals that we've been using for more than a year that seem to work pretty well for her when she's gagged in any way. If she's good to go, she gives me two thumbs up, the equivalent of a Green. If she needs to slow down a little and regroup, she gives me two index fingers, that's a Yellow. If she flips me off with one or both middle fingers, that's a Red and I know that something pretty serious is going on. It's only happened once, but I had gotten a little too 'in the moment' and she needed to bring things to a stop. Which we did. That's why staying aware and reading your sub's body language is important all the time, but it's critical when he or she is gagged and can't speak to communicate.

"But my slave's hand signals aren't the only way she communicates with me about how she's doing. I'm not sure if anyone else can catch the scent, but my little slut is quite aroused right now, and when I check, I'm sure I'll find she's dripping down her thighs in anticipation of an eye popping fuck. Which isn't going to happen here tonight, Clare! This is a punishment, there will be no reward at the end."

Sure enough, when Tommy ran his hand through Clare's slit, she was wet and ready. Two fingers inside her had her squirming on the bench in vain, but Tommy left those two fingers where they were, teasing her, tickling her G-spot as he administered the last five quick smacks to end her punishment.

The paddle dropped to the floor and Tommy was quick to come around and kneel by her head, removing the gag and wiping away her tears and drool with a warm, damp wash cloth someone had handed him.

He placed a tender kiss on Clare's forehead and asked, "How are you doing, lovely? Are you okay? You did beautifully. I'm so proud of you."

And she took a deep breath and nodded as tears continued to flow, exercising her jaws a little to ease the stiffness.

"Let's get you out of these restraints, baby, and get you some water."

Clare's restraints were removed and Tommy helped her to stand, moving her slowly to an upright position, and wrapping her in a huge hug, whispering encouragements in her ear. When he noticed her slight trembling, Jackson handed Tommy a blanket, which he wrapped around her, and then picked her up and carried her back to the waiting couch in the bar. She didn't realize until she was seated, drinking from a bottle of water, with Tommy massaging her ankles where the restraints had been, that the group had followed them back to the bar and were sitting or standing around them, looking at her. Portia was openly crying, and Marshall had her wrapped in a tight hug, whispering quietly in her ear to settle her.

Tommy finally pulled Clare into his lap and started to rub her wrists, then spoke to Will and the rest of the group. "Master Will, you asked me about the scars on Clare's ass, but I think that's her story to tell tonight, if she's willing."

And Tommy looked at her, but before Clare could speak, Will said "I have two questions, actually statements. First, that was an excellent spanking demonstration, I'm sure everyone enjoyed it. And maybe learned a little along the way. Thank you very much for that. Second, I don't want to make your sub relive some traumatic experience, but I think it would be good to reassure the group about what happened to her and when it occurred."

Tommy looked to Clare again, and she turned to the group and said "My Master would never do anything to me that would leave marks like you just saw. I got those scars a long time ago, from a cane wielded by an abusive Dominant. He did many terrible things to me while I was with him, but that caning was the one that left permanent scars and led to me eventually leaving him. There's a really fine line between giving a submissive what he or she needs, and being outright abusive. Even with the fascination with D/s right now, the vanilla world doesn't understand that fine line, and probably never will. So I encourage you all to embrace the connection between Dominant and submissive, enjoy your time together, communicate about EVERYTHING, and know that it's okay for either of you to walk away if something just feels wrong and can't be fixed. I placed my trust in a contract that my Dom ignored because I didn't know any better. I wish someone had shared a few lessons with me before I signed a contract with someone I didn't know anything about. And I wish I'd known I could walk away any time, regardless of what I'd signed. Try to make better choices than I did."

Surprisingly, the group all nodded and applauded when Clare finished speaking and she got embarrassed again. The small crowd started to disperse, leaving her and Tommy sitting on the couch, lost in each other as Tommy provided a little more aftercare. Jackson approached them and spoke quietly to Tommy, "Master Thomas, why don't you take your submissive home. I'll clean up here and see you tomorrow afternoon at my office to discuss training plans and potential member vetting. Master Will can join us and go over the plans he already has. And Clare, I want to reassure you that you never have to worry about seeing your ex-Dom in this dungeon. We're watching for him to drop by or apply once word gets out that we're here, but he will never be admitted to our dungeon. Never." And she nodded her gratitude.

Tommy looked up at Jackson with his own thankful expression and said "Thank you very much for the reassurance, Master Jackson. I'll see you tomorrow at your office around 1:30 with my training notes. Clare, baby, let's get you changed and back home, okay?"

"I'd like that very much, Master. Thank you for another wonderful, exhausting spanking experience. I hope I met your expectations."

"It was my pleasure, little slut. You exceeded my expectations, as always. You were spectacular this evening. Now let's get you moving and get you home."

Tommy helped her up from the couch and walked with her to the door of the women's locker room. "I want to have a quick chat with Master Will, slave, so you have about 10 minutes to get changed and get back out here. Okay?"

"That shouldn't be a problem if I don't shower, Master. May I shower when we get home, Sir? And then go to bed?"

"Yes, we can shower together when we get home and then I'll tuck you into bed and let you get some rest. Now get going." And he gave her a swat on the ass that was all sound and no pain, just a gentle massage on her tender behind.

Clare scooted through the changing room door and headed to her locker, but before she got there, she heard gentle sniffling in the corner and she felt the need to investigate. Her heart broke when she found sweet Portia huddled in a comfy chair, crying quietly, looking so distraught.

Clare sat down on the arm of the chair and held her hand, trying to give her the emotional support she needed without saying anything just yet. When she looked up at Clare, Portia whispered, "I can't do this, Clare. I'm not strong like you are, I could never let Marshall do that to me, especially in front of all those people. This is so important to Marshall, and I don't think I'll ever be able to do it. What am I going to do? I think I have to leave him so he can find a woman better suited to his needs. Before he walks away from me. I think that would kill me, but I don't see any other way." And a forlorn little sob escaped her lips, shaking her shoulders.

"Oh, Portia, honey, please don't cry. Master Marshall would never expect anything like that from you so soon. He knows this is all new to you, and I'm sure he understands how scary it all is for you. Don't worry. Just talk to him about how you feel. You have to communicate your feelings to him and let him communicate his feelings to you. This may be as scary for him as it is for you."

"But he always seems so strong, so in control. I think he has expectations I can't live up to. I'm afraid I'll disappoint him." And Portia's tears started rolling down her cheeks again.

"Portia, honey, no one is born to this lifestyle, everyone has to have a first time. I walked into my abusive Dom's house with zero experience. It was all new to me and he took advantage of my desire to please him. Just between you and me, I knew right away that I should leave him. I never really trusted him. Something just didn't feel right but I thought it was just because I was new. I thought it would get better. But it just kept getting worse and I didn't know what to do. There was no one for me to talk to, he kept me so isolated."

"How did you finally know you had to leave?"

"He put his collar on me without my permission. Then he beat me unconscious with a cane. At that point, it was pretty clear I had to find a way out. And I did – although it was just dumb luck, my contract with him finally expired and I was free to go."

"How were you brave enough to try again with Master Thomas? After everything you'd been through? He's so intimidating!"

"Everything with Edward felt bad, wrong, early on. Everything with Master Thomas just felt right. You probably don't know this, and don't ever tell anyone I told you this, but I've been with my Master since the day we met. He wasn't my Master yet, just a huge control freak who was so hot, I couldn't keep my hands off. I grew to love him so fast, it made my head spin, and I was afraid of what I felt for him. And then we got married.And then just a few months ago, he became my Master, and I couldn't be happier.

"Portia, I'm going to ask you one question. Have you ever been afraid of Master Marshall? Afraid he would really hurt you? Has he ever done anything to you that just felt like it shouldn't happen?"

"Never! I know he would never do anything just to hurt me. When he gives me pain, it's never more than I can handle and it's always to enhance the pleasure. I just don't think I could ever do anything in public like you did tonight. I don't know how long he'll agree to keep everything we do private. I'm afraid of losing him, but it might be better for him if I left now, before things got any more serious between us."

"Portia, I'll tell you another little secret. When I first met Master Thomas, sex of any kind in front of an audience was a hard limit for me. Hell, video and photography were hard limits for me until tonight! Sometimes my Master thinks he can just bulldoze through my issues, but when he gets too pushy about something, I stand up to him and tell him no. And we talk through it. Sometimes I win, and sometimes he does. But I always know that he won't ever push me too hard or too far. Even if I didn't love him with all my heart, I would still trust him with my life. Do you trust Master Marshall?"

"Yes, I trust him completely."

"Then talk to him. Be honest with him. Tell him how you feel about what you saw tonight, give him a chance to reassure you about all of this. The worst thing you can do for either of you is not communicate your fears, your apprehension, as well as your desires. It's his job as your Dom to see to your needs, physical and emotional. It wouldn't be fair to him to try to hide your feelings from him. I guarantee he'll know there's something not right between you, and the last thing you want is to let your Dom's imagination get away from him. Promise me you'll talk to him – soon, if not immediately. Okay, sweetie?"

"Okay, I promise."

"Good girl. Now I bet he's outside waiting for you and wondering what the hell is going on in here. I'm surprised he and Master Thomas haven't already come through the door looking for us."

"They both tried, but I decided they didn't need to hear this private conversation, and I kept them out."

Portia and Clare both whipped around to see Mistress Desdemona standing nearby with a very understanding look on her face. She looked to Portia and said "I think you'd better see to your Dom, Portia. He's starting to pace in the hallway, and that's never good. You've just gotten some great advice from your friend here. Talk to him tonight. You'll both feel better." And Portia nodded and headed for the door and her Dom.

Mistress Desdemona turned her attention to Clare as she headed to her locker, and she stopped to listen to what Des had to say.

"Clare, I overheard your conversation with our little sub. You seem to have a natural calming presence about you, and it certainly worked on Portia. You gave her some great advice. Master Marshall will be grateful. Clare, I wish I'd been around when you needed someone to talk to. I'm well aware of who gave you those scars. I was there the night of your Summer Solstice party. It's obvious to me now that you were in that dungeon against your will, but at the time, we all thought that you were there by your own choice. He told us all that you had begged him to let everyone have a go at you. It makes me sick to think about what Edward did to you, and what he let other people do to you without your permission. He's been a bastard for 30 years, it's a wonder no one has killed him yet. I'm glad you survived, and I'm glad you were able to find your soul mate. Master Thomas is devoted to you and I think you are to him as well. I look forward to seeing you continue to grow in your submissive role with your Master. The two of you are a pleasure to watch."

"Thank you, Mistress, I appreciate your kinds words. Speaking of my Master, did he look irritated that I wasn't where I was supposed to be 5 minutes ago? I hoped he would understand that I couldn't let Portia cry alone like that when I could reassure her just a little."

"Yes, I'm sure he's fine. But just in case, you should probably get moving. I'd hate think of your ass being any more red than it already is."

"Thank you, Mistress, I'll move quickly!" And she did, grabbing her things out of her locker and throwing her coat on over her dungeon wear in the interest of saving time.

Chapter 7

The next Thursday evening, Clare was in the kitchen cleaning up after dinner and the phone rang. Tommy had the house phone with him and she heard him answer from the living room.Two seconds later, she heard him swear loudly, and then she heard his office door slam. She was concerned about what might have made Tommy so upset, but she certainly wasn't going to brave the lion's den by going into his office after him if she didn't have to. Just about the time she was finishing up in the kitchen, Tommy came up behind her at the sink and wrapped his arms around her, but didn't say anything. He seemed edgy at first but after putting his hands on his submissive, he started to calm down.

"Is there a problem, Master? Is there something I can help with?"

"No problem, Baby Girl, just something with one of the businesses. Nothing for you to worry about at all. Now, if you're finished down here, how about a little time upstairs in the Jacuzzi? You can help take my mind off my little problem."

"I noticed something in the corner of the bathroom the other day, Master, something that looks a little like a camera. Are we making another 'training' video? Not that I mind, of course. I think I'm becoming something of an exhibitionist." And they both laughed a little, remembering what an almost hard limit video and photos had been for her when they first met.

"I hadn't thought of making a video tonight, my love, but that's not a bad idea. We can have a little fun, get a little creative. Good suggestion, little slut."

They locked the doors, turned out the lights and headed upstairs with a bottle of wine to have a little fun and calm down Clare's still too tense Master.

Saturday night was another training night at the dungeon, and on the way there, Clare noticed that her husband was still just a little off. For the past two days, Tommy had been more tense than usual, almost looking over his shoulder when he thought Clare wouldn't notice. Something was up but he refused to share, he just kept saying it was nothing, she shouldn't be concerned. That afternoon, she had pushed a little too hard and he yelled "Drop it!! Just let it go. It doesn't concern you."

It was the first time Tommy had ever raised his voice to her other than during play, and he was immediately sorry he had done it. But he couldn't take it back, it was too late, her feelings were already hurt. He stormed out the back door and paced around in the backyard for a while, and when he came back in, he went straight to his office and closed the door. She didn't see him again until it was time to get ready to leave, and whatever bug had crawled up his ass was still there. Clare was beginning to think it was going to be an ugly night at Asylum.

They didn't speak through the whole ride, and when they got there, he was very attentive, but still more distant that he'd been in a long time. Without warning, before Clare had a chance to go into the locker room, Tommy pulled a small silver key out of his pocket and unlocked her platinum collar, pulled it off and put it in his pocket. When she looked horrified, he said "It's okay little slut, I have a temporary collar in this bag. You won't need clothes for tonight. Just go get undressed and come back out. I'll be waiting right here, you will kneel and assume your waiting position next to me and I'll put your temporary collar on you."

"Why did you take my collar off? And what do you mean, I won't need clothes. I can't be naked all night!"

"Mind your tone, slave, and do what you're told! You've been pushing for some discipline for days and I just might accommodate you if you're not careful!"

"Master, you're scaring me a little. Please tell me what's bothering you."

With a gruff voice she rarely heard Tommy use on anyone, he said, "I told you, nothing is bothering me. Now go do what you're told. You have three minutes, and the clock starts now."

Clare hauled ass into the women's locker room, ignoring Portia and Bella, who stood watching her with confused looks on their faces. She tore off her clothes, fighting back angry, terrified tears, and headed back out the door to greet her asshole Master, using his favorite pose. Completely naked. With no collar on.

"Very good, slave, 15 seconds to spare. Now hold still while I put this temporary collar on."

Clare struggled to keep quiet, and held still while her Master fastened a thin leather collar around her neck, and then stood up when he offered his hand to assist her. When he fastened a leash to the collar and pulled her toward the door into the dungeon, her brat attitude started to mushroom, but she was controlled enough not to speak. She wasn't about to antagonize him just then, not in front of all of his friends. As they approached the bar area, where she could see other people already gathered, her embarrassment flushed pink across her skin, but still she held her control.

Half way to the bar, Tommy stopped and yanked on the leash a little – just to show Clare who was in charge. He was about to push her last button, and she didn't really care about the consequences.

"On your knees, slave, you can crawl the rest of the way."

Tommy knew how much she hated crawling, how demeaning she thought it was, but that bug up his ass seemed to be in charge, and Clare had to keep telling herself, "We're just playing. That's all it is. We're just playing." It was becoming more and more difficult to convince herself that was all it was.

As she lowered herself to her hands and knees, he said to the small crowd, "Follow us if you would please, we'll be doing tonight's training in the main dungeon."

He started to walk and Clare started to crawl, and her control began to disappear. Every yank of the leash, every sharp word, inched her anger higher, so that by the time they reached the table set up in the middle of the dungeon, she was a big ball of anger, and having trouble controlling her breathing. She could hear people talking very quietly, wondering out loud what was going on between Tommy and Clare. Jackson was openly staring at his friend, wondering when he was going to have to step in and stop the show.

Tommy stopped at the table, barely looked at Clare, and practically barked, "Stay!" And he walked toward one of the cabinets on the wall to retrieve a bit gag from a drawer. Once he had the bit gag in place in her mouth, he pulled her to her feet and pointed to the table.

"Up you go, slave. On your back, knees bent, legs spread, hands above your head."

Then he turned his back on her, leaving her to climb up onto the table and get into position without help. It took the last ounces of her control to not turn and walk back to the bar alone, but she knew that wouldn't solve the problem so she put herself in position without speaking the hateful words running through her mind. Assuming Clare had done exactly what he had ordered, Tommy addressed the audience, and started to offer an almost clinical explanation of what his demonstration would be. He stopped talking long enough to restrain Clare's wrists above her head and her ankles at the sides of the table, then turned away again and continued to talk. As she listened, her anger subsided, but her budding anticipation and arousal dissipated as her mind drifted and her anxiety grew. As Tommy continued to speak, she slipped back into a memory from her time with her abusive ex-Dom and she all but disappeared into the past.

"Our demonstration tonight will be erotic torture in the form of edge play, taking your sub just to the edge of orgasm and then pulling back. You can do this over and over again for as long as you enjoy the play. It doesn't matter whether your sub is male or female, they will get to the point where they're ready to beg you to stop or let them come. My sub loves this game and we have built up her tolerance so that I can take her to the edge 8 or even 10 times before she starts to beg. Just the anticipation should have her really wet by now."

Tommy moved so that he could still face the audience but could also begin massaging her clit, not really noticing that she wasn't nearly as wet as he expected. But he continued to torment her anyway, completely caught up in the demo. While he was stuck in top space, Clare was trapped in the past with Master Edward, reliving an evening when she had been gagged and restrained in a similar fashion, tormented to the point of extreme pain with no pleasure promised.

She closed her legs as much as her restraints would allow, reliving that past experience. Just like that past experience, Clare started to hyperventilate on the table behind Tommy's back, muttering through the gag almost to herself, "red red red red red red red..." Everyone but Tommy could see that Clare was not only calling her safe word, but she was using her non-verbal safe word as well. And still Tommy didn't stop.

Finally one of his students, lovely sweet sub Portia tried to get his attention – "Master Thomas? MASTER THOMAS!"

"What?!?!"

And from behind all of them, there was Jackson's voice yelling "MASTER THOMAS! YOUR SUB IS IN DISTRESS!"

"Oh, holy fucking shit!"

Tommy had finally turned to look at Clare, startled by her rapid breathing, incoherent muttering, and the distant look in her eyes. He was angered to see Jackson removing the bit gag, starting to release her wrist restraints, intent on helping her sit up. Tommy pushed him away and yelled "Don't touch her, she's mine to take care of!"

And Jackson yelled back at him, "Then do your job, asshole. You have not been a responsible Dom tonight, and I don't ever want to see this again. Now you take care of her properly, or I will!" And Jackson stormed off to the bar, taking the audience with him for a much needed drink.

As Tommy rushed to get Clare out of her remaining restraints, and helped her to sit up, he pulled her into a bear hug of an embrace, brushing the beads of sweat from her forehead, gently rubbing her arm and kissing the top of her head, muttering "Clare, I'm so sorry, I'm so very sorry. Please forgive me. You have to forgive me."

She had finally returned from the past, felt Tommy's arms around her, felt the tears he was crying run down his cheeks and mingle with her own. "Master, what happened? I was here, and then I was with Edward, and then I was here again."

"It's all my fault, Baby Girl, this was all my fault. I ruined this for you and for everyone else. We'll talk about it later. There's something I have to tell you, but we'll talk later. Just rest right now, baby, I'll take care of you."

Jackson appeared again with a blanket and a bottle of water, and encouraged Tommy to take Clare to a sofa in a quiet corner so that they could both settle a little more. But Tommy asked Jackson to please gather all the people from the class so that he could have a word before everyone started to leave.

Once the small crowd had gathered around them, Tommy addressed the group while Clare attempted to pull herself together a little more.

"I owe you all a huge apology, I ruined everything tonight, and I put my slave – my wife – in serious jeopardy. Something happened a few days ago and I've been brooding about it ever since. I went into the scene tonight in a bad place mentally, and that's something no Dom should ever do. I have to thank you all for trying to stop me, and I especially need to thank Master Jackson for getting my head back on straight without actually taking it off – which I believe he was very close to doing. I only hope that Clare will forgive me for my terrible lapse in judgment, and I hope that you'll all learn a valuable lesson from this. Never start a scene if you're not 100% focused on your sub and your play plan. This is how horrible accidents happen and I promise you'll never see anything like this from me in the future. And please be assured that if any other Dominant gets into the same situation in the future, someone will be there, ready and able to stop the scene, by force if necessary. My apologies again to all of you. Now, if you'll excuse us, I think Clare and I need a little more alone time before we leave."

And with that, the audience headed back to the bar for one last drink, leaving Jackson behind with Tommy and Clare.

Jackson gave Tommy one last look and said "If anyone else had done this, they would be out on their ass immediately. But I know what set you off so I'm going to give you a pass this one time. But never again, T. I'll drag your ass out of here so fast, you won't know what happened. And make sure you tell your incredibly forgiving slave what's going on. She's not stupid, I'm sure she's been worried about your attitude the last few days. She has a right to know." And Jackson walked back to the bar, leaving Clare and her Master to cuddle on the sofa and work things out.

Feeling safe in Tommy's arms, she said, "Master, this has something to do with Edward, doesn't it? Some kind of threat from him is the only reason you would lose your head like this."

"Clare, I'm not sure I'm quite prepared to talk about Edward, and what happened tonight, just yet."

"That's too bad, husband, because if we don't talk about this right now, I'll have Jackson take me to my favorite hotel, and I'll spend the night there. Or however many nights it takes for you to GET ready to talk about it. You've been putting me off for two days, and that stops now. You're all big and bad about communication until it's inconvenient or uncomfortable for you, but you're not even giving me the chance to do my job as your submissive – as your wife. To try to comfort you and reassure you that everything's going to be okay. That's not fair to either of us. I may not be successful in my attempt to solve the problem but you're not even letting me try."

"Mind your tone, sub. I'm still your Master."

"Yes, you are, and I respect and adore you. But I'm wearing some crap temporary collar instead of the one you gave me when you pledged so much of yourself to me. So you're just going to have to spank my ass red again, Sweetheart, because on this – right now – we're equals. Whatever is up with Edward, we're in this together, my love."

And he tried to give her that evil eye he was so good at, thinking to put her in her place. But Clare wasn't afraid of that look anymore, and she gave it right back to him.

Tommy and Clare were just about to go a few rounds right there on the sofa, when Master Marshall sheepishly interrupted. "I'm so sorry to interrupt your aftercare, Master Thomas, but I'm not sure what else to do. Portia was so upset by the scene tonight, and I can't seem to calm her down. She's never stood up to me before, and frankly, it's kind of hot, but she insists on talking to your slave to make sure she's alright before she'll let me take her home. Would it be alright for her to come over here and get some reassurance that everything is okay between you and Clare?"

Before Tommy had a chance to answer, Clare looked over at Portia, standing about 10 feet away, tears running down her cheeks, and she said loudly, "Portia, sweetie, come over here. It's okay, I'm fine and Master Thomas won't bite anyone but me."

There was a low growl next to her, but she ignored it and made room on the sofa, patting the cushion next to her, saying "Here, doll, sit down here and talk to me."

Still standing at a distance, Portia said, "Clare, I was so afraid for you, are you sure you're okay?" And she kept looking back and forth between Tommy and her, giving him her sweet sub version of the stink eye.

"I'm really fine, girlfriend, come on, sit down here with me." And Portia did finally sit down, and Clare wrapped her in the best hug she could come up with, still wrapped in her blanket. "Portia, honey, you have to understand something about my Master. He's a fierce lover, a fierce Dom, and sometimes he gets carried away. It's happened before, and I'm sure it will happen again, but that's okay, because we're a matched set, him and me. Yin and Yang all wrapped up in handcuffs. And I wouldn't have him any other way. My biggest problem tonight was getting stuck in the past at the same unfortunate time my Master was stuck in top space. I told you last week how important communication is in our lifestyle. He and I will talk this through, and we'll be stronger together for having had this experience. I still love him, and I still trust him with my life. Now you run along home. I think you and Master Marshall need to have a little conversation of your own about what happened tonight. So scoot on out of here." And she hugged Portia and sent her on her way.

When Tommy and Clare were alone again, and she looked back at him, he had a rather puzzled look on his face. "Clare, did you really mean all that you just said?"

"Of course I did, Master. I would never lie to Portia, she's too trusting and she feels everything so intensely. I love you and I trust you, and there is nothing you can ever do that will change that, my love. That being said, I think I should get at least one free brat pass, to be redeemed at the time and place of my choosing. In the meantime, I'm suddenly very tired, and I don't think I'm up to the long, soul-searching conversation it seems you and I need to have. Could we please go home and cuddle in bed? I think that would do the both of us a world of good. And we can have that conversation first thing in the morning."

"That sounds like an excellent idea, my lovely. Let's get you back into your proper collar. Then we'll get you dressed and back home."

Chapter 8

T ommy took Clare home, got her into bed and cuddled her to sleep, shedding a few more remorseful tears along the way. The next morning, he let her sleep in and then served their usual Sunday morning breakfast in bed. After they had eaten and he had cleared away the dishes, Tommy crawled back into bed and held her close, and they had the conversation they should have had three days before.

"Clare, you were right last night. Communication is something that's very difficult for me sometimes. I know we've talked about this problem I have. I have an expectation that you'll be 100% honest with me at all times, but I'm not always as forthcoming with information you need to receive from me. So here's the deal –

"You know there's been a big push to get members for the dungeon, and they're practically lining up down the street to apply. There was a munch at the café around the corner from the dungeon the other evening, just a little informal gathering for prospective members, and one of the people who showed up was Edward Livingston, acting all high and mighty, insisting that he should be given automatic entry because of his years of experience as a 'wise and knowing Dominant'. Well Jackson recognized him right away, pulled him aside, and told him he wasn't welcome, that he would never be welcome at

Asylum, and told him to leave. Edward tried to get back into the meeting and Jackson pushed him, and there was a scuffle. Luckily, Will and Desdemona were there to back Jackson up, and Edward finally left. But before he went, he told Jackson that he would not be kept out of the club, that he would see you again, that you would see what a poser I am by comparison, and you'd beg him to take you back."

"Oh, my love, you know that would never happen."

"I know that in my head, Baby Girl, but my gut thought something else, and it put me in kind of a mood. I was still in that mood last night and, in trying to prove something to myself, I actually proved the bastard was kind of right. I know better than to go into a scene in that state of mind, but I just couldn't stop myself. Clare, if I had hurt you, I would never have forgiven myself. It was bad enough as it was, and I just don't know how you can be so forgiving. You must have been terrified, being stuck between the memory of him and the reality of me."

And he started to cry again, remembering her tremors and the desperate look in her eyes as she lay on the table, unable to speak, or move, or breathe.

"Master, don't cry, I'm fine, and we both learned from last night's experience. But I do have a question I'm almost afraid to ask."

"What's your question, my love?"

"Do you think Edward knows where we live? Will he try to find me if he can't get access to the dungeon? I'm not really afraid of him, I can defend myself if I need to. But I'd really rather not see him again if I don't have to."

"Not to worry, little slut, he won't come near you without consequences. I have to assume he knows where we live, that's a matter of public record. But any time you're not with me, there will be eyes on you, watching out to make sure you don't have to see him again. If he does approach you, and you feel threatened, we'll get a restraining order to keep him away. I talked to the Police Chief the other day about what the process might be, explained the situation a little, and he thought there would be no problem getting a judge to issue one."

Clare pulled away a little to look him in the eyes and said, "Okay, I'll be safe, but will I be able to tell the good guys from the bad guys? Surely if Edward approaches me, he won't be alone, he always had people around him, protecting him. And what about the good guys? Are they prepared to see me pick a wedgie, or something equally disgusting, when I think no one's looking?"

And she laughed to think of Will or one of the other Masters from the dungeon, having to watch as she went about her daily routine.

With a very sarcastic tone of voice, he said, "Yes, slave, you'll be able to recognize the good guys with no problem. And yes, they've all been warned about your disgusting little habits. They all think I'm a saint to put up with you. My bratty little slut."

"Master, who will be watching over you?"

"Not to worry, Baby Girl, it's you he wants right now. He has no reason to come against me. You're the one we want to protect, little brat."

And then his tone of voice changed to one so soft and loving, she almost cried, and he said, "You may be a brat, my love, but you and I know who the saint in this relationship really is, don't we? I love you, Clare, more than life itself. Please don't ever leave me." And he kissed her gently and pulled her to his chest, where they lay in silence, just listening to each other breathe. One more crisis behind them. But was it really?

The rest of Sunday was sweet and sublime, just Tommy and Clare spending quiet time together, enjoying each other's company. They played music and slow danced in the family room, and spent some time in the playroom, easing back into their bondage lifestyle. It was a beautiful day, bringing their connection back to that intense level it had been before Saturday night.

Then it was back to another work week, a busy one for both of them, and they didn't have the opportunity to spend much time together. They were both looking forward to another Saturday evening at the dungeon, and this time, Tommy took a few minutes to show her his training plan, reviewing the 'what' and the 'why' of the upcoming session, so that she would know what to expect. He could always be so logical when he wanted to be...

Friday evening, Clare was cleaning up the kitchen after dinner and Tommy was in his office doing some paperwork. She heard his cell phone ring and a few minutes later, she heard his office door open, slamming into the wall in his haste to get out of the room.

"Clare? Clare! Where the hell are you?!?!"

"I'm in the kitchen, Sir! Right where you left me to do 'women's work' 15 minutes ago!"

He already had his leather jacket in his hand as he came through the dining room into the kitchen, looking like he was on a mission. He kissed Clare on the back of the neck, gave her a tight hug from behind, and said, "I have to go out for awhile, baby, I have some business to take care of. Don't wait up, I might be awhile. I love you, Clare. Gotta go."

And with a swat on her behind to show her he loved her, he was out the door, barely acknowledging her shouted "I love you too!" Clare heard his Harley fire up outside and he was gone, headed to a particular bar and a showdown that was long overdue.

Clare was restless after Tommy's sudden departure. She knew something was up but she had no idea what it was. She finished cleaning up the kitchen and then went in search of something to do. She watched TV in the family room for a while, but that didn't distract her from her unease. She even spent a little time in the playroom, remembering all the things she and her Master had done there since the remodel. She stared at the picture of the two of them from her collaring ceremony, remembering how it had felt when Tommy had snapped the lock in place, so much love in his eyes. But those memories certainly didn't calm her at all, they just made her want him back home again, where she could touch him, breathe in his scent, hear the moans deep in his chest when her tongue flicked his nipples or his cock. When she started getting wet just from thoughts of him, Clare decided the playroom was not the place for her to be right then.

So she grabbed her tablet from the family room sofa, locked up the house, turned off the lights and headed up to bed. She was in the middle of a good historical mystery on that tablet and she was suddenly tired enough that if she started to read again, she would fall asleep. So bed was the logical place to be. Sure enough, as entertaining as her book was, she was asleep by 11:00. She hadn't even turned off the TV or the bedroom light, she just dozed off with her tablet in her lap, half sitting up against Tommy's pillows.

Some time later, Clare woke to the sound of her cell phone ringing, and it wasn't Tommy's special ring tone she was hearing. When she looked at her phone, she saw the name James, and a phone number she didn't recognize in her sleepy haze, but she answered it, thinking if the number was in her contact list, she must know the person calling. Still half asleep, she said "Hello? Who is this?"

"Clare, this is James Porter."

"Who?"

"James! Your neighbor!" Their next door neighbor and one of Tommy's good friends.

"James, what the hell time is it? Are you okay? Do you need help with something? Tommy's not here right now but I can call him if you need him."

"Clare, it's 2:00 am. I'm outside your front door. You need to get up and get dressed and come with me."

"James, what are you talking about? Where do I need to go with you at 2:00 in the morning?"

"Clare, honey, you have to get up now. We have to go to the hospital. There's been an accident."

As the words 'hospital' and 'accident' sank into Clare's sleepy brain, she was suddenly a study in motion. She threw on a tee shirt and some yoga pants that were in the laundry hamper and flew down the stairs. She grabbed some flip flops and her purse on her way to the front door, yanked it open and almost knocked James down in her haste to get outside.

"James, what happened? Is Tommy okay?" When James hesitated to answer, she whispered "Is he still alive?"

"Clare, I just don't know what's going on right now, honey. Jackson Kelley called me a few minutes ago and said to come over here and get you and bring you to the hospital as soon as I could. We have to go, sweetie. We have to hurry."

There was no more conversation as James got Clare into his car and made the seven minute trip to the hospital, breaking every speed law along the way. He pulled up to the Emergency Room entrance, barely stopping for her to get out of the car and run inside. Where she ran into Jackson, standing by the inside door waiting for her. Ran into him physically, because she had such momentum getting into the building that she couldn't stop on the tile floor in time.

"Oh my god, Jackson, what's going on? What happened? Is he still alive? Please tell me!"

"Clare, he had an accident with the Harley. We were in Gennessee and when we left there to come back home, it had started to rain. He was pissed off and going too fast and there was another car involved that didn't stop. I was a little way behind him and I don't know exactly what happened, but T rolled the bike and was laying in the middle of the road when I caught up to him. Luckily we weren't too far from home so the squad got there pretty quick after I called 9-1-1. Clare, I'm so sorry."

"I have to find him. I have to see him. He needs to know I'm here."

She took off for the ER reception desk, prepared to see him immediately, also prepared to scream down the building if they didn't let her. But none of that was necessary, because her small town had her back, just as they had in the past. Tommy and Clare both worked at the hospital a few days a week, and the hospital staff was like family, a very caring, very understanding family. Before she'd even reached the desk, the ER doctor on staff was there waiting for her. He was the same doctor who had taken such good care of Clare the year before, after the insanity of Tommy's brother Shane. And now he was taking care of her husband, his friend, knowing how important it was to make sure that Tommy survived the accident.

"Clare, I'm so sorry we have to see each other under these circumstances."

"Dr. Morgan – David – I have to see him. Please. I have to see him and then you can tell me whatever you have to tell me."

"Clare, it's pretty bad. He hasn't regained consciousness yet. I'm not sure you should see him until we get him a little more stable and get him cleaned up a little."

"No. I have to see him. I don't care how bad it is. Please."

"Clare, this isn't normal protocol."

"David, I don't give a fuck about protocol right now. I need to see him and he needs to know I'm here."

"Okay, but just for a minute, and you can't blame me afterward for how he looks right now."

"I promise not to blame you for anything, just let me see him for a minute. Please."

Clare knew exactly where Tommy was from all the activity in the bay at the end of the hall – the one with the most sophisticated life support equipment. Dr. Morgan took her hand and led her to the end of the hall, and stopped in front of the curtain.

"Are you sure, Clare?"

"Yes, David, I'm very sure. I need to see him now, and he needs to know I'm here for him."

When Dr. Morgan pulled open the curtain, and she saw her husband lying naked on the gurney, Clare almost fainted. There was medical supply debris all over the floor, huge gauze pads soaked with Tommy's blood, tossed haphazardly on top of his shredded jeans, tee shirt and leather jacket. The helmet he'd been wearing was sitting on a chair in the corner, with a large crack down the back and deep scratches all over the left side. A ventilator was breathing for her husband and he was wearing a cervical collar. There was a large air cast covering his whole left leg, and his left hand was covered in gauze.

"You have 60 seconds, Clare, and then we have to get him upstairs for CT scans, x-rays, and an abdominal ultrasound."

She didn't waste any time getting to Tommy's right side, where there seemed less damage from the accident. She was able to grasp his right hand gently and whisper his name in his right ear, which seemed to make his EKG machine beep a little faster. Almost telling her he knew she was there. Clare whispered "I love you, Master, I'm here", bent down to kiss his right hand, and then she was being pulled out of the way so that his sizeable medical team could get him covered with a sheet and moved toward the elevator and all the diagnostic equipment he needed.

Clare followed Tommy with her tear-filled eyes as his medical team rolled him down the hall and into the elevator. When the doors finally closed, and she and Dr. Morgan were alone in the hallway, he said "He's going to be up there awhile, Clare. Let's go my office and have a talk."

She just nodded and started following him numbly, but before they got half way down the hall, she saw James and Jackson standing at the reception desk, waiting for some kind of news. They all walked toward each other without speaking, and she hugged them both to her, as if they could bring her the strength she knew she would need as she listened to what Dr. Morgan had to say. And as Tommy's close friends, they needed her strength and calm as they heard it too.

"Clare, guys, why don't you all come in and sit down, and I'll tell you what I know so far."

Chapter 9

She hadn't actually shed a tear yet, the shocking news of Tommy's accident had been too sudden and too acute. But as Clare sat in Dr. Morgan's office, flanked on either side by Jackson and James, waiting for some kind of good news about her husband's condition, those tears finally started to flow.

Jackson held her hand to steady her and started the conversation, almost breaking through Dr. Morgan's own shock at what had happened.

"Dr. Morgan, my name is Jackson Kelley, we met last year while Clare and Tommy were here in the hospital. Tommy is one of my oldest and closest friends. I'm the one who called 9-1-1 and waited with him for help to arrive, so I know he was just brought in a little while ago, but is there anything you can tell us about his condition?"

"We do know quite a bit, based on the Paramedic evaluation when they were bringing him in from the scene, and also from what we have observed since he arrived. Obviously, if Tommy hadn't been wearing his helmet, he would have died on scene. So be grateful that he was wearing it. However, based on the damage to the helmet, and the fact that he's still unconscious, he certainly has a concussion and some swelling of his brain that we need to monitor closely and possibly address with surgery at some point. He also has a large contusion to his left thigh with some swelling that would indicate a fracture of some kind, probably from the weight of the bike hitting his leg as he hit the ground. I understand the bike bounced off of him and into the ditch. It's probably a good thing he wasn't pinned under it, the damage to his leg could have been greater. The last visible damage is to his left wrist – it's broken but we won't know how badly until we see the x-rays.

"We can manage the femur fracture and the wrist damage, we just have to confirm that there's no cervical or other spinal injury that hasn't presented itself yet. The head injury is my greatest concern, and normally we would transport him to a larger facility if it was possible, but there's a sizeable weather front right on top of this whole region that makes an airlift all but impossible, and ground transport a last choice in my opinion. In lieu of moving him right now, I've contacted a doctor friend of mine who is a concussion expert, and just happens to be visiting family in Atlanta right now. I called him and explained what I know so far and he's on his way. He should be here this afternoon for a consultation, but in the meantime, he's given me the emergency treatment he would have started if he had been Tommy's admitting physician.

"The diagnostic tests we're running right now will rule out any injuries that were hidden from our initial evaluation. He'll be taken directly to ICU when those tests are done. Right now, we're considering his condition as critical, but I believe he's fairly stable right now, and I don't expect to lose him before Dr. Russell gets here. We're providing all of the care that Tommy would get in a larger facility with a more comprehensive trauma center. It may seem arrogant of me, but I believe he's in good hands right here at home."

Finally, Clare was able to speak a little, and she asked "Dr. Morgan, when can I see him again? Can I be with him in ICU?"

"Clare, I would tell anyone else to go home and get some rest while we're finishing our diagnostic tests and evaluation, but I know the three of you won't go anywhere until you can see him and maybe get a little more information about his condition. As I said, he'll be going to ICU as soon as the CT scans and the other diagnostic tests are done, but I expect all the diagnostics to take several hours. I'll take you up to the waiting room. It's just outside ICU and you'll all be able to see him as soon as they get him settled in the unit, but it won't be a comfortable wait. Are you sure you wouldn't rather go home and rest a little, then come back when he gets to ICU?"

"No, I'm staying."

"Okay, let's get you upstairs. I'm sure there's an available room just outside ICU you can rest in if the wait gets too long for you."

And he stood up, moving toward the door with the three of them following right behind him.

Unfortunately, they didn't get far before a State Highway Patrol officer approached them, looking very official. "Excuse me, folks, are you here with a patient who was brought in a little while ago? After a motorcycle accident? A Mr. Thomas Rollins?"

Jackson stepped forward, looking all big and bad and Dominant, and said "Yes, this is his wife, Clare, and we are Mr. Rollins' close friends. My name is Jackson Kelley. I was at the scene shortly after the accident. This is a family friend, James Porter. And this is Mr. Rollins' doctor, Dr. David Morgan."

"Mr. Kelley, I'm wondering if I could speak with all of you for a few minutes. It's about an incident that could be related to Mr. Rollins' accident. A homicide. The deceased is a Mr. Edward Livingston."

Clare gasped at the name and reached for Jackson's arm to steady herself as she asked without thinking, "Edward is dead?"

"Yes, ma'am, I understand from witnesses in Gennessee that Mr. Rollins and Mr. Livingston had an argument earlier this evening, during which Mr. Rollins threatened to kill Mr. Livingston. According to witnesses at the scene, it seems you were at the heart of the argument. Do you know anything about that?"

And Jackson stepped in front of Clare, looking at the officer but speaking to her, "Not another word, Clare. You know nothing about this, there is nothing you can tell him. Dr. Morgan, why don't you get Clare and James settled in that ICU waiting room, and I'll speak with this officer."

But the officer was persistent. "Mr. Kelley, I'd really like to speak with Mrs. Rollins, she might have some background information that would be helpful."

"Officer ... Daley, is it? Officer Daley, Mr. Rollins has been in a serious accident and is in critical condition. Mrs. Rollins' first concern is to be with him. Mr. Porter has absolutely no information that would be of help to you, but he can help Mrs. Rollins get settled and be with her while her husband is being examined and treated."

Jackson turned and hugged Clare close, whispered in her ear, "I'll take care of this and be up to ICU as soon as I can." Then he turned to Dr. Morgan and said "Go. Get them out of here."

When Officer Daley tried to stop any of them from moving toward the elevator, Jackson turned to walk the other way, toward the ER waiting room, saying over his shoulder, "Officer Daley, if you want information, you probably want to follow me."

Three hours later, James and Clare were restless but trying to keep each other occupied with unnecessary conversation, chasing after bad hospital waiting room coffee for each other, waiting for Tommy to get through his diagnostic tests and get settled in ICU. Jackson still hadn't caught up with them when Dr. Morgan came into the waiting room. He looked so very tired, and Clare read into his facial expression that there was something horribly wrong with her husband. It was obvious that Tommy's accident was taking a toll on the hospital staff almost as much as on Clare.

"Dr. Morgan, are the tests done? Is Tommy settled somewhere? Can I see him yet?"

"Clare, sweetie, all the initial tests are done, the results have been reviewed, and there's a little good news to tell you. There doesn't appear to be any vertebral damage anywhere along his spine, there's no evidence of any fractures, bone chips or swelling there. He has a few bruised ribs but no breaks were visible on the x-rays. He also has a very small chip off the top of his left hip bone, no doubt from the initial fall that should dissolve over time and not cause any problems. The femur fracture is very manageable, although he'll need a cast and possibly some surgery down the road. Eventually he'll need some physical therapy to get back to 100% use of his leg. The air cast on his leg will have to do for now to keep it immobilized. The wrist fracture is also very manageable, but again, he'll need surgery to put a few pins in place to stabilize two of the smaller bones. Physical therapy should get him back to almost 100% use of that wrist, but he won't be playing any fancy pieces on that piano of yours for awhile. That will all have to wait until he wakes up.

"The CT scan didn't show any skull fractures, again thanks to the helmet, but I don't want to speak to the concussion until Dr. Russell gets here and has a chance to check him out personally. Tommy seems to be in a pretty deep coma right now, he's not responding to pain stimuli at all, so there's no way to know if there will be any long term disability..."

"Oh my god, David, are you talking about brain damage? Paralysis? Memory loss? Will he know me when he wakes up? Will he ever wake up?"

This time it was James who spoke. "Clare, don't immediately go to the worst case scenario. Thomas is a strong, healthy man, with the constitution of a stud buffalo, and he's getting the best care he can get. Let's just get the specialist's evaluation of his head injury and give his body a chance to start healing itself. One step at a time, honey, you know that's what Thomas would say if he was awake right now."

And the doctor agreed. "Clare, James is right, we just have to wait and see what happens. Every 24 hours that we can keep him stable is a point in his favor. You know how stubborn T can be, he'll recover in his own time. He'll wake up when his body is ready, and then we'll know more. In the meantime, give me about 30 minutes to get him settled in ICU and then I'll take you back to see him." And the doctor stood and walked away, back through the ICU doors, shutting her out again.

It actually took 45 minutes, but finally an ICU nurse came to the waiting room to let them know that they could see Tommy, but only for a minute and only one at a time. Jackson was just coming off the elevator across from the waiting room, and Clare was anxious to hear what Officer Daley had to say, but she had to go see her husband first. She hugged Jackson and then went through the ICU door with the nurse.

When the nurse brought Clare to Tommy's ICU bay, the sliding glass door was open and she paused for a few minutes, getting her riotous emotions under control. She could hear the sounds of all the equipment – the repeated sucking sound of the respirator breathing for him, the even steady beeps of the heart monitor, the periodic sounds of the automatic cuff monitoring his blood pressure. But the most startling thing was the sight of her husband in the bed, surrounded by so much equipment meant to keep him alive. He was always such a big, vital specimen of a man, taking up most of the available space in any room, but he looked so small and pale in that bed. It made Clare realize how fragile human life was, and how Tommy must have felt, seeing her a year before when she had been in a similar situation. She took a deep breath and said a silent prayer as she made her way to Tommy's right side, where she reached out to hold his hand, but then hesitated at the sight of the IV line in his right arm.

Nurse Ethan stood beside her, his eyes flicking to all the different monitors, checking vital signs on screens, and noticed her hesitation. He said "It's okay, Clare, you can hold his hand, just don't jostle him too much. I'll need to leave the door open but I can pull the curtain and give you some privacy. Talk to him. If he can hear you, it might help him to know you're here. I'll come back for you in a few minutes."

"Thank you, Ethan." And the nurse left the room. And as much as she had already cried, her tears started to flow again.

Clare took Tommy's right hand gently in hers and squeezed just a little, half expecting to feel him squeeze her hand back, but there was no response. She leaned over, as close as she could get to his right ear, and whispered, "I'm here, my Master, your little slut. You've always been so strong for me, my love, now I'm going to be strong for you. I'll take care of things until you're better. You rest and recover." Her hand went instinctively to the platinum chain and lock around her neck and she said "I'll always be close by, ready for you to open your eyes and see your collar around my neck, see my love for you in my eyes."

She heard noise behind her and when she straightened and turned, it was Ethan, letting her know that it was time for her to go. "Clare, I know you won't want to leave anytime soon, so we're setting up a room with a bed just outside ICU for you to lie down and rest a little. It won't do Tommy any good for you to wear yourself out now. And I believe there are a few people outside who want to get a look at him for just a second. Come on, I'll walk you out."

She pulled Tommy's right hand to her lips and kissed it gently, whispered "I love you, baby", and then Ethan put his arm around her shoulder and led her out of the ICU to where Jackson and James were waiting.

Another nurse was just coming out of Clare's temporary room, and led her in to show her around and distract her a little. While she was getting comfortable, Ethan led first Jackson and then James to Tommy's bay so that they could both see him for a few minutes, and then they were all together again.

"Clare, before I came upstairs, I ordered breakfast from the Corcord Grill. It should be here in just a minute. You need to eat something. You need to keep yourself strong for whatever happens."

"Jackson, I appreciate your concern, but I'm not sure I can eat right now. Just tell me, is Edward really dead? What happened? Officer Daley thinks Tommy had something to do with it? Is that even possible? And what were you both doing in Gennessee last night?"

Before Jackson had a chance to respond, James asked "Who is Edward Livingston? You both seem to know who he is. What's his connection to you and Thomas?"

Jackson and Clare exchanged glances, not wanting to give away too much of the truth of her connection to Edward, so she was vague and said "Edward was someone I had a relationship with several years before I met Tommy. I left him because he was very abusive. It's been years since I've seen him or even thought about him."

Then Jackson summarized his conversation with the state trooper. "Clare, Edward is dead, he was hit over the head with a blunt object, a socket wrench that was left at the scene. One like T keeps in his Harley saddle bag for emergency repairs. The one that's missing from that saddle bag now. The police impounded what's left of the bike after the accident, and that's how they know that wrench is missing from the set.

"The coroner thinks Livingston was killed around the time Tommy left Gennessee, before I caught up with him. The police think Tommy could have followed Edward when he left the club, confronted him again at his house, and killed him. They think that's why he was riding so fast, and why he had the accident in the rain."

"Oh my god, Jackson. I can't believe Tommy would do anything like this. It can't have been him."

"I agree, Clare, he didn't have that much of a head start on me before I caught up to him – or at least got close to him. And I'm sure there was another car involved, like someone ran him off the road intentionally. An SUV flew by me and over a slight hill on the road and about two minutes later, I came up on the accident. I saw the tail lights of the car, it seemed like it was chasing T. Maybe a Jeep, I couldn't really tell, and I couldn't get close enough to really see. I just don't know what happened, and I'm not sure T will ever remember, especially if this coma lasts any more than a few days."

Their conversation was interrupted by the delivery of breakfast from the Grill. They all knew they were in for a long wait, and Clare forced herself to eat a little, as she struggled to keep her despair at bay.

Chapter 10

Five days later, Tommy was still in a coma, but his visiting concussion doctor had examined him thoroughly and determined that the brain swelling was indeed subsiding and that no surgical intervention was required – at least for the time being. Clare had sat by Tommy's side every day, for as many hours as the ICU nurses would let her, talking to him, reading the local newspaper to him, recounting the visits he'd had from the few friends who were allowed in to see him.

Even though the concussion expert, Dr. Russell, had given them all good news before he departed the hospital, Clare began to feel a sense of foreboding overtaking her. Optimism had always been difficult for her before she met Tommy, and the sudden realization that she might still lose him began to drag her down. Every day that he didn't wake up, or even stir a little, fed her desperation a little more.

On the evening of the eighth day since Tommy's accident, as she sat alone by his bedside, holding his hand, her despair completely swamped her. He had made no sound, no movement, other than those that machines had caused him to make, and Clare began to think that her loving husband would be in this comatose state for the rest of his life. She didn't see how she could survive on her own without him, and the hollow feeling inside her became a living thing. Her tears blurred her vision and created a puddle on the floor at her feet, and she began speaking to him quietly, hoping against hope that he could hear her.

"Master, I know I told you that I would take care of things until you were better again, but it's time for you to wake up. Please, Master, open your eyes and look at me. Squeeze my hand. I'll take any sign that you're still with me. I need you, Master, I can't make it without you." And she sobbed so hard, she barely heard the voice behind her, calling to her again, making her jump.

"Clare, it's time for you to take a break and get something to eat. Jackson is here, he'll stay with Thomas while you and I talk a little."

"James, you startled me. I'm not hungry and I don't want to leave him. Just as soon as I walk away, he'll wake up and be mad because I'm not here."

"Clare, let's go. Now."

"James..."

And Jackson spoke behind the two of them, "Clare, go with James. I'll stay here with Sleeping Beauty. I have a few things to say to him that his wife doesn't need to hear."

She finally let James pull her up out of her chair. She leaned down and kissed Tommy on the cheek, letting her tears run down his bruised face, then she turned and left the room.

During the next 45 minutes, while they ate a little in the cafeteria, James and Clare had a discussion about long term possibilities, and what options they might have if Tommy remained comatose for any length of time. James was speaking from experience – his wife had been in a persistent coma due to a stroke for the last year of her life. During that year, he had become well versed in long term care options available in their small community. After Clare had eaten more than she had expected she would, and was feeling a little stronger, they headed back toward the ICU. They had just come off the elevator when they heard ominous sounds coming from behind the heavy ICU doors. Knowing that her husband was the only patient currently being cared for in ICU, Clare leapt to the worst possible conclusion – she started screaming and running toward her husband.

Just as she was about to smash through the doors, Jackson came out and caught her. She could hear machine alarms and loud, terse voices shouting orders, a cacophony of sounds that meant the worst for Tommy. Clare was sobbing, struggling against Jackson's hold on her, trying desperately to get to Tommy, when everything went silent. Her heart fell and she would have collapsed if Jackson hadn't been holding her securely. She took the sudden silence to mean that her husband was gone, and she was alone with the despair that threatened to suffocate her. She could still hear voices – James and Jackson talking to her – but her vision faded to black as she imagined the future without the love of her life.

And then just as suddenly as all the noise had stopped, one machine started beeping again – a strong steady beep – Tommy's heart monitor. And Clare was buoyed by that sound, clinging to it just as Tommy was still clinging to life. And then her husband's doctor came through the doors with an exhausted but relieved look on his face.

"David, please, I need to see him. What the hell just happened?"

"Clare, Tommy just had a cardiac incident. His heart slowed down so much, it was all but stopped, and it set off all the monitors. We used the defibrillator to start his heart again, and it seems to have worked, at least for now. If he has another episode, we'll hook up a pace maker and that should keep him in rhythm. But I don't want to do that if we don't have to, so we'll hold off as long as we can.

"The up side of shocking his heart back into rhythm with the defibrillator is that the electrical charge seems to have jump started his brain a little as well. His brain waves have increased and there seems to be more brain activity in general, a lighter level of coma if I can use that term. You may not remember, but when he was brought in and we first evaluated him, Tommy wasn't responding to pain stimuli, which is a pretty basic autonomic activity. Now he's responding to several forms of pain stimuli and I'm taking that as a good sign. We'll keep up that pain stimulus, keep talking to him, keep moving him as much as we can with the femur fracture, and hopefully in the next few days, he'll actually wake up. Then we'll be able to evaluate the effects of his concussion and have a better idea what kind of long-term issues we may be looking at. I'm taking this as a good sign for his recovery, Clare, and you should also. Okay?"

"Okay, David, thank you for the update. Now when can I see him?"

"Give us about 30 minutes, sweetie, we're going to change things around a little in his bay, and get him settled again, and then you can come back in. Okay?"

"Okay."

·♥·♥·♥·♥·♥·

An hour and a half later, Clare was still waiting, sitting alone in an uncomfortable chair in the ICU waiting room. Jackson and James had left to run some errands for her, and she had just decided to rest her eyes for a minute, when she sensed a presence in the room with her that had been there several times before. Not a comforting spirit, as she had hoped, but a live body, wearing the boots of a state trooper – Officer Daley, back for another round of questions for which she had no answers. But this time, he had brought someone with him – a man in plain clothes, who sat down next to her without invitation and pulled his badge out of his pocket, showing it to her with a seriously smug look on his face.

"Mrs. Rollins, my name is Detective Jacobsen. I'm an investigator with the State Highway Patrol. I'm sorry to have to meet you under such circumstances, but I have questions that I hope you have some answers to."

"Detective Jacobsen, I'm sure you know that Officer Daley has been here many times, asking the same questions over and over again, and getting the same answers from me – I don't know anything, and I'm getting really tired of the interruptions while I wait for my husband to wake up. So even if you have new information, I just can't help you. My gut tells me my husband would never kill Edward Livingston, and that's all I have to go on right now. So please go away and leave me alone with my thoughts."

"Please bear with me for just a few minutes, Mrs. Rollins. I just want to clarify a few things and make sure my notes and timeline are in order."

"Fine, Detective, I'll give you 5 minutes."

"Thank you, Mrs. Rollins. I've been doing some digging into Mr. Livingston's past and I find that it intersects your past, which surprised me a little. It seems you had a relationship with him 7 or 8 years ago, a rather unusual relationship. According to people I've tracked down who knew you both when you were together, this relationship started out normally enough, but after you moved in with Mr. Livingston, things between you became a little – spicy, if you will. Some people would call it twisted and violent. Not that I'm judging or anything, I just want to make sure my facts are correct. Can you confirm that you had a relationship with the deceased around that time?"

"Who are these so-called people you talked to, Detective?"

"I was able to find a man who claims to have been Mr. Livingston's butler while you were in residence. I also located a friend of Mr. Livingston's – a man who has been practicing medicine without a license for more than 10 years. They were both eager to tell me what they knew. In one case, the man wanted his 15 minutes of fame. In the other case, the man didn't want to spend more time in jail than he already has. So, are both of these men lying about your relationship with Edward Livingston?"

Clare paused for a minute, trying to decide how she was going to answer the question, then decided a little truth wouldn't hurt any of them. "No, they're not lying. I had a brief relationship with Edward a long time ago. I haven't seen him since the day I moved out of his house."

"What was the manner of your relationship with Mr. Livingston?"

Again she paused to consider her answer and then said "Romantic."

"And did your husband know about this past relationship with the deceased? Is your husband a jealous man?"

"Don't answer any more questions, Clare." At the sound of the new voice, they all turned toward the entrance of the waiting room to see Jackson entering, followed by a stunning middle-aged man who exuded every bit as much dominant attitude as Jackson and Tommy, making Clare smile just a little. The man looked familiar to her, but she didn't think they had ever been introduced.

The stranger strode up to the man who had been questioning Clare and said "Detective, my name is Harrison Turner, I've been Mr. Rollins' attorney for many years, and I'm here to represent him and Mrs. Rollins in this investigation. I will decide what questions they should and should not answer during any future questioning. Since Mr. Rollins is currently incapacitated, and since I haven't had the opportunity to confer with Mrs. Rollins yet in this matter, we're finished with this questioning, and I'm asking you to leave. I need 24 hours to confer with my clients, and then you are free to submit any questions you have for them, in writing, to my office. Here's my card." He reached into his jacket pocket and pulled out a business card, which he handed to the detective.

"Mr. Turner, this isn't a formal questioning, I'm just trying to confirm information I've already obtained from other people. Mrs. Rollins has no need of a lawyer at this time. I don't believe she had anything to do with Mr. Livingston's murder, I'm just looking for her to fill in a few blanks."

"Be that as it may, Detective, my client is done answering questions for now. Your blanks will have to remain unfilled a little longer." Mr. Turner placed himself between Clare and Detective Jacobsen and stood silently while the police officers huffed and puffed and complained. There was continued silence on Mr. Turner's part until the officers left the room.

"Jackson, what the…"

"Not here, Clare, let's go to your room across the hall so we can close the door and have a little conversation."

"But I'm waiting to get back in to see Tommy again. I have to stay here until they come for me."

"Clare, honey, this will only take a few minutes and I'm sure if one of the nurses comes looking for you in the waiting room and they don't find you, they'll come across the hall and knock on the door."

She was suddenly just too tired to argue. The stress of the past two weeks had been too much. Between her husband's persistent coma and the almost daily visits from Officer Daley, and now the probing questions from Detective Jacobsen, Clare had reached, even exceeded, her emotional limits. She had no fight left in her.

"Alright, Jackson, whatever you say."

So they all walked across the hall into her temporary home and settled into the surprisingly comfortable chairs that were there.

When the door closed, she looked to Jackson to explain. "Jackson, do I need an attorney? Does Tommy need an attorney? Assuming that he eventually wakes up?"

Jackson looked to Harrison Turner, who looked to her and said "Clare, I know we've never been formally introduced but I've known about you almost since you moved in with Tommy. I've been his personal attorney for many years, and I've represented him in many of his business dealings. I actually handled the sale of your house in Blakeley, and I was at the closing. If I look familiar to you, I'm sure it's from there.

"Clare, I've already talked to Jackson about Tommy's altercation with Edward Livingston in Gennessee the night of the accident. It seems your incredibly protective husband and Master told Livingston that he would never live to see you or put his hands on you again."

Clare blanched at Harrison's use of the term Master, but he continued without a pause. "Yes, Clare, I know about your special relationship with Tommy. I've known for quite some time. You don't have to worry about your secret, I'm quite discreet. But as I was saying, I admit that on the surface it doesn't look very good for T, too many people witnessed his argument with Livingston and heard Tommy threaten to kill him. And it appears that the wrench that was found next to the body belonged to Tommy. It has his fingerprints on it, which would make sense if he's been keeping it in his bike saddle bag for emergency repairs. As his attorney of record, I've already requested access to all the information the authorities have that they think will implicate Tommy in Livingston's death but I have an expectation that the authorities will stall on that request. As much as I'd like to stay on this case, I'm not a criminal attorney, and I don't want to take a chance with T's freedom, at such time as he wakes up and either remembers or doesn't remember what happened that night.

"So I've taken the liberty of securing criminal legal counsel for Tommy and also for you, even though there is no chance the police would ever try to bring charges against you. The attorney is an old friend of mine, someone who knows Tommy almost as well as I do. His name is Price Tucker. He's very good at what he does, and he has one of the best investigators in the area on his legal team. I trust him to handle any defense that we might need to bring forward if charges are ever filed against T. I just need you to sign this paper, authorizing Price to begin investigating on his own and represent both of you if needed."

And Harrison pulled a piece of paper and a pen out of his inside jacket pocket and handed them both to her.

Clare looked to Jackson for a little moral support and he just nodded, so she took the paper and pen to the bedside table and signed and dated it. The language of the contract covered both Clare and Tommy, based on the fact that she had already activated her power of attorney on behalf of her incapacitated husband. She was just about to breathe a sigh of relief when the door of her room slammed open. Nurse Ethan rushed in, grabbed her by the arm, and without explanation, started dragging her toward Tommy's room.

Chapter 11

Clare was deposited unceremoniously at the entrance to Tommy's ICU bay, on the edge of what could only be called bedlam. The privacy curtain had been pulled all the way back, and there were alarms sounding from multiple machines. Two other nurses, plus Tommy's doctor, were pinching his arms, slapping his face, sticking needles in the bottoms of his feet. Nurse Ethan began monitoring all the machines, calling out readings every 10 seconds. Tommy was moaning and his head was flopping back and forth on the pillow, in obvious pain. Clare couldn't believe what she was seeing.

"What the fuck are you doing to him! You're hurting him! You have to stop!" And she tried to pull the closest nurse away from him, trying to stop Tommy's apparent agony.

Dr. Morgan shouted at her, "Clare, he's trying to wake up, and we're trying to help him! Pain stimulus is all we have to work with, unless you have some other suggestion!"

"You want him awake?!? You won't do it with pain! He won't respond to pain the way you expect – he's a fucking ex-Marine! He thinks he's too manly to let pain affect him! If he needs help waking up, I'll wake him up! Everybody just get away from him and let me at him!"

Everyone in the room, including new arrivals Jackson and Harrison, looked to Dr. Morgan for direction. When he nodded, they all stepped back from the bed and she ran forward. Her husband was going to wake the fuck up, and he was going to wake up right fucking now!!

"Master! Master! It's time to wake up! Please, Master, I need help and you're the only one who can do it!"

She gave Tommy five seconds to respond to her voice, and when he didn't, she took another approach. Ignoring the sounds of all the machine alarms, Clare pulled up his hospital gown and reached for his flaccid penis, thinking to give him a wake-up blow job, but realized immediately that he was equipped with a Foley catheter, which was going to get in her way. "Get this catheter out! Now!"

Dr. Morgan just stared at her and said "Clare, he still needs to have that catheter."

"Not right now, he doesn't! Get it out now, or I'll yank it out myself, and you really don't want that." The Doctor and the wife stared each other down for a few seconds, and then he nodded to Nurse Ethan, who made quick work of the catheter. As soon as the nurse had stepped away from the bed again, she went to work waking her husband.

Clare had to climb up onto the edge of the bed, and Jackson came up behind her, holding her at the waist to keep her from falling backward. She grasped Tommy's cock tightly and started moving her hand slowly up and down, rubbing her thumb over the crown on every up stroke like she knew he loved her to do. On the third stroke of her thumb across the head of his cock, a moan escaped from Tommy's throat, and they could all see the beginnings of an erection. Encouraged by this small but meaningful reaction to a hand job, she lowered her head to the cock she knew and loved so much, and quickly enveloped the head in the inviting warmth of her mouth. Her tongue lashed across the sensitive spot on the underside, just where the head mushroomed out, and there was another moan from Tommy. And moans from all the other men in the room with her!

Clare giggled to herself as she started bobbing up and down on her husband's hardening cock, going lower with each pass of her lips and tongue, while she gently caressed his balls in her hand. She turned away from him to get a better angle, and the room went suddenly quiet, other than the slurping sounds of her enthusiastic blow job. She was about to shift her position again when something touched her arm. She tried to shake it off, thinking Jackson or one of the nurses was trying to pull her away, but the grip tightened, causing her to turn toward it.

If Jackson hadn't been there to keep her on the bed, the sight of Tommy's eyes, open and heated with desire, would surely have caused Clare to fall from the shock. She let Tommy's cock slip out of her mouth, tears oozing down her cheeks, and whispered "Oh my god, baby, are you awake? Can you see me? Can you hear me?" He mouthed her name around the breathing tube and his responding nod answered every prayer she'd said since the accident.

As Tommy came more awake, he began to struggle against the breathing tube that had been keeping him alive since he'd been injured. He was trying to breathe on his own and communicate, and it was obvious that in that moment, he didn't need the tube. Jackson helped Clare off the bed and the medical staff went to work removing the breathing tube, replacing it with a nasal cannula that provided the oxygen Tommy still needed. It was ugly for a few minutes, watching her husband struggle against the tube being removed, but watching him take his first real breaths on his own was almost a dream come true. The love of her life was awake and they would go forward together, traveling his road to recovery.

For the next 24 hours, Clare didn't leave Tommy's side for more than a few minutes at a time. He would be awake for a little while and then doze for a while more. There were constant interruptions from his medical team, checking this monitor and that gauge – heart rate, oxygen saturation, muscle response. And most important, his memory. He knew his name, Clare's name, where they lived. When she sat on the edge of his bed, close enough for him to reach it, he would run his thumb around her wedding ring, or he would reach up and slide a finger across her platinum collar. They shared memories about her collaring ceremony, Christmas, the dungeon opening – and he even recalled some of a conversation Jackson had with him while he was unconscious. But he seemed to have no recollection of anything that occurred after he left the house the night of the accident. He had no memory of actually going to Gennessee, the confrontation with Edward, or whatever had happened after he left the bar that night.

During the next six days, Tommy continued to recover, gaining strength every day, and Clare began to get back to a normal routine that didn't include sleeping in a chair in his hospital room or in her room outside the ICU. She had vowed that she would never sleep in their bed at home until her Master was there with her, so she would sleep fitfully for a few hours every night in the guest bedroom at the house, or on the fainting couch in the playroom, looking up at the picture of the two of them on the wall. In the privacy of her home, she would cry tears of gratitude, relief, joy, every positive emotion, so very thankful that her husband was alive and awake, and remembered who she was.

Ten days after Tommy woke up, he was moved to an ICU step-down room, and a few days later, he got a consultation from the local orthopedic surgeon about fixing his broken femur and wrist. Every doctor on staff seemed to have an opinion and a say as to when those surgeries would take place, but everyone agreed that Tommy needed at least another three or four weeks to stabilize.

His visitor list increased gradually but noticeably in those few weeks, and he was eventually able to see all of his friends from the dungeon, plus all of the local hospital staff who had been waiting and praying for him to recover. Just a few days after Tommy was moved to his long term 'home away from home' in the hospital, he was also able to confer with both of his attorneys – Harrison Turner and Price Tucker. That meeting was unknown to Clare at the time, they chose to visit Tommy while she was at home taking a shower and changing her clothes.

After exchanging some words of gratitude that Tommy was awake again, Price started and led the conversation. "Tommy, what's the very last thing you remember before waking up here in the hospital?"

"I have a vague memory of Jackson being in my ICU room, rambling on and yelling at me about lots of things that didn't make sense to me, including him telling me that bastard Livingston was dead. Before that, the last clear memory I have is getting on the Harley and turning out of the driveway in the dark. The rest is a big blank."

"So you have no memory of going to Gennessee that night. Or arguing with Livingston at a bar? Nothing about the accident?"

"No, I have nothing at all. A few days after I woke up, Dr. Morgan asked me a few questions about what I remembered about that night, but I think he was just trying to assess the state of my long term memory, and he didn't tell me anything that might jog my memory. I'm glad to see both of you, but do I really need a criminal attorney? Do the police really think I had something to do with Livingston's death? Now that I'm awake, do you think I'm going to be arrested?"

"Well, T, I do have to tell you there's some pretty strong evidence against you that makes you a serious person of interest in Livingston's death, and it's likely that asshole Detective Jacobsen will place you under arrest as soon as he can get in here, but you still need too much medical care, and a few surgeries from what I understand, so it's not like he's going to be hauling you off to jail anytime soon. Just don't worry too much. I have Jake Sykes investigating this personally. He'll dig under rocks the police won't bother with, and he'll come up with the truth. Do you remember Jake?"

"Yeah, I worked with him when Jackson was arrested for killing Robert Malcolm. He's a really good investigator. He found clues I would have missed, and we were able to clear Jackson in pretty short order. If there's a way to prove my innocence or guilt, Jake will find it. Just promise me that you'll protect Clare, whatever Jake finds, and however this ends. Both of you."

And they both agreed that Clare would be Harrison's number one priority while Price was overseeing Tommy's criminal investigation. When she got back to the hospital that afternoon, she found Price and Harrison still in Tommy's room, but all she heard was the three of them reminiscing about past experiences – and women – they'd shared before she and Tommy had met. Not something she really wanted to hear but it was good to hear them all laugh together, at least that much lightened her mood.

Unfortunately, four weeks after he had woken up, Tommy had two visitors that Clare had tried to keep out, but ultimately wasn't able to – Detective Jacobsen and Officer Daley. When she heard they were in the hospital trying to get clearance to see Tommy, she had called Price to let him know Tommy was about to be questioned. Price told her to try to stall the police officers until he could get to the hospital, but not to worry about it if they got to Tommy before he did. Because Price would get to them before the Police got to the part of the questioning where Tommy needed the advice of counsel.

To hedge her bets, she had also called Dr. Morgan to see what he thought about the police questioning Tommy so soon, and he was adamant that he needed to be present for any interrogation, even if Tommy's lawyer was present. So by the time Detective Jacobsen got to her husband's room, Dr. Morgan and Nurse Ethan were already in the room. And their lead attorneys walked into the room just ahead of him.

When Detective Jacobsen walked into the room, he was openly shocked to see the number of people in the room other than his suspect. But he was also surprised to see the condition Tommy was still in. His face and body were still covered in bruises, fading from dark blue to red and yellow. His entire left leg was still in an air cast, with surgery coincidentally scheduled for the next day to finally fix the leg fracture. And his left wrist was encased in a temporary plaster cast, but with an oval hole on top to allow access to the surgical incision made the week before to stabilize the tiny broken bones.

Detective Jacobsen was introduced to Dr. Morgan and Nurse Ethan, and thanked them for allowing him access to their patient. He was cordial at first, and never referred to his meeting with Tommy as 'questioning', only as a 'conversation'. But it was quickly obvious to everyone in the room that the detective thought Tommy was guilty of murder, and he would pay for his assumed crime one way or another.

"Mr. Tucker, I understand that you might want to be present for my conversation with Mr. Rollins but I don't seriously think we need anyone else in this very small room with us. And I'm sure that Mr. Rollins would appreciate some privacy during our conversation. So how about I send my patrolman out of the room, and you send everyone else out as well."

"No, I don't think so, detective. I'm sure Dr. Morgan will insist on staying in the room, along with Mr. Rollins' nurse, to monitor his still tenuous medical condition. And I require Mr. Turner's presence as Mr. Rollins' long time legal counsel. And you certainly can't expect Mrs. Rollins to leave the room while you subject her husband to whatever 'conversation' you have in mind, so soon after he's awakened from his coma. But you're more than welcome to send your patrolman to the cafeteria for a cup of coffee while we 'chat'."

Detective Jacobsen's friendly demeanor left the room quite suddenly, but no one else left.

"Fine. Mr. Tucker, would you agree to my recording this conversation with your client? My memory isn't what it used to be, and I might have the need to replay the conversation in the near future to put my notes together."

"Fine, you are free to record the conversation. But I will make my own recording as well, just so that we can compare notes after the fact, if needed." And Detective Jacobsen's mood darkened further.

The detective pulled a small recording device out of his jacket pocket and turned it on, and Price pulled out his cell phone and started the recording feature, scanning the entire room to capture all of the people present in the room.

Price spoke first, recording the names of all the people present, as well as the date. Then he had a few questions of his own for Tommy – "Mr. Rollins, do you know where you are? And do you know who I am?"

"Yes, I'm a patient at Hickory Regional Medical Center, although I don't recall what caused my injuries. And you are Price Tucker, my criminal legal counsel."

"And do you know why I've been retained as your criminal legal counsel?"

"Yes, it appears the State Highway Patrol suspects I killed Edward Livingston."

"Very well, thank you, Mr. Rollins. Alright, Detective Jacobsen, you may begin your 'conversation'. I instruct my client to answer your questions honestly, but if at any point I think you've asked a question my client should not answer, I will let you both know immediately. Also, given Mr. Rollins' current medical condition, we're allowing 15 minutes for this questioning, but if at any time during the next 15 minutes, Dr. Morgan feels that it is in his patient's best medical interest, he is free to stop the meeting and we will all exit the room. Am I clear on that?"

And Detective Jacobsen took over the 'meeting'. "Yes, Mr. Tucker, I agree to those terms. Now, Mr. Rollins, are you acquainted with a man named Edward Livingston?"

"Yes, I know who he is. He was pointed out to me at a social event a few months ago, but I don't believe we've ever been introduced."

"Really. You don't think you've ever met him?"

"No. I don't recall ever meeting him."

"Convenient memory lapse, don't you think? We'll come back to that. Mr. Rollins, are you aware of your wife's history with Mr. Livingston? A romantic relationship she had with Mr. Livingston? One during which she was rather seriously injured?"

Tommy paused for a minute, exchanging looks with Price, and then answered, "Yes, I have been aware of my wife's previous relationship with him for quite some time. She made me aware of that relationship, and the injuries that ended it, just a few weeks after we met. To my knowledge, she has not seen him since she ended the relationship."

"Are you the jealous type, Mr. Rollins? Perhaps a little possessive? Maybe a little 'dominant' in your relationship with your wife?" Several of them caught the innuendo of the word 'dominant', but no one reacted.

"I love my wife very much. I don't think anyone could blame me for wanting to protect her."

"Have you ever threatened someone who might have made a pass at your wife? Have you ever threatened your wife because you misconstrued something she did with another man?"

Price interrupted immediately, "Excuse me, detective, I'm instructing my client not to answer that question at this time." And Tommy remained silent, looking slightly more sullen than he had before. He was getting upset, remembering the incident that Detective Jacobsen was referring to, that had occurred early in his relationship with Clare. He got jealous one night in a bar, and threatened her in front of witnesses. Witnesses who had obviously spoken to the police recently. And his blood pressure started going up.

And the detective continued his questioning. "Yes, well, we'll circle back around to that later also. Mr. Rollins, do you carry tools in your motorcycle saddle bags?"

"Yes, I always carry minimal tools to make emergency repairs."

"Is a Craftsman socket wrench among the tools you usually carry?"

"Yes, I have some, but it's a pretty universal wrench set, I think half the motorcycle riders on the road carry all or parts of that set."

"What would you say if I told you that Mr. Livingston was killed with a socket wrench that was left behind at the scene?"

"I would say that someone wasted a perfectly good wrench on a villainous pig."

"And what if I told you that the wrench that killed Mr. Livingston and was left behind at the scene had your fingerprints on it?"

"I would have no explanation for how my fingerprints could get on a wrench that was found at the scene of a murder. Because I didn't kill anyone."

"When was the last time you remember using any of your socket wrenches?"

"I did some routine maintenance on my Harley at the house right after Christmas. I haven't needed them since."

"Mr. Rollins, the murder weapon has your fingerprints on it, but you say you have no recollection of what occurred the night of the murder. Do you seriously want me to believe that you didn't kill Mr. Livingston? Purely based on your say so? When you can't even be sure of your innocence yourself?"

"YES! That's what I'm telling you! I didn't kill anyone!" And Tommy's blood pressure monitor sounded an alarm, causing Dr. Morgan to speak up for the first time.

"Gentlemen, I believe we're done here. Further conversation at this point would seriously jeopardize the health of my patient, and I'm stopping this now."

"Well, Dr. Morgan, I appreciate your concern for your patient, that's your job. But I have a job to do also. I have a warrant for Mr. Rollins' arrest for the murder of Edward Livingston.Obviously, I won't be taking him to jail today, but it is within my rights as the arresting officer, to make sure he doesn't go anywhere anytime soon." And he pulled out his handcuffs and attached Tommy's right wrist to the bed rail. "And I'll be posting a 24 hour guard on Mr. Rollins' room just to make sure there's no funny business while we continue to investigate and gather evidence." Then he handed the paperwork to Price to review.

Dr. Morgan objected vigorously but Price stepped in again. "Detective Jacobsen, I can't believe you're doing this, it seems a pretty petty move on your part. It's very clear to everyone present that Mr. Rollins isn't going anywhere, he has another surgery scheduled for tomorrow. These handcuffs cannot go to surgery with him."

"Mr. Tucker, I will concede the handcuffs during surgery, but when he comes back to his room, they go back on. The guard on the door will have a key to remove them and replace them. I'm within my legal rights to do this, and this is what's going to happen. Whether he remembers or not, Mr. Rollins is a murderer and he will eventually be brought to justice! The 24 hour guard starts now."

And with that, Detective Jacobsen left the room with Officer Daley, who took up his guard position right outside the door.

The doctor and the two lawyers all started talking at once, but Tommy and Clare didn't hear much of what they were saying, they were having their own tear-filled conversation. "Clare, I'm so sorry. I wish I could remember what happened that night. I would never put you through something like this. Damn it!! If I could just remember! No matter what happens, know that I would never do something that would hurt you like this."

All she could do was nod and sob so loudly that everyone else in the room stopped talking.

And Price took over once again. "Dr. Morgan, do whatever you need to do to take care of your patient. If the cuffs get in the way, get them removed. Cut them off if you have to. I'll file paperwork before the end of the day to get an official court order for their permanent removal, and I'll be in court tomorrow morning to make sure that happens.

Tommy, we'll get this all straightened out, just try not to worry too much. It's not good for your blood pressure, and you have another surgery to get through tomorrow. I'll be back to see you in a few days, or whenever I have something to report.

"Harrison, can you meet me in my office in 30 minutes? We'll track Jake down and see what he has so far. Clare, honey, we'll make this thing go away as quickly as we can. I know you've both been through a lot lately, just let your friends support you for a little longer. I'll be in touch as soon as I know anything at all." And he walked out the door, followed closely by Harrison.

When the two attorneys had left the room, Dr. Morgan made one final check of all Tommy's monitor readings, laughed a little, and said "You certainly know how to liven up a room! Now if you'll excuse me, I have to go scare up a bolt cutter – you know, in case we need to cut those cuffs off at any point." And he left the room as well, whistling as he went.

When it was just the two of them, Clare held her Master's hand through the bed rails, still teary-eyed, running her thumb over the hand cuff attached to his wrist. She sniffled, smiled just a little, and said "You know, under other circumstances, in a different place, you in these hand cuffs would be pretty hot. Maybe we'll try it sometime, once we get you home. How would you like that?"

"Oh, there will definitely be hand cuffs in our future, Baby Girl, but I won't be the one wearing them. Now how about a pre-dinner blow job, little slut – you know, to get my blood pressure back under control."

"Tommy, that was a one-time deal, just to get you out of that coma. I don't think it would be considered proper medical protocol for me to just jump up on the bed and rip you off any time you want. And there's no way for me to lock this door, so anyone coming in could see both of us, doing things we're not supposed to be doing in a hospital bed."

"I don't care about proper medical protocol, brat, I'm in charge and I say a blow job is just what I need to get my BP back where I want it. So hop to, little slut. Chop, chop! If someone comes in uninvited, they will see what they will see."

Two minutes later, Officer Daley was treated to a rousing chorus of moans as Tommy and Clare went about their 'business'.

Chapter 12

Tommy came through his femur stabilization surgery the next day with an excellent prognosis, and five days after that, he was deemed ready to be moved to the Physical Rehabilitation unit of the medical center. The advantage of being the only full-service health care facility within a hundred miles was that whatever a patient needed, he or she could get it somewhere within the large hospital campus.

He was still handcuffed to his hospital bed most of every day, and he wasn't handling it well at all. Which made him the punch line of so many jokes among the employees and his friends. Healthcare workers – doctors, nurses, physical therapists – all have the best interests of their patients at heart, but they rule their wards like dictators when it comes to uncooperative patients. Like Clare's sometimes unmanageable husband. The saying that healthcare professionals make the worst patients was certainly true in Tommy's case. And the combination of the handcuffs, the ever-present guard outside his door, the resulting jokes, and being ordered around his own hospital, was often more than he could handle.

And making matters worse was the lack of information from Price Tucker's lead investigator. Jake Sykes seemed to have gone off the grid and there had been no information at all for the past 4 days. Tommy had become a horrible combination of restless from lack of activity for so long, worried about where Jake was and what he was finding out, and angry that he still couldn't remember anything about his argument with Edward and the subsequent accident. Going into his room had become like braving a wounded bear in its den. Even Clare didn't want to go in some days. So it was without regret that his Medical/Surgical care team handed him off to the staff in the Physical Rehabilitation unit with best wishes for all involved.

Once he was moved, they fell into a new normal routine. Clare arrived each morning in time to help Tommy with breakfast and to 'cheer' him up a little. The staff had grown tired of interrupting hand jobs and blow jobs and whatever else she could think of to improve her husband's mood, so each day Clare would stop by the Nurse's Station and announce her arrival, check to make sure Tommy had received his morning pain meds, and then have 45 uninterrupted minutes for her husband to eat his breakfast and for her to eat him. They always tried to make as much noise as they could, for the entertainment of the staff and other patients, and to irritate the fuck out of whichever Highway Patrol guard was outside the door making sure Tommy didn't escape. And then, of course, Tommy had a 'stamina' reputation to maintain – he had led people to believe he could pound nails with his cock and he could do it for hours and hours! He had spent years building that reputation and he wasn't going to have a little thing like a life-threatening injury do damage to his larger-than-life sex god image among his friends.

Clare would stay all day, watch to see what changes the Physical Therapist would make in his exercise routine, and mostly to control who was stopping by to see him. After the second week of therapy, Tommy started sending her home for lunch every day, and several times when she came back for the afternoon, he was entertaining visitors – almost holding court in his room. Word had spread throughout the region about his accident and subsequent recovery, and people from his past showed up from far and wide to see him and reminisce about the 'old days'.

She came back from lunch one day and before she had gotten close to his room, Clare heard Tommy's very distinctive, and very loud, laughter. Wondering what the cause was, she walked a little faster toward his room. From inside, she heard an unfamiliar male voice say "T, these cuffs look good on you!! They kind of remind me of a cheap motel!"

"Shut the fuck up, bastard, we said we'd never talk about that night again!"

Ignoring the guard posted at the door, Clare walked into the room to the sound of booming laughter that she did not recognize. When the stranger saw her in the doorway, he flashed a huge smile and approached her for a hug, introducing himself.

"You must be Saint Clare!I heard the Beast got married but I didn't believe it until I got here today and one of the nurses told me it was true. I'm an old friend of your husband, from his 'Roadie Summer'. You can call me Hog."

"Get your fucking paws off my wife, Hog. Clare, don't let him touch you, you'll come down with some horrific communicable disease!"

"Your name is Hog? And what was his 'Roadie Summer'? Does it have something to do with the handcuff story? Because I could really use a laugh right about now. Tommy, a tow truck delivered the remains of the Harley to the house while I was at home. Good God, how did you ever survive? I got hysterical just looking at it. Baby, I so could have lost you!"

She started to cry and went to sit down on the edge of the bed, where her husband wrapped her in his loving arms – well, one arm – because he still had one wrist handcuffed to the bed rail.

"Shh, Baby Girl, I'm right here, I'm going to be fine."

"Clare, let me cheer you up. I'll tell you about the night your husband got handcuffed to a bed in a cheap motel by three groupies, one of which we think was a guy!"

"You tell one word of that story, Hog, and it will be your last!"

Hog moved far enough away from the bed that Tommy couldn't get at him, and started his tale.

"You may not know this about your husband, Clare, but back in the day, when he was fresh out of the Marines and sort of at loose ends, he got drunk in a bar one night where a bunch of us were hanging out. We were on roadie duty for a well-known Detroit rocker who's name I cannot mention, and pretty soon, we were all drunk and tellin' lies, including the Beast here. He looked to be all dumb muscle but it turned out he could play the piano pretty fucking well. Well, someone needed to look after the poor idiot bastard, so we took him under our wing."

"Yes, and you got me arrested that night!"

"Well, I could say you got US arrested! You were the one who threw the first drunken punch. And one of the muscle-bound boys got way beat up and spent 5 days in the hospital."

She looked at Tommy with a "you must be joking" look and Hog continued his story.

"Rocker came and bailed us all out the next morning and paid the hospital to take care of Pretty Boy. And he hired the Beast to fill in for Pretty Boy until he could catch up with the tour."

"So where do the handcuffs come in??"

"I'm gettin' to that! It had been about four weeks and we were doing two shows back to back in Atlanta so after we secured the stage and the equipment for the night, we hit a local bar and met up with a literal pack of groupies looking to hump anything with a dick. And these two busty beauties and their questionable friend talked your boy here into going back to their motel with them for a little party. When I finally caught up to them the next morning, the chicks and the probable dude were long gone and T was naked, handcuffed to the bed, and that big cock of his was all swelled up around a cock ring, so hard he could have pounded nails with the damned thing! He seemed to be in a lot of pain and swearing up a fucking storm!

"Well I wasn't gonna touch him and I didn't have a key for the cuffs, so I had to call one of the boys to bring a bolt cutter to get him free – from the cuffs, not the cock ring!" By now, Hog was laughing so hard he could barely breathe, and Tommy was silent, looking like he could shoot lightning from his eyes!! Clare laughed so hard, she almost fell off the bed.

And Hog finished the story. "We finally got the cuffs off, and grabbed T's clothes, ran out to the van with him still naked, and caught up with the rest of the team, heading back to the arena for that night's show. I have no idea how your husband got that cock ring off, or how long it took, but he walked funny for a few days after! I don't think he let any chicks talk him into a quick fuck the rest of his time with us. We kept in touch for awhile after that, and the last thing I heard, he was working at a hospital in Atlanta and had hooked up with a nurse. Was she freaky, T? You know what they say about nurses and crazy sex.And I heard she was into that BDSM shit you always talked about."

"She was a lying bitch and we didn't last long! And we don't talk about her in front of my wife!"

"Oops! Sorry, dude. I guess I wasn't thinking!"

Clare jumped into the conversation to ease Hog's worries. "No problem, Hog, I heard all about her, not long after Tommy and I met. She's way in the past."

"Good, I'm glad to hear that, 'cause I think you two have something real special going on here. I'm a little jealous, seeing as I just divorced wife number three."

Before they could start another conversation, one of the physical therapy interns came in and announced it was time for another session, so Hog said his goodbyes. They exchanged contact information and promised to catch up with him as soon as Tommy was up and around again, and he was gone.

Another day, not long after Hog's visit, when she came back from lunch, Clare walked into Tommy's room to find her husband's bare chest being caressed by a stunning woman, tall with a killer figure and long straight black hair framing dark eyes and a perfect porcelain complexion. He wasn't protesting or trying to pull away from her touch and he had a distant look in his eyes. As he continued to recall a past experience, it looked like she was moving down his chest toward more interesting body parts. Clare didn't recognize her but she had a funny feeling she knew who she was. Her husband didn't seem to mind the strange woman's attention, and Clare's jealous streak made an appearance.

"Excuse me, but you seem to have your hands on my husband. Unless you're some kind of medical professional, and a hospital employee, I would suggest you remove your fucking hands before you lose them."

"Clare, this is Veronica. I told you about her a long time ago. She heard about my accident and came to see me to make sure I was okay. Isn't that nice?" And the look Clare gave him made him flinch just a little. And then the stranger spoke, making the most of her low smoky voice.

"Yes, Clare, isn't that nice of me? I was quite concerned when I heard about Thomas's accident and I had to see for myself that he was alright. He's always held a special place in my heart, I always thought we'd find a way back to each other. He looks good in these handcuffs, don't you think? If it had been up to me, he would have been cuffed all the time. But I just couldn't talk him into it often enough to suit me. If I had managed to keep my hold on him just a little longer, teased him along just a little more, he would have been mine forever. He always loved the feel of my hands on his body, especially that long, strong cock. He struggled to submit, though, he has this misguided notion that he's a Dominant. Apparently it isn't manly for a male, especially one as virile as Thomas, to be seen as submissive. But in my opinion, there's nothing sexier than a strong man on his knees, restrained and begging for me to torture and pleasure him. But you probably wouldn't recognize the submissive in him. He keeps it buried so deep."

"Veronica, you may have thought you saw something submissive in him all those years ago, and there may have been some small piece of him that was curious about submission, he was curious about so many things back then. But I think you were just seeing what you wanted to see. Things that didn't exist. He may have allowed you to think you were topping him, just to get a sub's perspective for the future, maybe satisfy that idle curiosity, but that would be all it would have been. If anything, the way you tried to force him into a role he wasn't meant for was the catalyst that strengthened his Dominant resolve. That submissive perspective he got from being with you helped to make him the strong, wise Dom he is today. If you think there's anything submissive about him now, you don't know him at all. I guess when it comes right down to it, I owe you a small debt of thanks for the things he learned from being with you. A very small one, but a debt nonetheless."

"You're such a misguided little thing, Clare. Thomas needs a strong woman to bring out the best in him, and I'm the one he was meant to be with. If I'd found a way to get him back, I would have molded him into the quintessential submissive he's supposed to be. I would have taken him to every club around and shown him off. He would have looked spectacular all oiled up, wrists bound in leather cuffs behind his back, those huge biceps and pecs and quads bulging. Not to mention that tight little ass of his, so perfect for plugging him and whipping him into a frenzy of desire. Nothing ever got him harder than having me shove that plug in deep when he was completely restrained and couldn't do anything to resist it. Fuck, I would have taught him such control over his body, he would have been a model for every other submissive. He would have been eternally grateful to me and he would have kissed my feet in thanks.

"I would have kept that huge cock of his in a nice snug locked cage until I was finally ready to play with him and then take him. I would have been the key master and he would have been my prize stallion. He wouldn't be able to touch himself, and neither would anyone else but me. I still dream of walking him naked behind me on my leash, obeying my every command. A nice tight cock ring would have kept him so hard he could pound nails, and still show off that monster. I would have been the queen of every dungeon we toured. I would have tortured him for hours, held him off until he screamed and begged for release. And he would have loved every minute of it."

Clare couldn't help but notice that Tommy's cock was responding to the images of Veronica's broken dreams. Veronica noticed as well, and pointed to the obvious. "Oh, dear, look what I've done. Thomas, you never could resist me when I was in Domme mode. Maybe you're not so lost to me as I thought, my sweet." And Veronica combed her fingers through Tommy's overly long hair until he coo'ed.

"Sorry, Veronica, as much as you may think you're right, I know you're not. He loves me as much as I love him. And he married me. And he collared me. And you still have your hands on him. So remove your hands or you'll find yourself in a hospital room of your own."

"Clare..."

"No, Master, you and I will talk after she's gone, and trust me when I say you won't like what I have to tell you. Now get your claws off the man, bitch. I won't warn you again."

"Well, I see I've overstayed my welcome here. Thomas, it was very good to see you again. I'm glad you're on the mend. You have my card, baby. Call me if you ever want to pursue your true destiny. Clare, I'd like to say it was nice to meet you but it wasn't. But I don't take what obviously belongs to someone else so I'll say goodbye."

Veronica leaned over the bed rail and kissed Tommy on the lips – a slow gentle kiss that made Clare a little wet just to watch – and made Tommy's cock continue to engorge more and more. The kiss went on long enough that Clare was about to grab Tommy's ex by the hair and pull her off when Veronica finally stood up next to the bed. She gave Tommy's painfully erect cock a little pat and a firm squeeze through the bed sheet, making Tommy moan quietly.

"Call me, pet. You know you want to."

She smirked a little at Clare, and waved as she walked out the door.

The ensuing argument could be heard down the hall, and it was heated enough that one of the ward nurses felt the need to come into the room and break it up. That argument was also heated enough to deflate Tommy's spectacular erection without Clare having to do anything but yell at him. When the physical therapist came in for Tommy's treatment, Clare took the opportunity to go down the hall for a cup of bad hospital coffee.

·❤·❤·❤·❤·❤·

When Clare saw the physical therapist walking back past the waiting room, she headed back to her husband's room with a very apologetic look on her face. She crawled up onto the bed and snuggled next to him, and whispered "I'm sorry, Master. Sometimes I just can't stop myself."

Tommy reached down and ran his finger back and forth across her gold and platinum collar and said "Well, since I'm not in a position to administer any punishment for your horrible behavior right now, I guess we'll just have to add this to the list for later. And I'm sorry you had to meet her. I was shocked when she walked into the room. She's the one person I would have asked the guard dog outside to keep from entering the room."

There were no more treatments that afternoon and no more visitors, so husband and wife had a few quiet hours to just talk and cuddle. In the past few days, since the cast had been removed from Tommy's now healed wrist, Clare had started crawling up into his hospital bed with him during the day, and they would lie quietly together, sometimes talking, sometimes just holding each other, reveling in the knowledge that he was on the road to recovery. During those quiet times, they were Master and slave, and they both treasured each moment, longing for a time when they could get back home and establish a new normal routine again. They both knew there would be a few challenges ahead before that happened, what with continued therapy and the pending murder charges, and all – but for the time being, they were just happy they could be together.

Chapter 13

Another week passed and there was still no news from Jake Sykes or from Price Tucker about the investigation. The only bright spot in their dark lives was that Price had finally gotten a Circuit Court judge to rule that even though Tommy was technically under arrest, there was no need for him to be handcuffed to his hospital bed. The judge had visited Tommy at the hospital and decided that he wasn't going anywhere any time soon, restrained or not. More as a source of irritation than anything else, Tommy had started getting daily visits from Detective Jacobsen again, and by the time each visit was over, Tommy's blood pressure was high enough to raise monitor alarms. Jacobsen seemed to feel that if he couldn't take Tommy to jail, he would bring the jail atmosphere to Tommy, and he didn't care what effect his visits had on Tommy's mental or physical health.

After the last visit, Tommy and Clare had settled in to watch a chick flick on TV and she fell asleep cuddled up next to him. In the middle of the night, she was jostled awake by her husband, tossing and turning and crying in his sleep. She managed to wake him from his nightmare, but he refused to go back to sleep and wouldn't tell her what it had been about. They talked the rest of the night, and he finally dozed off around sunrise, but it was a fitful sleep and didn't last long. He was surly that whole day and tried to send Clare home twice, but she decided she needed to stay with him, if only to keep him from terrorizing the Physical Therapy staff.

Tommy resisted sleep for three more days, only dozing for an hour at a time, and waking loudly from a terrible nightmare each time. But now, he admitted that he was having nightmares about the accident. He still didn't remember his confrontation with Edward, but he clearly remembered the accident, and the green Jeep that attempted to run him into the ditch. It seemed that every nightmare took him back closer to the fight at the club, so he stopped resisting sleep, hoping that he'd finally remember whether he had killed Edward or not. With Tommy so agitated all the time, Clare opted to spend her nights sleeping either in his bed with him, or on a cot in the corner of his room. In the middle of the sixth night, she was awakened by Tommy's restless sleep and was just about to get up and wake him when a man she didn't recognize burst through his door, followed by Price Tucker – and they were both followed by the Highway Patrol officer who was guarding the door.

The commotion at the door woke Tommy from his nightmare and he looked relieved to be awake, but he was very agitated, and he wasn't making too much sense.

"Where's my phone! Give me my fucking phone! Quick!"

"Tommy, my love, why do you need your phone? Who are you going to call at 2:00 am?"

"I'm not calling anyone, I have to record something, quick, before I forget!"

Clare pulled his phone off the bedside table and handed it to him. He opened his Voice Memos app and started recording what sounded like random thoughts, almost like he was talking in his sleep.

"I just had it out with that cocksucker Livingston. What an arrogant pig he is. But it felt good to finally meet him and tell him what I thought of him. (Pause, with a look on Tommy's face like he was straining to remember something important.) Crap, it's raining, this is going to be a long ride home. To Clare. To my angel, Clare. (Pause, with a smile on Tommy's face when he spoke of Clare.) Who's there! Get away from my bike, asshole! I think he took something out of my saddle bag, but it's raining too hard to stop now and find out what it was. Gotta get home to Clare."

There was another pause in his rambling as he stopped that recording and started another one.

"Green Jeep skidding out of the parking lot. He's going to kill someone driving like that. Asshole!" And there was another pause, stopping the recording, as he squeezed his eyes shut so tight, like he was in pain, or trying again to remember something important. And then he started again.

"Green Jeep coming up on my left – the same one as before. It's raining so hard. He keeps swerving into my lane. Not quite in front of me. Swerved again into my lane – on purpose!! Fuck, he's trying to kill me!! He swerved again, clipped the front wheel of the bike. I can feel the skid start. I can't stop it! I hit the ground hard and the bike bounced off my leg into the ditch. Motherfucker, that hurts! He's backing up! He stops right beside me on the road. Then he peels out again, license plate KYT... What's the rest! I can't see the rest! He's gone."

One last pause and another recording.

"There's a car behind me, thank God someone stopped. Someone calling to me. Jackson?

(The rambling paused but he kept recording this time.) Bright lights, sirens, faces I should recognize. Clare, I love you. Don't ever forget me. I'll always love you. Please God, let me live." And he laid back on his pillow, closed his eyes, and stopped the recording with a heavy sigh.

It was only then that Tommy really looked around him. Clare had dissolved into tears at the first mention of her name and he reached out a hand to her to lace his fingers in hers. Then he noticed the newcomers in the room, and a look of recognition spread across his face.

"Sykes, you motherfucker! Where the fuck have you been? Did you find the information we need? Price? Somebody please tell me what's going on!"

And the man Clare hadn't recognized, who turned out to be investigator Jake Sykes, said "Yes, I found lots of information and your ramblings just confirmed what I found out. But first, I think we need to clear the room just a little." And he eyed the officer standing just inside the door.

Tommy's attorney, Price Tucker, looked at the patrolman and said "Officer, I believe I'm about to have a privileged conversation with my client. I need you to leave the room. I also need you to call your Detective Jacobsen and get him here within the hour. I have some information to pass on to him about this case and I don't believe it can wait until morning. I want this murder accusation hanging over my client's head to be lifted as soon as possible and only Jacobsen can do that."

"Mr. Tucker, I can only pass on the information and your request. I can't make him come here in the middle of the night."

"Well, tell him that I'm having Gordon Livingston followed until he sees fit to arrest him. Tell him if he wants to close this murder case, as well as solve another murder I believe Livingston committed, he should get here as soon as possible. Now out you go." With that, Price opened the door and ushered the officer out.

For the next hour, while Tommy held Clare close to his side as she shed joyous tears, Jake recounted all of the people he had interviewed since Edward Livingston's murder, and the eight days Jake had gone off the grid, waiting for a suspected murderer to make a mistake.

"Someone did take something out of your saddle bag, T, a man named Chappy Wickham. He was a small-time thief who was paid a few bucks to steal that socket wrench from your bike. He was paid by Gordon Livingston, Edward's jealous, greedy little brother. Gordon's the one who supposedly found his brother's body and called the police. And he drives a Green Jeep with North Carolina license plate KYT 1485.

"I managed to get a taped confession from Wickham about the socket wrench, and I had him in hiding, but he didn't think Livingston knew where he was, and he left the safe house. Livingston killed Wickham four days ago, starting to tie up loose ends. I have an eye witness to that murder in hiding, and she's a smart girl, so she'll stay where I put her. I believe we have enough information to get Livingston arrested for both murders. That should get you out from under the murder charges and put all of this behind you."

One hour later, Detective Jacobsen walked into Tommy's room, followed by the officer who had been guarding him. Price Tucker and Jake Sykes were still there, even though it was 3:30 a.m. Clare had fallen asleep in Tommy's bed, snuggled up next to him, while Tommy gathered and recorded his memories of the night of his accident and shared them with his legal team. There were still some gaps in his memory timeline, but he remembered enough to know that he hadn't killed Edward Livingston.

With the arrival of the Highway Patrol Detective, and with recording devices scattered around the room, Jake recounted everything he had learned about Edward's murder by his brother, as well as the murder of Chappy Wickham and the attempted murder of Tommy Rollins, also by Gordon Livingston. The ultimate motives were fear and greed – the relationship between the two brothers had always been adversarial, but Edward had taken care of his baby brother in the end, just not fast enough to suit Gordon. Gordon had piled up considerable gambling debts and he had 48 hours to pay up before someone tracked him down and broke a leg or two. And Edward had refused to give him any money.

Gordon was Edward's beneficiary on two very large insurance policies. He was also the primary beneficiary named in Edward's will, which meant he would inherit his brother's mansion and everything in it, including the posh BDSM dungeon in the basement. When Gordon witnessed the argument between Edward and Tommy, he saw a golden opportunity to get rid of his brother and lay the blame for the murder at Tommy's feet, hopefully after his untimely death in a motorcycle accident.

The fact that Gordon had managed to find someone to steal the murder weapon from Tommy's Harley saddle bag in the short amount of time that Tommy had remained at the bar after the fight was something that Detective Jacobsen had difficulty believing, but he was willing to go along with Jake's explanation if it meant he could close two murder investigations with one perpetrator. Closing out Tommy's attempted murder investigation, which Harrison Turner had been pushing hard, would be a bonus. Jake was able to verify that his witness to Chappy's death was still where he had put her, and he was also able to pinpoint Gordon's location during a conversation with his associate who had been tasked with following him 24/7. All that remained was getting local police to Gordon's location without being seen, so that Detective Jacobsen could swoop in and make the arrest without too much effort.

Satisfied that there was a plan in place to arrest Gordon Livingston, the Detective left Tommy's room with Jake and his officer in tow, leaving Tommy, Clare and their lawyer to celebrate a little that Tommy's name was about to be cleared. Ten minutes worth of discussion later, Price left Tommy and Clare to get some sleep, knowing that they would be awakened in a few short hours by hospital personnel starting another day of rehab. Five minutes after Price left the room, the lights were dimmed and husband and wife were sound asleep, peacefully dreaming in each other's arms.

·❤·❤·♥·❤·❤·

Three hours later, the sleeping couple was rudely awakened by the day shift hospital staff delivering breakfast and reviewing the day's therapy schedule. And gossiping about the lack of police presence outside the hospital room. The lack of sleep might have prevented Tommy and Clare from moving at their normal speed, but they were in such a good mood that nothing could ruin it. Hospital staff were in and out of their room all morning, getting in the way of the people who were supposed to be there, wanting to hear all about the huge change in Tommy's criminal status. At 10:30, when Tommy's first physical therapy appointment was about to begin, Clare decided to run home. She wanted to shower, change her clothes, sort through the mail, and take care of a few other errands before returning to the hospital.

Next door neighbor James Porter stopped by the house right before Clare was planning to leave, and she talked him into coming back to the hospital to see Tommy and let him tell the story of the day and night they had just had. Just as Clare was turning off the TV, there was breaking news being broadcast and she stopped to listen. The name 'Thomas Rollins' had caught her ear, but he wasn't the main focus of the news.

"James, come here!! Listen to this!"

"What is it? Is that a SWAT standoff somewhere? What channel are you watching, for heaven's sake??" The live broadcast showed about 15 police officers surrounding a suburban house, all with large weapons in hand.

"Yes, it's a standoff, and it's in Gennessee! That's Detective Jackass with the bullhorn! And look! That's Price Tucker and Jake Sykes in the background! They apparently didn't get any sleep last night."

As they continued to watch, the video cut away to some stock photos of a man Clare thought at first was Edward Livingston, but the caption indicated it was his brother Gordon.

"Oh, good heavens. He looks just like his brother. They could almost be twins."

When the broadcast returned to live video, something appeared to be happening inside the house, and the on-scene broadcaster's voice took on a high level of excitement. Several shots rang out from inside, and one of the officers positioned close to the house went down. It was obvious by his movement that he wasn't seriously injured, but when his fellow officers returned fire all around the house, it was clear they were shooting to kill. The live camera panned away from the house to the reporter on scene who summarized what had been going on, and shortly thereafter, the TV station returned to their normal news coverage.

"Crap, James, we have to go!" And they both ran out to their cars and sped toward the hospital to make sure Tommy knew what was going on.

Tommy had just settled back in his hospital bed after physical therapy, which that day included a walk up and down the halls of his unit, using a cane to balance himself. He felt stronger every day, but physical therapy always tired him out, and the lingering ache in his left leg refused to be mended.

"Steven, I appreciate everything you're doing to help me get back on my feet, but the sessions these last few days have been kicking my ass! I need to know what you think about this ache I still have in my leg. If I keep working on it, will that go away, or is this as good as things are going to get?"

"T, I wish I could tell you with certainty that you'll be back to 100% in another 3 months, or another 6 months, whatever. But I can't. All we can do now that the fractures are healed is to get all those muscles and tendons and ligaments strong and flexible again. I think another few weeks of therapy will get you as good as you need to get before you can go home, but even if your insurance doesn't cover any more structured physical therapy, you're going to need to keep up with all of your exercises on your own going forward.

"I've been to your house. You have a great exercise area off the family room that's already pretty well stocked, but I'll give you recommendations on a few extra machines I think will be of benefit. Beyond that, just going up and down those stairs will be a good workout, two or three times a day. Be prepared, my friend. You had significant injuries in that accident. You have to be in this for the long haul, or resign yourself to sitting on your ass for the rest of your life."

"What about a new Harley? Will that ever be a possibility?"

"T, I won't say never, but I don't expect Clare to let you on anything bigger than a bicycle any time soon. If you think I've been hard on you, just wait until you get home and she's overseeing your continued recuperation. She loves you more than life itself, and she will never let you settle for anything less than the best you can be."

"Don't I know it! She can be a real tyrant sometimes, especially when she's sure she's right and I'm wrong." And they both laughed as they continued their conversation, which was suddenly interrupted by a commotion at the door.

Both Tommy and Steven looked up as the door to the room slammed open. Clare and James rushed through the door and Clare grabbed the TV remote, switching on the flat screen. She quickly dialed in the right channel and they all looked in shock at what they were seeing.

"Tommy, you won't believe this. I think the police just killed Gordon Livingston, but I'm not positive because I couldn't get the news in the car!"

"What the hell happened?!? I thought the police were going to take him into custody quietly and without resistance. Isn't that what Jacobsen said earlier?"

"Yeah, well, we don't always get what we want, do we?"

As they all watched the final coverage of the police standoff, more people started drifting into Tommy's room, watching the news coverage and wondering exactly what this new development would mean for their friend. No one wondered more than Tommy and Clare what the next few days would bring.

One of the last visitors Tommy and Clare had at the hospital that evening was Detective Jacobsen, along with Harrison Turner and Price Tucker. The detective started the conversation with a summary of the earlier events of the day.

"Mr. Rollins, I'm sure you've seen the television coverage of our attempt to take Gordon Livingston into custody. Obviously, it did not go as well as we had planned, and Mr. Livingston is now as deceased as his brother. I would imagine they're together now in Hell."

"I only saw the end of the confrontation. What happened before that, what caused him to commit suicide by cop the way he did? And was there anyone else in the house with him or was he alone at the end?"

"We don't know what ultimately set Mr. Livingston off, but it was clear early on that he was aware of our presence in the neighborhood. Before we surrounded the house, we had quietly evacuated all of the residents on either side of his house, and also the houses behind him, perhaps one of his neighbors alerted him during that evacuation. I repeatedly attempted to contact him by phone to no avail. We had officers adjacent to every first-floor window, and they could hear his phone ring, but he never answered. When that line of communication failed, I attempted to make contact using a bullhorn. I laid out the basic evidence and anticipated charges against him, assured him that he had no means of escape, and that giving himself up was the best way to stay alive. I don't think he cared about staying alive at that point.

"You may have seen the coverage on TV, when he made the decision to end the standoff by firing at one of our officers. Luckily the officer was not gravely injured, and that may have been Mr. Livingston's plan all along, but all of the officers returned fire, through the windows and the front and back door. We quickly halted our fire and I again attempted to make contact, but he still wouldn't answer the phone. When the SWAT team entered the house, Mr. Livingston was found in a hallway between the living room and the kitchen, suffering from multiple life-threatening gunshot wounds. He was still alive when the team entered the house, but by the time paramedics reached him, he was gone. A subsequent search of the premises didn't turn up anyone else, but there was evidence that someone else had been in the house. We don't know who they were or when they were there, and we may never know.

"We were not able to get an admission of guilt from Mr. Livingston, but I would say that his actions, along with the statements from people Mr. Sykes was able to interview, would be tantamount to an admission of guilt. Technically you're still under arrest, but as soon as the County Prosecutor reviews all of the evidence, I'm confident he will clear you of all charges and we will put this business to rest. I'm not one to apologize for doing my job, Mr. Rollins, but I'm glad that an innocent man won't go to jail based on circumstantial evidence. Mr. Tucker will be notified when there is a change in the status of your pending charges. I'm sure he'll keep you informed. Now if you'll excuse me, I'm ass deep in paperwork and I have several other pending cases that require my attention. Good night."

Before anyone could respond or ask any questions, Detective Jacobsen was out the door and out of their lives.

Chapter 14

Clare hugged Tommy so tightly, Harrison had to practically pull her off. The few people left in the room all shared a quiet moment of thanks for Jake Sykes' work, and Clare cried again. The two attorneys stayed for a little while to chat and review the day's events once last time, then Clare and Tommy were alone.

She climbed into his bed and cuddled to his side, and they shared a gentle kiss, but soon that wasn't enough for Clare. She had been caressing Tommy's chest over his tee shirt, but soon her hand slid down to the hem of that shirt and up underneath. Her hand didn't stop until she could play with the light covering of chest hair, and rub her finger tips over his nipples, causing him to suck in a breath. She leaned over and started tonguing and sucking on a nipple through the tee shirt, almost like she was breast feeding.

While her tongue lapped at the nipple, her hand slid down to the waist band of his sweat pants and disappeared beneath, to where Tommy's cock had sprung to life. She began brushing her finger tips lightly along the underside, playing with the enlarging veins, massaging his balls, until she and Tommy were both panting.

"Clare, I know the last few days have been very stressful for you, but you're topping from the bottom again. You know that's a nasty habit that we're going to have to break as soon as I get home. You already have a large boatload of discipline coming, I'll just have to add this to the list. But in the meantime, I'm not going to make you stop, because your hand rubbing my cock and my balls like that feels so good, it's practically making my eyes cross. So you go on and scootch yourself down there and suck my cock dry. When you've made me come one time, I'll think about letting you ride me until we both come. And then maybe we can sleep through the night for a change. Let's try to keep the noise down tonight, okay baby? People are trying to sleep."

"Yes, Master, I'll do my best to keep my rapture to myself."

When Clare had made Tommy come, and he had allowed her to ride the two of them to silent glory in his hospital bed, they cuddled up again and dimmed the lights for sleep.

"Goodnight, sweet sub. Thank you for sticking with me through everything that's happened. I love you so much, I can never tell you how much your faith and fortitude have meant to me."

"Goodnight, Master. I love you too. You deserve nothing less than my honesty and my faith in your protection. I'll always be here for you, my love."

And she cried again, and fell asleep, surrounded by the strong arms of the man she loved more than life itself.

The next week crawled by, filled only with what Tommy considered uncomfortable, unproductive physical therapy, as well as bad moods and boredom. Then toward the end of the month, there was a monsoon of activity that would ultimately make life so much more pleasant.

The first good news came during Tommy's visit late one afternoon from Price Tucker and County Prosecutor William Briggs, bringing him paperwork stating that all charges against Tommy, related to the death of Edward Livingston, had been dropped. The County Prosecutor had reviewed all of the evidence that had been provided by Jake Sykes, along with the sworn testimony of the woman who had witnessed Chappy Wickham's murder by Gordon Livingston. That, combined with what Tommy could actually remember of the night Edward was killed, was enough to convince the Prosecutor that Tommy had nothing to do with Edward's death. And they didn't have to worry about

Gordon coming after Tommy for a murder he hadn't committed. That dark cloud over their lives had been lifted and he was free and clear.

Tommy's guests stayed for a little while after the paperwork was signed. Since Clare was at home taking care of errands, the three very relieved men celebrated with a bottle of well-aged Scotch that Price had smuggled in, and when she returned to the hospital, she found them somewhat intoxicated, telling dubious stories and snort-laughing loudly.

Then three days later, a panel of hospital physicians convened to review Tommy's medical records, and deemed that he could be released from the hospital. The panel was withholding approval for Tommy to return to work indefinitely. That would be reviewed again at some later date, should Tommy decide he wanted to try. There would be one final consultation with his physical therapist, getting outpatient orders and a list of exercises that he needed to continue at home. Beyond that, in 48 hours he would become Clare's problem to deal with, and the whole hospital was happy that their all-time worst patient was finally going home.

The night before Tommy's release from the hospital, Clare got dressed up and brought dinner with her to see him. She was a little emotional because they had completely forgotten a very special event.

"Tommy, I don't know how, but I completely forgot about our wedding anniversary. It's our first, and it was 10 days ago! The date completely slipped my mind, there has just been too much going on the past few months. Can you forgive me, baby?"

"Oh, Clare, there's nothing to forgive. Apparently, I let it slip myself. You look gorgeous tonight, baby, and I'm a little under dressed. Let's just enjoy this fabulous dinner you brought, maybe watch a movie, make out a little in bed, and get a good night's sleep. Tomorrow's a big day, you know. They're actually springing me from this joint. I didn't think that would ever happen."

"I'll be so happy to have you home again, Tommy. The house is all ready for you. I'll be able to have my way with you any time we want and we won't have to worry about someone walking in on us. And don't worry about exerting yourself for awhile, I'll do all the work, you just have to recline however you want and enjoy!"

"Fuck, I can't wait to get back into the playroom again. I've been cruising the internet the past few days and I've actually found a few positions that could be considered physical therapy for me! I can't wait to try them out. They're a little creative but I think we can manage."

"Maybe we can spend a little time on the fainting couch. Maybe a few restraints could be involved? Ever since Veronica was here, I've been having dirty dreams about topping you every now and then. That's never crossed my mind before, but I have to admit thinking about it makes me a little wet."

"Oh, there will definitely be restraints involved. I need to get my fill of topping you first, baby, and that might take awhile, but I don't want you to have unfulfilled dreams, so maybe we can talk about who wears those restraints down the road. Now let's enjoy this delicious looking dinner, maybe have an anniversary dance or two, and then I'll let you choose the movie. Or the position. I'll leave that up to you."

Clare and Tommy ate their lasagna, garlic bread and Caesar salad, along with a bottle of merlot Clare had brought. Then they set the flat screen TV on a classical radio station and danced until Tommy's leg started to ache and he needed to sit down.

"Baby, I'm sorry to interrupt our dance, but I just need a little break. Maybe we can dance some more later."

"Don't worry about it, my love. It's been awhile since I've worn any kind of heels, much less these stilettos, and I wouldn't mind sitting down for a little while myself. Did you get enough to eat? Would you like some more wine? I could roll you out to the patio and you could smoke a cigar."

"No, baby, I'm good. And since I've been here in the hospital, I've cut back on my cigars so much, I can probably go ahead and quit. How about we just cuddle a little and see what's on the movie menu for tonight?"

Before Clare could answer, the door opened and 20 people streamed into the room, laughing and singing a happy anniversary song someone had just made up. The Physical Therapy ward charge nurse was carrying a huge cake and one of the PT interns had plates and forks to pass around to everyone.

Clare teared up and asked "How did you know about this? We both forgot, with everything going on.

The charge nurse admitted "James Porter told me when your anniversary came and went and you hadn't celebrated it. We've been dating since you've been here, and he wanted to give your friends a chance to celebrate with you before all the commotion of moving you home again."

"Oh, Stella, this is so sweet. Is James here somewhere? He's such a dear friend, we have to thank him."

"No, his son's anniversary is today and James is babysitting his grandkids while they go out for dinner. He said he'd catch up with you when you get home tomorrow."

"Thank you all so much. This is so nice. Now let's cut this cake and have a little party!"

Stella started cutting the cake and as soon as plates of delicious, sugary goodness had been passed around to everyone, the story of Clare's surprise proposal and their wedding in Hawaii, all planned by Tommy, brought tears and laughter to the crowd.

Once the last of the well-wishers had left the room, Clare changed into an ivory satin negligee she'd brought from home, and the happy couple crawled into their hospital bed and snuggled, as they had done so many times since Tommy's accident. They talked quietly about everything that had happened since then, how much progress he'd made in his recovery, and how much work he still had to do to get strong again. As always happened when they were in close proximity, hands began to roam, tongues tangled, and soon Clare was riding Tommy very quietly to an exquisite shared orgasm that left them breathless and ready for sleep. They dimmed the lights, left the flat screen on the quiet classical radio station, and were soon asleep, both dreaming of getting back home and finding that new normal for their lives.

Tommy and Clare were awake early Friday morning, excited to be headed home. But before he could finally leave the hospital, Tommy had one more appointment with the physical therapist, and Clare wanted to be part of that consultation. They ate their last hospital breakfast, then showered and dressed. She dressed in a denim skirt and a white golf shirt, the last of the clothes she had brought from home, threw on some sandals, and was ready to go. Tommy put on his standard 'work' attire of sweat pants, a tee shirt, and running shoes, and the two walked together slowly to the Physical Therapy office.

An hour later, they had a complete list of exercises Tommy was to do twice a day, including two new ones he hadn't done before. He also had an appointment for the following Tuesday for a home inspection with Steven, to make sure there was nothing about their house setup that might impede Tommy's recuperation progress. Clare walked back to Tommy's room with him, and then waited for the doctor to make his appearance with all of the release papers to sign. While Tommy was finishing the paperwork, Clare went to the parking lot and pulled the car up to the Emergency Room entrance where Tommy was supposed to be waiting. After waiting five minutes for him to be wheeled out of the building, she decided to go in and look for him.

When Clare got into the Emergency Room, she was treated to a sight she would never forget. Tommy was seated in a standard wheel chair that had been fitted with an IV pole on each side, decorated with pompoms and crepe paper streamers. The very large wheels were equipped with playing cards attached to the spokes by clothes pins, just like kids did with their bicycles to make that flapping noise to mimic the sound of a motorcycle engine. His outfit was complete when his friends in ER gifted him with a new motorcycle helmet, which he was required to put on to finish his ride to the outside door. The last 'gift' from his hospital friends was a large banner over the outside door, saying "THANKS FOR FINALLY GOING HOME!!"

Tommy's doctor pushed the wheel chair out to the car, running a gauntlet of hospital employees lined up on both sides of the hallway, sending him off with thunderous applause. After being helped into Clare's Christmas present Ford Escape, very unhappy that he was not allowed to drive for another two weeks, Clare climbed in behind the wheel, kissed Tommy's repaired left wrist, and started to cry.

"I can't believe I finally get to take you home. I thought this day would never come."

"Clare, let's not get all emotional in the parking lot. Let's at least get out on the street before you make me cry too. I have a reputation to maintain, after all. Baby, I can't imagine what you went through those first few weeks, and I'm so sorry you had to go through this, but it's all behind us now, and we can move forward together." And a single tear trickled down Tommy's left cheek.

"I love you, Thomas Rollins. And if I have to hold you captive in our house to keep you safe from now on, I'm prepared to do that. There are handcuffs there, and I know how to use them!! Now let's go home. I know you're probably a little tired, but I have a feeling a few of the neighbors will be stopping by today or tomorrow to check on you, and then there are all your friends from Asylum who will want to see you and talk to you too. "

"I can't wait to get there. Let's hit it!" And she gunned the engine and raced out of the parking lot, making the ten minute drive to their house, breaking the speed limit just a little along the way.

Tommy was barely in the house when people started arriving, bringing snacks, beer, soda and everything else they could think of to welcome him home. It was a beautiful day so Clare settled Tommy in his favorite lounge chair on the deck in the back yard, in the shade of the gazebo he had built for her not long after she had moved in with him. He held court the rest of the morning and most of the afternoon, as people stopped by to chat for a few minutes and hear the story of his accident and subsequent arrest for murder. No conversation was complete without viewing the photos of the remains of his motorcycle, not only the official police photos from the scene, but also the ones that Clare had taken the day the remains of the Harley were dropped in the driveway. Every few hours, Tommy needed to walk a short distance, so he would take tours to the garage to view the remains live and in color.

In those few short months after the accident, Tommy had become a living legend among his friends, first for surviving such a horrible accident, and then for 'beating the rap' of Edward Livingston's murder. Tommy and Clare withheld many of the details of that incident. They both felt that no one really needed to know the history Clare had shared with the deceased, or the reason why Tommy had threatened him. But since most of the town had seen the shootout at Gordon Livingston's house on live TV, or taped versions after the fact, they shared what they could just to keep people's curiosity satisfied.

All of their friends were respectful of Tommy's need to rest periodically, so people wandered in and out, chatting for ten or fifteen minutes and then leaving, for most of the weekend. A few of his closest friends even joined in with the exercises he had to do several times a day. By Sunday evening, Tommy and Clare were ready for a little privacy and a little quiet time. And maybe a quick romp in bed. Clare had originally planned to bed Tommy down in the living room on the pull–out sofa, but he insisted that if he didn't get any other exercise each day, he would make the climb to the second floor to sleep in his own bed. She was a stern task master, making sure that he did his required physical therapy twice a day, but she also made sure that even if he was tired at bedtime, she would help him up the stairs and get him settled beside her in their bed.

The first two nights, all they did was cuddle and sleep, but by Sunday evening, Tommy was ready for a little sexual release. He was having trouble reconciling himself to the fact that he seemed to have less stamina at home than he had had in the hospital, and Clare had to have some straight talk with him.

"Thomas, I don't understand why you don't understand. You're the medical professional in the family. Everything was set up perfectly in the hospital and in the PT unit, they practically brought everything to you. Now you're back home and it takes a little more effort to do everything. You just have to be patient and do your exercises, and you'll get your strength back."

"Clare, you know patience isn't my forte. I understand all that in my head but my gut tells me I should be doing better by now. I should be able to take you to the playroom and have my way with you, but by the time I get down the stairs, I feel like I need a nap. I'm so tired all the time. That's not me and I hate it!"

"Master, it will all come back to you. Don't worry about it. You've only been home for two days. We're still in 'one day at a time' mode. I'm giving you five days to maintain what strength you have, and then we have to kick it up a notch, both of us. Walk a little farther every few days, add an extra rep to your exercise routine, make one extra trip down the stairs and back up again. You'll be ready to kick ass before you know it. I promise. But for right now, let's get you settled in bed, and maybe we can take care of each other, a little like the old days. Hmmm?"

"Fuck, woman, what would I ever do without you? I don't think I would have survived the accident without you to come back to. You're the bright light I kept reaching for when I was in that coma. I knew there was something I had to come back for. I love you, I always will. No matter what happens in the future, please believe that. Now let's get into bed. Make me hard and we can enjoy each other for a little while."

True to her word, Clare made sure that Tommy didn't need to do anything strenuous in bed that night, other than tease her nipples and clit just a little. She was more than ready to ride him until they were both fulfilled and relaxed and ready to sleep. If this was their new normal for awhile, she was more than happy to please him any way he wanted.

By Tuesday, they had settled into a routine of breakfast, exercises he could do on the deck while chatting with friends and neighbors, and then a slow trip down the stairs to the fitness equipment off the family room in the lower level of the house. It was back upstairs for lunch and a nap, then a slow steady walk on the bike path around the neighborhood with his trusty cane. Just as she had promised, each day he was able to do a little more, walk a little further, depend on his cane a little less, and make love a little longer at night.

Physical Therapist Steven's visit was delayed until Friday while he tended to another accident victim at the hospital. When he arrived at Tommy and Clare's house on Friday afternoon, Tommy was just waking up from his nap and was ready to get Steven out of his hair. The two men took a short walk on the bike path to see how he was handling walking on pavement, and by the time they got back to the house, Clare had drinks and snacks ready for them. After chatting for a few minutes while Steven got his assessment paperwork started on his laptop, they headed downstairs to see the exercise equipment and how Tommy was using it.

"So, T, how are things really going for you? It's been a week since you've been back home, and you seem to be walking pretty steady, but I'd like to see your stamina improve more than it has. I see you don't have an elliptical machine here at home. You can either come to the PT center three or four times a week and use one there, or you could get one to keep here at the house. It would help with your endurance and would make climbing the steps a little easier as well."

"I'm doing okay, but you're right, I'm still more easily winded than I would have expected by now. While Clare was out doing errands yesterday, I got a call from the Respiratory Medicine Department reminding me of a follow-up appointment. Apparently, I hadn't mentioned the first appointment to Clare and I forgot to go. The appointment scheduler volunteered to come and pick me up if needed to make sure I get to this one."

"You forgot to go to a Respiratory Medicine consult? They get really pissy when you don't show up! You know that could be part of your stamina problem. Any kind of problem with your lungs, even a minor one, can keep you on the sidelines for a long time!"

"What can I say? It's just a thirty minute consult to make sure my lung capacity is what it should be. I didn't originally think it was all that important, but when I can't catch my breath, it's a little frustrating."

"Maybe even a little scary?"

"I'm not sure I'd go that far but yes, if there's something going on with my lungs that's keeping me from making better progress, I want to know."

"Does Clare know? About the new appointment?"

"Yes, I told her about it last night. She's seen me struggle a little to breathe a few times in the past few days, and I'm still not allowed to drive, so I told her. I promised her awhile back, before the accident, that I wouldn't keep secrets from her anymore. This would be a bad time to make a liar out of myself. So, any other new equipment I need? I'll call the equipment manager at my gym and order whatever you think will help."

"I think the elliptical, and maybe a rowing machine for upper body rehab, would be the only other equipment I'd have you get at least for right now. Just make sure you follow the schedule of reps and times per day and I think you'll be fine. But before I leave, I want to check out the playroom and make sure there's nothing in there that you might hurt yourself on. I haven't seen it since the remodel but I've heard good things about the changes."

"Then follow me! I love showing off the changes we made."

As they were walking away from the exercise equipment toward the playroom, Clare stepped off the bottom step with fresh drinks and said "I seem to recall liking the changes we made as well. I just want to know when my husband might be cleared to play a little."

Chapter 15

Two weeks later, lots had happened with Tommy and Clare. The new elliptical machine had been delivered and was a big hit with both of them. Tommy's Respiratory Therapy consult and resulting chest x-ray showed a mild lung infection that responded almost immediately to antibiotics and his stamina and overall condition improved noticeably. And they had finally spent some quality time in the playroom together. It was nothing terribly strenuous for either of them, and they did have their friends, Marshall and Portia, sharing the playroom, just in case anything unexpected happened with Tommy's health while Clare was restrained, but it was a start. The four friends had dinner and then plenty of orgasms, a highly enjoyable evening all around.

The other big news for Tommy was that he had been cleared to start driving, and that seemed to be his trigger to start working again. Several of his businesses were in need of his attention, as none of his partners had wanted to bother him while he was still in the hospital. But when he put in three 12-hour days in a row and came home every evening looking exhausted, Clare took it upon herself to get involved. She made contact with all of his primary business partners and rather laid down the law about how much time Tommy was allowed to spend working. When one of those partners got pissy and intentionally let the cat out of the bag about his conversation with Clare, Tommy felt the need to put an end to her 'interference'.

Leaving his car parked in the driveway and slamming the car door on his way into the garage, Tommy stormed into the kitchen, yelling at the top of his lungs.

"Clare? Clare! Where the fuck are you?"

"I'm right here, Thomas! What bug crawled up your ass today? And why are you so late getting home? You look exhausted, baby. Did you have dinner? Please come and sit down and rest a minute before you dismember me!"

"Yes, I had dinner. It was a Partners business dinner and I got an ear full of what you've been doing lately. You have no right to meddle in my business affairs, and I'll have no more of it! You mind the house and keep your fucking nose out of things you know nothing about!"

In as calm a voice as Clare could muster, she responded, "I see. So you're the Master and I'm the slave and I'm just supposed to stay home and mind the house and leave you to work yourself to death? How dare you? Do you know nothing about me? When I committed to be your slave in this relationship, I committed to taking care of you, just like you take care of me. But apparently that only applies to how many blow jobs I can give you, until you leave the house, and then I'm just an ignorant little sex toy, on hold until you come back. It doesn't matter that when you do finally come back home, you're so wiped out, you can barely climb the stairs."

"That's not what I mean! I just don't want you interfering in my businesses, and that means not hounding my partners about how much time I'm spending on work. I'm doing what I have to do to keep things going."

"Tommy, you almost died – several times! And you were just fine with me taking care of everything until you came home and now I'm supposed to just let you run wild like you were before the accident. Master, you work too hard, you drink too much, and your diet sucks. I'm not sure why we worked so hard to get you well again, if you're just going to kill yourself, trying to prove to yourself that you're still Superman, when you're not!" And tears streamed down her cheeks as she pinned him with a look that told him her heart was breaking. But he wasn't swayed by her honest display of emotion, he was still just too angry.

"Clare, you're dangerously close to earning yourself some discipline. I appreciate that you think you're trying to take care of me, but I don't need your suffocating help or advice. Now it's late and we both have to work tomorrow. I'm really tired. Let's just go to bed."

"Well, Master, you can take your discipline and shove it up your ass! I think I'll just sleep in the spare room tonight. When you go to bed angry, you do a lot of tossing and turning and you'll keep me awake. As you said, we both have to work tomorrow, and I certainly wouldn't want to suffocate you with my help and advice."

"Clare, I don't like your tone and I don't want you to sleep in another room. I can't sleep without you beside me."

"I guess you should have thought of that earlier, Master. I'll see you in the morning." And with that, Clare left the room and headed upstairs, leaving Tommy stunned and a little confused about what had just happened. He just knew he was a little screwed, and not in a good way.

Tommy decided he should try to get some more work done, since Clare was pouting about their argument, so he went to hide in his office for awhile before facing her again. He pulled a contract out of his briefcase that needed to be reviewed, but his exhaustion got the better of him, and he dozed off while reading page 2 for the third time. About an hour later, he was awakened by his phone buzzing with an incoming text, and he picked up his phone to look at it, thinking one of his partners had a question or needed some help. Much to his surprise and dismay, it was from Veronica, the woman from his past who was trying desperately to become his future.

> *Thomas, I heard you were home from the hospital, congratulations on your recovery.*

He stared somewhat longingly at the text but didn't respond, and in a few minutes another one came in from the same number.

> *I can't tell you what seeing you and putting my hands on you again did for me. I've been craving you ever since, and I just couldn't resist making contact with you again. I think we have unfinished business, my pet. I know from the way you responded to my touch that you still crave my Dominance. You know Clare can't give you that special release you need. Come to my summer cottage and have lunch with me. I know you remember where it is. We'll talk. And maybe a little more. You know you want it, baby. Next Wednesday at Noon. It will be our little secret. V.*

Tommy stared at the new text message, read it over and over again, then threw the phone across his large desk. He was horrified to realize that he had gotten hard just thinking about Veronica's suggestion, but there was a tiny part of him that wondered what it would be like to be with her just once more – for old times' sake. He loved Clare with his whole heart and he knew that seeing Veronica again would be a huge mistake, perhaps one he could never erase, but that little something called to him irresistibly. He rubbed his hands over his face a few times, then stared at the phone for a few more minutes. He picked it up again with a shaking hand and sent an answering text.

> *Okay. I'll be there.*

And in his head, he screamed, "What the fuck have I just done?!?"

When he had hit Send on the text, he knew it was a horrible idea to see Veronica again, but he didn't send a retracting text. After a few minutes, he deleted the text and made sure Clare wouldn't find Veronica's number anywhere in his phone contacts or history. Then he turned off the phone and leaned back in his chair, closed his eyes, and drifted off to sleep again, dreaming of the last time he had submitted to his Domme.

A few hours later, Tommy was awakened by Clare, and he hoped he hadn't talked in his sleep, because the dream she'd woke him from was enough to make him feel like he'd already been unfaithful to his wife.

"Master, you know you shouldn't sleep in this chair. It's so bad for your back, and it makes you mumble things I can't understand. Come upstairs to bed, it will be so much more comfortable for you.

"Are you still mad at me?"

"Yes. Are you still mad at me?"

"Yes, but it's nothing I won't get over. I understand why you did what you did, but you have to realize that taking care of these businesses is my job, and if that makes it hard for you to take care of me the way you want to, we'll just have to work through it."

"Come to bed, baby. That dream must have been pretty hot because you seem to be in need of some release. I hope it was about me, Master." And she gave him an inquiring look but didn't say more.

"Who else would I dream about, little slave? Let's go to bed. But just to sleep for now, okay? I think we're both too tired for anything else." He stood and let Clare take him by the hand and lead him upstairs to bed, leaving his phone on his desk, not wanting it – and his possible infidelity – anywhere near them.

The next few days, things were a little off between Tommy and Clare, but she assumed it was because of the argument they'd had and the fact that Tommy's work hours were still longer than she thought was healthy for him. It felt like they were stepping around some issue that was going to jump out at them. But she kept ignoring it in the hopes that it would just go away.

Saturday was a big day for both of them. Visiting Asylum together for the first time since the accident gave them both a little anxiety, but they were very excited to see the club up and running, and see all their friends in their true 'habitat' again.

Tommy and Clare were both quiet on the drive to the club, but for different reasons. Tommy was thinking about expectations club members would have, wondering if he was still the same raging dominant he had been before the accident. He was wondering the same thing. For her part, Clare wondered how long it would take her to settle back into club life. Several months had passed since their last visit to Asylum, and that last visit hadn't gone well. Tommy had gotten stuck in top space during a training session while Clare was trapped in the past with her former Dom, and the combination was disastrous for both of them, as well as frightening for the members being trained. She didn't want a repeat of that performance, and she was concerned that she wouldn't be able to get back into sub space with that possibility on her mind.

When they pulled into the parking lot at the club, they were stopped by a tall metal fence and gate, along with a parking lot guard who hadn't been there before, more of Master Will's security measures come to life. Tommy's key card told the guard which parking space he had been assigned, and the guard directed him to that spot. When he and Clare exited the car, Tommy noticed that the club's main entry door had been moved from the front wall of the building, by the sidewalk, to the side wall inside the fence, and the door was protected by an updated key card reader. None of these facility changes had been in place when Tommy had been to the club for a meeting two weeks before, and he smiled to think of the changes they might see inside as well.

In retrospect, neither of them should have wasted time on needless worry and anxiety. When they walked through the door and into the well-appointed, but very vanilla, lobby, they were met by the founding club members offering enthusiastic applause for the return of Big Man and Baby Girl, as Tommy and Clare had long been known among their friends. They were both allowed a few minutes to go to their locker rooms and change into appropriate dungeon wear, and when they came back to the lobby, Tommy was dressed in his well broken in black leathers and Clare was in a black leather corset that was mostly a few thin straps that left her breasts exposed, paired with black lace and satin thong panties. And they both had a moment of pure lust when they looked at each other. But the crowd around them distracted them temporarily.

More hugs and handshakes pulled them slowly but surely from the lobby, through a substantial antique oak door, into the dungeon, where newer members of Asylum were waiting to greet them as well. After 15 minutes of congratulations and well wishes, the guests of honor were led to the raised seating area by the bar, where they were settled as a

Dom and his sub should be – Tommy on an antique wood and leather chair that looked like a medieval throne, and Clare on a large comfy pillow on the floor at his feet. The bar staff served them what they knew were Tommy and Clare's favorite drinks, and Tommy fed Clare little bites of her favorite hors d'oeuvres. Then Jackson settled everyone and proceeded to give a little speech, which Clare expected would not be short and sweet.

"Ladies and Gentlemen, welcome to Asylum, and thank you all for being here for the grand return of our Training Master and his beautiful sub. We've all felt their absence, and we're thrilled that they have been able to return to their D/s home.

"I was with Master Thomas the night of his accident, and I saw how serious his injuries were. Frankly, I was shocked when he lived through that first night. Since then, I've waited with all of you, first for signs of life in those early days, and then when he awoke from his coma, for the healing process to begin in earnest. And, of course, the murder investigation and the legal issues were a never-ending source of aggravation for our Master T. Welcome back to life, my friend, I've missed your presence here keenly.

"But I would be horribly remiss if I didn't acknowledge Clare as well, and extend a personal welcome back to the club. As hard as the last few months have been on Thomas, and all of his friends, it has been even more difficult for her. I was also at the hospital with Clare in the hours and days after the accident and I saw firsthand what a toll it took on her. Not knowing if her Master was going to survive was harder on her than we can imagine, but then having to deal with lawyers and police officers, and one especially arrogant Highway Patrol Detective, just piled on the agony and despair she faced each day. To you, Clare, I say 'Well done, my friend, you saw to your Master's every need, and you did your job exceptionally well. Now it's time for you to relax and let your Master take care of you again.'"

Jackson walked to where Clare and Tommy sat, knelt down, and kissed Clare's bowed head. With a finger under her chin, he lifted her face to look at him, and wiped her tears from her cheeks. A low grumble from her Master told Jackson that he'd spent enough time touching Clare, and everyone but Tommy laughed. Jackson stood again and stepped away, leaving Clare to mumble under her breath, "That's it?" And she immediately knew that there would be some celebratory 'funishment' in her near future.

·❤·❤·❤·❤·❤·

Tommy rose from his medieval throne like the sex god he was, and addressed the crowd. "Friends, thank you so much for attending this evening. I'm thrilled to be back in my element again, and I'm so proud of how Asylum has turned out. That being said, I see questions in the eyes of a few people this evening, wondering if my accident has slowed me down. In truth, I would say yes, it may have, but I'm still capable of meting out some punishment when it's warranted, even invited!" His last comment drew some murmurs from the crowd, along with a few chuckles. It drew a wince from his submissive.

"Up, Clare. I believe we have some discipline to attend to, and I want you to acknowledge to your friends exactly what you did to deserve it."

Almost under her breath, Clare started to speak. "I'm sorry, Master, I may have…"

"Louder, slave, your friends can't hear you."

Head bowed, and almost yelling now, Clare spoke again. "I'm sorry, Master! I may have hinted that Master Jackson's acknowledgement of my turmoil these last few months might have been a little shy of what I deserved! It was a joke! No one seems to have a sense of humor anymore!" And the crowd laughed, including Tommy and Jackson. But Tommy had more to say.

"Slave, we've been through this before, and you know what to expect when you disrespect another Master like this. Apologize to Master Jackson, and then we'll get on with your punishment."

"I'm very sorry, Master. I apologize, Master Jackson, your comments were quite heartfelt, and they are very much appreciated. I should not have joked about it, and I welcome whatever discipline my Master feels is deserved."

"Very good, little slave. Master Jackson, do you accept my submissive's apology?"

"I do, Master Thomas, your submissive is always good at the apologies. And so much fun to watch as she accepts your discipline!"

"Very well, then. Head to the spanking bench in the center of the room, Clare. Remove your panties and position yourself like you know I expect, and I will be there shortly."

Clare headed to the spanking bench that was positioned for the evening in the very center of the dungeon floor, slid her thong panties off and kicked them to the side of the bench. She then dropped to her knees, placed her hands on her thighs and bowed her head as she waited for her Master. Tommy went to one of the antique dressers on the wall near the bench, gathered several items, then joined Clare in the center of the gathering crowd. He placed the items in his hands on a wooden tray and turned to face Clare as she knelt at his feet.

"Up you go, slave, place yourself over the bench and allow Master Jackson to secure you in the bindings." And he reached his hand out to help Clare to her feet, placing a kiss on her head before he turned away from her.

While Jackson tethered Clare to the spanking bench by her wrists and ankles, Tommy addressed the crowd with a joy he hadn't experienced in several months.

"Fuck, it's good to be back here! I love this place, and you people, and most of all, I love this woman more than life itself. But loving someone often includes some discipline to keep her on the straight and narrow path. Luckily, Clare loves getting her discipline as much as I love giving it, so we're two halves of a whole spirit. Clare may be a little shy tonight, she hasn't done much in public lately, but I think by the time I'm done, there won't be a shy cell in her body."

Tommy turned back to Clare, not wanting to wait another second to put his hands on her. He knew what he had planned and his cock surged to life as he imagined every movement and every sound she would make for him. His hands reached out to caress the soft globes of Clare's ass, and they moaned together at the touch. He pulled the tray close and picked up the first item he needed, then bent over and blew gently in her ear. He spoke in a whisper to Clare, almost ignoring the group gathered around them.

"Do you trust me, Clare?"

"With my life, Master. You should never need to ask that."

"I love you more than I can ever make you understand. Don't ever doubt that."

As he rose to a standing position, he placed light, gentle kisses down her spine, making her tremble and break out in those goose bumps only he ever coaxed from her. He placed a final kiss on the ticklish spot just above her waist, and she felt the lube begin to dribble down between those globes. And then he began to play.

"You're not allowed to speak, Clare, but feel free to moan all you want. I love those little sounds you make when I'm playing with your ass. It goes without saying that you should use your safe word if need to stop me at any point."

"Yes, Master, I promise to use my safe word if needed."

But that idea went right out of Clare's head when Tommy started to massage the lube around the rosette of her ass, inserting one and then another finger into the channel that was drawing him in like a moth to a flame. The third finger proved to be a challenge, but before Clare knew what she could handle, the tip of the butt plug was rimming her and then sinking in, seating itself like it was destined to be there. And then the vibrations started, low at first and then noticeably faster, because above all, her Master had a sadistic streak that sometimes came out to play.

He gave her a minute to acclimate to the steady vibrations while he cleaned himself up a little, but very soon, his hands were back on her ass cheeks, squeezing and caressing, now and then pulling on the butt plug and then pushing it back in. And then the first slap of the crop came down on her left butt cheek, startling her and making her cry out. The next four slaps came in quick succession, peppering her butt and thighs, followed by big familiar hands that reached out to massage the hot pink flesh. The moan that Tommy wrung from Clare with the slaps of the crop was heard by everyone, but when the vibration of the butt plug increased, she wasn't the only one in the room to moan.

"What color are you, love?"

"I'm bright green, Master. I've missed this with you lately. Feel free to continue."

Another five slaps of the crop and another loud moan from Clare, and Tommy could wait no longer. In the span of ten seconds, he had dropped the crop on the tray and shut off and removed the vibrator, then let his lubed cock do the talking with one quick, vigorous slide, coming to rest as deep in Clare's back channel as he could get. He leaned over and let his hands lightly dance up and down her sides, brushing the outer edges of her exposed breasts, leaving open mouthed kisses up and down her back.

"Please, Master, you have to move. I need you to fuck me as hard as you ever have. I need it so badly."

"You're not supposed to be speaking, slave, but since you asked so politely, I will grant your request. Let's ride the wave together, my love, shall we?"

And he began to move – rapidly and fiercely – and still managed to reach down and circle Clare's clit with his middle finger, around and around, until she was right on the edge of a glorious orgasm. Two more hard strokes and they came together, almost drowning in the lusty wave. With a look from Tommy, Jackson was there to release Clare's wrists and ankles from the bench, so that when Tommy was able to stand again, Clare was free to rise with him. And that unnamed thing that had been sitting between them, getting in the way, seemed to disappear as they held each other tightly and just breathed each other in.

·♥·♥·♥·♥·♥·

The ride home from Asylum that night was as quiet as the ride to the club had been, but for different reasons. Clare had climbed into Tommy's lap in the driver's seat of his sleek, black Mustang, straddling him like she loved to do, and then she had promptly fallen asleep. Her gentle, measured breathing had been like a balm to her Master's soul, and he had made a decision that he couldn't tell her about. At some point during the evening, as they watched other couples scene together at the club, Tommy had decided that he would see Veronica one last time, but that nothing would ever happen between them again. He loved his wife too much to jeopardize their relationship.

When he pulled into the driveway at their home, he sat in the car with Clare for a few minutes, not wanting to wake her, but knowing he would have to if he wanted to get her inside and into bed. The love he felt for her swelled his heart and brought tears to his eyes, but the guilt he felt for what he had almost agreed to do made him shed bitter tears that Clare never saw.

When he had calmed his emotions and wiped away his tears, he gently woke Clare, took her inside and put her to bed, cuddling her back to sleep. And then he lay awake most of the remaining night hours, wondering how he would refuse his Domme, and still keep her from communicating with Clare about what Veronica had hoped would happen between them.

Chapter 16

The weekend flew by, but Tommy and Clare enjoyed every minute of it. They did silly things that they never seemed to find time for anymore, like taking a drive along the river, and stopping at a farm market to see what was in season. They bought fruit and vegetables, and then brought everything home and cooked way too much food for the two of them. That led to a picnic for the neighbors and everyone enjoyed just chilling and eating and gossiping. Sunday night, Master and slave spent time in the playroom, getting reacquainted again, then took a bottle of wine to bed and spent their last waking moments with some leisurely, relaxing slap and tickle. Not bad for a couple in their sixties.

Clare worked her part time hospital job on Monday, and Tommy spent the day with two of his golf course partners, checking out a potential new course that was for sale. But Tommy got home in time to have dinner delivered before Clare got home, so neither of them had to cook. Not that Tommy actually knew how to cook, but he did try from time to time, just to take the burden off Clare now and then. They watched a rom-com movie Monday evening, and got carried away with each other during the most romantic scenes. Neither of them actually saw the whole movie, and that was okay with them. They were just happy to be together, feeling like they had during their early months together.

Tuesday, Tommy was out all day for another partners meeting. Clare had library board meetings in the morning, but was home in time to do some cleaning in the afternoon. She put dinner in the crock pot and then started vacuuming and dusting in the formal living room and in Tommy's office. Her dusting in the office got a little rushed and she accidentally knocked some books off the bookshelf in the corner. As she was picking up the books that had fallen, she noticed a small card that had fallen out of one of the books. It looked like a business card and she almost put it back in the book without looking further, but something on the card caught her attention.

The side of the card she could see was white with a large red rose triskelion symbol in the center, which Clare associated with things she'd learned about BDSM. She hesitated to pick it up, wondering why this particular card would be in a book in Tommy's office. She sat down on the floor and stared at it for a few minutes, and then her curiosity got the best of her and she picked it up. When she turned it over to see the other side, she all but stopped breathing, and she dropped the card back to the floor. It was a very simple design, with a full red rose in the top left corner and trailing thorny vines surrounding the name.

MISTRESS V
The Key to Your Wildest Dreams

Veronica! That witch! Tears burned Clare's eyes and betrayal sat so heavy in her stomach that she knew she had only seconds to find a bathroom before she lost her lunch. She made it just in time to drop to her knees and hug the porcelain. And it wasn't a quick thing, every time she closed her eyes, she saw the name again, and that just made her wretch harder.

When there was nothing left in her system, she got to her feet and tried to think what to do. She thought she should leave but then decided that she needed to confront her husband about why he had kept that card, knowing how much Clare hated the woman. So she went back to the office, picked it up off the floor, and went to the kitchen table to wait for Tommy. She had no idea how long she sat there, staring at the business card of the only woman she had ever considered a rival for her husband's love.

Eventually she heard the garage door open, and heard Tommy come through the kitchen, greeting her with a kiss on her head. When she didn't respond, he looked closer at her and realized something was terribly wrong.

"Clare, baby, what's wrong? Did something happen? Are you sick?"

She still didn't respond, just lifted her hand away to reveal the business card that she had found. And Tommy immediately went on the defensive. He snatched the card away from her and shouted at her, "What the hell are you doing with this? Have you been snooping again?!"

"What the hell am I doing with it? What the hell are YOU doing with it? I watched you throw that in the trash can in your room at the hospital. How did it get in your office? Hidden in a book? Did you dig it back out of the trash while my back was turned? Or did she send you another one? How could you?"

"What's in my office is MY business, not yours. You were snooping again, and you have no right!"

"Are you seeing her again? Do you want my collar back? Do you want a divorce? You have to choose. Her or me. You don't get to have both of us."

"Clare, of course I don't want your collar back, and I don't want a divorce. You're overreacting again. You've gotten yourself all worked up over a business card that I forgot was there. If you would just stay out of my personal things, this would never have happened. What were you doing in my office?"

"I was cleaning! If I don't clean now and then, that room will fill up with dust and you won't find anything. And then THAT will be my fault. I was hurrying to get it done and knocked some books on the floor, and that card fell out of one of them. Like you were hiding it."

"Clare, I wasn't hiding anything. She means nothing to me. You have to know that. I love YOU. Only you. Please don't let her come between us."

"Tommy, I'm not the one putting her between us. That's all your doing. I'm not sure what I'm supposed to think, what I'm supposed to do. I can't unsee this, or pretend like nothing happened."

"Please, Clare, it means nothing. Look, I'll throw it away again. I'll put it down the garbage disposal if that will make you feel better. I can't stand this look you have on your face, like you don't trust anything I say or do, and I don't know how to convince you that you're the only woman I love. The only woman I need."

"I need some space. I can't be here right now. Your dinner is in the crock pot, eat whenever you want."

"Clare, where are you going?"

"I don't know, I just can't be here right now."

She got up from the table, turned her back on him, and walked out the garage door. And he let her go, because he was riddled with guilt and doubt, and he was afraid if he touched her right then, he would confess everything, and that would be the end of their relationship – the end of their marriage.

Three hours later, he was getting worried that she hadn't come back. He was sitting on the deck in the back yard, and heard her come through the garage door and into the kitchen. She tensed when he ran to her and pulled her into a hug, tears running down his cheeks, but she eventually relaxed a little.

"Tommy, I don't want to talk anymore about this right now, but we're going to have to clear the air eventually. Right now, I'm just really tired, and I want to go to bed."

"Of course, baby, come with me, let me get you into bed. We can cuddle until you fall asleep. Baby, you really have nothing to worry about, but we can talk in the morning. I love you Clare, I'll always love you."

Because of her sheer exhaustion, Clare let Tommy guide her up the stairs to their bedroom. She let him strip her naked and help her into bed, and she let him caress her body until she relaxed enough to fall asleep. When he was sure she was finally asleep, Tommy slipped out of the bed and went down to his office, pulled out his cell phone, and sent a text.

> *I can't see you. I can't see you ever again. Please don't ever communicate with me again. I love my wife and I can't let anything jeopardize that.*

Before he had a chance to delete the sent text and shut off the phone, a response came back to him.

> *Surely you can spare me five minutes to say goodbye, pet. Five minutes? My place, at Noon. If you don't come, I may have to track Clare down and tell her all the things we used to do. Things you still need to do. Maybe show her a few of my favorite photos of you in your submissive poses. Give me my five minutes and I'll leave her alone. You have my word. I'll see you at Noon.*

He didn't respond to the text, he just deleted all evidence of it from his phone, and headed back to bed, where he knew he would have another sleepless night. Because he knew he would see Mistress V one more time, and he had no idea what would happen.

Tommy woke up alone, surprised that he'd slept at all, surprised that Clare had left their bed without waking him. The house was deadly quiet as he looked in all the usual places where Clare might be hiding, and he finally found a note from her on the fainting couch in the playroom.

I'm not ready to talk about anything yet. I'm sorry I'm being such a coward. I decided that since I can't face you yet, I might as well work. We have a big computer update scheduled at Noon and I probably won't be home until around 9:00 tonight, maybe later than that. Have a good day. C.

Tommy was a little relieved that Clare was not only being a coward about talking to him, but also that she was going to be at work such a long time. That gave him time to say his goodbyes to Veronica, get a little work done himself, and then plan a late dinner to surprise Clare. If he got carry-out from Clare's favorite Greek restaurant, he might be able to worm his way back into her good graces. It would be a start anyway.

He spent the morning working out in their home gym, pushing himself extra hard to work off a little of the guilt he felt about what he'd already done, and about what he was about to do. He would have to tell Clare about his last visit to see Veronica, but he felt he needed some closure, to get things settled in his own mind before he could explain things to Clare. Once he thought he had an appropriate talk track in his head for both Veronica and for Clare, he showered and dressed, and headed out for the first of two very difficult conversations. He just hoped that at the end of the day, the woman he loved would be in his bed where she belonged.

Just before Noon, Tommy turned off the highway into an unmarked tree-shrouded gravel lane that ran a half mile under a shady canopy of branches covered in bright green leaves and large white flowers, ending at a large white stucco house with beautiful Southern landscaping. The Southern mansion Veronica had always referred to as her summer cottage. It was just as he remembered. He had stopped several times in that half mile drive, talking himself out of, and into, this last visit with his Domme. He knew it was the worst mistake in a life filled with horrible mistakes, but he couldn't stop himself, any more than he could stop time.

As he approached the open door of the screen porch under the huge live oak tree, he could make out the familiar scents – that sweet combination of patchouli, hashish and Veronica's almost too strong perfume. He had to keep his head clear, there was too much at stake to have his resolve crumble now. He would have the required cup of tea, explain why he wasn't staying, and be gone again in five minutes. Ten minutes tops.

As Tommy stepped into the screen porch, Veronica stepped out of the house to greet him. He hated to admit it, but she was dazzling. Her long black hair was up in a tight bun on top of her head, held in place by three crisscrossing emerald-topped hair sticks that made her look like she was wearing a jeweled crown. She was wearing a black skin tight cat suit and black patent leather over the knee stiletto boots, an outfit that almost made his mouth water. And which made him look embarrassingly shabby in his own tight black jeans and snug black tee shirt. But the smile on her face and the gleam in her eyes said she thought he looked absolutely delicious.

"Thomas, my pet, you're right on time. I knew you'd come. Only I can give you what you truly crave, sweet boy, and we both know it."

"Veronica, I can only stay a few minutes. I only came to say goodbye and wish you well."

"Nonsense. Come in. Have some tea. You promised me five minutes. Come, the tea is ready."

He knew he should turn and run, but something made him resist the urge. He had promised, after all. He took her offered hand and let her pull him into the house, where she settled him in a cozy little room off the kitchen, in a very comfortable chair with a high back and no arms to get in the way. The small table was set for tea, and she poured him a cup, then sat down next to him, so close their thighs and shoulders brushed against each other.

The scent of hashish was strong in the little room, and he turned to see a smoker pot in the corner, vapors wafting from the top. And sitting so close to her, the scent of her perfume was almost overpowering. The combination was heady, and he was already feeling more relaxed, even a little chatty.

"Veronica, I meant what I said. I came to say goodbye. You and I were never right for each other, and no matter how much you seem to think otherwise, I love my wife. She's everything I want, everything I need, and you can't change that."

"Thomas, pet, you break my heart. You've convinced yourself that such a mousy little woman can be your heart's desire, but if you would just be honest with yourself, you would have to admit that I'm the woman you need. I'm your Mistress V. Remember? Look! Up on the wall. It's my favorite photo of you, from our days together. Just look how strong you were, how virile, how aroused. All for me! Looking at that photo of you, naked and restrained, in a perfect submissive pose, always makes me hunger for more. That's why it's here it my tea room, where I can admire it every day."

"No, Veronica. That man in the photo isn't me. Not anymore. If that man ever really existed, he doesn't exist now. I can see that coming here was a mistake, I need..."

She leaned against him and laid her hand firmly on his thigh. Her perfume was spellbinding, clouding around him, and she used it to her advantage. "Pet, you promised. Five minutes. You need to drink your tea before it gets cold. I made it especially for you, just the way you like it." And she picked up the cup, brought it to his lips, and tipped it so that the tea poured, little by little, into his open mouth. And as he drank, he stared at the photo on the wall, admiring that strong man, never thinking to raise his hands to push the cup away. "That's my precious pet, drink your tea all down like a good boy."

Tommy wasn't sure what was happening to him, but he did remember the flavor of the tea she used to make for him. Peppermint, with something else he could never identify, not a bad taste, for tea. But the more he drank, the more fuzzy his mind got, like he could close his eyes and take a nap sitting right there at the little table. Except that he was starting to grow a substantial erection for some reason, and it was getting uncomfortable, trapped behind the zipper of his jeans. Veronica turned to him, took his face in her hands and placed a light, gentle kiss on his lips. Leaving one hand to gently grasp his chiseled jaw, she let her other hand drift down his chest to that zipper and stroked his enlarging cock through the denim, making him moan.

"Shall I continue, pet? Do you remember how I used to kiss you? What I used to do with my hands? I think you do, and you have a reward waiting for me right here, don't you?" Her hand settled on the denim covering his ever-growing erection, and the squeeze of her fingers made him groan with pure desire.

"Veronica, I..."

"What do you call me, pet? How do you address me when we're together? Say it, pet, tell me who I am."

"Mistress V, I..."

"That's right, pet, I'm your Mistress V. Shall we play a little? Would you like to play with Mistress V?"

With her hand still gripping his cock snugly through his jeans, all other thoughts left his mind and he whispered, "Yes, Mistress V."

"Excellent. Let's get you out of these uncomfortable clothes and play."

Mistress V pushed the tea cups to the center of the table and climbed up to sit on the edge, with her feet straddling Tommy's legs, boots resting on the chair rungs. She reached up and caressed his face, let her fingers tangle in his hair, and pulled him in to gently suck his bottom lip into her mouth, just for a moment, just like she used to do. And he gasped at the memory.

"Can you raise your arms over your head for me so we can remove this uncomfortable tee shirt?"

"Yes, Mistress V." And he raised his hands over his head as if he was in a trance, while she tugged the tee shirt up and over his head, tossing it in the corner.

"Oh, pet, you've taken such good care of your body. What I can see so far is magnificent. I'm going to play with your nipples for just a few minutes, maybe suck on them just a little, like I used to. Would that be okay? You used to enjoy it so much."

"Mistress V, I..."

"Pet, I won't ask again. I don't want to spoil our time together having to discipline you."

"Yes, Mistress V."

She climbed up to straddle his lap on the chair and rubbed the palm of her hand across one nipple while she breathed lightly on the other, and was immensely pleased when both nipples puckered tightly. He'd always been so responsive to her touch, and nothing had changed in all those years they'd been apart. When she pinched one nipple and sucked on the other one, he moaned loudly, and began to pant just a little. And she knew he was ready for anything she wanted to do. With the ease of a jungle cat, Veronica climbed off his lap and stood next to him.

"Thomas, my pet, can you stand for me? So we can remove these uncomfortable jeans? I think we can find something else for you to wear that would be more appropriate. Now up you go, pet."

Tommy stood obediently and didn't make a move to stop her when Mistress V unsnapped and unzipped his jeans, then pulled the jeans and his boxer briefs down far enough to free the monster she had created. Unable to stop herself, she wrapped a hand around his cock and squeezed until she heard the gasp she had known would come when she reached that grip just at the point of pain. And his cock grew larger in her hand.

She released her grip on his erection and knelt down to remove his shoes, then helped him shed his remaining clothes. She stood and stepped back a pace, and let her gaze rake over his naked body, until he thought he could feel her stare physically, like claws against his skin. "Oh, pet, that's quite a scar on your leg. Is that from your recent accident? It makes you look so rugged!"

"Yes, Mistress V. Thank you, Mistress V."

"Don't move, pet, stay right where you are for just a minute, and then we'll play."

When she turned her back on him, he suddenly felt deserted, and he began to step closer, but she stopped him with a cross stare over her shoulder. She reached into a cabinet in the corner of the room and pulled out four similar objects, but didn't show them to him right away when she turned to face him again.

"Close your eyes, pet, and stand very still. I have a treat for you but you must be very still, no matter what you feel. Is that okay?"

"Yes, Mistress V. I won't move."

"Perfect." She came close to him again and laid her items on the table, then picked one up and wrapped the soft object around his right wrist.

"Mistress V, I..."

"Hush, pet, let me finish this and then we'll play." She pulled his head down and placed a long kiss on his lips, sinking her tongue into his open mouth. While he was still enjoying the magic of her kiss, she wrapped a similar soft object around his left wrist. She took the other two objects, knelt down, and wrapped a fur lined cuff around each of his ankles, then stood to admire him again, with his wrists and ankles cuffed and ready for play. She stepped behind him and gently caressed his back, his shoulders, ran her hands down his arms, then with the skill of much practice over the years, she pulled his wrists behind him and buckled them together before he could react.

When she moved to face him again, his eyes were still closed but his breathing had become shallow and rapid, and she could hear the cuffs clinking behind him as he tested their hold.

"Open your eyes, pet, and tell me how you feel. Do you remember how much you used to enjoy this?"

"I'm uncomfortable, Mistress V, I don't think I like this play. I don't know what you're going to do to me that I need cuffs on my wrists and ankles like this."

Enjoying how his eyes were now somewhat dilated, she whispered in his ear, "Nothing to worry about, pet, you've always loved playing with me like this. Now let's have a little more tea and then we'll take a walk into the other room and we'll have some real fun. Okay?"

"Yes, Mistress V, if that's what you want."

Veronica poured another cup of tea from the pot and lifted it to his waiting lips, feeding him the entire cup, bit by bit. "You like my special tea, don't you, pet? It makes you feel so relaxed and so sensitive." To prove her point, she reached down and ran a long red fingernail up the impressive length of his erection, enjoying his shuddering reaction to her touch.

"Yes, Mistress V."

When Tommy had finished his tea, Veronica took a leather collar out of the same cabinet, and buckled it around his neck, thinking how stunning he still looked wearing her collar. There were two D rings on the collar, one in the front and one in the back. She took a fifteen inch, specially made silver chain from the cabinet and attached one end to the back D ring, and the other end to his linked wrist cuffs. It was the perfect length to pull the collar snugly against his throat if he didn't keep his arms bent just so. Then she attached a leather leash to the D ring on the front of the collar. When she tugged his head down with the leash for another kiss, she could hear him choke ever so slightly from the pull of the collar, and he quickly moved his wrists up high enough to remove the pressure. Such a smart pet, even dazed as he was, to figure out a solution so quickly. Satisfied that he was sufficiently subdued, and adequately restrained, she walked him out of the cozy little room, looking up and waving to a small camera as they went.

Chapter 17

Tommy felt like he was inside a dream as they walked, so there was no fear in him. Nothing in a dream could hurt him, he'd heard that from someone, so he followed obediently, curiously, as Mistress V tugged on the leash. They didn't have far to walk, but when they entered another room off the kitchen, he knew he had stepped into a completely different kind of dream. As they walked into the room, Mistress V closed the door behind him, then turned to him and said "Smile for the camera, pet. It's right there in the corner. It will capture our play, and if you're a very good boy, I'll make you a present of the video. But you have to be a very good boy and do everything Mistress V tells you to do, as soon as I tell you to do it. Can you do that?"

"Yes, Mistress V." And he looked directly into the camera with unfocused eyes and smiled just as she had asked.

In the fog of his dream, Tommy looked around the room and caught wisps of memories, like the room was familiar. There were no windows, but recessed green light circled the room near the ceiling. He saw walls covered in small river rocks from floor to ceiling and the floor was laid with black slate tile. There were muted gold sconces here and there on the walls to give a little more light to the room, and as he looked closer, he saw things attached to the walls, some large and some small.

Mistress V tugged on the leash attached to his collar, pulling Tommy toward one of the smaller wall decorations, what looked like a ballet barre attached solidly to the wall at a height just below his waist. When they got close, he noticed another barre set a few inches off the floor, directly below the first one. Mistress V read correctly that her pet was becoming anxious, so she spent a few minutes holding him, stroking his chest, licking his beaded nipples, talking quietly to him as she turned his back to the barre.

"No need to be nervous, pet. Nothing bad will happen to you here. We're just going to play a little. It will be great fun and you'll see what I can do for you that your little mousy girl will never be able to do. You'll see that I'm clearly the right woman for you. Now take a deep breath for Mistress and calm yourself, and we'll get started. Okay?"

"Yes, Mistress V. I feel a little better."

Veronica gave Tommy a final kiss and then a number of things happened quickly. Running her hands down his arms behind his back, she quickly removed the chain at his back from his wrist cuffs, and attached the cuffs to a ring on the upper barre. Showing him that he could support his weight and steady himself with his hands on the upper barre, she knelt and moved his feet about 24 inches apart and attached each ankle cuff to a ring on the lower barre. As she moved from ankle to ankle, she passed his erect cock, and stopped to take a few short licks, teasing him and making him enlarge even more.

The last thing she attached to a hidden wall ring was the chain on the back of his collar, leaving him about four inches of movement from side to side. The leash remained attached to the front of his collar, hanging down across his chest, just to the level of his waist. Then she stepped back to admire her handiwork, while Tommy gazed at her with growing trepidation, testing his restraints, finding himself solidly attached to the wall.

"You are a work of art, pet, I always thought you were so beautiful like this, restrained and erect. I think I'll take another photo of you like this to hang in the tea room with the other one. It will be a perfect counterpoint to the original, younger virile Thomas alongside more mature, equally stunning Thomas. Is that okay, my pet?"

"I don't know, Mistress, I don't think..."

"That's right, pet, you don't think. You don't have to. I'll do all the thinking right now, okay?"

"Yes, Mistress V."

Veronica walked to a short library table by the back wall and picked up her portrait camera, then stood in the center of the room. "Smile for the camera, my darling, show me how much you enjoy being with me." She raised the camera and took several shots of Tommy in his restrained pose, as she moved here and there around the room, looking for the best angle.

When she had what she thought was the ideal shot of him, she placed the camera back on the table and said, "Now let's get the smoker going so you can relax a little more, okay? I don't want you to be nervous or afraid, I'll always protect you from harm. I know how much pain you can handle and I'll never take you beyond your limits. I love you, pet, always know that. I am your one true Mistress."

"Yes, Mistress V."

Veronica went to the corner of the room and pulled a small table to stand close to Tommy. She lit the smoker that she had placed on the table and the hashish vapors that emanated from the pot drifted straight up to his face. In just a few minutes, his growing stupor was visible and Mistress V was ready to play.

Making sure that she was well visible, not only to Tommy but to the camera on the wall, Mistress V removed her boots and her cat suit, revealing a black latex demi bra that lifted and supported her ample breasts but left her nipples exposed, along with a matching black latex thong that covered nothing. She climbed back into the over the knee stiletto boots because she wanted the height they gave her, then walked to a cabinet in the corner, selected several things she needed, and returned to stand a few inches from Tommy, who was all but unconscious from the hash smoke.

Mistress V pushed the small table a few feet away, grasped and stroked Tommy's fading erection back to life, and started to speak softly. "Wake up, pet, it's time to play! First I'm going to punish you for making me wait so very long to get my hands on you again, and then if you're a very obedient boy, I'll let you lick me to orgasm. If you can make me come, I'll let you come. But you're not allowed to come until I say so. Just like before, remember? You'll like that, right?"

"Yes, Mistress V."

"Oh, louder, pet, we want to make sure the camera can hear you too."

"Yes, Mistress, I'll do my best."

"Oh, pet, you always have. But I think I need one or two other things from the cabinet before we get started. Just to heighten your arousal and my pleasure. Can you guess what they might be?"

"No, Mistress V."

She walked back to the cabinet again, opened a different drawer and took out a blindfold, then took a small bottle of peppermint oil off a shelf. Her pet had always been sensitive to the oil, and he had enjoyed the persistent tingle when they played with it in the past. Now she felt she had everything she needed to get started.

Walking back to Tommy, tethered to the wall, she held up the blindfold and rubbed it against his face softly. His unfocused eyes made her laugh but it was obvious he knew what she held. He groaned a little and then pleaded, "No, Mistress V, please don't blindfold me. I have to be able to see you."

"Now, pet, just relax, you know I'm right here. I would never leave you unattended. You can trust me. How about just for a few minutes until you get comfortable with it again? I'll be right here with you. You wouldn't want to disappoint me, now would you?"

"No, Mistress V, I would never want to disappoint you. I'll try the blindfold."

"Good pet. Now here we go." She kissed him on the cheek and then slipped the blindfold over his eyes, remaining in physical contact with him until his suddenly rapid breathing returned to normal.

"There now, pet, is that better now? Do you feel safe now?"

"Yes, Mistress V."

"Very good, pet. Let's continue."

Mistress V picked up the clamps she had taken from the cabinet and held them up to the light to admire. She placed a drop of the oil on each of his nipples and then massaged them gently until they beaded to sharp peaks that made him gasp and whimper. Then she attached the clamps snugly to those puckered nipples, relishing the increasingly loud moans she considered his gift to her. When she felt he was reaching his pain/pleasure limit with her play at his nipples, she grasped and squeezed his cock, until he was a monster in her grip again. She did a little moaning of her own thinking about finally sinking down onto that monster and staking her claim on him once and for all.

She leaned over and breathed lightly on each nipple a few times, making them engorge against the clamps, causing him to wince and moan again with a combination of pain and arousal. Then she knelt down and put her lips on his cock, sucking hard and drawing out the dew she wanted to see and taste. Another moan from Tommy made her laugh as she stood, and she realized how much she was enjoying herself with her favorite pet finally back in her care.

She reached for the peppermint oil again and applied a few drops to his impressive erection, massaging it in with her fingertips, knowing how much more arousal he would gain from it when she used the last item she had pulled from the cabinet.

If Tommy had been able to see the crop Veronica had in her hand, he would have tried desperately to get away. As it was, he was completely unaware of what she was about to do. Blindfolded as he was, he was startled when Mistress V stepped close to him and tapped his face lightly with the crop, getting his attention. She ran the wide end of the crop across his shoulders, down his arms, and up to his chest, where she suddenly placed a harsh strike against one clamped nipple. He shouted and shuddered at the pain, and then moaned from the pleasure, and his Mistress smiled. Several more strikes of the crop against his nipples and down his abdomen coaxed louder moans from him, and she grinned at the satisfaction that punishing him gave her.

Tommy's fuzzy attention was now fully on the crop, fearing where she would strike next. He shivered in anticipation and dread, and when a fast series of harsh strikes landed against his massive erection and his testicles, drawn up so close to his body, he came all over his Mistress and himself.

"Oh, pet, look what you've done. That wasn't very obedient of you, was it?"

"No, Mistress V, I'm very sorry, Mistress V. I couldn't help myself, Mistress V."

"Well, I guess I'll have to think of a way for you to make it up to me, won't I?"

"Yes, Mistress V."

Hours later, Tommy and Mistress V had both had multiple orgasms, and she thought her time to play for the day had come to an end, because Tommy was quickly coming to his senses and she had a decision to make. Should she leave him tethered to the dungeon wall and see how he reacted to his predicament? Or should she get him cleaned up and back to the little tea room before he realized what they had done together? In the end, it was a little of both. He was alert enough to realize what room he was in, and that he was naked, but she had managed to remove all the toys and the cuffs, and hide them away before he was fully conscious. To say that he was not happy was an understatement.

"What the fuck did you do to me, Veronica? Why am I naked? Where are my clothes? And what time is it? I have a feeling I've been here way more than five minutes! What did you do to me, bitch? I feel like my head is splitting open!"

"Bitch? So I'm not Mistress V anymore? All we did was play a little, pet, you were never in any danger, and you had quite a good time. That submissive streak of yours is a freaking mile wide, just as pronounced now as it ever was. You would make such an excellent slave, if you would just let go and embrace that part of yourself."

"My clothes, Veronica, where are my clothes?"

"Just calm down and we'll go back out to the tea room so you can get dressed. Although that's quite a shame, putting clothes over that glorious body of yours."

"Get me the fuck out of here before I call the police!!"

"You'd never call the police on me, pet. You enjoyed yourself way too much and I have photographic evidence to support that statement. Now when can we do this again?"

Twenty minutes later, he was dressed and flying down the lane, after telling Veronica that there was no fucking way he was ever seeing her again. He hadn't believed that she would really record everything she'd done to him, since she had drugged him and restrained him against his will. She decided that he didn't need to know just yet that she'd really done it. She was a little concerned that he might become physically violent if he knew the extent of their activities that day, but she was quite confident that the authorities would never become involved.

As soon as he was gone, she ran to her computer and pulled up the first video from the tea room. She would review everything that had been photographed and recorded that day. She couldn't wait to select just the perfect photo to send to him, and the perfect video clip to send to his little mouse. Mistress V had been the smartest of the three of them, and she was excited to see everything that had been captured on video for posterity. And a little blackmail. But first, she needed to order a new bottle of her special perfume, since it worked so well on her favorite pet.

·❤·❤·❤·❤·❤·

When he got to the main road at the end of the lane, he sent a quick text.

> I'm in trouble, I need your help.

And got an immediate response back.

> Come to the house.

Feeling a little better, knowing help was on the way, he headed back to town. There was a large gap in his waking memory, with flashes of remembrance here and there, but he couldn't fix that right away. There was a more urgent conversation he had to have, but not with Clare. Not yet. Not until he knew more.

Chapter 18

istress Desdemona answered immediately when Tommy knocked on her door. She might be the only one who could help him salvage his future with the woman he loved, his very life. She wasn't just a master whip handler and astute businesswoman, she was a celebrated psychoanalyst, adept at hypnosis. And she was known internationally for her ability to help men and women in the D/s community find their true calling, as a Dom/me, a submissive, or a switch. Tommy had never thought he would need her counsel on anything other than proper whip technique, but he wasn't too ashamed of what he'd done to refuse help when it was available.

They shared a quick hug and then she led him into her office.

"Is Clay here? Am I interrupting something? I'm so sorry, I should leave."

"Tommy, my sweet submissive boy is away on business this week. Who would ever have thought that Clay would turn out to be some kind of advertising genius? I never saw it in him, but apparently everyone else does. Anyway, we have all the time you need. Who did you kill? And do we have time to bury the body?"

As Des laughed at her own joke, a text pinged on Tommy's phone. He paled visibly and froze in place, half seated, when he saw who the text was from and what it was.

Seeing himself in a photograph taken without his permission, one that he didn't remember posing for, was unsettling, to say the least. But it did bring up a sudden, clear memory of a conversation he'd had with Clare early in their relationship, and empathy for her feelings hit him like a brick.

"No audio or video recordings of any sex acts I'm involved in – absolutely none! I don't intend to see my ass up in the air on YouTube, Facebook or any other internet site – and I would prefer that you ask my permission before any photos are taken."

"Whoa. Are you all right? What's going on, T."

Allowing himself to fall into his chair, he cursed his stupidity, and regretted his decision to bring Des into his problem.

"Talk to me, T, tell me what's going on. Who's the text from and what does it say?"

"Des, there are a lot of things going on, but at the heart of it, I've done something incredibly stupid and it's going to cost me my wife."

"Start at the beginning, T. Like I said, I have all night. If you don't mind, I'm going to record our conversation, because I don't want to miss any details in the heat of the moment. Okay?"

"Fine. It seems I've already been photographed today, I may as well be recorded too."

Des set up her audio recording device and then said, "First, let me see the text." He passed his phone across her desk to her, and she made a few notes as she viewed the photo of Tommy, naked, restrained, and incredibly aroused, the photo that Veronica had taken earlier that day. The only comments in the text said,

> *I didn't get my fill today, pet, I need more time. Friday, Noon, same place.*

"Tommy, is this what you texted me about? Did this just happen today? T, was this consensual? Is there something you've been hiding from everyone?"

"Yes, it was today. Des, I never intended for anything to happen. I was meeting with her one last time, just to say goodbye. I needed closure with V to take care of a problem I caused between Clare and me."

"Wait. V? As in Mistress V? 'The Key to Your Wildest Dreams' V? Oh, Tommy, how could you? You fell right into her trap, didn't you?"

"Yes, I did. I started feeling fuzzy as soon as I walked in the door of her house, and now I have a fairly long memory gap. I'm not sure exactly what happened in that house today. I'm getting flashes of things, but nothing clear, and there's not much. She had a hash pot burning in the room, and I think she put some kind of date rape drug in my tea. And what the fuck is up with her perfume?!? Whenever I was near her, I couldn't think straight, all I could think about was her next touch, her next kiss. Des, I'm so fucked. Clare's already furious with me about something, and this is just going to make things worse. I'm going to lose her. And I don't even remember everything V might have done!"

"Please, Tommy, take a deep breath. I'm going to take some blood really quick, and I need a urine sample, too, just to see if there's anything left in your system. I have a very cooperative lab technician who can rush it through for me. Do you remember anything other than the hash and the tea?"

"I don't remember anything but that doesn't mean there wasn't something else while I was out of it."

"Okay, let's get your samples really quick."

Des turned off the recorder, got up from her desk, and led Tommy into a separate locked room that looked like a medical exam room, but the table had restraints that wouldn't normally exist in a standard exam room.

"Uh, Des, is this where you and Clay... do things??"

"Yes, you prude, we do things in here, but it's also where I keep all of the drug supplies I need for psychoanalysis and for regression hypnosis. Trust me, T, I'm well qualified to take your blood. Here's a urine container, pee in this quick while I get the vials ready. Please don't be shy, I'll be so disappointed."

She didn't wait for him to respond, she just handed him a specimen cup to pee in, and then motioned to the exam table and had him sit. As a well trained emergency room nurse, he knew the drill about getting urine samples and taking blood from a patient, so the process went smoothly, and they were back in her office in just a few minutes. She made a phone call to her lab tech friend, and then started the recording device again.

"Okay, Tommy, let's get back to your situation. Take me back as far as you need to, back to where Clare got involved in all this."

·❤·❤·❤·❤·❤·

Twenty minutes later, Des had taken copious notes during Tommy's explanation of why his life was spiraling into hell. In their early days together, Tommy and Clare had both had secrets that had to be shared, and one of Tommy's most painful secrets was his relationship years before with Veronica Smith. Veronica had been convinced that Tommy was a submissive, and Tommy was convinced that he was a Dominant. Their short relationship was explosive, but at times it was extremely fulfilling for both of them. Clare had been very understanding at the time, and they hadn't seen a need to discuss Veronica again. Until V visited him in the hospital after his accident.

Veronica had left a business card with Tommy which he had made a point of disposing of in the trash for Clare's benefit. Unfortunately, Mistress V's visit had brought back memories and created new feelings that were foreign to him and needed to be investigated, so he pulled the card back out of the trash and kept it hidden while he decided what to do. His relationship with Clare had been somewhat strained after he came home from the hospital, and those feelings about submission kept nagging him. He wasn't sure if it was just seeing Mistress V again, or possibly his traumatic head injury, or maybe a combination of both, but he just couldn't let go of his sudden new interest in submitting to a Domme. Specifically, Mistress V. And then Clare had found the business card the day before and felt betrayed.

"Tommy, I have to get one totally unprofessional thing out of the way before we continue. Dude, you may not think you have submissive tendencies, and maybe you don't, but you rock in this photo. You are a freaking rutting bull!! If I wasn't in a committed relationship, I might be tempted to have a go at this part of your personality. Drugs or not, this is one seriously hot man!"

"Des, you are not helping me!!"

"I know, I'm sorry, I just had to get that out of the way. Now about the drugs. You say there was a hashish burner in the first room you were in. And you said that after you had been effectively subdued by that and whatever might have been in the tea, you think she took you into this other room where the photo was taken. Was there hash in that other room as well? Is there anything during the time you were in the second room that you remember with clarity? Or is everything just the dream-like state you described?"

"Des, I wish I could remember everything clearly, but if I hadn't been out of it, none of it would have happened. As a matter of fact, when I first arrived, when she first came out to the screen porch to greet me, I was already starting to getting fuzzy headed. I could smell the faint scent of patchouli and hash coming from inside the house, but the very strong scent of her perfume almost knocked me on my ass before I ever got into the house. I had an initial urge to leave then and there, but I couldn't make myself go. And it all went downhill from there."

"That, my friend, was her pheromone perfume. It really should be illegal. She has it custom made somewhere in Europe and it's super strong. She only wears it when she's on the hunt, and I dare say even a gay man would struggle to resist her charms when she wears it. The perfume, combined with the hash and whatever Rohypnol derivative was in the tea, would have dealt your determination to resist her a fatal blow."

"She wants to see me again. In two days. I know if I don't go, she'll go right to Clare, and that will be the last straw. Clare will leave me and never look back. Des, I can't lose Clare, that's my first priority, but I need to investigate this sudden attraction I've developed to submission, and that can't wait long either. You're the only one who can help me with that. I know this is a lot to digest, I'm sorry I brought my problems to you, but I wasn't sure where else to go."

"T, I've been trying to catch Veronica abusing her submissives like this for years and I've not been able to. She's got 16 houses that I know of, and she keeps moving around, so I can't ever find her or anyone who might be willing to testify against her. I'm glad you thought to contact me. We'll work through all of this, we just have to prioritize. And if I can finally nab that witch, that's a bonus! Now I think the first thing we need to do is get to Clare, before Mistress Witch does. You need to tell her your whole story, but I'll be there to support you, if you feel comfortable with my presence."

"Des, I would be thrilled to have you backing me up. Hold on, I just got another text. It's from Clare. Oh, I am so fucked."

Clare walked into the house, exhausted, almost glad to see that Tommy wasn't home yet. She still wasn't ready to talk about the threesome they seemed to have with Mistress V, and she just didn't know what to do about it. She wanted to trust her Master, but he hadn't given her any foundation for trust to grow, and she was floundering. She sat at the kitchen table with a large glass of wine, wondering what the hell to do. She wasn't sure how they would move forward from this point, but she didn't want to give up on their relationship, not yet. She decided that if Tommy wasn't home in fifteen minutes, she would just go to bed and try again tomorrow.

The fifteen minutes came and went and she was just getting up to turn off the lights and head upstairs when her cell phone pinged with a text. She thought it might be Tommy letting her know where he was and when he would be home, but when she looked, it was a phone number she didn't recognize. She sat back down at the table and opened the text, still not sure who it was from. The text comments were brief and to the point, and there was a video attached.

> *Thought you might enjoy seeing how your Master spent his day while you were at work. He certainly did have a good time while you were slaving away at your little job, mouse. It seems I win after all. V.*

Through her tears, Clare watched the attached video clip, unable to look away. When it ended, she watched it again. And again. She just couldn't believe what she was seeing, but she was certain about one thing. It was time to go. She wasn't sure where she would end up, but she was done being a doormat for her husband and his new Mistress. Feeling faint from the shock of what she'd seen, she walked out to the deck, thinking a little fresh air would clear her head. After a few minutes, she decided the dizziness was passing, and her path became clear - she needed to leave, for good. She came back inside and took off her wedding ring. She had to break the lock on her collar to get it off, and it took a few minutes, but she finally managed it. She placed it next to her ring on the kitchen table. She sat at the table and cried more bitter tears, and then forwarded the text to Tommy, with her own comments. Then she went up to their bedroom and packed enough clothes for a few days, went out to her car, and drove into the night.

> *Master, I'm leaving, for good. I'm not sure where I'm going, but you probably don't care anyway. You're welcome to spend the rest of your miserable life with Mistress V. You seem to be enjoying yourself quite a bit in this video she sent me. Have a nice life. I'm leaving my collar and my wedding ring on the kitchen table. Not sure you'll have anyone else to give them to in the future but I don't need them anymore. You'll hear from my lawyer in a few days. C.*

He clicked on the video and almost vomited in his lap. He was in the same room as in the photo V had sent him, but now he could actually see some of what Mistress V had done to him. That Clare had seen her do to him. Des walked around the desk and knelt beside him so that they could view the short clip together. They could see Tommy blindfolded, tethered to both barres, and they could see the collar, the leash hanging down across his chest, the nipple clamps biting into his flesh. And his massive erection, larger than he could remember having in a very long time. They watched as Mistress V slapped Tommy's erection so hard with a crop, he came all over both of them. The volume on the video was turned up high enough that they could hear everything.

"Oh, pet, look what you've done. That wasn't very obedient of you, was it?"

"No, Mistress V, I'm very sorry, Mistress V. I couldn't help myself, Mistress V."

"Well, I guess I'll have to think of a way for you to make it up to me, won't I?"

"Yes, Mistress V."

"So, pet, how do you feel about anal play? I recall you struggled with it quite a bit. Let's see if you do any better with it now."

Tommy and Des watched as Mistress V walked to the cabinet and returned with a medium sized butt plug and some lube. His active memory had recorded none of it, but he recognized himself in the video, triggering a sense of dread at what he was about to see. And it just kept on going.

"Pet, you should be grateful that I'm a kind and considerate Mistress. Otherwise, you'd be getting this plug without benefit of lube. Now be a good boy and take your punishment. Maybe you'll enjoy it after all."

"No, Mistress V, please don't. I don't want it."

Mistress V reached up and ripped the blindfold off. She grabbed Tommy by the nape of his neck, pulling him forward and choking him on his collar. In a deep voice, she hissed, *"Who's in charge here, pet? I believe I am. You have no say in what happens in this room. Now you will take the plug and then you'd better be able to make me come, or I'll come up with a worse punishment and you'll still take the plug."* At that last comment, she pushed him back into the wall, and stepped back.

"Yes, Mistress V. I'm sorry, Mistress V. Please don't hurt me, Mistress V." And the sound of his sob was so loud, it made Tommy sick to his stomach to watch.

"Just relax, pet, and I won't have to hurt you. Now hold still and unclench those cheeks. This is going to happen whether you want it to or not."

"Yes, Mistress V."

What came next was almost too much for Tommy to watch. Mistress V covered her fingers with the lube and reached around behind him. The video didn't catch exactly what she was doing but it was obvious she was using her lubed fingers to open his ass for the plug. The video sound was filled with his whimpers and moans and with her laughter at his discomfort, telling him to take his punishment like a man. Eventually Mistress V took the plug, covered it with lube, and reached around him again.

"Here we go, pet. Once I get this plug in, we'll continue, but if you let it come out, we'll start all over again, including more of the crop. Do you understand, pet?"

"Yes, Mistress V." And there was another audible sob from Tommy along with a look of fear that couldn't be denied.

It only took a few seconds for the plug to seat itself, and when it did, Veronica stepped out of the frame, leaving video Tommy tethered to the barre, tears running down his cheeks, moaning loudly, with an almost rapturous look on his face. And the video stopped. And real time Tommy ran to the bathroom to vomit, wondering if Clare had done the same thing.

"Tommy, assuming she really has left, where would Clare go in the middle of the night? Is there a particular friend she might run to? Somewhere special she might hide out?"

"Let me make a quick phone call." He pulled up his phone contact list and called their neighbor, James Porter. "James, this is Tommy. Yes, I'm good. Listen, is Clare there with you? She doesn't seem to be at home and I'm not sure where she is. No? Okay. Listen, if you talk to her, just text me and let me know. No, nothing important, I'll see her later at home. Yes. Goodbye."

"Any other tricks up your sleeve? No other friends she might tell where she's at? I'm a little surprised you haven't found a way to put a tracking chip in her little ass."

"Oh, Des, I can be so stupid sometimes, but YOU'RE a genius! I have an app on my phone that tracks her phone! She keeps leaving it on the golf course or at the grocery store. We're constantly running somewhere to pick the damned thing up. Let me check it quick. BINGO! Oh, crap. She in Old Town, at the Benedict Hotel. At least her phone's there. Des, she really left."

"I think you need to leave her alone for right now. At least you know where she's at tonight, you know she's safe. If you text her now, she'll probably go somewhere else and she might remember the app on her phone and remove it. Then we won't know where she's at. In the meantime, we need to get the founders group together and brainstorm how to handle this. You call Jackson and have him call Will. I'll get Rodney and Marshall on a conference call. Tell Jackson to get Will and come here."

"I need to text James first and let him know Clare's okay. Then I'll call Jackson. At least that will give me something to do.

Chapter 19

Thirty minutes after the initial calls went out, they were all gathered in Desdemona's family room, waiting for someone to explain the details of what was going on. All anyone knew was that their friend Tommy was in trouble and needed their help. The group consisted of Des, Tommy, Jackson, Will, Rodney and Marshall. They were the founding members of Asylum, and they always stuck together. They'd been together long enough that if one of their group was in trouble, they would all be there.

Once everyone had a drink in hand, Tommy finally spoke up. "I can't tell you all how much I appreciate all of you dropping what you were doing this evening to come here. You all have great instincts about how to get in and out of trouble, and I need your brain power on this one. I've done something really stupid, and if I don't do something quick, my mistake will cost me Clare."

Jackson, considering himself the brains of the group, had a few questions to get them started. "T, I've seen you do some really stupid things in the past, but no one here has done stupid things like I have, so whatever this is, I'm in. Did you really kill someone this time? Is there a corpse we can abuse? A body that needs burying? Are you in danger? Is someone after Clare?"

As Tommy looked around the room, his friends were all in agreement, they were there to help. Marshall, always wanting to cut to the chase, said "How about a 50 thousand foot level picture of the situation, T? We can get to the low level details once we know the highlights." And they all nodded in agreement.

"Okay. Do any of you not know Veronica Smith?"

"Mistress V? The Key to Your Wildest Dreams? I've run into her a time or two. I think we all have." And everyone agreed with Jackson that she was a known entity. And not a well respected one, at that.

Tommy agreed and was ready to give his friends that 50 thousand foot level analysis of his dire situation. "Yes, that's her. I had some history with her when I was younger, and I actually moved here to get away from her in Atlanta, but it seems she's always wanted what she couldn't have. She came to visit me in the hospital after the accident, and had a run-in with Clare. She left me her business card that day, and Clare thought I threw it out, but I pulled it back out of the trash behind her back and kept it. For reasons you'll all find out eventually." As he looked around the room, he could see heads shaking and pained expressions on their faces, as if the group at large was saying "You freaking dumbass!" But no one said anything out loud so Tommy continued.

"Yes, my grand plan dissolved around me yesterday when Clare accidentally found the card and went ballistic. I thought I had smoothed things over with Clare, but I needed closure with Veronica so I went to see her today, and things got way out of hand."

A chorus of "Noooooo!" and "You idiot!" assailed him, and they weren't stopping so he held up a hand to silence them. Once he had finished his very quick story, they could pile on all they wanted.

"I know. It gets much worse. Once I was inside the house, she drugged me and chained me to a wall in her home dungeon and... Did things. Apparently, a lot of things, although I don't remember everything, which is probably just as well. After a few hours, the drugs wore off and I booked ass out of there, and I swore I would never see her again. And I called Des, because there are some side issues that she can help me address later. The big problem right now is that Veronica recorded everything and photographed me. She sent me a still photo that Des says rocks, because she's an insensitive clod. I could deal with that. But Veronica sent Clare a video clip earlier this evening starring Mistress V and me and a butt plug, and Clare has left me because she thinks I crave submission to V. And I'm afraid V will go after Clare just to punish me for staying away from her for so long.

She thinks she has blackmail material that will keep me with her, and she's demanding to see me again on Friday. The woman is totally deranged, and right now, I'm quite afraid of her." His last few words were almost a whisper, and he shuddered as he took his seat again.

Tommy wiped the tears from his face and waited for his friends' comments. Will was the first to speak, and his assessment was spot on. "T, you probably should call the police in, but date rape drugs usually don't last long in a victim's system, and you're probably never going to get your hands on the whole video. If Veronica were to let the police see selected parts of the video, it would probably support her claim that your affair was ongoing and consensual so not much real help there. So we take matters into our own hands. Once we actually get some kind of evidence, we'll bring the police in, but for right now, I think Clare is our biggest concern. Do you think Veronica would actually hurt Clare? Regardless, we need to get eyes on Clare and keep her safe. Do you know where she went when she left the house?"

"I tracked her phone to the Benedict in Old Town, I assume she's there with the phone. And just so you all know, Des got a blood sample and a urine specimen just a little while ago, and sent them with Secret Agent Lab Tech, to see if there's anything I can use to prove my claim. We'll just have to wait now."

"Have you actually talked to Clare? Does she know the whole story?"

"No, I haven't tried to call her. She sent me one text with the video clip and told me she was leaving. She says she left her wedding ring and her collar behind. Des thought it would be best for me to leave her alone for the night. If she thinks I'm following her, she might really run, and she might delete my tracking app from her phone so I can't find her again. I can't protect her if she's in the wind."

"Okay, I know a guy. He can be very discreet when I pay him enough. He'll get eyes on her tomorrow and protect her from a distance for as long as she's in danger. Now about those texts. We need to see them."

Tommy groaned but he had already resigned himself to the fact that his friends would have to see the photo Mistress V had sent him, and the video she had sent Clare. He handed his phone over to Will and walked to the window so he wouldn't have to watch his friends view his latest humiliation. Since Des had already seen everything, she joined Tommy at the window and they talked quietly while they waited for the group to view the photo and video, and start to come up with more next steps.

"Tommy, you don't want to wait too long to see Clare, so I'm going to suggest that maybe she'll talk to me more readily than she will talk to you. You and I can go to the hotel in the morning, and I'll text her from there, ask to see her, and lay the foundation for the two of you to see each other again. You need to be very honest with her about everything. Your feelings for V, your newfound curiosity about submission, V's latest demands. Most important, she needs to know how much you still love her, how sorry you are that all this has happened. Answer any questions she has as honestly as you can. Once we get the two of you back together, we'll proceed with a plan to retrieve all the photographic evidence we can find, maybe even catch V in the act. Okay?"

"Yes, Mistress Des." And he leaned down and kissed her cheek. And then he had to deal with the sarcasm that was raging behind him.

"Dude, Des IS an insensitive clod, but in this case she's so correct. You ROCK this photo. The video, on the other hand, makes me shudder to watch. I did one butt plug, one time, when I was in Dom training, and I swore never again. I think I cried! Portia loves her some butt plug but not me!"

Jackson punched his friend on the arm and said, "Marshall, if that's all you have to offer at this time, just shut up. Now, T, do you even remember this happening? You look and sound really dazed. You think she gave you some kind of Rohypnol drug? In your tea? You drank tea, dude? And is that a hash pot off to the side? How long were you breathing that shit in? And how was V not falling down with that much smoke in the air? She must have built up some serious tolerance over the years. That is one seriously demented chick. But I have to say, she has certainly kept herself in shape. Those legs go on for fucking miles!"

Des felt the need to bring the discussion back around and said, "Jackson, you're drooling! Maybe you should have T set you up with her some time, take some of the pressure off him. In the meantime, Tommy and I have come up with a plan to get him in the same room with Clare for a frank discussion, and we'll see how things go from there. Rodney, you've been awfully quiet. You have the most logical brain of anyone in the room, and I think you're putting puzzle pieces together in your head. Tell us what you're thinking."

"I keep seeing myself and Bella in this same situation and I'm not sure what I would do if I thought I was losing her. Thomas is showing extreme restraint, not going back to V's house and just killing her. Although maybe his recent brush with the law has changed his thinking on homicide. All that being said, there has to be a reason why she stayed away for so many years, and then reappeared now. It almost feels like she's tying up loose ends. She looks so thin in this video, and Jackson did mention the tolerance she seems to have built up to recreational drugs. Did she act like she was in pain at all? Did she seem physically sick?"

"I only have clear memory of walking into the house around Noon, and then running screaming for the door hours later. When she came to see me at the hospital a few months ago, she seemed a little thinner than I remembered, but she didn't seem to be in pain or anything then."

"Bella is going to own me after this. I just disciplined her severely for spending time in places on the internet that she shouldn't be and now I'm going to have to go home and actually ask her to do a little sleuthing for me. If there's anything about Veronica or her alter ego Mistress V anywhere on the internet, Bella can find it. This can't leave this room, but my wife just finished up a contract working with the feds on an internet bank hacking ring that netted multiple high-level arrests. She got a big bonus and orders not to talk about it. So don't talk about it! But be ready for a big pool party in about six months!! Anyway, those are my thoughts about T's situation right now."

Will stepped back into the conversation, clearly taking charge. "Okay, here's how I think we should proceed."

The conversation that evening went quite late, but they had a plan they hoped just might work. If it didn't work, they could lose Tommy, but it was a risk he was willing to take. The cornerstone of the plan was the text he sent Mistress V before the group broke up for the night.

> You want to see me. I want to see you. Friday. Noon. Your place.

> I'll be here, pet. Perhaps I can talk you into staying this time?

The plan for Friday was all set, but Thursday's plan was still unsettled. It all depended on how persuasive Des might be, and if she could talk Clare into seeing Tommy. Des and Tommy met at the hotel at 8:30 Thursday morning, hoping to catch Clare still in her room. When Room Service confirmed they had just delivered breakfast to her, Des sent her a text.

Thirty minutes later, Clare had cried and yelled and cursed Tommy's name and got all of the venom out of her system. Des had somehow talked her into seeing Tommy, listening to what he had to say, and then she could decide how she wanted to go forward.

Des texted Tommy to come to the room, and in the few minutes it took him to get there, Clare changed her mind about seeing him multiple times. In the end, she answered the knock on her door and she let him in.

"Clare, I'm so sorry this has happened. I know I should have talked to you about this long before now, I'm just a stupid man and I thought I could handle it. Baby, there's so much going on in my head, and in my heart, right now, I'm not sure where to start. Will you let me just ramble for a few minutes and see if I can make sense of any of this?"

"Des told me just a little about what happened yesterday, about the drugs and these new feelings you're having. Just tell me why you went to see her to begin with. If you hadn't gone there, we wouldn't be here right now." And she stroked the place on her neck where her collar used to be, as a solitary tear ran down her cheek.

"Clare, I really am just a stupid man. That day V came to see me in the hospital, she brought out feelings in me, and questions, that I wasn't sure what to do with. I'm still not sure what to do with it. But Des says she can help me figure things out. But I can't go forward without you by my side. Our relationship might change, we might end up on more equal footing than we have been, I just don't know. I do know that I love you with all my heart and nothing V did yesterday, or might do in the future, can ever change that. I went to see her yesterday to get closure. I just wanted to put her behind us, out of our lives forever. But I got caught in her web. Sending me a photo of myself that I don't remember her taking, sending you that video that I don't remember participating in, that's her way of drawing a line in the sand.

"Clare, can you ever forgive me? Is there any way we can put this behind us and move forward together somehow? I'll do whatever I have to do to put Mistress V in the past, but you're my future. I have to know that at the end of the day, you'll be with me."

"You really are one sorry son of a bitch, Master. You've hurt me so much with all of this crap, but then you've done that before. And I keep coming back for more. I'll give you one last chance. If you hurt me again, I won't walk away, I'll just shoot your ass. Is that clear?"

"Yes, baby, it's crystal clear. No more secrets ever again. I know you're a good shot and if someone else comes after me in the future, I'll just stand behind you and let you handle it. Fair enough?"

"Yes. Fair enough." And she closed the gap between them and fell into his open arms. A few minutes later, Des cleared her throat to get their attention.

"Okay, lovebirds. Here's the deal. Master Will has some friends in seriously low places. One of them is going to keep eyes on you, Clare, and keep you safe until this is all over. He brought you room service this morning so he knows what you look like and you know what he looks like. Stay in your room if you can, but if you need to go out, he'll pick you up in the lobby and follow you discreetly until you're back in your room again. There's no negotiation on this, okay?"

"Okay, Mistress D. So while I'm trapped in my hotel room for the duration, what is this fool going to be doing? I have a feeling it's more stupid shit. Just tell me so I don't have to imagine the worst."

"Baby, I love you so much, and I'm so grateful for this one last chance, but you won't like what I have to tell you. Des says I have to be honest and answer all of your questions so here it is. Mistress V wants to see her boy toy again. Tomorrow. I'm going to go, and I have to expect that she'll do the same thing she did yesterday. I won't be able to wear a wire and I won't be able to defend myself for long."

"No, Master, absolutely not, I won't allow it! You can't put yourself in harm's way with that woman again. I might never get you back! Just call the police and let them handle her."

"No, baby, we can't bring the police in, we have no evidence – yet."

At this point, Des stepped back into the conversation. "Clare, before you panic too much, another one of Will's incredibly low friends who seems to be adept at B&E is working to get a few bugs into her house while she's out today. We figure we have the morning to get that done, because Bella found an appointment on her calendar that will take most of the morning. If we're lucky, we'll have our own video and audio feeds so we can keep track of the boy toy and not let him get in too deep."

"Tommy, baby, this is so dangerous. Please be as careful as you can, and let your friends protect you as much as possible."

"Not to worry, baby. I may be the official boy toy, but I won't be alone. Will's running the op, and I've seen him in action. He's awesome at stuff like this. They'll all be on the grounds and maybe even inside the house, monitoring the situation and getting as much evidence as we can for the police. Once we have that, the police can handle the rest. And if she does what she did yesterday, I'll probably be asleep for most of it. She won't really hurt me, not if she expects me to stay for any length of time with her. She thinks she can blackmail me with this, but she doesn't know who she's dealing with. I'm a different man this time, and I have a much better team at my back."

Des heard her cell phone ping as she watched Tommy and Clare embrace and kiss, and she smiled up at them when she read it. "The game is on, kids. Bugs are in place and tested. We're a go for tomorrow."

"Please stay with me, Master. If I can't leave the hotel for awhile, I need you here with me, at least for awhile."

"I'll stay for as long as I can, baby, but we have a meeting at Will's condo this evening to go over the physical layout and the plan. Rodney said he thinks Bella is close to cracking V's system security, so we may have a complete copy of the video from yesterday, and I can finally see what she really did. It will help to know what to expect from her tomorrow. Des, just text me when it's time to meet at Will's place, and I'll be there."

Des left the room, and Tommy and Clare fell on the bed together, lost in the moment. They didn't know if at the end of this road, they would still be Master and submissive, but they would still be husband and wife, partners for life.

"Okay, listen up boys. And Des. We've been through the plan three times, everyone knows where they're going to be and what they're supposed to do. But be on your toes. Ops like this seldom go as planned and we won't all be armed. There could be lots of variables, including other people in the house. T, you said you don't think there was anyone else there, but you don't know for sure so just be prepared for the unexpected. Just let her do her thing, and don't be surprised if she changes things up a little this time. Go with the flow, man. Know that we've got your back and we won't let her hurt you too bad. Like you said, you'll probably sleep through the whole thing anyway."

"Will, I know you're trying to lighten the mood and I appreciate that, but you guys are all risking a lot for me and Clare, and we won't ever be able to repay you. If anything goes wrong, and I don't come out of this in one piece, take care of Clare for me."

"That goes without saying, brother, rest easy on that. Now everybody hit the road. Get some sleep tonight, we'll meet up at the carpool lot near her house at 11:00. Park in the back of the lot where we can't be seen from the road. Rodney, tell Bella to get some sleep as well. Whatever she has right now is fine, she can get back to it again after V leaves for her appointment in the morning. I'll have someone watching her place to make sure she actually leaves, then we'll start monitoring our bugs while Bella digs deeper. See you all tomorrow."

"Okay, I talked to my guy just a little while ago. He knows we're hiding in this carpool lot, and he's parked a mile down the road in the other direction. He says V left her house at 8:00 a.m. and according to her schedule, she had some diagnostic test scheduled from 8:45 to 10:00 and then a followup appointment with her doctor. She has her calendar blocked from Noon on, so she's planning a party. Snoop says it doesn't look like there's anyone in or around the house. He checked the bugs and said there's no noise inside except the fridge and the A/C. Hold up, he just sent me a text. V just drove up the lane, he's got eyes on her walking into the house and she's alone. Our video is picking her up nice and clear, and it will as long as she stays in the tea room, the kitchen or the dungeon. He placed a few extra audio bugs in other rooms, just in case she takes her guest on a tour, but we'll know either way. Des, are you sure you want to be in on this? Maybe hang back for plausible deniability? So you can bail everyone out if this goes south?"

"No way you're going to leave me out of this. I spent more time in the military than half you macho bozos, and I never get to have this much fun anymore. I'm armed and I'm in."

"Okay. Recording is up and running, time to go. T, relax and be the submissive little boy toy she craves. We'll be right behind you, buddy, no worries."

Tommy got into the Mustang and headed up the drive while the rest of the team hung back. They would give him time to get into the house, and then they would be right behind him. Comms were checked one final time, everything seemed to be working as it should. It was show time!

Chapter 20

Tommy didn't think he'd ever been so nervous, so afraid, as he was now, sitting in his car in Mistress V's driveway. Not even in all the years he'd spent in the Marines, saving men's lives on the battlefield, had he felt so alone. He had no comm device to hear or communicate with his team, and he felt abandoned, even though he knew that wasn't true. He had a fleeting thought that, if he never got out of his car, nothing bad would happen to him, but that wasn't possible. His team was about to come up the lane. He had to get himself and Mistress V into the house, and he needed to do it now.

Just as before, as soon as he stepped into the screen porch, Mistress V came out to greet him. He looked closer at her this time, and he noticed little lines around her mouth and around her eyes, hints that she wasn't as well as she let on. There was no bun or decoration in her long hair today, she had pulled it into a low ponytail at her neck, as if she'd rushed to get ready for him. But the tug on his senses was still there, maybe stronger than it had been two days before. And he wondered why.

"Thomas, my pet, you're back. I knew you'd come, you've seen the light, haven't you? You know that I am your heart's desire, the woman you were destined to serve."

"How are you, Mistress? You look lovely today. Red is a good color for you, and the boots are spectacular. Mistress, I think we have some things to talk about. I have some questions."

"You would question your Mistress, pet? Isn't that a little presumptuous of you? Shouldn't you know that my way is always the best way for both of us?"

"You're asking a lot of me, Mistress. I have to admit that our time together on Wednesday stirred new feelings, new desires, ones I would never have considered before, if you hadn't taken matters into your own hands. But you seem to want a long-term relationship that is completely foreign to me. There would have to be a period of adjustment for me, wouldn't you agree? A transition from Dominant to submissive would require a substantial mind shift. Yes?"

"Very well, pet, I see your point. I'll answer a few questions before we begin. Shall we go inside? I have tea ready."

He took her offered hand, just like the last time, and as soon as he was in close proximity to her, his mind began to cloud, pulled down by the swirling effects of her perfume. The familiar scent of patchouli and hashish reached out to coax him inside, and when she closed the door behind him, he had the briefest tingle of anxiety, as if no matter what happened in this house, he would be changed forever. But his job today was to just let things happen as they were meant to happen, to be the live bait, so that his team could gather the evidence they needed. So he smiled at Mistress V and let her lead him back into the tea room, where he would inhale hashish smoke and drink drugged tea, and let her take control.

Back in the commuter lot, Tommy's 'team' were anxious to get moving so they could be close if Tommy needed them.

Will touched base again with his guy on camera detail. "Snoop, can we move in? What do you see? Are they on camera yet?"

"They just went inside, Will. Don't get impatient on me! You have to hold back until they get into the dungeon or you might be seen or heard. I have clear video, cams are rolling. He's okay. I'll let you know when you can move."

"Roger, we don't have video, but I just picked them up on audio. We'll hold here."

As they waited for the go sign, Will remembered the fear on his friend's face as he drove out of the parking lot and up the lane. And he remembered why he had always admired Tommy so much. Action in spite of fear. Always. Tommy knew he would come out of this a changed man, but he was doing it anyway. For himself and for the woman he truly loved. And now the team would wait while Tommy started the information gathering process.

When Tommy and Mistress V entered the little windowless tea room, the table was set as it had been before, tea cups and teapot ready. The earthy scent of patchouli and hashish was still the same. But something was different this time. He turned his head slightly to a new display light that hadn't been there before, and a new photograph that he'd only seen in a text. Mistress V had worked quickly. Other artwork had been removed from that wall, and only two large framed photographs remained, attention drawn to them by the light. He walked to the wall so that he could view the photographs side by side, and felt a rush of sadness he didn't understand.

The first photograph was the one he had seen during his original visit, the one Mistress had taken in their early time together. A younger Thomas, in a kneeling submissive pose, naked, restrained, erect. A striking example of the male form at the peak of his manhood. The other photograph was an older Thomas, also naked and restrained, also erect, still a striking example of the male form, but this Thomas was standing, the scar from his recent leg surgery clearly visible. This Thomas seemed to be declaring that life and time had not beaten him down, but his eyes seemed to reflect the sadness of a lifetime lived alone.

Mistress V came to stand by him, a hand on his arm, watching him as he looked at himself on the wall. "What do you think of my little art gallery, pet? Aren't the photos stunning? I love the juxtaposition of the subjects – younger vs more mature. So much to read in each face."

"You have quite an eye, Mistress, you've captured these two men well."

"Thank you for that, pet. A serious photographer appreciates the approval of her subject and her audience. Now come and sit, have some tea and we'll chat."

And she took his arm and guided him to the same chair, where he could admire the photographs while they talked.

Once they were both seated, Mistress V got right to the point. "So you have questions for me, pet?"

"Just one right now, Mistress. Why did you wait so long to come for me? It's been years since we saw each other last, and then all of a sudden, there you were in the hospital, visiting after my accident. You told Clare that you had hoped we would find each other again, but I don't recall that you ever reached out to me. Maybe it's the combination of your tempting perfume and the hashish affecting my thinking, but I have to wonder if you're planning on tying up a loose end here. Is this a last hurrah? Are you going to kill me today?"

Her eyes clouded for just a moment, and then she answered, "That's more than one question, pet, but I understand what's troubling you. I always thought we had all the time in the world to reconnect. Then I discovered the critical nature of your injuries and I realized time wasn't going to wait forever. Here, sweet pet, have some tea, I made it just like you like it. To answer all of your other questions, of course I'm not going to kill you. Why on earth would you think that? I'm hoping we have a long, happy life together, pet, just you and me, right here in my favorite house. We'll burn our hashish, and drink our tea, and play together in our dungeon. It will be great fun, yes?"

"Yes, Mistress V, that sounds like fun."

"Very good, pet. Now drink up and we'll talk about what games we want to play today. Are you feeling all right, love? Shall I help you with your tea?"

"I'm feeling a little fuzzy, Mistress, a little help with my tea would be very nice."

So Mistress V helped him drink his tea and Tommy let his muddled mind roam elsewhere. He entered that dream-like state where there was no fear, and he barely realized that Mistress had helped him remove his tee shirt. She didn't try to hide the fact that she was attaching cuffs to his wrists, and he barely acknowledged that she had linked the cuffs together with his hands behind his back.

He simply smiled as she straddled his lap and kissed each cheek sweetly, before taking his lips and invading his mouth with a passionate kiss. Her soft caresses of his shoulders and arms, her gentle play at his nipples, and the ever-present draw of her perfume on his senses, led him further down his dream path.

She offered him another cup of tea, which he allowed her to feed him, and the real world floated farther away. Her perfume was intoxicating, the hashish was soothing, and Mistress V's touch was mesmerizing as the drugged tea did its work. In his dream, no one else existed but the two of them – and the massive erection he could feel behind his zipper.

Mistress helped her pet to stand, and after caressing his upper body and licking her fill of his puckered nipples, delighting in the sounds of his little whimpers, she let her hands wander down to grasp that erection through its denim prison, eliciting a long, low groan from deep in his throat.

Anxious to get her pet into the dungeon, but not wanting to disturb the calm moment they were sharing, she continued to stroke his cock lightly over his jeans and whispered in his ear, "You must be so uncomfortable in these incredibly tight pants, pet. Shall I help you free yourself from your discomfort? I'm so looking forward to our time together in our special room. Shall I prepare you for our afternoon of play?"

"Yes, Mistress, that would be lovely."

After placing a light kiss on his lips, she helped him out of his shoes and jeans and boxer briefs. They both smiled as he sighed at the relief of his cock being liberated once again. Once he was free of his clothes, Mistress decorated him again, with his ankle cuffs, his collar and leash, and the silver chain that attached his collar to his wrist cuffs.

She smiled and waved again to the camera in the tea room as they walked out, not noticing that this time, she was waving to more than one camera. Mistress led her prized pet by his leash, through the kitchen, and into the dungeon where they had played before. She closed and locked the dungeon door, and the world outside disappeared for both of them.

Once the dungeon door closed, Snoop gave the go sign and the rest of the team moved from the parking lot to the top of the lane, in two separate cars. Will was in his Jeep with Des, Jackson had Marshall and Rodney in his SUV. They parked as quietly and as invisibly as they could, ducking behind bushes growing here and there in the large yard, then checked their equipment again, noting the time Tommy actually entered the house, and then the dungeon.

Will made contact with his bug expert, hidden away in the brush, having parked his own car about a half mile down the road in the opposite direction. "Snoop, can you slip inside and get a sample of that tea? I want to know everything that's in it. T seemed to slip out of touch really fast so she may have boosted the dose to speed up the process."

"Already on my way in, boss, I'll be back outside with the sample in two minutes."

"Copy that."

·❤·❤·❤·❤·❤·

"Do you remember this room, sweet boy? We played here just the other day. Did you enjoy that?"

"I don't recall, Mistress V. Did I enjoy it?"

"Oh, pet, you had a wonderful time. I'm hoping that someday soon we'll be able to play in here all day and your mind won't be so fuzzy, and you'll remember what fun we have."

"Yes, Mistress, if that will make you happy."

"I do love you, pet, you make me so happy. Someday very soon you'll realize that, and you'll see that you love me too. Shall we play now?"

"Yes, Mistress V."

Almost giddy with her success getting her pet into the dungeon so easily, her mind raced with all the things they could do together. She decided she would dress him up first, and then get him tethered, and then they could play for hours. She would just need to keep an eye on him and start the hash burner if he started to slip out of his lovely buzz. She wasn't prepared for the eventual confrontation just yet, there would be time for that later.

"Stand right here, pet, I'm going to get some things from the closet and the cabinet for our playtime."

"Yes, Mistress."

She got his custom-made chaps out of the closet, and another anal plug and some lube out of the cabinet, just to get them started. When she returned, Tommy was standing right where she had left him, and she rewarded his obedience with a deep kiss and a strong grasp on his naked erect cock. As always, he responded to her grip with a sultry moan, which made her smile. She had him move his feet a little apart and got him dressed in his chaps, specially selected because they left his ass, his cock, and his testicles fully exposed for her attention. They were also designed for easy dressing of a submissive who was already, or was about to be, restrained. Two snaps around his waist, and a few buckles down each leg and he was dressed for play. She walked him to the mirror wall to show him how virile and manly he looked. A nearly naked vision in supple black leather, so stunning it made her wet just looking at him.

"What do you think, pet? Don't you look spectacular in your chaps? With these, I can caress your shapely ass, and I can do anything I want with your beautiful cock and those heavy, bouncy balls. Oh, we're going to have so much fun, aren't we, pet?"

"Yes, Mistress."

His huge erection, so close and so exposed, was too much to resist, so she reached down and grasped him tightly and stroked him until he panted for her, watching their reflection in the mirror.

"That feels so good, doesn't it, my pet? Mistress knows how to take care of her pet, doesn't she? You love when Mistress plays with your big cock, don't you?" And she gave him another tight squeeze to prove her point.

On the edge between pain and pleasure, he gasped, "Yes, Mistress."

"I'm back out of the house, boss. Sample is secure, and everything is recording perfectly. The hash is really strong inside that little room, I don't know how they're not both coughing up a lung from the smoke. How long are we going to let her go on before we go back in and get him out of there? Surely we have enough video to hang her by now."

"I picked up on her comment that someday soon they could play together without his mind being so fuzzy, but I want just a little more self-incrimination before I pull the plug, so to speak. T is totally out of it and he doesn't seem to be stressed, so I think we're good for a little longer."

"Copy that."

·❤·❤·♥·❤·❤·

Mistress V seemed to lose herself in a memory as she stared at Tommy in the mirror, but that old memory faded, replaced by a new one. She had expertly captured the Thomas of today in the photograph taken two days before, the Thomas she intended to keep one way or another. If it was up to her, and it was, her pet would never return to his old life. Whatever arguments he might have for not staying, she would counter. She had to have him. He might not have the stamina his younger self had, but his body was more well defined now and his eyes had taken on a maturity she didn't often see these days. Like he knew exactly what to do when he was with a woman. She couldn't wait to have him in this room without the drugs, and see firsthand what he could do for her when he was in his right mind. She just had to hope she hadn't waited too long. Taking a chance, she unclipped his wrist cuffs, letting his arms drop to his sides.

"Come, pet, let's go to the barre and get a little more dressed up. Would you like that?"

"Yes, Mistress, if it will please you."

"Oh, sweet boy, it will please us both. Just you wait and see. Now stand right over here and bend at your waist. Grip the barre with both hands, like a good boy." And he did as he was told.

"Like this, Mistress?" And he smiled up at her as she tethered his wrist cuffs to the ring on the barre. A genuine smile that brought tears to her tired eyes.

"Yes, just like that, pet. Now stay very still for me. You enjoy wearing an anal plug but sometimes you feel discomfort getting it inserted. So I'm going to burn a little more hashish, it will relax you and make you more comfortable. Okay?"

"Yes, Mistress."

She made quick work of lighting the hash burner and satisfied herself that it was having the desired effect on her pet. As she lubed her fingers and inserted them, one at a time, into his anus, he whimpered and squirmed, and without warning, he moved his feet to stand up. She pushed him back down and reached between his legs to pull his testicles toward her behind him, just far enough to give him a touch of pain and get his attention.

"I'll have none of that, naughty boy. Do that again and you'll find yourself in a humbler and we'll have a completely different kind of play that you won't like one little bit. You just stand still and let me do what I want to do and then we'll have some fun."

"Yes, Mistress. I'm sorry Mistress. I'll try not to act up again, Mistress."

"That's my good, obedient boy. Now I've made more than enough room for this big anal plug in your sweet behind, so this should take no time at all. Be absolutely still while I work it in." She brought the tip of the lubed plug between his butt cheeks and started to ease the plug in, pushing in, pulling out, pushing in again, gaining ground with each press forward. Despite his whimpers, he remained perfectly still and the plug seated itself quickly. "There we go, pet. All done. Mistress is so proud of you. That doesn't hurt at all, does it? It looks so manly peeking out between your cheeks. You make Mistress so very happy, pet. Stand here just like this for me, I'll be right back." She patted his ass over the plug a few times, and kissed each butt cheek for good measure, and then walked away as he responded to her command.

"Yes, Mistress. I'll try not to move, Mistress."

She went back to the cabinet and brought out the blindfold and the crop, but just couldn't resist picking up her camera as well. She zoomed in on her pet, capturing his restrained position and the pink flared end of the seated plug on display between his cheeks. She giggled as she walked back to where he stood so patiently, thinking that was another photograph that might end up on her new submissive Thomas art wall. He balked when she slipped the blindfold over his eyes, but a few whacks of the crop across his ass settled him. A quick caress of his ass and a gentle jiggle of the plug settled him almost as much as the hash smoke, so she spent a few minutes alternating between hard slaps and soft caresses and easy jiggling of the plug, keeping him slightly off kilter.

"You're doing so very well, sweet boy. Have you had enough of a spanking to behave while we change things up a little?"

"Oh, yes, Mistress. Quite enough, Mistress."

"Good. I know it will be a little awkward with the blindfold on, but you'll be fine. I'm going to stand you up and you have to keep that plug in or I'll be horribly disappointed. Keep gripping the barre, pet. You'll have to move your feet forward toward the wall as you stand, okay? Then I'll give you a seat so that your wrists and shoulders and your leg have a little rest. Come along, pet. That's it, just like that. That's perfect. Now let me unclip your wrist cuffs and you can turn your back to the wall. Very good, just like that, pet. Okay so far?"

"Yes, Mistress."

"Okay, now sit down on this padded stool, yes, just like that. Sitting on that plug gives you a little extra sensation, doesn't it? Are you okay so far?"

"Yes, Mistress. It feels tingly but it's okay."

"Very nice, pet. Now lift your arms out to the sides and rest them on the barre for me. Grip the barre with your hands while I adjust the restraints." With practiced ease, she quickly attached his collar to one ring on the barre, and then clipped each wrist cuff to its own ring. Satisfied that she had him adequately secured, she went back to the cabinet one more time and got a condom and two more chains. She paused to push the hash burner away, and then removed the blindfold so that he could see her, and she could see how dilated his eyes might still be. "Is that more comfortable, pet? I know you love being restrained like this, don't you?"

"Yes, Mistress."

"Very good, pet. I want you to spread your feet a little wider and open your knees for me, just like this." And again, she made quick work of securing the chains to his ankle cuffs and then to the lower barre on the wall. "Can you smile for me, pet? You look so regal like this, the obedient prince of my castle. I want to take your picture." And he smiled blankly at the camera until he heard the click of the shutter.

She knelt down beside him to whisper in his ear, "Pet, I'm going to stroke your mighty cock and get it all ready for me. Once you're like steel, I'm going to put a condom on you and then we're going to fuck each other blind, just like we did the other day. Can we do that, pet?"

"Yes, Mistress."

And she took him in hand, and stroked him until he was long and thick and ready for action. And then she pulled the condom down on him, admiring his length and his girth. Her stiletto boots made it easy to straddle his lap on the stool, and after opening the crotch of her tight red catsuit, she sank down on his raging erection, riding him until they both came explosively. Until they could both barely move.

While she sat on his lap, with his cock still inside her, she grasped his face gently with both hands and looked deep into his eyes, looking for any sign of recognition, but there was none yet. "Are you in there somewhere, my love?"

"Yes, Mistress."

She laid her head on his shoulder and started to ramble, tears running down her cheeks, knowing he wouldn't remember anything she said or did. Such a sad, depressing thought, it steeled her resolve to carry out her final plan, just a little ahead of schedule.

"I have something to tell you, pet. I've been sick for some time, and the doctor says I don't have much longer to live. He has described how the end will go and I don't want that for myself. So I'm choosing the time and place, and who goes with me when I go."

Mistress climbed off his lap and went back to the cabinet one last time. She dissolved a large packet of white powder in a large glass of water and took six large capsules from a prescription bottle. She brought the pills and the glass of water back to his side, looking down at him and smiling, knowing they would soon be together forever in a place where there wasn't any more pain. She sat down on his lap again, cradling his semi erection against her core, and looked longingly at him.

"Open your mouth, pet, nice and wide. Take these big pills for Mistress and I'll give you a drink of water to help them down. There you go, take a big drink, love. Yes, just a little more. Perfect. I see that bad face you're making, pet! It doesn't taste so bad, does it? Such an obedient boy, right to the end. Now I'll take my pills, and I'll drink my water down. See? Just like that. All done. And now we'll just sit here and rest until the end. Okay, my sweet pet?"

"Yes, Mistress, whatever you say."

She placed the empty glass on the floor next to them, and then rested her head against his shoulder, letting her hands roam across his arms and chest, tears of joy and sorrow running down her cheeks. The end would come quickly for both of them, she'd made sure of that, and they would be found, eventually, with her sweet pet wrapped in her loving embrace.

"Will, what the fuck did she just say? What was that about pills? What did she give him? Somebody call 9-1-1!!! Drug overdose!! Oh my God! Oh my God! I'm going in!"

"Jackson, wait up! Snoop says she locked the dungeon door and it will take a few of us together to break it down! Fuck, man, this is all my fault! I left him in there too long!"

"No, Will, we all left him in there too long. We're all to blame."

And they all ran for the house like their lives depended on it. Because Tommy's life did depend on it. He was their responsibility and they had failed to keep him safe. But he still had a chance if they could get to him in time, and if the paramedics got there in time, and if all the fucking stars aligned perfectly. If all that happened, they might still save him.

Chapter 21

Marshall, Will and Jackson were hammering on the dungeon door, throwing everything they could find at it, and it wasn't budging. Until Des walked in with her big-ass 9mm and blasted away the lock – and half the door frame. Rodney had gone back down the lane to direct the paramedics up to the house, but help was still three or four minutes out and Tommy's friends weren't sure what to do.

Snoop ran around the house and gathered up all his bugs and video gear, but left what Veronica already had set up in the house. As he threw Tommy's clothes into the dungeon, he saw Des on the floor trying to revive Mistress V, doing chest compressions to supplement her weak, shallow breathing.

Marshall went to the cabinet and saw the empty packet next to the prescription bottle, but resisted the urge to grab them both, because his fingerprints would taint their evidence of attempted murder. They needed Veronica's fingerprints to be the only ones found on the bottle and the packet, especially if this turned out to be a murder-suicide. Will and Jackson had managed to get Tommy untethered from the barres, and onto his side on the floor, but they had no idea how to make him throw up the pills and the water his Mistress had coaxed down his throat.

They had just gotten instructions off the internet on inducing vomiting, when Rodney burst through the dungeon door with two paramedics hot on his heels.

"Oh, thank God you're here. She gave him something and then took some of it herself, and we have no idea what it was, and we don't know if we should induce vomiting or what!"

"Jackson, stop rambling, I think I found it. It's right here in this cabinet where she left the remains, this has to be it. Do you guys recognize this stuff? I can't begin to pronounce it, it's like 17 letters long." One of the paramedics took the pill bottle and the empty packet and secured them both in a large plastic evidence bag, assuring Marshall they would call it in as soon as they got back into the ambulance.

"Marshall, you're rambling as bad as Jackson! We need to get these two to the hospital likity-split. Pack 'em up and move 'em out!!" At least Will wasn't rambling like the other two!

Rodney was just helping Des up off the floor so that the paramedics could tend to both victims when a second rescue unit arrived. Tommy and Veronica were hustled out the door, into two ambulances, with Des riding in Tommy's unit. The last thing Jackson heard from inside Tommy's ambulance was "gastric lavage" and he knew both victims were about to have a really bad day.

Then he realized they were all about to have a really bad day when a local police car and a highway patrol vehicle passed the rescue vehicles coming up the lane. Snoop was long gone, along with their electronic evidence and the spiked tea sample, leaving Jackson, Will, Rodney and Marshall to do damage control with the authorities.

Two hours later Jackson and his friends walked into the Emergency Room, followed by a local police officer. Luckily, after observing the scene, aka the dungeon, the Highway Patrol officer didn't think he needed to take charge of the scene, that mess would be best handled by the local authorities. Between the hashish pots and the suspected drugs in the teapot, along with the alternative lifestyle equipment in the dungeon, low man on the totem pole won jurisdiction. The local police would be spending hours on scene, photographing and cataloging everything, and trying to figure out what had really happened in the house. They preferred not to have the victim's four friends under foot, contaminating possible evidence, while they worked. The four men gave brief statements (ones they had rehearsed in advance) and Jackson assured the officer in charge that any of the four of them could be reached 24/7 for as long as necessary to answer any questions he might have, but they really needed to get to the hospital and see about their friend.

The fifteen minute ride to the hospital seemed to take an hour, but Des was waiting at the door for them when they arrived. She was the one to tell them that Veronica had coded shortly after arriving at the hospital, and attempts to revive her had been unsuccessful. Bella had determined through a little benign hacking that Mistress V had a brain tumor that was growing unchecked, and her doctor had just that morning given her the news that she only had a few weeks left to live. Her compromised system just couldn't handle the large dose of sedatives and chemo drugs, and she had passed away, by her own hand, just like she had planned.

Luckily she didn't take anyone with her when she died. Tommy had gotten his stomach pumped during the ride to the hospital, and Des couldn't wait to show everyone the video she captured of the procedure. She really was an insensitive clod, but she was a great friend, and she'd had Tommy's back all the way.

Clare had been sprung from her hotel as soon as the 9-1-1 call had been placed, thanks to a timely text from Will, and she had been waiting at the Emergency Room door when Tommy was brought in. Des had held her hand until Tommy was stable, and Clare couldn't stop hugging her for helping to save his life.

Tommy had been moved from the ER to ICU, just to keep a close watch on his vital signs for a few hours, and then late that evening, after he had regained consciousness, he was moved to a regular room. His doctor gave Clare 24-hour access to her husband for the duration of his hospital stay, but he only allowed Tommy's friends a few minutes each that night, to see him and reassure themselves that he had survived a very close call.

After they had all seen Tommy, and Clare was settled in his room for the night, his doctor took his friends into a closed waiting room down the hall from his room and locked the door to prevent accidental interruptions.

Once everyone was seated, with a cup of surprisingly good hospital coffee, the doctor spoke to the group.

"I have a feeling there's a lot to this story that will never make the nightly news, and that's okay, I don't need to know everything. But I have a few questions I have to ask. Like, where the hell was he? And who was he with? He came in here with a huge pink butt plug, wearing assless chaps and fuzzy cuffs, and he had ingested massive doses of a very strong sedative and an experimental chemo drug, along with a heavy dose of Rohypnol. And someone mentioned hashish somewhere along the way? I'm guessing he was playing somewhere, and things got terribly out of hand, but what the fuck?!? A woman is dead! And he almost died himself!"

"Doc, we could be here all night explaining everything that's happened in the last three days, but I don't think you want all the gory details right now. Maybe someday, with a lot of beer and a whole lot of time, he can tell you what he remembers. Or maybe he'll eventually gather his closest friends around him, and finally watch all of the video, and see for himself what really happened. What she did to him. He doesn't remember much right now, and he may never remember some of it, unless Des can get to those memories with a little hypnosis. But..."

"Jackson, I hope someday you'll all be able to put this nightmare behind you, but that certainly won't be tonight. You all look like death warmed over, and you need about twelve hours of sleep. So at least tell me the connection between T and the woman who came in with him. I can't imagine that any of this was his doing, but I don't know anything about her. Were the drugs hers? Was she trying to kill herself? Was she trying to kill him? Or was it all a terrible accident and not intentional?"

"Doc, we can't tell you everything until we've unburdened ourselves to the Chief of Police, but I can tell you a little. The woman's name is Veronica Smith and she knew T when he was living in Atlanta after he separated from the Marines. They had a... relationship of sorts. Fulfilling and yet not. And it didn't last long.

"He didn't see her again until a few months ago. She had heard about his accident, and came here to the hospital to see him. Veronica wanted him back, and she had a run-in with Clare in his room. Clare had nothing to do with any of this, by the way."

"No, I would be shocked if any of this was Clare's doing. Continue."

At this point, Will took over the conversation, afraid Jackson might say too much without thinking. "They exchanged a few texts in the past few weeks and he agreed to see her one more time, just a few minutes to get some closure. To say goodbye. She wasn't ready to let him go, so she drugged him with hashish and some Rohypnol derivative and took advantage of his inability to think clearly. In his highly suggestive state, she was able to talk him into doing things with her that he would never have done if he was in his right mind. And she captured it all on video and photos, no doubt for blackmail purposes. Luckily the drugs started to wear off prematurely and he was able to get away. That was on Wednesday,"

"This gets worse before it ends, doesn't it?"

"Yes, I'm afraid so. Veronica sent T a text on Wednesday evening with a little photographic evidence that he doesn't recall, telling him she needed more time with him. She also sent Clare a text with a little more photographic evidence that devastated her enough to leave him. The veiled threat to Clare was more than T could handle and he went to Des, asking for help. Then we all got involved. He went back to see Veronica again today and you've seen the unfortunate results."

"Is that why you were all so close by? Because of some ridiculous plan that you cooked up to catch her in the act? Because the police are so inept, they couldn't have handled the threat? My God, he almost died!!!"

This time Des felt the need to speak, wiping away tears as she did. "Doctor, no one knows more than we do how close we came to losing him. This is the second time in five months that someone has tried to take him from us, from Clare, and we are keenly aware that it would have been our fault if he had died. We reacted the only way we know how. And we will have that conversation with Chief Davis as soon as we can. And we will take whatever punishment the Justice System sees fit to lay on us."

As Des was about to continue, there was a knock on the locked door and a voice outside, calling the doctor to attend to another of his patients. He turned to the group on his way out the door and said "Go home. Get some sleep. You can see him in the morning. I'm sure he'll be in better physical shape by then. But be prepared for a few emotional issues. If his memory is as spotty as you say it is, and there's past history between them, there will be regret and doubt and more than a little self-loathing to deal with. Give him time."

And Des whispered, "I'll be there to help him all the way. We all will."

·♥·♥·♥·♥·♥·

Early the next morning, Tommy stirred in his hospital bed and Clare was immediately by his side. He pulled her into the bed with him, allowing her to straddle him and lay on his chest, mindful not to disturb the saline IV. They lay like that, quiet and still, listening to the steady, hypnotic beat of his heart monitor. They had an hour before his next scheduled nurse visit, so they occupied themselves, kissing, caressing, reconnecting. They had been through so much in the past few weeks, it was almost therapeutic to be here together, safe, knowing that it was – mostly – over.

"I don't remember anything between V's tea room yesterday and getting to this room last night. Is everyone okay? Did we get enough evidence to lock V up? And why am I back in a hospital bed? No one would tell me anything last night. Please, Clare, at least give me the bare minimum."

"I'm not sure what that entails, my love, and I'm not sure what you're strong enough to handle just now. I don't know much either. Maybe we should wait until Jackson or one of the others gets here, and Dr. Schneider can be here."

"Just tell me what you know, Clare, I may have slept through most of it yesterday, but I can take it. Please tell me what you know."

Just as she was about to spill her guts to her husband, Jackson walked through the door, followed by Will and Des. Clare attempted to climb down out of the bed, but Tommy held her where she was, not wanting to lose contact with her again.

"No one is telling me anything, Jackson. I'm sure I don't want every detail right now, but I need to know what happened yesterday and why I'm back in the hospital. Someone tell me something."

"Okay, buddy. Turns out, it was a crap plan. We didn't have all the intel we needed and we almost lost you. Good enough?"

"Not nearly!"

Tommy turned to Will, thinking he might get a little more information out of him than Jackson, and he was right. In all the years Tommy had known Will, he had never sugar coated anything, and he didn't start now.

"T, Jackson's right, it was a crap plan. We should have given Bella a little more time to gather intel for us. She did find a gold mine on V's server but not before you almost died.

I know you're going to say that V wasn't giving you more time, but we should have forced her hand and waited. If we had, you probably wouldn't be here right now."

"More details, Will. Like, what happened to V? Is she in jail? Did she run?"

Jackson, Will and Des just looked at each other, deciding who was going to tell him, so Clare took matters into her own hands. "She's dead, baby. She loaded you up with a deadly drug concoction, gave herself the same drug cocktail, minus your date rape drug, and waited for the two of you to die. She planned for the two of you to be found eventually, locked in her dungeon, with you wrapped in her deadly embrace. She didn't make it, but you did. Luckily you have the constitution of an alpha male buffalo and somehow you survived long enough for your friends to get to you."

"No suicide note? No explanation?"

Des stepped up and put her psychoanalyst hat on. "Tommy, are you really sure you're ready for any of this? I don't think it's good to pile too much on, too soon. There's plenty of time to get into it later when you're stronger."

"When she first took me into the tea room, before I got too fuzzy to think, I asked her why she had waited so long to come for me. I asked her if she was tying up loose ends, if this was a last hurrah for her. I asked her if she was going to kill me. She said no."

"T, there's no way of really knowing what was going through her head yesterday. Bella found some information we're not supposed to have that probably explains it. She's been getting experimental treatment for an aggressive brain tumor and her doctor told her yesterday morning that she only had a few weeks to live. At some point while you were in the dungeon with her, she decided to take her own life and take you with her while she still had you in her hands. We heard her telling you that last part right before she dosed you and herself with the drugs."

"I think you're right, I don't need to hear any more right now. Thanks for being honest with me."

"Boys, we have an appointment with the Chief of Police in thirty minutes. Let's sync up our stories before we get there, okay?"

Jackson and Will laughed as they followed Des out the door, leaving Clare and Tommy to figure out what was going to happen next.

·❤·❤·❤·❤·❤·

Jackson, Will and Des walked into the Police Station, right on time for their appointment with Chief Gray Davis. They had opted to keep Marshall and Rodney out of the initial conversation, and out of the matter in general for as long as they could, to protect their professional reputations. They hoped to provide as much buffer for Bella as they could, considering her periodic work with the Federal Bureau of Investigation. Chief Davis was in a surly mood when they were escorted into his office.

"I am so pissed off at you people right now, I can hardly think. But because of all your backgrounds, I'm going to give you the benefit of the doubt, listen to what you have to say, and then try really hard not to throw all of you into the darkest depths of my rat infested, antique jail and let you all rot. I have a woman in the morgue and a man who almost died, and some really good officers who were shocked and dismayed by what they saw in that house!"

"Chief Davis, I'm a clinical psychologist. I'd be happy to sit down with your officers and talk things out with them, see if I can help them come to terms with what they found at the crime scene."

"Dr. Wyatt, you're the last person I would ask for help right now. Don't speak again until I ask you a direct question. Mr. Kelley, you seem to think you're the leader of this little gang, so I'm asking you why you didn't have enough respect for me and my officers to bring me your suspicions and let us handle this. We may not have the big city experience some of you do, but we're pretty fucking good at our jobs. So tell me why you thought you needed to handle this yourselves. Then maybe I'll tell you a few things you may not know."

"Chief, we all have the utmost respect for the work you and your officers do. You put your lives on the line every day for this community, and we three, more than most, appreciate the sacrifice you make. When we found out about the threat to Tommy and Clare's lives, Will did bring up coming to you with what we had, but the unanimous decision – all six of us, including T – was to see if we could gather a little concrete evidence that you might actually be able to act on.

"All we had was a text and a photo of Tommy, and no actual proof that any drugs had been involved in his first interaction with her. She would have claimed that their affair was long standing and consensual, and she would have had video evidence that appeared to prove her claim. It would have been his word against hers. In retrospect, we didn't count on how unhinged the woman had become and just how much of a threat she really was. And we didn't allow enough time for the results of Des's lab tests to come back. Ms. Smith was pushing hard for another meeting with T, sooner than we could get hard evidence. We should have called her bluff and waited, but we didn't. If we had lost our friend, I would have been the first one through your door, begging to be locked away for the rest of my life. And these two would have been right behind me."

"So, Dr. Wyatt, you took blood and urine from Mr. Rollins the evening after the first assault, and sent it off somewhere, but didn't wait for the test results? Is that standard practice for you?"

"No, Chief, of course it isn't. I know where you're going with this. We were too close to the situation, and probably weren't able to be objective. All the more reason to bring our suspicions to your office. But as they say, hindsight is 20/20, we can only regret our actions and thank God our friend is still alive."

"You three are fucking lucky I'm not throwing the book at you. At a minimum, interfering with an active investigation almost cost T his life and let an incredibly guilty woman go free."

"What!?!" The shocked response issued from all three of them simultaneously.

"Hah! So I DO know something you don't know!! Yes, we've been quietly investigating Ms. Smith for several months. Just between us four, one of her on again, off again sub-missives finally decided she'd gone too far after she drugged him and held him prisoner for a weekend. She had photographic evidence then as well, and thought she could blackmail him, threatened to ruin his reputation in the community. After a long talk with his wife, the two of them decided not to let Ms. Smith get away with it any longer and they came in to see me. She's been a wiley witch, there's no doubt about that, but we were getting closer. You managed to neutralize a threat to the community, but in the process, we wasted six months of time and effort for nothing.

"In the meantime, I walked the scene myself last night and quietly appropriated a few items from the house that I didn't think needed to be entered into evidence. I'm going to assume that somehow you already have copies of the videos that were on her server. Our IT tech could see that the system had been compromised but he says he has no idea who or where from. If you do have all the video, you know that there were a total of ten men she was trying to, or actively blackmailing. No one ever needs to know about those other nine men. We're in the process of identifying and notifying each of them about the current disposition of those videos and photographs. Do I make myself clear?"

"Crystal clear, Chief Davis. No one will ever be compromised by what we might have in our possession at this time."

"Good. I'm about to throw you three out on your incredibly lucky asses, but I have a few things I'm going to give you. Please pass them on to Tommy when you feel he's ready. The first is a duplicate of the SIM card we found in her camera in the dungeon. I've already removed the photos of the other victims, only his photos are on it, and there are only a few, but he might not be prepared to see them just yet. The other thing I have for you is this box. There are two large framed photographs of T that were in a little room off the kitchen in Ms. Smith's house. At this point, they're not pertinent to the case we were working, so they're not going to be considered evidence. Be assured that any other photographic images we might find as we close out our investigation into Ms. Smith will be destroyed. Now take this crap and get out of my office. I have multiple cases to close now that the wicked witch is dead, and there's a shit ton of paperwork involved."

"Thank you, Chief Davis, we appreciate your tact and your candor. We'll go now and get out of your hair."

And the three of them, Jackson, Will and Des, walked out of the police station free as the breeze and feeling like the luckiest fucking people on the planet. And anxious to see all of Tommy's cheesecake photos for themselves. It seemed they were all insensitive clods at heart.

That evening, during nursing shift change, while Clare was in the cafeteria with Bella and Des, Tommy got out of bed, glad that his IV had been discontinued earlier in the day. He put on his hospital issue robe, opened the door to his room, and checked to make sure no one else was in the hallway. He walked quietly to the stairwell and headed down three flights to the basement level of the hospital – where the morgue was.

He needed a little more closure than his friends had been able to give him, and the only place he was going to get it was here. He knew Veronica would still be there, she would probably be there for days. She had no next of kin, and her will would take time to get through probate. No one was banging down the doors to get her body, so he had time to say goodbye.

When he walked through the door, the County Coroner looked up in shock, never expecting to see anyone else here at this time of the evening.

"Thomas, this is a strange place for you to be visiting this evening, don't you think? What can I help you with, my friend?"

"I want to see her. Veronica Smith."

"You know this isn't standard hospital protocol, but I guess it was to be expected. You know the hospital grapevine here is an amazing thing. I've never seen anything like it. Gossip covers the campus at the speed of light. How are you feeling tonight, by the way? Any lingering side effects from the drugs?"

"Not really. My memory still sucks but my friend Des thinks she can get most of it back with hypnosis. Not that I'm sure I want it all back, but if I do, heaven knows there's enough fucking video available to see every minute I spent with her."

"Yes, I've seen Des Wyatt do some incredible things with hypnosis, she's helped a lot of people over the years. She's a good friend to have. Now it seems I need a bathroom break, Thomas, and I'll be gone from this room for ten minutes. What you're looking for might be located in drawer five. Don't dwell on this, Thomas. She didn't ask for her illness, and in the end, she couldn't handle it. Not her fault, not your fault. She did what she did for many reasons, most of which we'll never know. Give her the benefit of the doubt. Say your farewells and be at peace. Don't be here when I get back."

The smells of a working morgue were always just a little beyond what Tommy could take, but this was an errand that wouldn't wait. He opened drawer five and pulled out the shelf just far enough to look down on the face of the woman who had almost killed him in the name of perverted love. She looked old, tired, ill. Certainly not the ravishing young beauty he had first met. He searched his memory for any indication that what she had believed all those years ago was actually true. That he was not a Dominant, but a submissive, one she craved to have for her own. The twenty-year age difference between them was a monumental issue for him, but the few times he had willingly submitted to her had been explosively fulfilling. She had been confident, capable, loving and kind in her own way, a lover of punishing his ass whenever she could.

She had still been all those things the last two times they had been together, and he found himself disappointed that he couldn't give her what she so desperately needed, not without benefit of mind-altering drugs. He wished he'd known three months ago what he knew now. Maybe they could have worked something out. But there was nothing more he could do for her now. Her spirit was in a much better place now and he had to let her body go. He pushed the shelf back in and closed the door, and as he turned to leave, Des was standing in the doorway. She gave him a sympathetic look and said, "I knew you would be here, saying goodbye. Let's go somewhere quiet and talk, before they call out the hospital guards to find you."

Chapter 22

"It's only been three weeks, T, are you sure you want to do this? There's plenty of time to look at these videos later. There are lots of other things we should talk about. Like why you and Clare haven't been in your playroom since you've been home. And why you haven't been to Asylum since all this happened. You told me yourself you've been playing pretty vanilla lately."

"I'm not here so you can psychoanalyze every part of me, Des. Just this part. You said yourself I need to face what happened, confront my fear. Well, I don't know what I'm afraid of because I don't know what she did and I don't know how I reacted. Bella went to a lot of trouble to get these videos from V's system. The least I can do is watch them."

"Shouldn't Clare be here to watch them with you? Shouldn't she know what V did? Her whole world is upended, too. Yes, you had the experience, for better or worse, but Clare has become collateral damage in this. You're treating her like she doesn't matter anymore, like you're the only one who suffered because of this experience you had. If you push her away again, V wins after all."

"Des, I'm not even sure I want YOU here when I see these videos, except to hold the bucket for me while I puke. There's no way I want Clare here to see this, to see me. Not until I know what V did. What I did. So let's just watch the first one, from her system, the first time I went to the house, just the tea room part. That can't be too bad, can it? And then we can talk about how I reacted to her, and maybe why. I have to make a start to move forward, and this is the first baby step. Clay isn't going to come home in the middle of this, is he? Although getting his reaction might not be a bad idea. He's the pro at submission, I'm just a newb."

"What you are is a smartass, and I'm not sure I feel comfortable with your cavalier attitude. But we'll see how you are once this first video is over. And if Clay comes in while it's running, he can provide color commentary. He's really good at the sarcastic shit."

"He must be if he's been with you this long. Roll tape, Mistress D!"

"Okay, T. Should I make popcorn?"

"Insensitive clod."

"That's what they call me."

"Tommy, when we get to the part where nothing looks familiar, where you don't have a clear memory of what's happening, let me know, and we'll stop the video and talk for a minute. I just want to make sure you're not pushing yourself too fast."

"I think you'll know when that happens."

Des started the first video Bella had sent her and prepared to watch both the flat screen TV and Tommy's reactions to what he saw. The video started as Tommy and Veronica entered the tea room, and his reaction to the scene was immediate. He appeared to have a fairly clear memory of the initial encounter, but he was definitely affected by seeing her again, and hearing her voice. He watched as V led him to a seat at the table, and then sat next to him, with their bodies touching.

"I remember this, but I was starting to get cloudy and I was struggling to keep my head clear."

As the video continued, their conversation was easy to hear.

"Veronica, I meant what I said. I came to say goodbye. You and I were never right for each other and no matter how much you seem to think otherwise, I love my wife. She's everything I want, everything I need, and you can't change that."

"Thomas, pet, you break my heart. You've convinced yourself that such a mousy little woman can be your heart's desire, but if you would just be honest with yourself, you would have to admit that I'm the woman you need. I'm your Mistress V. Remember? Look! Up on the wall. It's my favorite photo of you, from our days together. Just look how strong you were, how virile, how aroused. All for me! Looking at that photo of you, naked and restrained, in a perfect submissive pose, always makes me hunger for more. That's why it's here it my tea room, where I can admire it every day."

Tommy watched himself glance at something to the side that the camera couldn't see, but that much he remembered, if not completely clearly. The photograph of young Thomas. Then video Tommy turned back to Veronica and continued. *"No, Veronica. That man in the photo isn't me. Not anymore. If that man ever really existed, he doesn't exist now. I can see that coming here was a mistake, I need..."*

He watched as she leaned against him, and he had a vague memory of the touch of her hand on his thigh. He even touched his thigh, on that spot, as if remembering the feel. And he watched himself as his eyes clouded and his face visibly lost its focus. Des had paused the video and Tommy admitted, "I barely remember this. Can we continue a little longer?"

"Of course, T, just tell me when you need to stop." And she started the video again.

"Pet, you promised. Five minutes. You need to drink your tea before it gets cold. I made it especially for you, just the way you like it."

And he watched as she picked up the cup, brought it to his lips, and tipped it so that the tea poured, little by little, into his open mouth. Des was intrigued by Tommy's response, actually opening his mouth and leaning his head back slightly, as if Veronica was right there, helping him to drink the drugged tea. He licked his lips as if he could taste the flavor of the tea. He could see himself turn his eyes to the wall again, obviously staring at the photo, and even though he didn't have a real memory of it, he knew that, at that point, he couldn't stop her from doing anything she wanted to do. Des paused the video again.

"What did the tea taste like? Do you remember that much?"

"Yes, it tasted of peppermint and something else that must have been the Rohypnol. It actually didn't taste all that bad, at least by then it didn't. Keep going." And Des started the video again.

"That's my precious pet, drink your tea all down like a good boy."

Des paused the video one more time, as Tommy struggled to capture an elusive memory that danced just beyond his reach. He had nothing to match the video against his fading memory of the scene, and the frustration accelerated his breathing noticeably. He glanced over at Des, having a telepathic conversation with her. Then, as if making a decision in his head, he said "Keep going. And don't stop until it's over or I use my safe word." Knowing that Tommy's safe word had always been 'Pansy', she started the video again, and prepared for the inevitable.

They watched as Veronica turned to video Tommy, took his face in her hands and placed a light, gentle kiss on his lips. Keeping one hand on his stubbled jaw, she let her other hand drift down his chest to his zipper and stroked his enlarging cock through the denim, making him moan loud enough to be heard on the video. He had the vaguest memory of her touch on his cheek and then on his erection, but nothing else about the scene looked familiar.

"Shall I continue, pet? Do you remember how I used to kiss you? What I used to do with my hands? I think you do, and you have a reward waiting for me right here, don't you?" Though he had no real memory of the scene they watched, he had just the slightest remembrance of the squeeze of Veronica's hand on his cock, and he groaned along with video Tommy as she groped him.

"Veronica, I..."

"What do you call me, pet? How do you address me when we're together? Say it, pet, tell me who I am."

"Mistress V, I..."

"That's right, pet, I'm your Mistress V. Shall we play a little? Would you like to play with Mistress V?"

"Yes, Mistress V."

"Excellent. Let's get you out of these uncomfortable clothes and play." In the video, Mistress V pushed the tea cups to the center of the table and climbed up to sit on the edge, with her feet straddling Tommy's legs, boots resting on the chair rungs. Des and Tommy watched intently as she reached up and caressed his face, let her fingers tangle in his hair, and pulled him in to gently suck his bottom lip into her mouth, just for a moment. Video

Tommy gasped and real time Tommy began to cry silent tears as he touched his bottom lip.

"Keep going, please. I have no memory of this but I have to keep going. I have to know."

"Can you raise your arms over your head for me so we can remove this uncomfortable tee shirt?"

"Yes, Mistress V." And they watched as he raised his hands over his head as if he was in a trance, while she tugged the tee shirt up and over his head, tossing it in the corner. It was easy at this point to see Tommy's drug-dilated eyes and blank face. Des slid over on the sofa to grasp Tommy's hand as they watched, and they clung to each other, ignoring each other's tears.

"Oh, pet, you've taken such good care of your body. What I can see so far is magnificent. I'm going to play with your nipples for just a few minutes, maybe suck on them just a little, like I used to. Would that be okay? You used to enjoy it so much."

"Mistress V, I..."

"Pet, I won't ask again. I don't want to spoil our time together having to discipline you."

"Yes, Mistress V."

The video seemed to go on forever but by that point, nothing, not even her touch, was familiar to Tommy. They watched as Mistress V climbed into Tommy's lap and played with his nipples, then she helped him to stand so she could remove the rest of his clothes. They watched as she put wrist cuffs on him and linked them behind his back, and he never once tried to resist. They could see the lost look on his face as she turned her back to get other things out of the cabinet, and they watched as she finished preparing him for what V continued to call playing in the dungeon.

"Open your eyes, pet, and tell me how you feel. Do you remember how much you used to enjoy this?"

"I'm uncomfortable, Mistress V, I don't think I like this play. I don't know what you're going to do to me that I need cuffs on my wrists and ankles like this."

"Nothing to worry about, pet, you've always loved playing with me like this. Now let's have a little more tea and then we'll take a walk into the other room and we'll have some real fun. Okay?"

"Yes, Mistress V, if that's what you want."

Video Mistress V poured another cup of tea from the pot and lifted it to Tommy's waiting lips, feeding him the entire cup, bit by bit. *"You like my special tea, don't you, pet? It makes you feel so relaxed and so sensitive."*

Tommy and Des watched as Mistress V reached down and ran a long red fingernail up the impressive length of his erection. Video Tommy's shuddering reaction to the touch was clearly visible, and his eyes seemed to cloud even more.

"Yes, Mistress V."

Real time Tommy put a protective hand over the erection he was hiding under a pillow and he shuddered along with the video. Even without actual memory of that touch, just watching it made his skin crawl.

When video Tommy had ingested enough drugged tea to make him a willing participant, Mistress V took a leather collar out of her tea room supply cabinet and buckled it around his neck. The camera angle was not good now, but the collar had at least one D ring that she could use to attach other things. They continued to watch, and sure enough, she took a fifteen-inch silver chain from the cabinet and reached around behind him to attach one end to another D ring on the back.

As she continued to work with her back to the camera, it appeared that she then attached the other end of the chain to Tommy's linked wrist cuffs, although they weren't sure why. Then video V attached a leather leash to the D ring on the front of the collar. When she tugged his head down with the leash for another kiss, they could see him start to choke, and he quickly moved his wrists up high enough to relieve the pressure. Des felt a rush of pride in her friend. Even in his drugged state, he had enough sense of self-preservation to remove the perceived threat. Apparently satisfied that he was sufficiently subdued, and adequately restrained, Mistress V walked him out of the tea room, looking up and waving to the camera as they went. All that remained was a tea room filled with hashish smoke and impossible dreams. And the video stopped. And real time Tommy reached for his little plastic bucket and puked up his breakfast, just like he'd known he would do.

"Here, drink some water. I promise there's nothing in it but hard water minerals and fluoride."

"Thanks. Do you have any crackers? My stomach feels terrible."

"Yes, here, munch on these little cheesy things. Slowly. Do you think you can talk about what we saw in this first video? Any questions stand out in your mind?"

He munched a few crackers and sipped a little water, avoiding her determined gaze. Finally he looked at her and pulled the pillow away from his lap, embarrassed to let his friend see his uncomfortable erection. "I understand that my reaction to her in person could have been from her pheromone laced perfume, but she's not here now. The only thing that's here is video of her dominating me, and doing a fucking fine job of it. Was she right all along? Have I been fooling myself all these years about being a Dominant? I'm ashamed of my reaction, Des. I don't know what to believe anymore and I've been taking my confusion and self-hatred out on Clare."

"T, all of your feelings are to be expected. It's good that you're confused, that you're willing to see that maybe there's been a little shift in your mindset. That's healthy, and I'm glad to hear it."

"A LITTLE shift? Are you fucking kidding me? Isn't that a fucking 180 shift? How do I explain to my wife, to my friends, that 'oh yeah, remember when I used to be a kick ass Top? Well now I'm a pansy little bottom, so feel free to get in line to take your shot at me.' I can just see that. I may never be able to show my face at Asylum again."

"Okay, so now I want to just slap the shit out of you."

And a new, deep voice said "Yeah, so do I."

Surprised and embarrassed by the sound of another person in the room, Tommy looked up to see the submissive young man Des loved. "Clay, I'm so sorry, please don't take that personally. You know I have the utmost respect for you. I just don't know how to handle what's going on in my head."

"Master Thomas, believe me, I understand what you're experiencing. I guess Mistress Des has never told you my story."

"Clay, love, that's never been my story to tell. But maybe, in this particular instance, you could share your experience with another confused soul."

"Clay, what's she talking about? Are you both saying what I think you're saying?"

"Master Thomas, I started out in BDSM thinking I was a Dominant, a real bad-ass Dominant. I topped every submissive woman in every club I went too, I was like a big old manwhore. And I thought I was having a great time. And then, one night in a club in Atlanta, a woman walked in looking like sex on a really big stick, all tits and legs and leather. She took my breath away, and I couldn't wait to get her cuffed to a wall and under my control. She just laughed at me, wouldn't give me the time of day, so I went to the bar, found a quiet corner, and just watched her the rest of the night. I watched her top every male sub in the place, and sometime during the evening, I started wondering what it would be like to have her top me. Just once, just to say I'd had the experience. I thought it would make me a better Top myself.

"Well, all I did that first night was watch her, and drool all over myself, and then go home with the biggest boner I'd ever had, so big I couldn't get rid of it all night. So I went back to the club the next night and there she was. And she still wouldn't have anything to do with me. Except just before she left for the evening, she stopped by my table in the bar and said 'you're a looker, little boy, but you've got everything backward. Think about what you really want, what you really need, then call me.' She tossed her business card on the table and walked out. I was scared shitless, but I couldn't get her, or her advice, out of my head."

"T, it's been a really long day for all of us. I have a lovely sub who's in need of my attention, and lord knows, I need a little attention from him too. So your homework for tonight is to call your wife and tell her you're on your way home. Tell her the two of you need to talk about what you saw here, and then tell her to wait for you, naked, in your playroom. I've found that's the best place to have intimate chats. Really talk to her, T. Be honest about everything. She deserves nothing less. Call me in the morning and we'll set up another appointment. We have more video to get through, and maybe, if you're okay with it, Clay can sit in and give you his viewpoint. He is an advertising genius, after all." And she giggled as she stared at the love of her life.

Tommy got up, thanked Des, kissed her on the cheek, and headed for the front door. As he was walking through the living room, he heard Des giggle again and say, "You're still a looker, little boy."

"And you still take my breath away, Mistress."

"I think you need to spend some quality time on the wall, sub." And she laughed, like it was coming from deep in her throat.

And as Tommy pulled the front door closed, he heard Clay's moaning response, "Oh, Mistress. Yes, please."

And he suddenly couldn't wait to get home and make his own submissive moan a little.

Instead of calling, Tommy sent Clare a text.

> *"Little slut, I'm on my way home. You have ten minutes to meet me in the playroom, on your knees. Be naked, and be ready. T."*

When he got into the house, Tommy all but ran through the kitchen and down the stairs to the playroom. The door was ajar, and he could see muted gold light spilling out into the dark family room. He wasn't just nervous to be with Clare in this room again, he was afraid. Of what he would say, of what she would think, of what she would do. But if they stood any chance of moving forward together, they had to talk things out. When he opened the door, he was stunned by the vision of his wife, his slave, kneeling in the center of the playroom, head down, hands at rest on her thighs, back stick straight. And he wondered one last time if he was good enough for her, if he could still be the man she needed him to be. And if she would forgive him when he had finally told her his story.

"Clare, you look lovely. Once you finally mastered that pose, you never wavered. You're a submissive vision."

"Thank you, Master. I appreciate your kind words. How may I serve you this evening?"

"If you're not too tired, lovely, I'd like to have a chat. But first, I have to apologize for not spending time with you in this room recently, and I'd like to make that up to you now. Would you play with me? For just a little while?"

"It would be my pleasure and my honor, Master. I'm yours to command while we're in this room. I'm sure you know that, Sir." And he smiled at her little insinuation that while she might be his slave in this room, she might not be outside it anymore. Maybe she could transition with him after all.

"Rise, little slut. Into the bondage throne with you." And she rose gracefully from her kneeling position and walked to the leather and wood, custom made chair. Tommy smiled as he helped her onto the half seat, then secured her thighs over the cushioned armrests with comfortable leather straps. She leaned back into the chair, placed her hands over her head, and sighed when he had secured her there as well.

"Comfy, lovely? Yes? You always look stunning in this chair, safe and secure, awaiting your pleasure – and mine."

"I'm here to satisfy your every desire, Master. I love you, and I'm thrilled to be here with you."

"Thank you, little slut. I don't deserve you, but I'm going to make sure we both enjoy this time together."

He stepped back into the center of the room and began a little striptease for her. He grabbed the back of his tee shirt in his fist and pulled up slowly, revealing his abs, little bit by little bit, until the material was over his head and only clinging to his well-developed shoulders and upper arms. He threw the material off to the side as he crept back to the chair. Their eyes were locked on each other, reading lust and love in the dark, dilated pupils. When his hand went to the erection she could clearly see behind his zipper, and he stroked himself through the denim, her breathing ticked up visibly.

Tommy unsnapped his jeans, and lowered the zipper inch by inch, eventually revealing that monster cock, making Clare practically drool between her legs. He slipped his jeans and briefs off, kicking them aside, and stood before her like Adonis, god of beauty and desire. Unable to resist touching her any longer, he stepped forward and took her face in his hands. His lips moved slowly toward her and in the hair's breadth that sat between them, he whispered, "Yes, little slut?"

"Yes, Master."

With her permission, his lips finally met hers and they fused together as one being, and the world dissolved away. While the kiss continued, his hands moved down to caress her breasts, tease her nipples. His fingers tickled their way down her abdomen until they reached her mound, making her gasp and whimper. And safe in the knowledge that she was secure in her restraints, he let the monster play.

They had no idea how much time passed while they made love, bringing each other to orgasm over and over. But eventually, Clare's whole body trembled from the strain and Tommy could barely stand. Using the last of his strength, he released her from the bondage throne and carried her limp body to the fainting couch in the corner, laid her down, and then collapsed beside her, pulling a soft, warm angora throw over them. A few kisses were all they could manage before falling into a dreamless sleep in each other's arms.

Tommy awakened before Clare, and took the quiet time to watch her as she slept and then stirred. Her face was lovely at rest, and when her eyelids fluttered and opened, there was a gleam in her eyes that he hadn't seen for some time. He hoped it would still be there when he had finished speaking.

"Clare, baby, it's time. I have things I need to tell you. Please don't say anything, just let me get it all out and then you can tell me what you're thinking and how you feel.

"I'm not even sure where to start, there are so many things spinning around in my head. I've always thought of myself as a Dominant, I didn't think I ever had a desire to submit to a woman. I did submit to Veronica – Mistress V – three times while we were dating, but I thought I was just humoring her, giving her an opportunity to be in control. It was certainly interesting, I got a lot of sexual pleasure out of it, but it wasn't something I thought I would ever want on a regular basis. I've never had those feelings about another woman since I moved away from her, I never imagined I might feel that way again. And then she came to visit me, and seeing her, being near her, brought it back to me, and confused the hell out of me.

"Des says traumatic head injuries can change people, that maybe I've experienced a fundamental shift in my sexual orientation, so to speak. She also thinks that V's pheromone perfume had a lot to do with my reaction to being around her. All I know is that the more time I spent with her, the stronger the attraction was. I'm so confused, I don't want to hurt you while I'm trying to figure out what's happening to me, but I know one thing. I love you, and I know I'm being terribly selfish, but I don't want to go forward without you. I'm afraid that you only love the Dominant me, and if you find out I'm not really a Dominant, you won't love me anymore."

"Tommy, stop. I don't…"

"Please, Clare, let me finish. You know Bella found a number of videos of me with V, and there is another set that Snoop recorded from the second time I went to see her.

I watched the first one today with Des. It's the beginning of V's recording, before she took me in the dungeon that first time. My reaction to watching the video was alarming and painfully arousing. It makes me think that maybe V was right all along. I'm not really a Dominant, I'm a submissive, pretending to need control. That would make our relationship a lie, and I can't live with that. Clare, if you don't believe anything else I say, ever again, please believe that I love you with all my heart, and I will always try to give you what you need, regardless of how I feel."

"Master, please let me talk. It breaks my heart that you doubt how much I love you, that you think I would ever stop loving you because something about you changed. Baby, I know that you're confused about the feelings you had, that you might still have for Veronica, but nothing you feel for her changes what you feel for me. A part of you may always be drawn to what she was able to give you, but that won't keep me from wanting the best for you, always. The wonderful thing about the human heart is that we're able to love more than one person, and one love doesn't diminish the other. I may be jealous of her from time to time, but the heart needs what the heart needs. I would never ask you to choose one part of yourself over another.

"I may be selfish as well, baby, I think I'd rather share you than lose you altogether. So I would like to suggest a compromise of sorts. Consider yourself a Switch, if you will, and have the best of both Dominant and submissive. I don't think I can ever really top you, but I would be willing to try if you wanted to experiment a little. Or we can find a Domme who might be willing to top you. Or both of us. I don't know, we're in uncharted territory with all of this, but there are certainly things we can try that would let you be my Master, and still allow you to experience the joy of submission when you want or need to. Baby, you told me at the beginning, our relationship is what we make it. If it changes over time, maybe that's not such a bad thing."

"Clare, are you sure? You're proposing a major change in our relationship, it could end really badly."

"Or it could be a good thing. We won't know unless we try. But I do require one thing from you. I need to see the videos. I need to watch them with you. I need to see how you responded to V in person, and how you respond to just watching yourself do it. If you can't share that with me, then maybe I'll have to rethink this after all. Your newfound submissive desires are a part of you that I won't let you hide from me or from yourself."

"Clare, I love you so much. Knowing that you're willing to walk this new path by my side means so much to me. Des and Clay will help us along the way, I know they will. I think it would be really creepy for her to top me, but she could help us find a Domme we can work with together. If you're sure."

"I'm sure, Master. Now I don't know about you, but I'm suddenly feeling a little old, and a lot tired. Life with you can be exhausting, and that little nap we took wasn't nearly enough! Let's go to bed and see how the world looks in the morning. Okay?"

"Okay, Baby Girl. One day at a time."

Chapter 23

"Oh, Master, they're stunning. As much as I hate to admit it, Veronica was quite the photographer. Just terribly unscrupulous for someone who proclaimed to be a caring Dominant."

"I completely understand your point of view, Baby Girl. As a matter of fact, when I saw this picture here in the text she sent me, I was suddenly very empathetic of your hard and fast rule about no video and no photography. And I felt guilty about that one little photo I took of your freshly waxed mound the night before we went to court that time. But I suppose she did capture my best side – the front! She loved those full-on poses, except for this one here. From the side, I almost look like a ring toss game."

"Stop! I'm trying to be serious, and you keep making jokes about this. As good as they are, she took them without your informed consent, and that's terribly unethical. That being said, these are so striking, what would you think of having them printed and framed, to hang in the playroom? Maybe your photographer friend could come and take a few of both of us to hang in there as well. There is that one wall that really doesn't have anything on it. One or two of these would give me something to focus on when I'm on the bondage throne."

"Definitely something to think about, although the picture of the bright pink butt plug is never getting printed. Ever. Now, we haven't opened this big box that Chief Davis removed from the house right after, and I have a feeling I know what's in it."

Clare nodded and Tommy picked up the large box and laid it on his desk. Once the tape holding it closed had been cut, he lifted off the top, and stared. And Clare gasped. "My god, Tommy, they're breathtaking. These were hanging in the house? Where anyone could see them?"

"Yes, the first time I went, young Tommy was already hanging in the tea room. That was the day she took this photo in the text. By the time I went back the second time, she had removed all of the other artwork on that wall and it was just these two, side by side. I don't think we'll be able to see them in any of the videos, and I believe she hung them that way on purpose. So that only she and her special guests could see them."

"Do you think any of those other men saw her in that house? Do you think they know what happened to her? And all of her blackmail material?"

"I don't know if they saw these photos or not, but I'm sure Chief Davis has been able to identify and notify all of them by now. When I spoke with him last, he seemed to be on a mission to put an end to her little reign of terror. His words, by the way, not mine."

"Well, I can't wait to hang these two downstairs. We'll need new frames for them, these white frames won't go well with the gold wallpaper, but the black and white photos will be perfect. Now what time are we supposed to be at Des's house? Do we need to get going?"

Clare was surprised to see so many people when they arrived at Des's house, and more surprised when they were all escorted by Clay down to the dungeon Des had created in the basement of her huge home. Everyone greeted everyone else and they took convenient seats facing a large flat screen TV on the far wall. It all seemed a little surreal to Clare, sitting in a very well-equipped dungeon, knowing they were about to see her husband, unable to defend himself, being erotically tortured – in a dungeon – by a woman who claimed to love him. But she didn't have time to dwell on it long, because Des took control of the room.

"Listen up, you pack of insensitive clods. Tommy hasn't seen some of this video yet, and Clare hasn't seen most of it. If you can't understand the gravity of what we're about to see, you can just haul ass out of my house right now. Most of you aren't even supposed to be here. Tommy wanted to see this last video of the second visit, inside the dungeon, and he obviously wanted Clare here. He wanted me and he wanted Clay. You four fools just piled on as soon as you heard about it. Now here this! No food, no beer, no smartass comments. Put yourselves in their position and act accordingly. Am I clear on this? Because if anyone forgets, I have my single tail right here, and I know how to use it."

"Des, remember, most of us were there that day, and while we didn't have video, we had the audio, starting on the screen porch and ending at the point V tried to kill Tommy. No one understands more than we do what happened that day, and what almost happened. And whose fault it would have been if the worst had happened. Speaking for Rodney, Marshall, Jackson and myself, watching this video might be almost as difficult for us as it is for Tommy and Clare. But I would like to make one request. This is the copy that Snoop put together for me, and it starts with the screen porch audio and then fades into the video as soon as it started to record in the tea room, continuing right up to the point where the EMT's charged in and Snoop stopped recording. I know that Tommy was laying it on a little thick at first but I think it's important for Clare to see how soon he tripped out and wasn't himself anymore."

"I appreciate your thoughtful comments, Will, and I understand your request. If it's okay with Tommy and Clare, it's okay with me."

Tommy looked to Clare, snuggled up next to him, tissue in hand for those tears she knew were inevitable. She nodded and Tommy looked back to Des. "Let's just get this over with so I can have that beer! Roll tape, Mistress D. Please."

Des felt the need to narrate a little, more for Clare and Clay than for anyone else. With the exception of those two, they'd all been there listening in.

"This is the audio Snoop was able to grab from the screen porch when Tommy first arrived. If you listen closely, you can tell he's pushing a little for incriminating background, and I think she fell into his trap here."

"Thomas, my pet, you're back. I knew you'd come, you've seen the light, haven't you? You know that I am your heart's desire, the woman you were destined to serve."

"How are you, Mistress? You look lovely today. Red is a good color for you, and the boots are spectacular. Mistress, I think we have some things to talk about. I have some questions."

"You would question your Mistress, pet? Isn't that a little presumptuous of you? Shouldn't you know that my way is always the best way for both of us?"

"You're asking a lot of me, Mistress. I have to admit that our time together on Wednesday stirred new feelings, new desires, ones I would never have considered before, if you hadn't taken matters into your own hands. But you seem to want a long-term relationship that is completely foreign to me. There would have to be a period of adjustment for me, wouldn't you agree? A transition from Dominant to submissive would require a substantial mind shift. Yes?"

"Very well, pet, I see your point. I'll answer a few questions before we begin. Shall we go inside? I have tea ready."

"There's some white noise for just a few seconds and then the video kicks in – right here. You can see when he notices the photographs on the wall and walks over to them. It's too bad the angle on the camera doesn't catch them on the video."

"What do you think of my little art gallery, pet? Aren't the photos stunning? I love the juxtaposition of the subjects – younger versus more mature. So much to read in each face."

"You have quite an eye, Mistress, you've captured these two men well."

"Thank you for that, pet. A serious photographer appreciates the approval of her subject and her audience. Now come and sit, have some tea and we'll chat."

Des stopped the video and said "Here you can see where she takes him by the arm and leads him to the table and he gets her to talk about her plans again."

"Des, speaking for the four of us who weren't invited to this little party, can we knock off the narration and just watch and listen? It's hard enough to watch without your play by play."

"Sorry, Marshall, I didn't realize you were so squeamish."

"Please, will the two of you stop sparring? Clare and I are sitting right here."

"Sorry, T, we'll all shut up until you need to stop or until we get to the end." And Des started the video again, silencing the audience.

"So you have questions for me, pet?"

"Just one right now, Mistress. Why did you wait so long to come for me? It's been years since we saw each other last, and then all of a sudden, there you were in the hospital, visiting after my accident. You told Clare that you had hoped we would find each other again, but I don't recall that you ever reached out to me. Maybe it's the combination of your tempting perfume and the hashish affecting my thinking, but I have to wonder if you're planning on tying up a loose end here. Is this a last hurrah? Are you going to kill me today?"

A tiny gasp beside him made Tommy turn his head toward Clare, who was trying to bury her face in his chest.

"It's okay, Baby Girl, I'm right here. She didn't originally intend to kill me that day. It's okay, baby." And he looked to Des, who had stopped the video, and said "Keep going, please." And the video started again.

"That's more than one question, pet, but I understand what's troubling you. I always thought we had all the time in the world to reconnect. Then I discovered the critical nature of your injuries and I realized time wasn't going to wait forever. Here, sweet pet, have some tea, I made it just like you like it. To answer all of your other questions, of course I'm not going to kill you. Why on earth would you think that? I'm hoping we have a long, happy life together, pet, just you and me, right here in my favorite house. We'll burn our hashish, and drink our tea, and play together in our dungeon. It will be great fun, yes?"

"Yes, Mistress V, that sounds like fun."

"Very good, pet. Now drink up and we'll talk about what games we want to play today. Are you feeling all right, love? Shall I help you with your tea?"

"I'm feeling a little fuzzy, Mistress, a little help with my tea would be very nice."

The silent little group just watched as V continued to drug Tommy, then dress him up and parade him out of the room with a wave to the camera. Clare ran into the bathroom and Des stopped the video, looking to Tommy for direction on whether they would continue or not.

Clare returned to the room after a few minutes and silently nodded to Des to start up the video. She sat down next to Tommy again and whispered "It's a good thing she's dead, because I'd really like to kill the bitch myself." She turned to the TV on the wall and steeled herself to view what happened in the dungeon.

"Do you remember this room, sweet boy? We played here just the other day. Did you enjoy that?"

"I don't recall, Mistress V. Did I enjoy it?"

"Oh, pet, you had a wonderful time. I'm hoping that someday soon we'll be able to play in here all day and your mind won't be so fuzzy, and you'll remember what fun we have."

"Yes, Mistress, if that will make you happy."

"I do love you, pet, you make me so happy. Someday very soon you'll realize that, and you'll see that you love me too. Shall we play now?"

"Yes, Mistress V."

"The sound on this last part didn't pick up on V's original recording in the dungeon but Snoop accidentally picked the perfect spot to place one of his extra mic's. Clare, I'm really sorry, but this will probably be the hardest part of the video to watch. But once we all ran through the door, Snoop cut the recording. You'll see the video pause and then go black. And we'll be done. Okay?"

"Thank you, Will. I think I'm about ready to be done." And Tommy hugged her closer, as much for his own comfort as for hers.

Clare didn't think it could get any worse than watching Tommy chained to the wall, with Mistress V bouncing up and down on his raging erection. She tried very hard to convince herself that he had no idea what she was doing, and that it wasn't really him being unfaithful to her, it was someone else who looked like him, being forced to do her bidding. But then the very last part of the video started and she knew this would be the worst.

"I have something to tell you, pet. I've been sick for some time, and the doctor says I don't have much longer to live. He has described how the end will go and I don't want that for myself. So I'm choosing the time and place, and who goes with me when I go."

They all watched in silence as Mistress V climbed off his lap and went back to the cabinet one last time. The angle on the camera wasn't perfect but they could see her dissolve a large packet of white powder in a large glass of water and take six large capsules from a prescription bottle. She brought the pills and the glass of water back to his side, looking down at him and smiling. She sat down on his lap again, cradling his semi erection against her core, and looked longingly at him.

"Open your mouth, pet, nice and wide. Take these big pills for Mistress and I'll give you a drink of water to help them down. There you go, take a big drink, love. Yes, just a little more. Perfect. I see that bad face you're making, pet! It doesn't taste so bad, does it? Such an obedient boy, right to the end. Now I'll take my pills, and I'll drink my water down. See? Just like that. All done. And now we'll just sit here and rest until the end. Okay, my sweet pet?"

"Yes, Mistress, whatever you say."

They watched a silent screen for several minutes, as Mistress V cuddled her beloved submissive into unconsciousness. Just as they both stopped moving, a shot rang out, and on the far end of the room, the dungeon door frame exploded around the lock, allowing four terrified people to race into the room. And then the video paused, and then went black. And Tommy and Clare both raced for the bathroom, serenading their friends with the sounds of stereo vomiting and sobs.

From the bathroom, Tommy and Clare could hear Will's distinctive Boston accent. "I'll have that beer now, Mistress Des, if you don't mind! As a matter of fact, how about a round for the whole bar? Put it on my tab."

"Get it yourself, you insensitive clod." And it was just enough humor to chase away the ghosts of the past three hours.

"Clare, what's this legal envelope on the kitchen table? Did it come in today's mail?"

"Yes, love, the postman brought it to the door and I had to sign for it. I've never heard of this law firm before, I have no idea what's in it. It's addressed to you, maybe you should open it."

"I think I will, smart ass. And then I think I'll be taking you downstairs for a little discipline. I've been letting you slide quite a bit lately and you're getting a little cocky."

"Oh, Master, I'd love to get a little cocky with you, any way you want."

"Enough, woman, or you'll get a spanking and no orgasm to go with it. Now let's get into this envelope and see who's in trouble in this house."

He carefully opened the large heavy envelope, read the cover page and cursed loudly.

"Master, what is it? Is someone suing us?"

"No, we're not getting sued. I've been named as V's sole heir. This will is dated right after she came to see me in the hospital. She's left me everything! Fuck! I don't want anything from her. According to this summary page, she has real estate all over the Southeast, plus insurance policies, cash, stocks, bonds, you name it, she left it to me! What the fuck am I supposed to do with all of this?"

"Maybe we could have Harrison and his new wife over for dinner tonight and let him go through it. He might be able to suggest some charities that could benefit from all of this, and that way, you don't have to get as involved. I have lasagna in the oven, we'll have plenty if he's available."

"I see once again, you're not just another pretty face. No wonder I married you! I'll give him a call and see where he thinks we need to start.

"Clare, thank you so much for the dinner invitation, it smells delicious. And timely! With Martine out of town for the past week, I'm depending on carry-out from every restaurant I can think of."

"You've barely finished your honeymoon and she had to go out of town already? She's a lawyer, just like you! Surely she can set her own schedule."

"We knew when we got married that she was in the middle of a big case. She'll be home on Friday, and we're taking a long weekend for a little second honeymoon at the beach. In the meantime, it looks like your husband has just handed off a lot of research on the lovely and demented Veronica. T, I wasn't kidding when I said you have homework on this mess. I'm sure we can sell off most of these properties and donate financial assets to your favorite charities, but I want you to take one more look at the house here."

"Wait, you mean the one where she drugged me and tried to kill me? That house?"

"Yes, I want you to take Clare with you and don't just look at the house, look at the whole property. Think big picture. Think about other uses for the land. Then call me when you've been there and taken a few notes. Now how about we eat before we start arguing about this mess again? And then I'll have to go. I'll be up reading half the night on this ridiculously big inheritance. Plan on a higher tax bracket for a few years, buddy, we won't be able to unload all of this overnight."

"Tommy, this is Harrison."

"It's a little late, don't you think, buddy? Clare and I just went to bed."

"I've been reading through Veronica's will and I thought you'd want to know about the clause she had tucked away in the fine print."

"What else could she possibly have done?"

"It says if she predeceases you, she wants to be cremated and you get her ashes. I'm sure in her mind, she thought that if she died first, you'd be so distraught, you'd build a shrine in her honor. I know that the Court considered donating her body to UNC Medical, but that never happened. Apparently, the university thought they had enough whack jobs for now, and they declined. She couldn't hang out in the morgue any longer so she was quietly cremated and her ashes are being held at the funeral home pending the reading of her will. Tag, buddy, you're it."

"Are you fucking kidding me? I don't want anything from that woman, especially her ashes! What the fuck am I supposed to do with them?"

"Sorry, buddy, I'm just telling you what it says. There are no specific instructions for interment of last remains, just that you get them. I guess it will be up to you to decide where she ends up!"

"Fuck and double fuck!! I'm hanging up before you find anything else in that damned will!" And he disconnected the call before Harrison could say anything else.

"Clare, we're going back to the playroom. I need to burn off some steam!!"

"Master, I don't think I have another orgasm left in me tonight! How about you go spend some time on the elliptical and I'll keep the bed warm for you."

"Clare!"

"Coming, Master."

"According to the survey, this is a huge lot. I can't imagine what it cost her, even knowing she bought it before market value increased with the new highway going in. I'd rather not go inside if we don't have to, at least today, it's just a little too soon after... You know.

Just look around the outside and think what else the land could be used for. Think local charities, things like that."

As they walked the lot surrounding the house, comparing different sections to the survey, Clare took in a deep breath, marveling how clean the air was, and how quiet the lot was, set a half mile off the highway. And she had a sudden thought. "I was reading the other day about an organization run by a group of Priests and Ministers and Military Chaplains, focusing on children of service men and women who were wounded or killed in action. These kids never have the opportunity to just be kids, to experience places like this, many of them have no idea what nature is, because they have too many responsibilities at home. What if you donated the land to this organization, and offered to tear down the current structure and replace it with something more rustic, something that was more in keeping with the setting and with their needs. I know Master Rodney is more a commercial architect, but I'm sure he'd love to get involved with something like that. And Master Marshall would love to be part of that as well, he could be the general contractor for the project. We could start with the kids, and maybe expand over time to include wounded service people as well.

"This is a big, beautiful house but it's out of place here. You could do better with a great big log home with lots of bunk rooms and a big open kitchen and dining room. Library rooms with movies and books and TV's. The barn up on the hill would be perfect for a few sheep or goats, maybe some chickens for egg production. Let these kids come here and get a different taste of life. If you could help one kid remember what it's like to just be a kid, it would be worth it. What do you think, Master?"

"I think, once again, you amaze me, lovely. I'll call Harrison tonight and see what he thinks, but I'm sure he's going to love the idea. We can sweep away all the bad that's happened here, and start fresh with an idea that will actually do a little good in the world. I love you so much, Baby Girl, I'll never be able to show you just how much."

"Well, we did just get that new Hitachi wand vibrator, maybe we could..."

The Hitachi had to wait a little while. When Tommy and Clare got home, their neighbor James was standing at their front door with a small box.

"James, it's a little early for Christmas, isn't it? What have you got there?"

"It's a package for you, dumbass. I had to sign for it. The return address is UNC Medical Science Department. Are they finally returning your brain?"

"Oh, fuck. I know what that is. And it's going right back. They can process their own damn medical waste."

"Tommy, baby, you don't mean that. You knew this package was coming. At least you would have if you'd read more of the letter they sent you two weeks ago. I know he was a total whack job and he tried to kill us, but he didn't ask for his mental issues, and he deserves a decent burial. James, these are Shane's ashes, and Tommy is in denial about his final responsibility to his brother."

"So what would you have me do with him, Clare? Put him in a nice urn and display him on the mantle? I don't think so!! He can sit his ass on a shelf in the garage until I decide what garbage dump to sprinkle him on. Thanks for nothing, James. You can go home now!" And their neighbor shook his head, laughed a little to himself, and walked away.

"Tommy, Master, please. I don't want him in the house any more than you do, but we do have to do something with him soon. We'll both feel better once he's been laid to rest. Maybe when Veronica's ashes arrive, we can put them in the same niche at the Columbarium. The loons can keep each other company for all eternity. Now come in the house. I believe we had some plans to test drive a new vibrator. It will make us both feel better once I've had two or three screaming orgasms, don't you think?"

"Topping from the bottom again, slave? We'll just see how many screaming orgasms I let you have, baby."

And they deposited Shane's last remains on a shelf in the garage on their way to the playroom and a little distraction for both of them.

On a rainy day at the end of June, Shane Rollins and Veronica Smith were finally laid to rest, side by side in a niche at the Heaven's Gate Cemetery Columbarium, on a hillside overlooking a lovely quiet pond. Tommy thought they had gone to too much trouble for two people who had both tried to kill him, but Clare somehow found it in her heart to forgive both of them, and she would have nothing less for them.

After the very quick service, Tommy and Clare met their friends at Clare's favorite pub for a long lunch, too much alcohol, and tales of Big Man and Baby Girl that grew with each telling. And life went on as it should.

Epilogue

SIX MONTHS LATER...

"And the phoenix of their love rose from the ashes once again. The end."

Clare closed the manuscript, looked up at her husband from her seat next to him in the family room, and said, "So what do you think? I found a literary agent who's very interested. She thinks she can get one of the major publishing houses to publish it, market it, get it in all the big book stores, maybe do a book signing here and there if it actually sells. But I don't want to make any decisions without you. The book is about you, after all. Come on, Master, tell me what you think!"

"I think it's a spectacular story, Little Mistress. You flatter me with your descriptions and your attention to detail. You make me look better tha I really am. For the most part. But I have some questions, so I'll make you a deal. I'm going to take the manuscript and read it all the way through, in private, and make some notes. Then we can discuss the areas I'm not completely crazy about. In the meantime, if you've researched the literary agent and you have confidence in her reputation and her work history, make contact with her again. Start the negotiation process and see what you come up with. Just let me know before you sign anything."

And she threw herself at him, straddling his lap, and covering his face in kisses. "Oh, Master, have I told you today how much I love you? How hot I think you are? What a great Master you are? How much I love the orgasms you give me?"

"Yes, Clare, you may have mentioned all of that about an hour ago."

She pulled him close to her, allowing her lust to grow as she considered her next words. "Very well then, Thomas, turnabout is fair play. I believe I owe you some play time. You have five minutes to get into the playroom, strip and present yourself next to the spanking bench. Make sure that cock is nice and big and hard when I get there. After I've warmed you up, I may treat you to a little time on the fainting couch with that new plug I got for you. Would you like that, Thomas? Do you need that?"

"Oh, yes, Little Mistress, I think I need that really badly. Look what just thinking about that has done to me?" And he pulled her hand to his zipper so that she could feel the erection growing by the second inside his pants.

She loved how his eyes dilated at the thought of her discipline and how raspy his breathing became, thinking about the plug. She was still learning how to read his needs, when to submit to him and when he needed her Dominance, but her confidence when it came to seeing to her husband's needs increased with every lesson she got from Mistress Des and Mistress Kitty.

Her thoughts went back to the previous weekend, when Tommy and Clare had scened with Mistress Kitty at Asylum for the first time. Tommy, the consummate Master, had locked Clare into her favorite bench and spanked her ass red, just because he could. And then he had fucked her so well on that bench, she almost lost consciousness. After she had roused enough, Clare watched from her comfy seat next to that same bench as Mistress Kitty stepped forward and placed a black leather collar around Tommy's neck, stirring whispers and smiles around the room.

Mistress Kitty ordered him to strip and present himself, on his knees, before her. After she had accepted his submission, Mistress Kitty firmly grasped his sizeable erection and pulled him to his feet, smiling when he winced and moaned from the pain and the pleasure. She adjusted the spanking bench slightly to allow that steel rod cock to hang free, then strapped him down and reddened his ass as well, using her favorite cane. To finish the scene, Mistress Kitty had broadened Tommy's submissive horizons by donning a fairly large strap-on and giving him an intense fucking of his own. Watching as the scene played out, Clare had found herself becoming very aroused, and at the last thrust of Mistress Kitty's strap-on, with their eyes locked on each other, Clare and Tommy climaxed together, more in love than ever before.

After he had come down from his orgasm, and had been allowed to kiss Mistress Kitty's stiletto boot in thanks for her splendid Dominance, he came to sit with Clare and bask in the afterglow of his new Switch dynamic. And Mistress Kitty went back to her own precious female submissive, doling out a little more discipline and some love of her own to complete the evening.

When Clare returned to the present, she realized her five minutes were up. She walked to the playroom door and looked inside, seeing the love of her life, naked and on his knees, with his favorite crop in one hand and the new plug in the other. His cock was indeed big and hard. She had never dreamed, all those months ago, when she met an arrogant man on a lovely golf course, that they would end up in this emotional place, so comfortable with the changing dynamic of their relationship. She stepped forward, took the crop and the plug from Tommy's hands, and prepared to let the phoenix of their love soar once again.

Enjoyed the ride? Let the world know.

If this story stirred something inside you, made you blush, bite your lip, or fall just a little in love—why not share the experience?

Leaving a review takes only a minute, but it makes a *huge* difference. It helps other readers who enjoy erotica and BDSM stories find their next favorite escape—and it helps me keep writing the stories you crave.

Leave a review where you bought this book. I'd love to hear what you think.

And if you'd like to stay connected, get sneak peeks, or just hang out in a space where passion and pleasure are celebrated, follow me on:

Facebook: Lorelei Tiffin writes

Instagram: Lorelei_Tiffin_Writes

Your support means the world to me. Until next time... stay curious, stay bold, and always choose pleasure.

With love,
Lorelei

Bonus Material

CLARE'S JOURNAL

Friday, August 8, 2003

Holy hell, what is going on with my body?? I've been so horny lately. And so unfocused I can hardly concentrate on my work. And moody – I almost slapped someone today. Losing weight without trying is a little scary. Menopause was two years ago and all of a sudden, it's like I have PMS 24/7. I was awake at 3:00 AM, so torqued I was climbing the walls – old vibrator just couldn't take the strain. I'm not going through that menopause crap again. All my research online leads to cancer diagnosis. I need to see a doctor. And I need a new vibrator – quick!

Sunday, August 10, 2003

Found a great website, ordered two new vibrators, will have to stock up on lots of batteries. Found a few scary websites along the way, a lot more BDSM than I'm prepared for. Medical fetish?? Holy hell!!

Thursday, August 21, 2003

Finally got in to see my primary care physician. You'd think a medical professional would be more empathetic. Or sympathetic. Or something. I expected a little humor, I did not expect him to laugh so hard at my symptoms that he almost fell off his exam stool. Would have served him right. He doesn't want to deal with this, so now have a list of gynecologists to pick from. I think I want a woman doctor for this!! Good news – vibrators arrived today in the mail. I'd rather sleep through the night than be up at 3 AM screwing myself, but at least with new equipment, maybe I won't be awake as long??

Tuesday, September 16, 2003

I should just be shot – all the 20-something boys at work are hotter than snot and I can't stop staring at asses and packages. Although some packages are a little harder to see than others! No pun intended! Even old bald guys are looking pretty good these days – yikes!! At least I haven't reached out and grabbed anyone yet.

Wednesday, October 22, 2003

Burned a vacation day for Gynecologist appt but I liked her. She was very thorough, sympathetic, laughed a little but not so much I wanted to punch her. Official weight loss so far is 20 lbs since August – who knew masturbation could be a fitness program. Butt is looking better these days and less jiggly. Pap test was less uncomfortable than past ones. Vag ultrasound was an unusual experience but not horrible, they drew lots of blood for hormone tests. Now lots of waiting for test results. Oh yeah, happy freaking birthday to me!

Friday, November 28, 2003

Test results review with gynecologist. Everything came back normal. Too bad I'm still riding the midnight vibe almost every night. Not so normal. Gynecologist isn't giving up – next step is referral to endocrinologist to see if hormone levels are really normal for post-menopause. Waiting again.

Thursday, January 8, 2004

Guess doctor offices are closed all of December? Finally got a call from gynecologist's office, working on my endocrinologist referral. Still no symptom changes and I'm getting really tired of not sleeping through the night.

Monday, January 26, 2004

Would you believe, just got my referral to the specialist – it's in April!! Fuckin-A!! Both vibrators gave up the ghost over the weekend – overuse? Maybe they're not as waterproof as they claim. Back to that website for more.

Wednesday, January 28, 2004

BDSM websites keep drawing me back – why is that stuff so hot??? Concerned about my state of mind.

Friday, April 2, 2004

God I'm so tired. I can't remember the last time I slept through the night. Nights are just a series of short naps anymore. Two more weeks until the endocrinologist appt – she'd better have something constructive to say or I will just cry.

Monday, April 19, 2004

Normal??? How can everything be normal?? Holy hell, I actually cried in the office. She suggested maybe I should seek psychological help – maybe the problem is in my head and not in my pussy. Maybe she's right but I'm not spending another freaking dime on this. Maybe I just need some sex. Time to start warming up my golf swing – and my alcohol tolerance. And I need another new vibrator. At this rate I should buy stock in Doc Johnson! Fuckin-A!!

Saturday, May 29, 2004

Picking up men is harder than I remembered. Spent the day on the golf course and the evening in the bar and ended up with nothing more than a sun burn and a hangover. Maybe I just haven't invested enough time. Sure would like some help – I'm not doing a very good job giving myself an orgasm and it's not helping my mood at all.

Tuesday, June 8, 2004

Ladies night at the local bar. No action. Need to find a bar that has Guys night.

Sunday, June 20, 2004

Finally – a guy with a condom and 20 minutes to kill. Unfortunately he didn't have a whole lot to offer in the dick department, but he was good with his tongue. I got what I needed and so did he. He wasn't all crazy about seeing me again and that's a good thing. I'll just have to be careful when I play that course again.

Saturday, August 21, 2004

Well I got what I needed but I can't go back to that golf course again. Thought I was alone on the back nine, got caught with my hand in my panties by a guy wanting to play through. He had a condom in his wallet and a big cock to put it on, and he knew how to use what God gave him. Got some abrasions on my back and on my ass from the tree bark, but he made me come and got his rocks off in the process. He even said thank you. Wouldn't mind running into that again but I promised myself no double dipping so I need to find another golf course. Can't believe this has been going on for more than a year. I'm so tired of this. Maybe I do need a shrink.

Saturday, October 30, 2004

Official tally – now persona non grata at 6 local golf courses and 3 area bars – I may have to leave the county next Spring if I actually want to play golf. Found 1 bar that welcomed me with open arms. Only go when I can't get an 'O' on my own but the guys are decent looking, clean and carry their own condoms. If I buy a drink or two, I can usually get what I need. Haven't had to double dip yet, enough local guys know about this place. Just afraid I'll run into someone from work and then my dirty little secret will be out.

Friday, December 31, 2004

Happy fucking New Year. Beginning to think this is never going to end, getting a little depressed. Tried pot, pills, booze, prayer – nothing has helped so far. The shrink option is looking better all the time. That endocrinologist told me to just ride it out – I'd like to see her function when her panties light up for some stranger who walks by. I'll be back when I have something new to say.

Thursday, March 31, 2005

Horrible winter appears to be just about over – hit a long 'O' dry spell. Getting ready for golf, bar hopping and hopefully some sex.

Sunday, May 1, 2005

Golf game is getting pretty good but only two "encounters" so far – one in the bushes on the course and one in the back seat of my car – no skyrockets but got what I needed. Started carrying condoms in my golf bag, just in case. Favorite bar closed last week, so much for the bi-weekly fuck fest.

Friday, May 27, 2005

Finally talked to my boss today about going part time. Just can't concentrate, too many short sleep nights, I cry too often. He approved it, effective June 24. Hope this helps – hope the budget can handle less income. Will have to cut back on my vibrator/toy/video spending.

Saturday, June 18, 2005

One last vibrator purchase, promise of free videos with my order, no telling what will arrive.

Friday, June 24, 2005

Last day full time – big party after work. Drank too much, almost fucked a co-worker in the parking lot. I'm such a slut. Gotta get a handle on this. Semi-retirement, here I come. New vibrator arrived and some scary BDSM movies. Again – why is this stuff so hot?? Too many romance novels and not enough skin to skin interaction? Holy hell!!

Friday, August 26, 2005

Semi-retirement going okay – finances holding up okay. Job is suddenly more interesting now that I'm only doing it 3 days a week. Haven't accidentally tried to fuck anyone from work yet, my luck is holding out.

Sunday, October 30, 2005

Last golf of the season – fuck it was cold out there!! I've acquired 2 friends with benefits at this course. They know about each other and don't seem to mind banging the same woman when it's convenient. Still have all the hornies but at least I can find a cure now and then, trying not to take advantage of either of them – they're both nice men, lots of fun, great in the sack. We're all looking for the same thing right now – no relationship – just sex. Not sure how long this will last but I'm going to ride the crazy train until it crashes.

Tuesday, February 21, 2006

Someone can't keep a secret. Everyone at work seems to know about my friends with benefits and behind my back I have become the cunt of the county. At least I don't have to sneak around anymore but none of my female co-workers will look me in the eye and all of my male co-workers are staring in the direction of my tits and pussy these days. I think it may be time to find a new job and move.

Wednesday, May 3, 2006

Got groped in the elevator by one of the firm's partners. Married guy – all hands when no one was around to see – really limp dick. When I mentioned having a chat with HR, he threatened me – said he could make my job go away really quick. No job is worth this crap. Need to decide where I'd like to move to, and start looking for alternate employment. How depressing!!

Tuesday, August 29, 2006

Was really hoping I could just get a new job and not have to relocate but I was wrong. Not sure if it's my current reputation or that there just aren't any decent jobs available, but I haven't even had a nibble. Well I had one nibble but he was a total lech and was looking for a quick roll before he would consider me for his crappy office job. It was all I could do not to slap his face and knee him in the balls. Might as well stay put a little longer.

Monday, October 2, 2006

Took a long weekend trip to Wilmington NC and scouted small towns on the NC/SC border. Lots of small factories, law offices – and tons of golf courses. Would love to live in this area. Need to find a job first.

Sunday, October 22, 2006

Happy fucking birthday to me. Got one card – from Carson. As much as she doesn't approve of my lifestyle, she never forgets my birthday. She's never understood how difficult my horniness has been to deal with – alone time for her is an infrequent blessing, not a nightly curse. She just doesn't understand her baby sister at all. Saw my one remaining friend with benefits Friday – wild night – naked birthday cake. He's a good guy but he's moving on so I'll be on my own again for awhile. Started running recently, official weight loss since this all started is 60 lbs. Hasn't helped my hornies but I am looking better, and maybe feeling a little better physically these days. Thank God for Harlequin Romance – bought 20 new books, hoping to get through the dry spell I'm anticipating this winter.

Monday, December 18, 2006

Work has been a nightmare – I've become such a pariah, hardly anyone talks to me unless there is something case related. Only a few friends left. Feeling pretty much alone right now. Going home for Christmas, I don't think that's going to help my loneliness and it adds that level of family crazy that I don't really need right now. But it's cheap and I will just deflect questions as needed. BDSM web sites still calling my name. Why so hot??? Budget holding up okay right now. Sanity not so much.

Monday, January 1, 2007

Back home yesterday afternoon, family time tense as ever, stopped by a local bar for a New Years Eve drink and struck up a conversation with a woman a few bar stools away. She moved down next to me and we continued to talk. She invited me to a party she was going to last evening, said I'd have a great time. Great times have been off my radar for awhile, after two Jager shots, a party sounded good. Went home and changed, came back to the bar and followed her in my car to a huge house, she introduced me to our host – holy hell – how have I not run into this guy before now? Practically run over by his looks – almost my age, quintessential tall, dark and handsome. Felt a little dangerous – kind of Dom dangerous – he could be a Harlequin hero – or villain. And so smooth!! Never left my side all evening, treated me like such a lady.

When we danced, he would put his hand on the small of my back and press me into his cock – really hard and really big. But at midnight, he touched my cheek and gave me the most chaste New Year's Eve kiss I've ever had. By then I was horny as hell but he was too good to be true and I started to freak a little – decided it was time for me to go. He apologized for not being able to see me home himself, kissed my hand and thanked me for coming, had his butler follow me home – can you believe that?? Insisted that I call him on his cell phone when I got home to let him know I was out of the car and in the house safely. Which I did. Talked for a few minutes and then hung up.

Didn't sleep all night – kept seeing his face, hearing his voice, feeling that big cock right where I wanted it. Hang on – phone. He just called!! Said he just wanted to hear my voice again. Didn't tell him I wanted to feel his dick nudging me again. Said he was going out of town for a few weeks but wondered if he could call me again when he got back, maybe we could have dinner – at his house. Got the jumpies just thinking about it – something nagging me about him – but I said yes. Fuck – something to look forward to! Haven't been excited about anything or anyone for so long. Guess I'll just have to wait and see if he really calls. God, I hope he calls.

Wednesday, January 24, 2007

Work still sucks but the hottie called right after I got home. His name is Edward, we're having dinner Saturday night at his house. He wanted to send a car for me, but I insisted on driving myself. I tried to explain that until we know each other a little better, I need a little extra control. He finally agreed. Need some new razors – haven't shaved my legs for awhile!! Will have to dig in the back of the closet and find something appropriate – aka sexy but not too sexy – to wear – not sure what's back there that might actually fit – weight loss continues. Need to make a good "second" impression. Really need to get laid soon or my eyes will be permanently crossed. I'm putting too much pressure on myself and how this dinner goes – just need one thing to work out for a change. Not even looking for a relationship, just a male voice to talk to now and then. I miss my friends with benefits. My state of mind lately is sad and pitiful. Maybe this will perk me up.

Saturday, January 27, 2007

Got the look I was going for – so nervous I want to throw up. Clean panties and a toothbrush in my purse – just in case.

Sunday, January 28, 2007

Dinner went well – I think really well. Just the two of us, whoever cooked knew what they were doing. Couldn't remember what we ate, though, I was too mesmerized to pay attention. We had three different kinds of wine with dinner and then brandy after – didn't do a very good job pacing myself. I talked too much about myself, he didn't talk nearly enough about himself. He's so freaking charming, I'm getting too caught up too fast, just like always. After dinner, beautiful slow soft classical music – we danced – Edward and me and that big cock. Whew!! We sat for awhile and talked some more. When he leaned in to kiss me the first time, I couldn't breathe. Damn, he's a really fine kisser. BP jumped about 20 points. Kissed and fondled for a really long time and I was ready to hit the sheets, but he was not. Said he didn't want to rush me, wanted to take things slow and not scare me off. I couldn't argue that – I was the one who needed time to get to know him. Hold on – phone. Edward – just called to say what a good time he had last night, I agreed. Feel a very strange attraction to this man – don't know what it is and I feel like I should be afraid, why am I not? Seeing him again Saturday – he's picking me up this time – have to clean the house this week!!

Saturday, February 3, 2007

He's here – why am I so nervous? He's coming up the front walk – damn, he looks so hot! Got my purse panties and my toothbrush, just in case.

Thursday, February 8, 2007

I should be more agitated than I am – I hated that job so much by Tuesday that knowing I don't have to go back there is somewhat comforting. Right now I'm pretending I'm on vacation. Plenty of time to freak later.

Sunday, February 4, 2007

Holy hell, this guy is fucking with my head. Had an incredible dinner last night at a super new restaurant, then went dancing – who does that anymore? It was cold last night but I didn't really notice – we took a walk hand in hand to the downtown ice rink and then back to the car. Talked a bunch during the evening, mostly fluffy stuff – school, early work history, stuff like that. Came back here, had a few glasses of wine, fucked until 3 am. Damn good in bed – pretty good with his tongue, and he knows what to do with that big cock of his. He stayed until dawn, kissed me goodbye and then left. He called a little while ago – said he needs to see me tomorrow night – something important we need to discuss. Said we will have dinner and then talk. Getting way too emotionally involved with this guy. I know I should be hearing warning bells about this but I'm getting too attached. I'm feeling a little impetuous and that's never good.

Monday, February 5, 2007

It's late and I just got home – I cried all the way – holy hell! I knew I got that Dom vibe from Edward – because he's a freaking damned Dominant!! He even showed me his fucking dungeon – yeah, apparently a lot of fucking goes on down there! He spent the evening trying to convince me that I'm submissive and that we would be so good together. Played on the fact that I'm really tired of taking care of myself and wouldn't I like to have someone else take care of me for a change? Says he just wants to make me happy. Wants me to quit my shitty job, give up my apartment and move in with him. Soon. If I decide to do it, there's some contract I have to sign – really not sure what that's all about – something about a six month trial period. No talk of marriage or anything beyond six months so far. He almost had me convinced and I freaked again – told him I needed to come home and think about everything. In some ways, the offer is very attractive – I AM tired of taking care of myself – it's been a tough few years. But there was some scary looking shit in that dungeon – things I might not survive. Just thinking about it makes me think I'm going to vomit. Why isn't just the word dungeon scaring me off? Don't know what I'm going to do, but for now, I have to get to bed – have to work tomorrow.

Tuesday, February 6, 2007

Didn't get much sleep last night – got yelled at by my boss today for something that was not my fault – got groped by the lecherous partner in the elevator again – everyone talking about me behind my back in the lunch room. Went back to my desk, typed my resignation letter, signed it – crumpled it up in a ball and threw it at my boss on my way out. I actually quit my job. Sitting in my car in the parking lot crying, Edward called my cell – I couldn't talk – he got upset. He's out of town the rest of the week, promised to come see me as soon as he gets back – maybe Friday or Saturday. I have a feeling I just made my decision about moving in with him. Carson will shit gold bricks when she finds out. I'll deal with that when I have to.

Saturday, February 10, 2007

Edward showed up here at midnight – called my cell and said he was outside, I needed to let him in. Opened the door, took one look at his face and started to cry again. He folded me in his arms and held me – told me this was a sign that moving in with him was the right thing to do. Took me back to bed and screwed my brains out, then we fell asleep together. We were awake again at dawn. Made love again and then I made him breakfast. He just left 15 minutes ago. Didn't tell Edward yet that I'm leaning toward making the move. What the hell? I have no job and I live in a tiny shit apartment. What have I got to lose?

Monday, February 12, 2007

Impetuous isn't the word for it. Made my mind up – I'm moving in with Edward – soon. Gave my moving notice to the apartment complex so there's no turning back. Haven't told Carson yet, she'll totally freak.

Saturday, March 3, 2007

It's moving day. Packing away this journal now, old life behind me and new one in front of me. My adventure with Edward deserves a journal of its own. If the next 6 months are half as good as I hope they will be, it will be pretty awesome. Wish me luck.

Sunday, October 14, 2007

Guess I'm lucky to still be alive. Survived my stupidity one more time. Spent 6 months in hell with Edward and when the torture was over, I left with my car, a key to a storage locker, a bunch of scars on my ass, and a check for $75,000.00 – hush money, I guess, so I don't go to the police. Not that I would – I walked into that nightmare with my eyes wide open. And signed a contract. Went to the bank with the check right away and it didn't bounce. All the money I had in the bank when I moved in with him was still there, plus 6 months of pension checks and 401k distribution deposits. Grateful that at least he didn't steal any money from me. That was last month. Since then I bought a little house and had a mover bring all my stuff from the locker to the apartment. Couldn't find another full time job so temporarily, I'm working at Meijer 3ʳᵈ shift stocking shelves. At least it will help keep my mind off the last 6 months. Fucking A-Fib is back – the stress of the last 6 months, I guess. Back in the *monthly Cardiologist blood test cycle again. I could just kill that bastard Edward. Called Carson today, let her know where I'm at – told her some of what had happened – she was very upset and so was I – not prepared to tell her everything that happened. Didn't mention the A-Fib. She already thinks I need to be committed. Found this journal in one of the boxes I unpacked today. I managed two months worth of entries in my Edward journal before he found it and burned it. Got the shit beat out of me that night. But beyond this entry, I'm just not prepared to put anything else on paper. Not yet.*

Tuesday, October 22, 2007

Crap. Now that I'm without Edward – and sex – I'm horny all the time – looks like I'm off and running again. Found the box of romance novels, and two vibrators that still work. I know which one I'm starting with, that should help ease the hornies. Happy birthday to me – seriously glad to still be alive.

Friday, November 16, 2007

Good news from the Cardiologist – A-Fib is gone, three cheers for sinus rhythm!! Still have to see the doctor monthly, but it all looks good right now.

Sunday, November 18, 2007

Thanksgiving means a little more this year than most – I'm still alive. Haven't seen or heard from Edward since he let me go and that's a good thing. Things are actually going well. Budget is holding up okay thanks to not spending any money for 6 months. Have made a few new friends and reconnected with a few old ones. Old friends wanted to know where the hell I've been the past 8 months but I didn't go into detail – just said I was in a relationship that didn't work out. Got a new vibrator, managing the hornies, so far, so good. Need to get all the ugly out of my head – soon – putting everything on paper will be almost too difficult but it needs to be done. Hopefully very soon.

Sunday, November 25, 2007

It's 5:00 am and I'm in the mood to clear some shit out of my head. So here it is – the Edward Chronicles. First two or three weeks were really good – I felt a real connection to him – after the fact, don't know what the hell I was feeling. Foreplay always started with spankings, which I didn't mind, but escalated to getting paddled hard with whatever implement was close by. The few times I tried to get away from the beating or defend myself, I got beat worse – learned to accept it because – the nightmare continued with some serious emotional abuse – really fucked with my head. By then I was glad we slept in separate rooms. He soon decided I needed to lose 20 lbs but continued to almost force feed me every day. For the next month, if I didn't lose a pound every few days, he would scream at me. God forbid I should gain a pound – he would chain me up in the dungeon and beat me. One minute I was a big fat pig and the next, I was a beautiful goddess and he couldn't get enough sex. Started making myself vomit every night after dinner so that at least I wouldn't die in the damned torture chamber. Not for that anyway. When I had lost the 20 lbs, we never talked about it again. He found other things to beat me for – I wasn't smart enough or pretty enough, my blow jobs weren't good enough, there was always some way I was lacking. We would start out making sweet tender love and then I would realize he was withholding my orgasms. Seemed to go on for hours some days and would become extremely painful – physically and emotionally. The more I cried and begged the worse he got – had the most cruel laugh I've ever heard. Hope I never hear it again. Family and friends would call and he wouldn't let me talk to them. Then he threw away my cell phone. May 1st I woke up with his collar on me, had to start calling him Master Edward. We had talked about a collar a few weeks before – I said I wasn't ready for that level of commitment – he wasn't happy and finally made the decision for me. It had a lock on it so there was no way I could get it back off. So much for that sacred BDSM symbol. I never left the house after that. He had a party for Summer Solstice in June – lots of people invited – I was chained in the dungeon naked, on display – Edward gave tours – brought guests down so they could look at me, touch me, beat me, fuck me, deep throat me – sometimes two or three of his friends going at me at the same time – whatever they wanted – Master was the consummate host. Had to say thank you and pretend I enjoyed it so that it wouldn't get any worse than it already was. Still didn't want to die in that damned dungeon.

By the time everyone left, he was so hot, he butt fucked me into unconsciousness before he unchained me. I was counting down to September 3rd so I could leave, just hoped he would honor his own fucking arrangement. Early August, he beat me with a cane so bad I passed out – woke up – passed out again – don't even remember why – there may not have been a reason – it was days before I could walk again – longer for the cuts from the cane to heal. God awful scars on my ass. I watched and waited, and when everyone's back was turned, I snuck out. Almost made it to the road before he caught me. That night he dragged me down to the dungeon naked, handcuffed me to the wall again with a bucket between my legs so I wouldn't pee on the expensive wood floor, and he left me there in the dark for the weekend.

When he came back on Sunday I was barely conscious, hanging by my handcuffs, almost frozen by the overzealous A/C. In a fit of remorse, he carried me up to my bedroom and called his friend, the doctor. Heard the doctor stayed with me, taking care of me for three days. When I finally woke up, the collar was gone. I only saw Edward twice after that and he never stayed more than a few minutes – never did say he was sorry for anything but the last look I saw on his face was almost apologetic. I never left my room – the butler brought all my meals and meds to me. Where the hell was the fucking butler when I was freezing in the fucking dungeon for a whole fucking weekend?? Three weeks later, the contract had expired, the doctor said I was well enough to leave, and that was that. I left with my car, the key to the storage locker with all my stuff in it, and a big check. Didn't see Edward that last day and never looked back – hope I never see him again. I know that I should have gone to the police right away and filed a complaint but I was convinced that what he did was as much my fault as his. Maybe I do need to be committed. Hopefully now that it's on paper, I can put it behind me and move forward. Hell, it might make a great book some day!

Sunday, December 2, 2007

Thanksgiving with the family was good. Carson was a little tense but never made me feel bad about anything that had happened. We didn't even talk much about it. Probably a good thing.

Sunday, December 23, 2007

Volunteered to work Christmas Eve and the day after Christmas so that a few co-workers with families could get some time off. Learned how to work the register and customer service so I can be scheduled just about anywhere they need help. No medical benefits through work but signed up for health insurance during open enrollment – it's pricey but at least I'll be covered as of January 1. Still no full time employment opportunities but I'm okay working part time for now.

Tuesday, January 1, 2008

Stayed home and watched TV last night with a bottle of wine and a steak. Wasn't even awake at midnight – par for the course. Despite everything that happened last year, I think

I'm in a pretty good place mentally right now. Talked to a shrink at the free clinic the other day, he had a few insights on putting the Edward shit behind me, but thought that until I call the police and report what happened, there will always be a piece of Edward with me. Guess I'll just have to live with that. Still horny a lot of the time, a tiny piece of me misses Edward – he could be hot in bed. Guess I'll just have to live with that too.

Friday, January 25, 2008

Started going out with friends from work, a few quick drinks, maybe some bowling, it gets me out in the world once a week. People have actually been nice to me here. Not sure I understand, but I guess I have to be nice to people before they can trust enough to be nice to me. At least it's a start.

Thursday, March 27, 2008

Still going out on Friday night after work with friends. I forgot how social I could be – it's nice to have friends again. We're going to a local bar tomorrow for one drink and then we're going bowling – it's been ages, but I'm looking forward to it.

Sunday, April 27, 2008

I've been in the hospital – let the wrong guy pick me up at the bar last month and it was very bad. I hadn't planned to let him in my house – I just needed to pick up a coupon before the bowling alley. I went to the kitchen for something and when I came back into the living room, he sucker punched me and knocked me down. Before I could get up off the floor, he sat on me and just kept punching me in the face and in the gut. I woke up in the hospital a few days later – he must have had a great time but I'm a fucking mess. According to the doctors, I need a few surgeries to fix some things. Luckily I don't remember much of anything between the punching and waking up at the hospital. He stole my car and my credit card, charged a whole lot of shit on my card, tried to open up two new credit cards before I was able to freeze my credit. Carson is taking me to her house to recuperate – she may never let me leave. Josh and his financial advisor are working on cleaning up my credit. Can't look at anything in my house – lots already at the dump, including the bed. Will have to sell the house and move, not sure who will buy it, it has a reputation now. But I can't stay there any longer. Fucking A-Fib is back AGAIN!! This is getting really tiresome.

Wednesday, June 4, 2008

One surgery down, one to go. Doctors and police are pushing me hard to try hypnotherapy to bring back my memories – maybe something will come back that might identify him. May never be ready for that. Good news is A-Fib is gone again, back in rhythm. Thank God!

Tuesday, August 26, 2008

Second surgery done, prognosis is good. Also face back to normal – as normal as it will ever be. Nose is definitely different from original but I can live with it. Agreed to hypnotherapy, scheduled for mid-September. Not sure I want to remember anything that happened that night but I guess I can't move forward until I do. I'm afraid I'll remember him – that he's a local guy – but I'm also afraid that he's not local – still out there – hurting other women – waiting for an opportunity to come after me again.

Friday, September 19, 2008

Fuck, I wish he had just killed me – I feel like I'm walking dead right now. Hypnotherapy was successful – I remember just about everything – but nothing that would identify him. So I'm saddled with all the ugly memories and no way to get justice or get this bastard off the streets. Every filthy thing he said to me, every humiliating thing he did to me, the sickening sound of his voice, the evil look in his eyes – the way I got so turned on a few times – I am one fucked up little lady. The cuts, the blood, the pain. The memories are all there, waking, sleeping, doesn't matter, I'll never get them out of my head. Psych therapy starts next week. I wish I was dead. I have to vomit.

Wednesday, September 24, 2008

First psych therapy session today. The doctor wanted me to verbalize everything that happened so he could videotape it. I couldn't do it – couldn't say the words. What a quack this guy is – don't know how he ever got a license to practice psychiatry. Part of my "homework" for next week is to put everything in writing – in lieu of saying it out loud. So here it is – Diary of a Rape – I must have lost consciousness on the living room floor – when I came to, I was in the bedroom, naked, gagged, hands tied together and to the bed. I was on my knees, face in the pillow, and he was butt fucking me – hurt so bad I screamed but no sound came out. He kept calling me cunt and whore and fat pig – kind of like Edward all over again, but worse if that's possible. I could smell smoke – he was a chain smoker – when he was done with one cigarette, he would light another one from it, and then he'd stub the cigarette out on the backs of my thighs. I prayed for death, lost consciousness again.

Woke up again on my back, blindfolded, hands and feet tied to the bed, spread wide. He'd been busy with the cigarettes again – this time on my breasts and my pussy – he actually set my public hair on fire just to see how fast it would burn. For some reason, it didn't torch like he hoped and he gave up on that. He became obsessed with my pussy. He found my butterfly vibrator and duct taped it to my clit, turned it on high and sat back to watch my reaction. Too soon it was so painful, all I could do was scream, but no sound came out through the gag. When he thought I was going to pass out again, he shut off the vibrator and ripped it off along with the duct tape and a big chunk of my pubic hair. He laid down next to me and started to caress and suck on my breasts. His hand slid down to my clit and he started rubbing. As much as I loathed his touch, his hand on my clit, his fingers in my cunt got me so hot I couldn't stop moaning and pressing my body into his hand, I soaked the mattress with my juice. He got so torqued, he rolled on top of me and started slobbering on me, pumping his cock into me so hard – more silent screams through my gag. Lost consciousness again.

When I woke up again, the blindfold was gone and he was slapping my face – he wanted me awake. He wanted me to see his face. I could see it was light again – he started moving around like he was leaving. Taunting me, telling me he'd be back so we could party again. Right before he left, he gave me what he thought would be a permanent mark – he carved his initials in my breasts – deep – so much pain, so much blood – I couldn't stop screaming but only gurgling noises came through the gag. Passed out again – drifted in and out for days – woke up in the hospital with no memory of what had happened.

Friday, October 31, 2008

Got my medical release, conditional on psych therapy continuing. Completely missed my birthday last week, but some anonymous group paid all my medical bills, paid off my car loan and my credit card bills, so happy birthday to me. Must not have checked my mail in the last week, just found the birthday card from Carson today. Not sure what's up with all the financial assistance, but I'm free and clear and I'm moving. Everywhere I go, people look at me and I know that they know what happened. Conversations stop when I walk into a room. I can't take it anymore. I have to get out of here.

Thursday, January 1, 2009

House sale is final, closing took forever. Now I'm in my new apartment, finished unpacking this morning. Moved about 80 miles east, new place is about the same distance to Carson's house. She really wanted me to move in with them, but Christmas was so tense, I think she finally agrees that the two of us living together would be hazardous to someone's health. Will start looking for some kind of part-time job next week. Part of my psych therapy includes working at a rape crisis center about 25 miles from here. I don't know what the hell they think I'll be able to do for some other woman, I can hardly get through the day myself. Maybe they think interaction with other victims will help me – and them – recover – I'm skeptical. But I can't avoid it. Fuckin-A.

Monday, March 2, 2009

So much for my time at rape crisis counseling. I actually had a woman who had been beaten and raped by her uncle for seven years try to comfort me when I started to talk about my own rape experience. I was completely useless – no help to anyone else at all – but I think it actually did me some good to hear about women who had experienced so much more evil than I did. I've done my 60 days of counseling, for all the good it did, and I don't have to go back. I just have to see my psych therapist once every other month for the next 12 months and then I should be good to go.

Friday, May 29, 2009

Starting a new job on Monday, working for an attorney who chases ambulances, trolling for clients, but he seemed nice during the interview and the job isn't going to be terribly challenging – just mornings, scheduling appointments, filing, all that fun shit. But it's some place to go for a few hours every day, which I really need right now.

Tuesday, June 30, 2009

The boss is a handsy pervert. Good god, he's young enough to be my son!! But the job isn't horrible. And the attention reminds me that I don't look half bad in my old age. Lost all the weight I wanted, plus a little extra that I should probably try to put back on. The other day, I caught sight of myself in a full length mirror and from a certain angle, I look like a concentration camp survivor. Maybe I could treat myself to a little ice cream now and then?

Thursday, September 17, 2009

The boss got hauled away in handcuffs this morning. There goes my job!! It seems he's been running a scam with a local doctor and some petty criminals. They jump in front of moving cars, the doctor certifies their injuries, my boss settles for large amounts of money from the insurance companies and they all split the cash. But dumb ass got greedy when one of his "clients" actually died from his injuries – boss refused to share the proceeds of the settlement with the grieving widow and she went to the cops. Boss is totally fucked, the doctor will lose his license, and I'm not allowed to leave town until I've been cleared of any wrongdoing. So I have to keep working and there's no one to pay me? So much for life in a small town!

Monday, November 2, 2009

Finally cleared of all possible charges in the dumb ass case. He's going away for a long time. Office got closed and padlocked last week, files all hauled away to look for possible additional charges. But I'm free and clear. Was shopping at Meijer on my birthday and applied for a job – surprise, surprise, I start tomorrow!! 3rd shift stocking shelves again – not a lot of brain power required but I do have experience with that. I really need to make a few more friends and I'll meet more people at Meijer than I did in that damned law office.

Thursday, December 31, 2009

Carson and Josh came to visit for Thanksgiving, things were much more comfortable on my turf. And they only stayed two days because I had to work so it was all good. I went there for Christmas, she's getting nosy about my love life – wanting to make sure I'm not putting myself "in a position where I might run into the wrong sort of man <u>again</u>". She'll never let it go and it could get really ugly between us if she doesn't find a way.

Friday, March 12, 2010

Got my release from the psychiatrist – don't have to see him again EVER! Bought a bottle of wine on my way home and celebrated.

Friday, April 16, 2010

I'm in trouble again. Not with the law, but with Carson. I met a guy at the golf course last month and we hit it off. He wanted me to sleep with him and I finally told him it wasn't going to happen. I told him about the rape and how I just can't stand to think about *having sex, and he started giving me his own sob story. I ended up giving him $10,000 out of my Edward stash – he promptly took the money and left town. Carson found out from my big mouth accountant, who happens to be her friend. This will get much worse before it gets better, if it ever gets better again between us. The good news is people in this town don't seem to care if I throw money at complete strangers. These people are all a little nuts and they aren't treating me any different than they were before.*

Tuesday, August 10, 2010

Got hauled into court in handcuffs this morning by the local sheriff. He pulled me off the golf course, needless to say, I resisted "arrest". Carson has started commitment proceedings on the grounds that I'm mentally unstable and can't take care of myself anymore. The judge did not order confinement but I have to submit to court ordered psych eval Friday morning. I will kill her before this is all done and then I will absolutely be put away somewhere. Again, no one around here seems to care that the sheriff carted me away this morning, or that I ended up in Family Court for a commitment hearing. I love this town!

Friday, August 13, 2010

Friday the fucking 13th!! Great day for a psych eval. If I had a weapon, I'd kill my sister. She was leaving the psychiatrist's office when I got there for my appointment. Had such a smug look on her face, like she was finally going to get me out of her hair without any guilt. I wanted to punch that smug look right off her face. The psychiatrist was a smug bastard, too. But I have to say that when I walked out three hours later, he looked a little less smug, and a little less convinced that I was crazy. Unfortunately I have to meet with this guy four more times before he will make a determination whether I can take care of myself or not. The next four weeks are going to be a little slice of hell.

Wednesday, August 18, 2010

News of my commitment hearing has really spread. The foofoo people around town are treating me like I have leprosy, but everyone I work with has been cool. I think half of them have been through Family Court a time or two themselves, so apparently it's not a strike against me. One of the joys of small town living?? Again, I love this town!

Friday, September 24, 2010

Final commitment hearing – I have been cleared to conduct my own affairs as I see fit. The court psychiatrist determined that I am not a danger to myself and the presiding judge agreed. Carson was pissed about the final ruling and went after the judge – she paid $500 in Contempt of Court fines before she left the courthouse. She's lucky she didn't have to go to jail. Yay me!!

Monday, September 27, 2010

Party at work last night to celebrate my mental health victory!! I work with some scary-ass people, but they all treat me well, and I think they watch out for me in their scary way. I'm thinking of moving again – my bitch sister doesn't need to know where I live. I don't need to see her ever again.

Friday, October 22, 2010

Happy birthday to me. No one here knows it's my birthday and Carson's still pissed so no card from her. I made myself a birthday cake and ate the whole damned thing. Will have to run a few extra miles to work it back off but it was worth it.

Saturday, November 13, 2010

Moved again – hahaha. I should get a new cell number but that would be too much of a pain in the ass. We'll see how long it takes Carson to track me down – or if she even bothers.

Friday, March 11, 2011

Looks like our crappy winter is just about done – really tired of hearing about snow storms and Alberta Clippers and Polar Vortexes. Met a guy at the golf course this week, he asked me out on a date. Not sure why I accepted, I'm tired of stringing guys along when there's no way they're going to get any sex from me. I can barely stand touching myself. Can't even imagine letting a man touch me. I have to be up front with this guy, he seems really nice and I shouldn't be a bitch.

Saturday, March 19, 2011

Had a very nice time with Ricky but I explained about the no sex thing and why. He was very understanding, but explained that he isn't getting any younger and he's looking for someone he can have a relationship with. I totally understood where he was coming from. If I can't get my shit together and start having a physical relationship with a guy, then I should stop accepting invitations to go out. It's just not fair to the guy or to me. Kind of sucks to be afraid when there are so many really nice, really good looking guys around.

Saturday, May 28, 2011

I'm so fucking horny these days, I don't know what to do. Touching myself still makes me want to vomit but I have to get over that or I'll never get back to normal. I ordered a new vibrator last week, it arrived today. I tried to use it – stared at it for almost an hour before I turned it on. I just held it in my hand for awhile, trying to get used to the sensation. Worked up the courage to actually slide it toward my clit, got the shakes so bad I could hardly hold it. The damned thing slid by accident across my clit and I screamed – not from any kind of sexual release but from terror. I shut it off and put it in a drawer, took me 15 minutes to stop crying. Guess I'm not quite ready.

Monday, July 4, 2011

Happy Independence Day!! Gave myself an orgasm with the damned vibrator!! Not a big one by any means but it was nice all the same. I was beginning to think I would never be able to have another orgasm, and I was wrong. Not getting overly confident – will try again in a few weeks and see how things go.

Friday, August 12, 2011

I'm getting pretty good with the vibrator. I don't come every time but it's nice when I do. I met a guy at work the other day, he's a traveling salesman – no joke – and he comes to town every few months. All the managers know him and they all say he seems pretty nice. He asked me if I'd have dinner with him the next time he comes to town. I said yes. I think I could fuck this guy – I just have to not panic when he touches me. We'll see what happens.

Saturday, October 22, 2011

Fuck. Celebrated my birthday with Charlie, the traveling salesman. He took me out for dinner, even had a little birthday cake for me, and then we went back to my place. We had a few glasses of wine and things started to heat up on the sofa. I really wanted to make love to this guy, and everything was okay as long as we were just kissing. Then he started feeling up my breasts, moving his hands up under my sweater. I thought I could handle it, I really wanted to handle it, I wanted it to be good for both of us. But when his hand started to slide up my skirt toward my pussy, I started to panic a little and I started to breathe hard.

He thought I was getting hot for him and kept pushing higher and higher. My voice got so small, I could hardly breathe, and he couldn't – or wouldn't – hear me begging him to stop. Just about the time he put his hand on "the promised land", I pushed him off and jumped up off the sofa. I fell on the floor on my hands and knees and started to hyperventilate. With my shaky breath, I could only whisper "I'm sorry" and "Please don't hate me" over and over again. He was actually quite the gentleman about the whole thing. Stayed long enough for me to settle down and then left. I was so embarrassed, I cried for an hour. I called his cell phone, no answer. I left a message apologizing again, asking him to let me explain, but he didn't call me back.

Sunday, October 23, 2011

Charlie stopped by on his way out of town to make sure I was okay. I invited him in for coffee, tried to explain why I looked like such a prick tease last night. He was very understanding. He said his sister had been raped a few years ago and he never really understood the emotional part of what she'd been through because she hadn't let him see her upset like I was. He's determined now to make her open up to him and maybe heal a little. I wish him luck with that. He gave me a sweet kiss on the cheek on his way out the door and said he'd stay in touch. Why can't I get past the damned rape? I'm letting that bastard ruin my life.

Sunday, December 25, 2011

Got a call from Charlie wishing me a Merry Christmas. He wanted to thank me – apparently he and his sister are really talking these days, and she's starting to put what happened behind her – a little. She has agreed to go to group therapy at a Rape Crisis Center, and he says she never would have done that if he hadn't pushed her – which he wouldn't have done if I hadn't panicked all over him that night. He told me he got a promotion and is moving to the West Coast so we won't see each other again. He's a good man, I hope he finds someone who can give him what he's looking for. Lord knows that isn't me.

Tuesday, January 3, 2012

Found a rape therapy group about 30 miles away, meetings start next week. I'm finally ready. Hopefully telling my story can help me put it in the past, and maybe help a few other women at the same time. Thank you, Charlie's sister!

Wednesday, April 25, 2012

Met a guy at the golf course. This could be it. He's coming over on Friday. I bought condoms today!!

Saturday, April 28, 2012

Fuck!! I'm finally ready for sex, the guy is hot – and couldn't perform. Isn't that just the fucking story of my fucking life?? We tried for hours last night and nothing – I started to take it personally after awhile. I got a good blow job out of it, but he didn't get anything but embarrassed. Like I don't know how that is! He doesn't seem willing to seek professional help for his problem so I'm guessing I won't be seeing him again. Fuck!!

Friday, June 29, 2012

Got laid off today. I will miss Meijer and all the people I've worked with. It's been a good job, and the people have been nice to me. The job search starts again Monday. Luckily I know the drill.

Saturday, August 11, 2012

No job yet and no man! Heard the other day about a hospital hiring to fill clerical positions, but it's about 90 miles from here, I'd have to move again. But what the hell. I'm going to go there, spend a few days, and try to fill out an application and see what happens.

Friday, August 17, 2012

Drove to Hickory Creek Monday, isn't that a cute name for a little town? Spent some time getting a feel for the town, seems pretty nice. The hospital is regional, no other medical facility for miles around so it's pretty big. I found the HR department on Tuesday and filled out an application, left a resume with it, not expecting much, and left. Wednesday I got a call to come in for an interview. I liked the HR manager, she seemed pretty cool. I think I interviewed pretty well. Got another call yesterday morning, went back for an interview with the IT manager, who is very young and new to the job. We talked about a lot of things, my experience, his plans for the department. He wanted to know if I would be available to start an entry level position in Medical Records in October. I said yes, if the job materialized, I would be available. Holy hell!! I'm moving! If this job doesn't pan out, something else will – Hickory Creek has a big Meijer store!! It's a nice town, tons of public golf courses in the area, my perfect spot to maybe finally settle down.

Friday, September 14, 2012

Got moved into my new house this week – holy fuck, I bought a house!! It's in an even smaller town than Hickory Creek, about 30 minutes from the hospital, just about all I can afford right now. Less than perfect neighborhood, and it needs a lot of work, but I need a project while I'm waiting to find out if I have a job or not. Little Church right down the street. Minister seems nice. Hoping I didn't bite off more than I can chew – AGAIN!!

Friday, September 28, 2012

Got a call from the IT manager at the hospital, offered me a job!! It's only part time, which is fine, and it comes with medical benefits!! Good lord, it's been so long since I've had medical! I'll be working in Medical Records, but also working in the server room a little. I will go in Monday and sign the employment letter, starting date tentatively Monday October 22. Could be a really happy birthday this year??

Friday, October 26, 2012

Started my new job Monday, serious happy 60th birthday to me. Working in Medical Records seems like fun, at least so far. Server room full of young people who aren't interested in much of anything but their computer games. I don't have much in common with them yet, but I'm determined to win them over. Everyone seems nice so far, but I've been there before. We'll see how things go. God, I hope this is my last move, I really need to settle somewhere and put down a few roots. I'm tired of my life flapping in the breeze, hanging on by my fingernails. Still looking over my shoulder for the rapist, maybe I've moved enough times that he won't be able to find me again. It's been more than four years – haven't had a bad nightmare about the rape for more than a year. Hopefully he's dead. I have to start living again.

Saturday, October 27, 2012

Called Carson to tell her where I'm at. She didn't seem very interested. No birthday card again this year, no invitation to spend Thanksgiving or any other day. She's still pouting about the competency hearing. We'll both get over it someday – at least I hope like hell we do, I feel like an orphan.

Monday, December 31, 2012

This is my last entry. I'm making a conscious effort to put the past behind me. I'm 60 years old – I can't live under a fucking cloud anymore. I made a new friend last week at the golf course – her name is Sasha – and I think it will be good for me to know her. She has an incredibly positive attitude even though life has not been kind to her. She makes me think 2013 will be a good year for me, I just have to keep my eyes open and notice when good things come my way – and do something about it! Maybe I'll actually find a man to have sex with. I'm so ready for that. Finally. I think. Karma, wish me luc

Acknowledgements

Sequels are a little more difficult to write because they are, as they should be, stand alone reads. But they should also contain some back story for those readers who didn't catch the prior novel. That means including a little extra 'past history' than a normal stand alone book might have. It also means that fans of prior books in a series have a little bit higher expectation – for quality and for entertainment.

This book started exactly where I planned, and then took so many unexpected twists and turns, it practically wrote itself. But when all was said and done, it ended exactly where it was supposed to, and I wouldn't change a thing about it.

As an author, no one knows more than I do how important the support of friends and family are – especially when things are difficult. Writing this book was not without a certain amount of drama, a little angst on my part, every time something took an unexpected turn. I would be remiss if I didn't call out a few anchors – those few people who read early versions, offered suggestions, found all of my typos and copy/paste errors, talked me down off a ledge from time to time, people who continue to love my characters as much as I do. My biggest help came from Laura and Hawley, the best beta readers in the world. They never turned down a request to read yet another version, provide feedback, or have dinner and drinks to decompress a little. Doing that in the midst of a global pandemic was no small feat, and I am forever grateful.

Beyond those two, so many of my friends continued to ask how things were going with the book, asking questions, looking for and suggesting plot line hints, and just providing emotional support that every author needs. I love you all, thanks so much for your support.

My family may not be local, but they provide more support than they know. And even a few suggestions for future scenes and plots in books I haven't written yet.

Most of all, I want to thank my parents. Madeline and Ray, you showed me what real love is, demonstrated what it takes every day to keep that love alive, and along the way, you gave birth to my love of both reading and romance. You've both been gone for many years, but I think of you both every day, and I like to think you would both love this book, and all of my books, as much as I do.

To everyone who reads this book, I want to say thank you. I hope you enjoy it, and I hope you continue to read my Southern Dom series as it continues to unfold.

About the Author

Lorelei Tiffin is a Baby Boomer who writes romance stories about sexy, spicy baby boomer characters who like a little bondage mixed in with their spice. Her characters have experienced the worst life can throw at them and come out the other side, strong and ready for their own happily ever after.

Tiffin learned about deep and abiding love from her parents, who were not ashamed to show their physical affection for each other in front of their children. She was born and raised in the American Midwest, and still lives there today, always keeping an eye out for her next bossy hero and the independent leading lady who will become the everlasting love of his life.

For more details, visit www.loreleitiffin.com.